One Breath
from Drowning

One Breath
from Drowning

KENT QUANEY

THE UNIVERSITY OF WISCONSIN PRESS

Publication of this book has been made possible, in part,
through support from the Brittingham Trust.

The University of Wisconsin Press
728 State Street, Suite 443
Madison, Wisconsin 53706
uwpress.wisc.edu

Gray's Inn House, 127 Clerkenwell Road
London EC1R 5DB, United Kingdom
eurospanbookstore.com

Printed in the United States of America
This book may be available in a digital edition.

Library of Congress Cataloging-in-Publication Data

Names: Quaney, Kent, author.
Title: One breath from drowning / Kent Quaney.
Description: Madison, Wisconsin : The University of Wisconsin Press, [2022]
Identifiers: LCCN 2021043289 | ISBN 9780299337148 (paperback)
Subjects: LCSH: Gay men—Fiction. | LCGFT: Fiction. | Novels.
Classification: LCC PS3617.U364 O54 2022 | DDC 813/.6—dc23
LC record available at https://lccn.loc.gov/2021043289

The quotations from *Cloudstreet: The Play* in chapter 3 are copyright © Tim Winton,
Nick Enright, and Justin Monjo; reproduced with the permission of the publisher.

One Breath
from Drowning

I

Ryan

The thumping grew louder, a deep rhythmic pounding rattling the headboard against the wall. He lay on the bed frustrated, nearing panic, dripping in sweat.

"Shut up!" Ryan shouted at the empty room.

It had been going on for at least an hour now, shaking the bedframe, vibrating his spine, and jarring his shoulder blades, picking up speed like a washer going into a spin cycle.

"It's just a bread-making machine," Sam had said that first night. "Chinese bakery downstairs. It only goes for a couple of hours. You'll get used to it."

But it had been three months now and it still drove him crazy. Starting up at two in the morning like clockwork, not ending until three, sometimes four. Banging. Thumping. He'd try to get to bed by midnight so he would be in deep sleep by the time it started, but it still woke him up half the time even then. And on the nights he didn't beat it? Disaster.

Sam of course could sleep right through it, one of the lucky ones who could nod off anywhere, snoring away while Ryan cursed the night. He'd tried a couple of Sam's sleeping pills once, and slept through, yes, but woken up with a hangover worse than any night out at the pub could bring on.

Nothing could be done now but wait it out and try to not freak out about tomorrow.

First day back at school. First day of auditions for every production that semester. Crucial to be at his best. He'd even kicked Sam out of the flat that night, pushed him out the door to go clubbing, hoping for some time to focus and prepare and get some sleep, but here he lay again, miserable, not even able to wake Sam up to commiserate. His heart thumped in sync with the banging of the bread-monster, racing as he grew more annoyed.

He threw the sheets back and got out of bed, the wood floor blissfully cool to his bare feet. By shutting the windows to keep out the street noise, he'd boxed in the brutal February heat. Summer in Sydney. Merciless. And they didn't have "air con," as the Aussies called it. Sam had just ordered two fancy reverse-cycle units that were

3

already a couple of days late (with deepest apologies). In the meantime, they roasted.

He padded over to the window and turned the crank slowly, carefully, avoiding the fresh paint around the pristine beveled glass Sam had rescued from a teardown in Summer Hill. They had finished painting yesterday, but in this humidity the surface couldn't possibly be dry. He stood back as far as he could from the frame, cranking impatiently, the window tilting open millimeter by slow millimeter toward the street.

The flat was Sam's baby. A gorgeous corner unit in a Federation sandstone with views of Rushcutters Bay. He'd been rehabbing it for the last year or so. A design junkie's dream. But a dream situated smack in the middle of Sydney's old red-light district, and, as much as there was talk of the neighborhood transitioning, Kings Cross still clung to its shady past with mongrel's teeth. The new array of award-winning restaurants, galleries, and cafés grudgingly shared Darlinghurst Road with a sketchy collection of leftover strip joints, porn shops, and youth hostels. At first he'd liked the buzz of the neighborhood, the seediness, the edge. He had even convinced himself that the patch of bay he could see from the lounge room windows meant he was still beachside, but after his first week there with the strip in full swing every night, he figured he may as well have hung a hammock between the pool tables at the all-night pub next door, with its never-ending crowd of screeching drunk British backpackers.

"You're an idiot," Katrina had told him as he shoved his suitcases and laptop into the boot of the Uber in front of her rambling old Bondi flat, the beach spread out before him in full summer glory. "Walking away from all this for the crash-bang of the Cross?"

But he and Sam had been in drooling-stupid love, and it had seemed like the right thing to do. Impulsive? Sure, but as scared of this new life as he still often was, it felt like this might be the real thing.

And to be fair, the flat was honestly gorgeous. Sam had a real knack for the work, so of course Ryan posted carefully curated pictures all over social media highlighting the features of the architecture, the views, everything shot from the perfect angle. But just the architecture. The fact of his relationship with Sam, the fact of his sexuality at all—both were still fiercely guarded secrets. Questions from back home were fielded with casual vagueness. Roommate. Friend of a friend. Work done on the loft for lowered rent. He even talked up the added bonus of it being walking distance to the Mormon chapel on Hyde Park, but he hadn't entered that building, or any Mormon chapel at all, since his first weekend in Sydney, when he'd gone to Sacrament Meeting jetlagged and emotional, nervous at what he knew he was about to do, but awakening to a sense of unbridled freedom that complete anonymity in a new country would give him. As he left the service, he realized he'd only gone in to say good-bye.

He would tell them, tell her, eventually, but as long as he was here and they were there it just seemed easier to keep things separate. Months had gone by, a year, and he'd stopped thinking about it. He would manage it before he went back home—that is, if he ever did.

He leaned out the window further, arms down, still mindful of the paint, trying to catch a breeze. Down the block, drivers gunned their motors in the bumper-to-bumper night traffic, edging past neon nightclub signs, honking at drunks and hookers in the street, shouts and laughter floating up from the patio of the pub. Eyes closed, he let the breeze drift over him and admitted defeat. He should have just given in to Sam's teasing and cajoling and gotten in the cab.

Rest and focus had been the whole point, but he'd insisted, and here he was paying for it. Hot. Irritated. Panicked. He and Lucy had rehearsed their monologues together all summer, and anything less than perfection was unacceptable. Third and final year of his MFA and he had yet to nab a lead role. Sure, lots of encouragement, supporting roles here and there, Lucky in *Waiting for Godot*, Mitch in *Streetcar*, but he needed to crack into the top or what was the use of coming all the way down here from Utah in the first place? A siren shrieked from somewhere up the road, followed by a distorted, amplified voice through a police megaphone ordering someone to pull over.

He whispered the opening lines of Vanya's speech, sending them out to the traffic and chaos below, wallowing in the Russian farmer's regret at never asking Yelena to marry him, the smash of beer bottles against the pavement punctuating each word. The character took hold and his voice grew louder, rising and falling as he stepped back from the window stomping back and forth across the bedroom in his underwear, expressing the regret of a life not lived, of a love not acted on. Imaginary applause rang in his head and he bowed slightly, then walked to the kitchen while running vocal exercises, thee-ing and thou-ing, humming and shouting. He turned on the kettle for a cup of hot water with lemon and eyed the dreary steamed veg plate he'd left on the table before bed. Calorie cutting. Had to look as lean and fit as possible when his instructors saw him on stage.

The kettle bubbled and hissed, and he dug into Chekhov again, energized, finding more depth in the words, more pain. He picked a limp stalk of asparagus from the plate, chewed quickly, and swallowed the cold mess. It was good he had sent Sam out after all. Only three months in, but he found himself needing a night off more and more lately. Adjustment period, he told himself. A matter of time before they settled into a mutually agreeable routine. Work and study took a lot out of him, while Sam seemed to have boundless energy, always up for fun, for a night out with mates, and always hot for sex. It was intoxicating, even mind-blowing in its newness, but it could be exhausting. The house had felt blissfully empty tonight . . . until the bread-banger had started in.

Stop. Focus. Back to work.

He walked back through the bedroom and leaned out the window again, hands on sill, paint sticking to his palms, and launched into *Richard the Third* at the top of his lungs:

"Oh, I have pass'd a miserable night, so full of ugly sights, of ghastly dreams," he shouted to the street.

"Shut the hell up, ya bloody wanker!" someone yelled over the roar of the pub patio. The smell of smoking beef and sausage hit him from the kebab cart below. Steamed veggie plate be damned, he was starving. At least the Cross had all-night takeaway. He grabbed his jeans from where he'd left them on the kitchen floor, pulled on a threadbare South Sydney Rabbitohs T-shirt, kicked on his flip-flops, and jogged down the stairs two at a time, the rhythmic *thunk* of the bread machine still vibrating through the recently installed Tasmanian oak banister (another of Sam's salvage finds, another installation nightmare).

A crash of sounds on the street: music, shouting, clinking bottles and glasses. Fragrant eucalyptus branches heavy with fairy lights hung above the wooden fence of the pub patio, giving the sidewalk a pale glow. Drunken zombies milled about, smoking and chatting, while taxis lined down the block, their motors idling, waiting for fares.

"Fucking brilliant!" a chubby girl in a miniskirt yelled. She and her much skinnier friend leaned against the rough brick wall of the gallery across the street. "It's bloody brilliant. Pubs don't close here. Ever! And it's dead hot in the middle of bloody February. I'm never going back to Manchester!"

"I know! Right?" the other girl squealed. She grabbed her friend's arm and pulled her into a twirl. "And the beach is on your bloody doorstep, right? We're staying forever!"

Ryan waved at them and they burst into fits of giggles. "Evening, girls." He remembered his own first weeks here, shocked and seduced by the decadent ease of it all. It had been so simple. Revelatory.

He turned to face the bakery window, give them their moment. Through a half-open curtain at the back, a young Asian girl, maybe fifteen, pulled a metal handle back and forth over a bathtub-sized steel vat, oblivious to the party in the street, her dark hair pulled back in a ponytail, sweat-drenched T-shirt stretched tight against straining back muscles.

"I hate you," he whispered, his breath making a steamy circle over a placard taped to the inside of the glass. It was done in black marker in a crooked freehand script. "Slice cake cuppachino 10 dollers," it read. Someone had drawn a picture of a kitten on it.

Food. Right. The whole purpose of his mission to the street. He stepped off the curb, watching for a break in the line of cars, ready to shoot across to the kebab stand, but stopped short as a taxi jerked to a stop in front of him. He took a step back, waiting for whatever random mob of backpackers it was to spill out and ramble into the pub, but it was Sam. Giddy, wobbly, his boyfriend lurched out of the car and pointed a finger at Ryan. "Hey, Spunky," he shouted as he fell back against the door. "What you doing standing out on the road in the middle of the night? Trying to pick up chicks?" He righted himself, his tight T-shirt straining against his rib cage, brazenly advertising his six-days-a-week gym routine, a drunken grin on his face.

"Welcome home, you maniac." Ryan stepped into the street to grab him before he stumbled again, but Sam had turned back to the cab. "You coming, mate?"

A young guy, lean and toned, dark hair and eyes, pulled himself out of the back seat. Both arms were covered with tattoos, his clothing the western suburbs uniform of track pants and tank top (the Aussies called them singlets but he felt silly saying it). Lebanese? Greek? Another one of Sam's friends crashing at their place to avoid the taxi fares back to Bankstown or Cabramatta. Perfect.

Sam passed some cash through the window to the driver, then stepped to the curb, running his hand over his newly buzzed hair, his blue eyes bloodshot from drinking. "Sexy," he growled as he leaned in to kiss Ryan's cheek, catching him in a bear hug.

Ryan leaned into him, inhaling. Sam smelled of beer and smoke and sweat. Sexy. "You're back early."

Sam broke the embrace and grabbed Ryan's shoulders. "It's three thirty in the bloody morning. How long did you want me to stay out? Thought I'd done well. Thought you'd be all rehearsed out and ready to relax."

The guy from the cab still hung back at the sidewalk, and Sam motioned for him to come forward. "This is Alky," he said. "He's crashing with us tonight."

"Hey, mate." He jogged toward them out of the traffic.

The cab gunned its engine and inched back into traffic.

Ryan hitched his thumbs in his jeans. "Nice to meet you. Alky, is it?"

"Real name's Alakos, but yeah, call me Alky." He stepped closer and looked Ryan up and down. "Sam said you were a Yank. Love the accent."

"Yeah. American as . . . well . . . American. So . . . you're Greek then?"

"By extraction, yeah. Lived here me whole life though."

Sam wrapped his arm around Alky's shoulder and gestured toward Ryan. "I was right, wasn't I?"

Ryan hugged his chest and leaned back against the bakery window.

"So how do you know Sam?" he asked, trying to sound friendly, calm.

"Just met him, mate. Leaving the club. I live in Earlwood with family. Chilling with you blokes tonight. You up for a good time? Sam says you're great fun."

"Thought he might be asleep, but all the better for us now." Sam pushed past him, fumbling for his keys, and unlocked the door. "Come on then, boys." He jerked his thumb toward the staircase.

"Too right," he said. "Gonna be a good time." Alky slid past him and started up the steps, sweat glistening on his neck and shoulders. Ryan held back, still trying to take in what was unfolding.

Sam motioned him in. "You coming, babe?" he said. "Not thinking about those chicks, are you?" He nodded toward the girls in the pub doorway. "Hey, ladies," he yelled at them, "you're out of luck. He doesn't like girls anymore."

The one in the short skirt giggled. "Too bad for him," she said, and pitched her cigarette into the street.

Sam put his hands on Ryan's waist and walked him toward the doorway.

"What are we doing?" Ryan asked. He ducked out of Sam's grip and stepped back. "You know I have auditions tomorrow. I've got to be rested and ready."

"Come on, Ryan," Sam said, his voice lower now, an attempt at sexy. "Alky's looking for a good time and I thought you'd like him. You've rehearsed yourself out the arse at this point, I bet. Need of a little recreation, right? Might even energize you a bit for those auditions. You can sleep in a bit tomorrow. It'll be fun. Come on, be a sport."

"That's ridiculous. You know I need to be asleep."

"But he's totally into you."

"So, what if I didn't like him or . . . I mean, okay, yeah, he's good-looking, hot." His voice rose as he got more and more agitated. "Geez, Sam. What are you doing?" Hands flapping, almost yelling, he realized he was getting hysterical and stopped.

"You blokes coming?" Alky yelled down.

"But you do like him, right?" Sam hooked his thumb at the staircase. "And we talked about this, you know, opening up the relationship."

"You talked about it. I pretty much just listened, and as far as I remember we hadn't agreed on anything yet."

"I thought once you saw him, you know. Come on." Sam made a playful jab at Ryan's belly. "Besides, he loves Americans."

"Oh, well that makes everything all right then. Stupid of me. What was I thinking?"

"Christ, Ryan. Don't be so bloody Mormon," Sam said, agitation in his voice. He turned and did a rat-a-tat-tat on the brick wall with his open palms. "Unless you're going to dress up in your white shirt and tie and wear your Elder's name tag, that is." The drunken grin was back. He was relentless.

"Not funny at four o'clock in the morning, Sam." His mind flipped forward to auditions, him exhausted. Blowing it.

Sam put his hands on Ryan's waist and leaned his forehead in, locking eyes with him. "Oh, come on. Don't be a pussy. Let's have some fun."

Ryan knocked Sam's hands away. "You're drunk as a skunk and trying to start a random three-way in the middle of the night, so just because I'm trying to get some sleep, because I don't want to jump in bed with a stranger, I'm a . . . a . . . whatever. I'm not going to say it." His distaste for cursing was something he still held strongly to, even as he put the church further and further behind him.

And Sam's ribbing him about his Mormon prudery had been accelerating lately. He knew it was meant in fun, in that take-no-prisoners Australian way of joking. Sam was just as likely to mock his own Catholic past, but it was getting under his skin. There was something to be said for moderation, for loyalty. Just because he had left the church didn't mean he had to leave all its values behind. After those first few intoxicating months of freedom, the hedonism of the dance clubs, the newness of sex, he found he really longed for stability. When Sam had asked him to move in, he had thought that was the end of it. Settling down. Married bliss again, just with a man this time.

"Oh, come on," Sam said, "you know you'll have a good time. Relax."

He leaned in to kiss him again and Ryan felt that heat, that draw. Why fight it? No reasoning with drunk Sam anyway. Maybe calm things down a bit once they were all inside. "All right," he said, and followed Sam up the stairs.

Alky stood in the middle of the lounge room, hands on hips, appraising the freshly painted gray walls, the stark white furniture. "Nice place," he said. "You blokes do the rehab?"

"I've been working on it piece by piece for a bit," Sam said, walking toward the kitchen. "Bought it a couple years back. Been working on it when I can. Ryan moved in in November, and he helps here and there." Cupboard doors slammed, followed by the ring of glass hitting countertop.

"Nothing like free labor," said Alky.

Ryan busied himself collecting the debris of his rehearsal—scripts, highlighter, half-empty teacup.

"Yeah, well. He nearly knocked a hole in the wall the first time I gave him a hammer, but he looks good so I let him stay," Sam yelled.

"That's not true," Ryan yelled. "It was—

"Rum? Vodka? What'll it be, fellas?"

"Bundy and Coke, thanks," Alky said. "You having a drink, mate?"

"Yeah, why not. Vodka tonic," he yelled. It might even help him sleep.

Alky looked at him and raised an eyebrow.

Maybe it would be fun after all.

Ice rattled in glasses, and Sam returned with the drinks. "Right," he said. "No need to stand around like nervous kids at a school dance. Come on, boys."

"Ta. Thanks," Alky said. He took a swallow of his drink and followed Sam to the bedroom. "You blokes been together long then?"

"Nine months or thereabouts. He says he loves me but I think he's just using me to get his resident papers." Sam ended his sentence with that Aussie uptick that implied

9

a question but wasn't one. "Take what I can get though." He turned to Ryan. "Turn on some music, Spunky. And make sure you switch the speakers to the bedroom."

Ryan fiddled with the switches and a low beat kicked in, one of Sam's better jazz-chill-out mixes. He took a sip of his drink and walked into the bedroom. Sam and Alky stood in front of the bed, already kissing. Hands groping, gripping each other's shoulders and arms, chests pressed together, grinding. Sam broke the kiss, pulled Alky's shirt up over his head, and threw it to the floor, revealing a muscular chest covered with an array of crudely drawn tattoos: cartoon characters, Chinese lettering, slot machine cherries. Sam looked over his shoulder at Ryan, jerked his chin at him to come forward, then pulled Alky into a clinch as the two of them fell onto the bed together.

Ryan stood frozen, his heart racing, like a child who had walked in on his parents, guilty of witnessing something he had battled to convince himself wasn't a sin. In the low light, Sam didn't even look like Sam anymore. The bed was all sharp edges and strange angles. Just do it, he told himself as he took another drink. He's right. You're a prude. Prove him wrong.

Sam straddled Alky, pulled off his own shirt.

You've got to do this. Move.

He took a step toward the bed. "Right, I'm coming," he said, but his foot caught on Alky's shirt and he slipped on the polished floor, falling toward them. Glass still in hand, he put his arms out to break the fall, knocking Sam's head with his drink, ice scattering across the sheets. The glass bounced once, then shattered. Vodka dripped from Sam's hair.

"Holy shit!" Sam yelled. "What are you doing?" He rubbed the back of his scalp, his face dark red. "Jesus, Ryan. Did you hit me?"

Ryan sat on the floor among shattered glass and discarded clothing. "Shoot. Sorry. I didn't mean to. I slipped." He grabbed the window ledge and pulled himself up, the paint still damp and gummy to the touch. "Is everyone okay?"

Alky sat up and scooted forward. "All good here. You cut?"

"I'm fine. I'll just get this cleaned up."

"Calm down, buddy. It's okay." He shoved a pillow aside and grabbed Alky's thigh. "He just gets nervous. Mormon boy, you know. Still learning the ropes."

"Serious? Suit and tie and the name tags? With all them blokes in Hyde Park?"

Ryan picked up a couple of the larger shards. "Well, I went to Ecuador, not here, but yeah. Sam loves to talk about it." The bottom half of the glass was still in one piece and he used it now as a collection bin. "It was a few years ago."

"Sexy. Always liked the look of those blokes. So scrubbed up and polite. You must have got hit on heaps."

"You know he did." Sam leaned back against Alky's chest and gave a low growl. "Come on then, mister missionary. We can leave it till later."

"If I leave it, someone's going to cut their foot," Ryan said, shattered glass in hand. "It needs vacuuming."

Sam stood up. "Honestly, just leave it."

Ryan pointed toward the kitchen. "It'll just take a minute." He walked out of the room, carefully now, eyes out for further obstacles, and dropped the glass into the bin.

"You okay?" Sam whispered. He stood behind Ryan now, nuzzling his ear with his chin. "What was that all about? You're not really that nervous, are you?"

Ryan ran his hands under the tap, rinsing the smaller crystals down the drain. "I'll be all right. I just fell. Sorry. Just let me get things cleaned up."

"Sorry. Right then. I'll help." Sam grabbed a cloth from the dish drainer and walked toward the bedroom. "Don't move, Alky. Hazard cleanup first, then back to it."

Alky's voice was deep and rich. "Take your time, gents," he called from the bedroom.

Sam turned back to Ryan and waved the towel at him. "Come on, then. We'll have it sorted in two ticks."

Ryan reached under the sink for the hand broom. "Look. Maybe I'm just not up for this."

Sam stopped, broom in hand. "What do you mean?"

He stayed hunched in front of the cupboard. Dish soap. Furniture polish. He reached out for the dustpan but stopped short. "You guys go ahead." It came out a hoarse whisper. "I'll sleep on the couch."

"You can't be serious." Sam's voice was agitated. "We're halfway there," he hissed. "You're not pulling out now."

"I'm serious," Ryan said. He stood now, whisk broom still in hand. "I can't do it," he said.

"Come on now, Ryan. Don't embarrass me."

"You're embarrassed?" He slammed the dustpan onto the countertop. "What about me?"

"Why are you freaking out now?"

"I thought I could do it, but I can't." Ryan waved his arm toward the bedroom. "For hell's sake, Sam. You just pimped me out to a stranger."

"So now you're going to get all righteous on me?"

"Is everything okay, boys?" Alky shuffled into the living room buttoning his jeans. "Maybe I should go. No worries, really. Trains start up soon again anyway."

"Hold on, mate," Sam said. "He's new at this, just talking him through it. We'll be back in no time. Three-way virgin here."

"You can't let up, can you?" Ryan said.

"Calm the hell down." Sam dropped the broom to the floor, disgust in his voice. "We're not in Salt Lake City anymore, the righteous lightning can't find you here, now come on."

"Honestly, I can just go." Alky walked toward the stairs.

"Wait," Ryan said, whiskbroom still in hand.

Alky stopped.

"He promised you a good time. Don't let me stop you two. Go on and enjoy yourselves. I'm outta here." Clutching at his pockets for his keys, his wallet, he walked to the top of the stairs, hesitated a moment, hoping Sam would say something to make him stop.

"Go then. Fine!" Sam yelled at him, his voice still hoarse from drinking. "Just tying me down anyway."

Ryan's heart sank while his head burned with rage. He thumped down the stairs, two at a time again, back out into the night. The girls from Manchester were gone, a group of guys smoking and bullshitting in their place. Ryan ducked around partiers, hookers, and druggies, past the neon-lit strip clubs and tourist pubs of the Cross toward the all-night Indian food stand at the end of the block. He could still get a curry and sit down for a minute by himself, cool off in the air-conditioning. It was packed though, mobbed, and he was too angry to wait. He breathed in the comforting aroma of heavy spice and recycled cooking oil, turned around, and faced the street. The bright-yellow CityRail sign flashed directly across from him. Kings Cross Station. Why not? He looked back at the curry stand, still no open seats, then jogged through the slow-moving traffic across to the station entrance and jumped onto the escalator down to the platform.

Sydney wasn't anything remotely like it was supposed to be. Not even close.

He had arrived from Utah starry-eyed and ready to conquer the world, dead set on winning over his classmates and neighbors with his charm and talent, ready to be the cool American guy who had fearlessly come halfway around the world to attend one of the world's best acting schools. But images of idyllic beach days and overnight stardom had given way to frustrating shifts at his café job; endless homework and exhausting rehearsals; harsh criticism from his professors, who seemed to be making him work twice as hard for being American; and endless crap from his classmates for taking a spot from an Aussie. Why come all the way down here when Broadway's in your backyard? Poor baby couldn't get into Juilliard? You just came down here to party, didn't you? Even with his first paying gigs trickling in that summer—a mobile phone print ad, a bit part on a nighttime soap opera—he still wondered if he had made the wrong decision.

And the gay scene was crazy—far more intense than he'd imagined. Fit, confident guys who traveled in packs and spoke a language of jokes and banter he just couldn't figure out, or dancing queens who triggered every fragile conservative idea of masculinity his religious upbringing had pounded into him. He'd been totally thrown off when Sam had chatted him up. Thought he was out of his league, all confidence and manly swagger, and now nine months later here he was, fleeing his boyfriend's flat in the middle of the night in righteous indignation. Over what? A drunken failed three-way? How utterly Mormon of him. A Mormon prude. Sam had called him out on it, and it stung, because as much as he was playing the worldly gay guy in Sydney, it was just that, playing. He'd passed the religion thing off as a quirky part of his past he'd moved well beyond, as easily shed as his childhood worship of superheroes and Santa Claus, but he'd been entrenched in the church right up to the point when he'd gotten on that plane for Sydney. Entrenched in the church, and in his marriage.

It had made sense for Megan to stay in the States. She had a good job with the school district—middle school drama and choir—and she supported him in this endeavor 100 percent. Summers and Christmas breaks were of course promised, but with the price of tickets back and the need to build his résumé with any professional work he could get, those breaks had given way to "fingers crossed, see you right after graduation." The phone calls had gone from daily to weekly, to now occasionally monthly, with texts and Facebook messages taking their place, and even those becoming less and less frequent.

Neither one of them had brought up divorce. It went against everything they stood for.

And of course he hadn't told her his real reason for coming to Sydney, or anything about Sam.

And he hadn't told Sam anything about her. It hadn't seemed necessary when they had first started dating, but now, well. He promised himself he would clear the air once the stress of auditions was over.

It just wasn't something you shook overnight: faith in God, the church; and he often found himself reacting to his new world through the lens of his upbringing, torn between his new life and his long-held sacred beliefs. But Salt Lake City was long gone, and so was that way of life. No use even thinking about it. His choice had been made.

Not many people waiting for a train at this hour—a few drunks escaping the heat, a bunch of teenagers horsing around. A young woman in pub worker's black-and-whites, clearly just getting off shift, looked around nervously, clenching her rolled-up apron. The monitor above the platform had shorted out, its blue screen a scramble of letters and dashes, so he had no idea if there was even a train at this hour. He pulled out his phone. No service in the underground stations, but he didn't know who he would call at this hour anyway. He put his phone away and stared at the huge billboard at the far end of the station, a larger-than-life photo of a pale, heavily lipsticked woman in jodhpurs and riding blouse staring lustily at a stable groom. It was an advert for some cheesy television outback romance starting next month on the ABC. Weren't they supposed to be above this crap? The woman in the picture looked familiar, though. Classic cheekbones, arched brows, expression sexy but still condescending. He realized it was a girl he knew from the conservatory who had graduated last year. Smart, talented, and capable. All business. They'd only spoken a few times. And here she was the lead on a new show. As much as his new world felt totally out of control at times, at least he'd picked the right acting school.

Beneath the billboard, an older man sat on a bench wearing a cardigan and tattered scarf, far too much clothing for the Sydney summer. Ryan took no notice of him as he read the credits on the billboard, scoping for any other names he might recognize. And in the silent station, the man started singing. Something Ryan didn't recognize. A song about love and a girl named Mandy. For a moment he wished he had brought his headphones, to block out the interference, but the man had a good voice, beautiful, and he found himself humming along to the old guy's raspy melody, feeling the lyrics. The harmony was simple, and Ryan started improvising, fleshing out the minor chords. The debris on the station floor—napkins, empty candy wrappers, and takeaway containers—began rustling and fluttering in the gust of wind growing stronger from the tunnel, the shriek of metal on metal growing louder, both of them singing louder until the train stopped in front of him, ending their duet. A brown Styrofoam coffee cup fluttered to the floor at his feet, and in her prim British accent, the recorded female voice of the Sydney Train system announced: "The Train on Platform One goes to Bondi Junction."

The doors of the carriage slid open, and he stepped inside, dropping onto an empty bench and closing his eyes, imagining he was somewhere else, somewhere calm and quiet. The hiss of the brakes releasing pulled him back to earth, and the train lurched forward and rattled through the tunnel toward Edgecliff station, briefly running above ground as the steep hills of the Cross fell down to Rushcutters Bay, the lights of New South Head Road blinking and flickering in the last hours of darkness, then back into the tunnel, slowing as it reached the end of the line, the trip to Bondi Junction gone in a haze. He stood as the train slowed, the only person left in his compartment, as Her Ladyship of trains announced the end of the line.

Ryan stood, his exhaustion and worry overwhelming him. Calm down. Deep breathing. The doors slid open and he stepped toward the escalator, relishing the smell of the sea, present even underground. The beach would clear his head.

The streets were deserted and silent except for light morning traffic and the occasional shriek of a crow. He felt salt and sand sting his lips as he walked down the cracked and root-buckled sidewalks of Bondi Road toward the water, beneath palms and frangipanis, past metal grating and graffiti-covered roller doors guarding closed groceries, cafés, used bookstores, and secondhand clothing shops. The darkness was just starting to fade, and he stumbled as he stepped around a middle-aged woman unlocking the doors to a restaurant.

He turned down Denham Lane without thinking. Between the rehabbed brickworkers' cottages and new glass and concrete apartment blocks, Katrina's building was a bit of a relic, beautiful two-story courtyard flats, sandstone, standing since the early 1900s. She was vehement in her hatred of the new style: glass-walled boxes that lined the beachside streets as more and more of the old buildings were torn down. She and her co-owners, mostly old Bondi hippies who had been there since the seventies, had resisted many an exorbitant offer to sell and move out so the place could be razed for a hotel or a high-rise. They clung to the place in protest of the rapidly modernizing urban landscape. The courtyard was floral and fragrant, the doorway overgrown with mature frangipani and bright-red bottlebrush trees, almost obscuring the ornately carved stone lintel that announced the name of the building—Tavistock. She had been there for years now, collecting art and books and furniture, and the place had taken on a sort of regal shabbiness. Ryan always felt safe and cared for there, and he hit her buzzer without hesitation. She was often up at this hour getting ready for yoga or a jog, and if she wasn't, he would play dumb when she complained to him over coffee about a stranger ringing her bell at the crack of dawn.

The intercom box crackled.

"Hello?" she called. Her voice reserved, tense. Of course she would be wondering who the hell was ringing at this hour.

"Katrina, it's Ryan. I couldn't sleep. Want to go to the beach?"

"Ryan?" Her voice relaxed. "What are you doing here? Isn't this the middle of the night for you?"

He pushed through as he heard the buzzer and jogged up the steps to her flat, his exhaustion fading at the thought of a chat with his friend.

"Beach at this hour? What are you playing at, you crazy boy?" She beckoned him from the open doorway, already dressed for the gym in tank top and leggings. She was in her late fifties, but as fit as a woman fifteen years younger, the few silver-gray streaks in her otherwise honey-blonde ponytail the only clue to her age.

She caught him in a brief fierce hug, then looked him up and down. "I take it you haven't been to bed."

"Got an hour, maybe two?"

"Cup of tea then, or just a nap?"

"Tea, thanks. Beautiful."

He sank into his old favorite armchair and pulled the familiar mauve and green afghan around his shoulders. Scripts lay scattered across the coffee table, prickly with sticky notes, her handwriting scrawled across coversheets and folders.

She had graduated from the conservatory years back and had been on a wildly popular television show in the nineties, a soap opera set in an idyllic northern beach town populated by the usual bunch of eccentrics and charmers. Katrina had played the local schoolteacher, widowed young, who every season dated a series of men who couldn't live up to her beauty and brilliance, until she finally met her match and the show ended with the television wedding of the year. It had been better than the average soapie, and she had gone on to good parts in small films, even picked up a couple of critics' awards, but the parts had dried up after forty, ageism just as bad in Australia as it was in Hollywood. She hadn't let it stop her, though. She had channeled her energy into writing and had met with a string of successes beginning with a courtroom drama on SBS, and was now in her third year as staff writer on a multi-generational family drama for Foxtel. When they weren't shooting, she occasionally led workshops at the conservatory, and she had taught his accents and dialects class first semester. They had ended up chatting long after the first class was over, comfortably griping about America and the state of the world, how all the best scripts and actors were on television now. She had offered him her spare room at shockingly low rent, something she occasionally did for a more promising grad student—and she paused as she said this—if she sensed they were serious. He had assured her he was, and had given notice at his run-down flat in Redfern that day and moved in the next week. Mentorship had quickly become genuine friendship, and he now considered her his best friend in Sydney.

"So, why no sleep?"

"Same old, same old. And I've got auditions tomorrow. Three monologues: Chekhov, Shakespeare, and Contemporary Australian. I had it planned perfectly. Pushed him out the door to the club and figured I'd rehearse all evening and be asleep when he got home. But then the bread machine kicked in downstairs, and Sam turned up drunk in the middle of the night with some random guy in tow, some guy he just met, and expected me to just drop my pants and have a three-way."

"Oh God," she called from the kitchen. "You gay boys and your sex thing. What happened to getting to know people? What did you do?"

"I'm here, aren't I?"

She came back into the lounge room balancing teacups, creamer, and sugar bowl on a tray. "Here, this will help." She set the tray down on the low table and sat down on the sofa opposite him, cross-legged. Her face still carried the regal beauty of a classical actress.

"Well, you're always welcome."

"Bless you for that. I love him, but sometimes . . ."

"He's a lovely boy. Well, at least at first viewing, but you did move in awfully quick." She took a sip of tea and set her cup down next to her reading glasses. "And his energy, you know, it's a bit chaotic."

"But I like a little chaos."

"It's a world that doesn't suit you, though, isn't it?"

"It's not that, so much as . . . I don't know. I don't think you've given him a chance."

"Maybe. But you're destined for so much more, you know. He's perfectly harmless, I'm sure, even lovely for the right guy, but you're serious about your career, your future. He's serious about, what? Surfing? the clubs?"

"Well, yeah, he is into that."

"And apparently sexual escapades as well. I don't like thinking of you in that situation."

"I can take care of myself." He curled up in the chair and tucked the afghan around his feet.

"Yet here you are."

"Right."

"You could have stayed here as long as you liked, you know." She nudged the tray toward him. "Drink your tea."

He took a sip. Earl Grey with a touch of milk. She always made it perfectly. "I know that. I'm not saying you kicked me out."

"The flat was peaceful when you were here. Having a kindred spirit to talk theater with, watching all the new American television shows on your computer. I'm terribly behind in my research since you left, by the way." She tapped the pile of scripts on the coffee table. "And what about auditions? If you were living here, I'd have run lines with you all week and helped you prepare. Made sure you were perfect."

She was right. It had been perfect, really. "I felt like he was the right one, though. Take the plunge. Now or never. We've even been talking about me staying on after graduation next year. Applying for interdependent status for residency and all that. So even if it falls apart, I'd get to stay. That's a good thing, right?"

"Did you really move in with Sam just to get residency? I don't believe that for a minute."

"Oh, gosh no, of course not. I've still got the coming year to sort that all out." He squirmed lower on the cushions and shut his eyes. "I love him. I don't know what I want. I want him. I want to stay. I want to stay with him. He's the most wonderful guy on his best days, witty, romantic, charming as hell. But last night was a mess."

"And it's not the first time."

"Why couldn't I just be from Myanmar or Indonesia?" he said. "They always get residency."

"Stop being so fatalistic." She pointed a finger at him. "And please don't ever say that in public. Be glad you're not from a war-torn country having your civil rights denied based on your religion or race."

"Sorry, sorry."

"I know you're just upset, but really. Try to be a bit more aware."

"I will try. Sorry."

"It's fine." She waved his gaffe away and picked up her cup, blowing ripples across the gray surface. "What about Sam, then? What are you going to do?"

"I don't know, Kat. It's a mess. I mean, I could go back to him tomorrow and he'd laugh it off and take me out to dinner and turn it all into a joke, but it's just, I don't know. This isn't the only problem."

"Here's an idea. Why don't you stay with me for a bit while you think it through? At least for a couple of days. The beach is good for you, Ryan. It calms you and centers you. You're a different person out here than you are in the city. Your energy has definitely gotten more unbalanced since you left. That Sam chaos is rubbing off on you. Your artist's soul is drowning."

"Please don't get all new-age woo-woo on me. You know I don't believe that hippie-dippie stuff."

"You know I'm right."

He looked out the window. The sun was up now, the reflection off the vast sweep of ocean near blinding.

"Okay, maybe, but Kat, what am I supposed to do? Everything is going to shit."

"Everything is not going to shit. Your personal life's just gotten a little too intense, that's all. Calm down. You're doing well at school. You're getting work on the breaks. That play you did over Christmas was wonderful, and your bit on telly is coming up. You're on your way to being a professional actor."

"I'm a bit part actor about to start his last year of drama school. I don't see how my two scenes in next week's *Harbour Cops* qualify me as a professional."

"You're underestimating things. So what if the job is small? They auditioned dozens of actors and cast you."

"Yeah, but the shoot's over and school's starting again, and you know we're forbidden from taking professional jobs during the term."

She picked up a heavily marked script from the coffee table and waved it at him.

"It's all part of it. You start building your résumé during summer break, you get back to work at school. You graduate. You get another part, and then another. We build. You know that. People will see you're bloody brilliant, and this conversation will be a hazy memory."

"I know you're right. I just get panicky."

"Of course you do. You're at a crossroads. But for now, you just need to focus on those auditions. When are you on?"

"First appointment's at ten."

"You've got four hours. Go lie down and get some sleep before you go in."

He shut his eyes against the morning sunlight. "Lost cause. Sure you don't want to go to the beach?"

"I need to go for my run." She got up from the couch and leaned against the wall, pushing her legs backward into calf stretches. "And you're so exhausted you'll blow your auditions. Go to bed. Now." She pointed down the hallway, a mother sending a toddler to his room. "When you get up, meditate and run through your lines.

Message Sam and let him know where you are. Tell him you'll call him after school, that you're going to focus. We can cook dinner here later, get you centered, back on track." She leaned over and kissed him on the forehead, then grabbed her keys from the coffee table and walked to the door. "Sleep," she said, then pulled the door shut behind her, her soft footfalls barely audible on the stairs.

He stood and stretched, walked into his old room, the bed still covered with the same lacy rose-covered duvet. He'd always thought it a bit much when he lived there, real old granny style, but its familiarity comforted him now in his exhaustion. He shed his clothing in a heap on the floor and pulled back the bedding. The shades were already pulled down, casting the room in half light, and he lay back and pulled the sheets up to his chin, breathing deeply, telling himself it would be all right.

2

Sam

Surfboard balanced on his head, Sam jogged down the beach and out into the icy water. Rain streaming down his forehead, he kicked against the rough tide until he was waist deep, then jumped onto his board and paddled away from the city, cresting the waves that surged and crashed from the growing storm. The unexpected rain had scared the end-of-summer crowd off the beach, so he had the entire stretch to himself. He needed it. His head was still rough from last night, and he prayed the cold water would help his hangover, get his mind off things.

A storm-dark wave broke right in front of him, and he flipped his board, rolling under while it passed, then righted himself and pushed out further toward the big swells, his arms straining against the current as he banked and bobbed in the rough water. Just past the break line he stopped, sat up on his board waiting. Back on the beach, hordes of gulls screeched, pecking at sandwiches and ice creams abandoned by the crowds now huddled under café awnings along Bronte Road, watching and waiting. A growing gray mist obscured the slope behind them, a crisscross of houses and small apartment blocks, palm trees and frangipanis, rising to the top of the peak that cut Bronte off from the rest of Sydney and gave it the vibe of some tiny beach town miles from anywhere.

After Ryan ran off, Sam had sent Alky on his way—"Sorry, mate. Three-ways, yeah, cheating, no."—but still he'd hardly slept. He'd dragged into work late, making apologies to Jenny again. She'd told him not to worry—he was the boss after all—but he sensed the stress in her voice when she said that Kyle had rung twice from head office. Shit. Bastard was a clock-watcher for sure. He'd kissed her on the cheek and rung back, assuring Kyle that there had been a cock-up on the trains, then spent his first hour fiddling with paperwork he'd already reviewed, trying Ryan's number again every so often. He didn't expect an answer—he'd be in auditions—but he wanted there to be evidence that he had tried, that he'd kept trying. He'd been an idiot and he knew it. It had seemed like a great idea at the time. Sexy. Wild. Sharing his boyfriend with a hot piece of arse from the club. He shuddered now even thinking of it.

Ryan had texted just before lunch—I'm okay, stayed at Katrina's, at school now, probably stay over again tonight, talk later—so at least he knew where his boy was, even if he was still mad. He thought about heading over there after work, showing up at Katrina's and asking him to come home, but his gut told him no. If Katrina was there, it would just blow up in his face.

Katrina. Her. Ryan's best friend. He couldn't seem to do anything right in her eyes. Her place wasn't far from his office, just up the road on the Bondi side of the Tamarama Gully, in a block of what could be multimillion-dollar flats in the hands of the right renovators. Spacious and well appointed, all the solid craftsmanship of the 1920s, crazy ocean views. He'd mentioned this to her the first time he'd been invited over to dinner, and she'd smirked, said the lack of updating was exactly what she loved about the place. Quality craftsmanship, sea air, and nothing more. No delusions of grandeur. Leave the neighborhood as it was meant to be. He'd apologized, but she seemed put out for the rest of the meal, and made a point of deriding realtors and renovators and what they'd done to old Bondi more than once during the meal. He'd never found his footing with her after that. Always felt like he had to apologize for what his ilk had done to her precious old hippie Bondi of the seventies. A place that only existed in memory now.

So yeah, trying to talk to Ryan with her there would never work, but a surf would help. Get his blood pumping, sort out his thoughts, get through his hangover. They could talk later tonight. Meet somewhere neutral. Sort through this mess.

Most of the Bronte flats still stood from decades ago, modest red brick affairs, two or three floors, no more than six or eight units apiece, except for the property he'd been tasked with selling. It was a massive old concrete block clinging to the end of the southern promontory that separated Bronte from Clovelly, a 1950s brutalist slab that had been nothing special until the developers had gutted and rehabbed its flats within an ultra-modern inch of their lives. The developers were counting on the Bondi real estate boom to trickle down through Tamarama and hit Bronte next, and they'd booked his firm to sell them at top dollar. Sam had scored the lead agent position. His own building. Finally. And now he worked from the swanky on-site sales office with Jenny, a tatted-up Newtown hipster girl who had zero real estate experience but laughed at his jokes and didn't mind if he got to the office a little late, or if they knocked off a bit early on Friday for drinks.

But the units weren't selling.

Bondi and Bronte, while similar in name, couldn't be more different in style. Bondi was flash, mobbed with an ever-growing cluster of hip cafés, high-end hotels, local artisan boutiques, and yoga studios, the perfect gentle slope to the ocean giving almost every building astonishing views of sparkling blue water. Crowds of students and techie rebels crowded Campbell Parade and Hall Street, tourists abounded, and every unit sold hit top dollar.

Bronte's stretch of beach was just as gorgeous, but aside from the crowds at the one organic coffee shop and the surprisingly good Greek café, you'd be hard-pressed to rattle up any excitement. And that was what worked about it: its separateness, its slow pace. The residents were mostly young families and diehard surfies from back in the day, and the developers had misread the market and priced the units far too high.

Sam and Jenny often sat alone all day, praying for a potential buyer to walk in the door. He hadn't made a commission check in two months, putting him further and further in arrears as he tried to make things work on his base pay, cutting costs where he could, dodging phone calls from the bank about his mortgage. He'd called his dad again, past source of similar bailouts, but his dad had refused this time, subjecting him to an even harsher scolding than usual.

"Not this time, son, you've broken me this year."

"But Dad, I can get it right back to you. Commission check just around the corner."

"You said that last winter and I've yet to see it. You're in over your head. Dropped out of uni for this? You'd be better off moving back home and finishing at W.A."

Like that was going to happen.

He'd hated uni. Not at first. The first few weeks had been wonderful. The new friends, parties, all of Sydney at his feet. Amazing. But by the end of year one, he couldn't have gotten away fast enough. Not that he'd had much choice after being called out for an entire semester of missed lectures and failed exams. He'd been totally lost when he finally started to apply himself, months behind, but he was too proud to start over as his class moved on, so he'd walked out the door. He even liked real estate, but it still felt like some sort of consolation prize for failing at architecture school, especially since his dad had called in a favor to get him the job.

None of that really mattered, though. He could hope and regret and second-guess till his head exploded, but the mortgage still wasn't paid. He didn't know what he was going to do when the bank called again, but here, in the water, alone in the freezing Pacific, instinctively bobbing and weaving with the rhythm of the tide, he was in his element. For a moment, all was forgotten.

He ducked his head under the dark water again and reveled in the cold shock of the sea, then pointed his board straight east and paddled further out, watching, waiting, until a long rippling line appeared on the horizon, jumping and rolling as it swelled into a wave. It would be perfect. He shook the water out of his eyes, pointed the nose of his board parallel to the current, and started paddling hard as it rushed toward him, frothing and churning. The wave crested, he hopped up onto his board, and carved into it, the curl forcing him forward faster and faster, rain and wind in his face, his toes gripping the board, feeling the pound of the surf through the fiberglass, until the wave crested and broke, crashing around him as he went under, his leg band pulling tight as his board dragged him up. He surfaced, elated, catching his breath, ready for more.

Waist deep, he rubbed salt water across his board, banishing the last clumps of sand, while a few remaining rain-dodgers still fretted and huddled along Bronte

Road. He couldn't understand it. People came to the beach and then were afraid of a little water, running for cover like schoolgirls worried about ruining their hair. They filed into the cafés, or simply gave up and got in their cars, everyone gone but two scrawny kids walking down the beach toward him. They were both in rain-slick wetsuits, boards under their arms, both with that scraggly curly shoulder-length hair the high school boys were wearing around Sydney. They waded into the water a few yards down from him and dropped their boards. Whole damn beach open but they picked his spot. Sam scowled, flipped onto his board, and paddled further north toward the cliffs. Further out, the smaller boy bobbed over a small curl. Effortless. Smooth. Sam paddled further north, trying to give them a bit more distance, and looked back out to sea. The kids pushed further north as well. Sam growled. He wasn't going to let a couple of teenagers push him off his turf, so he stopped, determined to mark his territory.

After a few duds, he saw another good line forming, so he shoved further out and caught the wave right as it began to flip. He wobbled for a split-second, then hit a perfect balance at the front of his board, crouching, cutting through the wave like a skier in fresh powder. The smaller kid had caught it too, but couldn't keep up, and swerved toward Sam, bearing in almost on top of him. As he fell, Sam jumped, but it was too late. He scraped across the kid's board, lost his balance, and flipped backward into the water, landing on top of the boy, his rope twisting around his arm, tying them together and pulling them both down. The kid thrashed and kicked, sinking them deeper in the freezing cloudy water, until Sam's foot dragged painfully along the gritty bottom, dirt and sand clouding his vision. *Don't panic*, he mentally messaged the kid. He fumbled in the dark, lungs burning, until he grabbed the boy's arms, holding them in a tight clench, not letting him move, until the wave dragged them in and they floated to the surface in waist-deep water. The rain had stopped.

The boy gasped for breath, shaking.

"Jesus Christ, kid!" Sam grabbed him by the collar of his wetsuit and dragged him toward the sand. The kid skipped and stumbled to keep up with him, his face set in an embarrassed grimace. Sam stopped at the water's edge and stooped to untangle the ropes from their feet and each other. "You can't drop in on someone's wave like that. One of us could have drowned."

The kid looked terrified. His chin was bleeding. "Sorry. I'm sorry." He wheezed and coughed out a bit of water. "I thought I could handle it."

Close up, he saw that the kid was maybe fourteen, probably younger. Not even in high school yet. His arms and shoulders were thin, just starting to gain a little muscle. He looked like he was going to cry.

"It's okay, mate." He dragged his board out of the water and threw it ahead of him onto the sand. He grabbed the kid's shoulder to steady him and felt him tense up. "You all right?"

"I think so." He stared at the sand.

Sam guided him out of the water, the kid's board dragging behind him on his ankle rope, his breathing beginning to even out.

"I'm okay, really," he said. "I didn't mean to."

"You sure you're all right?"

"Yeah. Sorry. I just thought I could shadow you, you know, since you were such a good surfer, right? You'd know how to pick the good ones and I could follow. I didn't mean to crash into you."

"That's all right, mate, you're doing fine out there, you've got pretty good form, but you have to keep a safe distance. You see how unpredictable the water is?"

"You're bleeding, mister."

Sam looked down and saw the gash on his ankle, blood dripping down his heel onto the sand. "Shit," he said.

"I'm really sorry," the boy was whispering now, shaking.

Sam brushed the blood away, smearing it across his foot. "I'm fine. Don't worry."

The other kid had wandered closer bit by bit as they talked. He was a bit taller, pudgier, a dazed, mean look on his face. He stood just a few yards down the beach now, staring. "I'm going home, Perry," he said, then turned and walked toward the road.

"Perry, is it?" Sam asked the boy.

"Yeah."

"Some friend you've got there, Perry. Ducks out at the first sign of trouble?"

"It's his fault," Perry said. "He was the one who said we should shadow you. Probably leaving because he's afraid you'll kick his arse." He kicked at the sand, not looking at Sam.

"Ah, well. Let him go then." The clouds shifted again and a streak of sun hit the wet sand. "Be careful what you let your friends talk you into, though. What's his name?"

"He's called Spaz. He's not even really my friend. He just lives in our block of flats. He's an arsehole."

"Spaz? Really? What the hell is that short for?"

Perry shrugged. "Never asked him."

"Want to scare him?"

The boy smiled. "Hell, yeah."

"Hey Spaz!" Sam yelled. The other boy stopped and looked back. "Yeah, you!" Sam took two steps toward him. Spaz backed up a bit, nervous. "Watch who you mess with when you're surfing next time. You almost got your mate killed." Spaz looked up at the road, then back toward Sam, tensed for flight.

Bronte Beach was small as Sydney beaches ran, a slight crescent ending at sandstone cliffs, maybe a hundred yards in total. Spaz stood only a minute's run from the concrete steps that led back up to Bronte Road and the safety of shops and people.

Sam took another step forward. "Better run, Spazzo, I'm coming for you!" Sam jogged a few more steps and Spaz broke into a run up the beach, stumbling once on the steps, dropping his board, and lunging at the railing to pull himself up, hurtling toward the safety of shops and people. Perry laughed and brushed the crust of drying sand from his arms.

"There. Now he won't push you around anymore." He turned toward the ocean. "Let's give it a minute and we can go out again. Stay back but watch me and I'll signal you when to pop up. Looks like the rain's decided to stop for now anyway, so it'll be easier to see."

Perry looked up at him. "Really?"

"Of course," Sam said. "Someone's got to teach you, haven't they? Come on."

He slapped the kid's shoulder, threw his board over his head, and walked toward the surf.

"Perry!" a female voice called. "What are you getting up to?" Sam stopped. A woman walked toward them across the beach, waving, her loose tie-dyed skirt blowing in the wind. "Leave that poor man alone!" she called.

Sam shouted out to her. "He's fine. Just had a bit of a dustup."

She continued her approach, sandals in one hand and a woven tote bag in the other, long blonde hair still damp from the rain, her skin that deep tan that only comes from years on the beach. Classic Aussie surfie chick.

"I hope he's not making trouble for you."

"It's okay. He's okay. Learner's mistake. He knows now."

"He just got his first board a few weeks ago with his birthday and Christmas money. I guess I forgot to teach him a few of the rules." She pointed at Sam's foot. "You should have that looked at. That's quite a nasty gash."

"Nah. It's nothing. I'm a bleeder. It'll stop in a minute."

"It's my fault," Perry said.

"Course it is. Be more careful," she said. She pulled a handkerchief from her bag and held it out to Sam. "Hospital up the road. Happy to drive you to casualty. Better safe than sorry."

Sam took the handkerchief and dabbed at his ankle. "Really. It's fine. If it's still bleeding tonight, I'll come find him and drown him."

"You'd be doing me a favor."

"Mum!" Perry shouted.

"Oh you. You know I'm kidding." She tousled his hair, wooden bracelets and silver charms jangling on her wrist. "Raising a boy on my own. Never thought it would be my life, but we get along fine. Thanks for being cool."

"You surf?" Sam asked. She looked fit, athletic.

"A bit in high school. Grew up in Perth." She waved her hand in a westerly direction, as if the Indian Ocean was just down the street. "Wembley Downs."

"Great beaches there. I'm from W.A. myself. Down the road a piece from you, though. Margaret River."

"Ah, so you're posh then." She dropped her sandals and brushed a clump of sand from Perry's shoulder.

"Oh, we weren't as posh as all that," he said. "Working-class Margaret River."

"Like there is such a thing," she said. "You don't have to pretend for my sake."

She was right. The lie usually put people at ease and diverted unwanted scrutiny, but obviously if she'd grown up there, she knew what that part of the coast was like. Sam's father was an award-winning architect and he'd grown up in a huge house on prime coastal property. The surf had been his backyard.

"Well, yeah, I suppose . . . It's all the same neck of the woods, isn't it?"

"I don't think anyone in Wembley Downs would call Margaret River the same neck of the woods." She ruffled Perry's hair. "Seems you're taking surf lessons from the lord of the manor."

"Ah, well, we both ended up here, didn't we?" Sam worked the point of his board deeper into the sand, bracing himself with it like a shield. The rain had stopped, the water now a blissful calm. "What brought you to Sydney?"

"I'm the new art teacher at Randwick Primary School. Perry and I came over this summer." She waved in the general direction of the city. "I'm a painter."

"Lovely. You do showings?"

"Not recently. The move was a bit hectic, but I've started working again as we're getting settled."

"Let us know. Love to see your work sometime."

"Know any gallery owners?"

Perry grimaced. "Mum!"

"Oh, you." She patted his shoulder. "He's at that age where everything I do is excruciating."

"No galleries, but I'm a real estate broker. Sometimes we need paintings for staging flats. Be happy to hang your stuff for showings."

"That's kind of you."

"Ta. Just let me know when you've got something ready."

"Thinking about painting this. Don't usually do landscapes but no beaches in W.A. are this dramatic." She gestured toward the jagged red rocks below the Bronte cliffs. "What brought you out here?"

"I came out here after high school," Sam said. "Went to Sydney Uni, but school wasn't my thing. Itching to get into the working world. I do real estate. Mostly beachside stuff. I'm selling those new flats at the old Ocean Club building just up the road." He waved toward the end of the bluff.

"Ah, those are nice. A little too rich for our blood, though. We live in the flats above the Greek café on the corner."

The clouds had cleared now, the sky a brilliant blue, and people had begun venturing back out of the cafés and heading down toward the water again.

"His dad's in Indonesia. Works for an oil company. We divorced a year ago. Jack was going to teach Perry to surf this summer, but . . ." She glanced quickly at Perry and paused. "So you playing hooky from work today?" she asked Sam.

"Sort of," he said. "It's my lunch break, but I just sold a unit to a couple from Singapore looking for a second home on the beach. Got top asking price, so I'm rewarding myself a bit and taking a long one. Stretching it out. I'll head back in shortly."

He was bragging, puffing up. That sale had been over a month ago. He stopped, lowered his voice again. "Should honestly be back at work, though. But surfing clears my head. That is until young lads knock me off my board." He winked at Perry.

"He's a handful now and then, my Perry, that I'll say. You're good at it. I was watching from the café. Maybe you could give Perry some surf lessons, save yourself from future harm. I'd do it myself, but I can't tell you how much work it is getting settled in at a new job."

It struck Sam that her request was a bit bold. She was one of those women used to getting men to do things for her, he imagined. She was definitely attractive. But he hadn't thought about women in years and shook it off. His bisexual phase was long in the past. Still, the kid was cool, and clearly needed help.

"I was just offering, now that you mention it." He knocked his board three times with his fist. "Get him back up in no time. He has pretty good form already."

Perry looked up at his mother, sand spackled across his narrow chest. "See, Mum, I'm good at it. Told ya!"

The breeze rustled her hair and she pushed a stray curl behind her ear. "Was that good form as you knocked him down?"

Perry squinted up at her. "I said I was sorry."

"Well, the potential's there anyway," Sam said. "We'll knock him into shape."

A trio of young men in wetsuits, boards tucked under arms, jogged past them, kicking up sand.

"Of course you probably wouldn't want to teach him now that he's mortally wounded you. You really do need to see to that ankle." She tugged at her necklace again and held out her hand. "My name's Amanda, by the way."

"I'm Sam," he said, holding up his sand-crusted hands. "I'd shake but I'd cover you with muck."

"Rain check, then." She held both hands up, palms open. "And this is Perry, but of course you probably figured that out already," she said.

"Yeah, got it. And Spaz was the one who ran from the scene."

"Oh, that little shit. He says the cheekiest things to his mum, and I see him sneaking cigarettes behind our building. I can't wait until Perry starts making better friends at school."

"The kids here are all dickheads. I hate Sydney."

A group of teenagers stopped spreading their towels on the freshly sunbaked sand and looked up.

"Perry!" Amanda said.

"Well, they are." Perry pressed his forehead to his board. "I wish we were back in Perth."

Sam looked out to sea. Some real beauties were forming again. "I hated Sydney when I moved here, too," he said. "Thought Sydney Uni was full of wankers, but ended up making the best mates of my life. You'll do fine." He faced Amanda again. "He'll do fine at school. Soon enough he'll be a great little surfer, pull in all the chicks."

"Just what I need, a ladies' man at twelve," Amanda said. "I could barely manage his father. Maybe you can give him a few pointers in the gentleman department, too, so I don't have irate dads ringing me up to complain about him."

"Don't know if I have much to teach him in the gentleman department."

"Well, you've been more than a gentleman with my little monster. You'll have to come by for dinner sometime. Least I can do for you if you're serious about the surf lessons."

"Totally serious, and dinner sounds great."

"Give us a few to get settled and we'll set up a date. I mean, you know, a suitable day." She twirled her hair again, bracelets jangling. "And bring someone if you like, that is if . . ."

Sam realized she was fishing for his marital status.

"Think it'll just be me. Boyfriend seems to be making himself scarce," he said, trying to sound jovial but feeling the sting of it, replaying the image of Ryan disappearing down the stairs for the hundredth time.

Her eyes raised a bit at "boyfriend," as people's often did. He was used to it. Can't believe a manly bloke like you is gay, and all that. He had a rehearsed little speech along the lines of "not all of us are dancing down Oxford Street to Kylie Minogue," and was just ready to go in for the old joke, but her startle was only momentary; she'd masked her surprise and jumped back into the conversation.

"Well, I'm sorry to hear it. I'm sure it's his loss. And definitely his loss since he'll be missing out on my pasta Bolognese. This one loves it, anyway."

Perry sat next to his surfboard, tracing a finger along the aboriginal design, a swirl of dots twisting up from the edges to form the curved body of a goanna lizard. He was clearly bored with the adults now.

Amanda looked back toward the road. "Come on now, Perry. Let's leave the man to his surfing. You can sort out lessons later."

"Aw, no sorting needed. I'll be here Saturday, sometime around eleven a.m. Just turn up with your board and we'll get started."

"Awesome," Perry said. He tucked his board under his arm. "I'll be here for sure."

"It's really sweet of you." Amanda took her son's free hand, but he shook it away. "Be nice to your mum, Perry." She grabbed it again and held tighter. "G'day, Sam." They turned and walked toward the steps.

"See ya!" Sam called after them. He looked up the road toward the flats. Jenny was probably wondering where he was. To hell with it. He had no appointments and Jenny could manage things till he got back. He picked up his board and jogged back down to the water, his eyes scanning the dark-blue Pacific for the next wave.

3

Ryan

"Look at me. Whatever I'm gunna get, I've had, and damn near all that's been lost." Ryan drew out the word *lost*, made it rich, deep, resonant. "You can bear it when you lose money and furniture. You can take it when you lose your looks, your teeth, your youth."

He leaned into the words, the intonation not quite as he'd rehearsed. His voice a bit wobbly, higher pitched than it should eb.

Am I capable of this?

He took a deep breath and propped himself up further, leaning forward, his eyes focused on the ceiling. "But Jesus Christ, when your family goes—"

"Good God, Ryan. Stop there, please."

Ryan looked down from the makeshift hospital bed he'd fashioned out of a row of classroom chairs to see Graham frowning and waving his clipboard at him from his seat in the front row. Shit! Not now. He was at the best moment in the monologue, one breath before that wonderful, brilliant moment when his character, the dissolute patriarch of Tim Winton's *Cloudstreet*, having cut off all the fingers on one hand, having lost his wife, declares himself useless, declares all hope lost. Please just let me get that far. He'd even taped his fingers down with some dusty old gauze bandages he'd found in Katrina's cupboard and dripped them with a bit of pomegranate juice for blood seepage. Keep going. Grab the moment. He took a deep, gut-filling breath and picked up the line.

"It's more than a man can—"

"I said stop, Ryan." His teacher's voice was abrupt, annoyed. "Enough!"

He stopped, face burning, a moment of controlled breathing, then grabbed onto a wobbly chairback and hoisted himself up. In the semidarkness of the theater, his classmates huddled in groups of two and three, frozen, waiting for his fate to be decided, for judgment to be called. Graham held a silencing finger up while he continued scribbling on his clipboard.

That it had been a rough day was an understatement. He'd managed to catch up on some sleep at Katrina's, but he was still totally agitated from the previous night's antics. His heart was racing, his emotions manic, but he had to focus. Today was it.

Casting decided for the semester, and he couldn't let one stupid night of bullshit with Sam ruin it. He had every reason to be confident, he'd told himself over and over on the train on his way to school. His work had been well received last year, and he'd managed to book a couple of professional jobs over the break. He was nailing it, as they said. Lead parts should be his now. This should have been a cakewalk. But it felt wrong, sideways, his voice brittle and sharp, too loud, like the clatter of dishes smashing on a tiled floor. Not that the other students were faring any better. After Charlotte's piece, Graham had asked her if over the summer she'd lost her mind.

The earlier sessions had gone much better, still hopped up on coffee and indignation, but it had been hours now, a grueling afternoon of criticism and questions, and his energy was sapped. He was exhausted and frustrated, a perfect recipe for self-doubt. This was their third and final monologue of the day, and Graham had ripped them all to pieces from the start, not letting people finish, calling out sloppy character work, vocal tics, unnatural movement, and that cardinal sin, overemoting. "Not working hard enough over the summer," he kept saying. "Forgetting everything we've taught you. We should keep you all locked up." Lucy gave him a thumbs up from the back corner, but he knew it was half-hearted. At least everyone else seemed to be screwing up too.

"Why did you choose *Cloudstreet*, Ryan?" Graham asked, his unwavering eye contact unnerving.

Karen Flanagan, his second-year voice coach, looking mortified, focused her gaze on something far above his head.

Was that sarcasm in Graham's voice? Boredom? Ryan could never figure out how to read him. Head instructor of the drama division, Graham could be your champion one moment, encouraging and complimentary, then seconds later rip you to shreds, no encouragement, no teaching moments, just brutal bitter criticism. They'd all experienced it. First-year hazing, someone had said. Weeding out those who weren't ready to sacrifice absolutely everything for their craft. Of course it could be that he just sucked, as he sometimes secretly suspected, and that they'd only let him in to cash his double-digit international tuition check with no intention of really making an actor out of him. But he was being paranoid. Stop.

He pushed the lack of sleep out of his head, buried his worries about Sam, and grasped a moment of clarity. His juice-spotted makeshift bandages now made him cringe. Just add a broom handle for a sword and he could be a ten-year-old playing pirates. Why had he chosen it? It felt like a loaded question. To be honest, he'd never even heard of *Cloudstreet* before his web search for Australian monologues began a few weeks back, when they'd all gotten the audition schedule email. He had barely heard of Tim Winton, but he'd wanted to show them he was aware of Australian dramatic literature, that he wasn't just some cocky American who thought everything was David Mamet and Tennessee Williams. He'd stumbled onto it and read it in an afternoon. It was a rip-roaring play. Drowning, dismemberment, alcoholism, poverty, adultery, reconciliation—it was gripping stuff, but that answer wasn't going to fly, was it? What was he supposed to say? He didn't want to sound like a shallow soap opera fan. What was the smart answer? He punted.

"Well, I chose it because the character is incredibly complex, full of agony and regret for the results of a life lived without true purpose. Quintessentially Australian, of course, but the play is universal in the way it dissects working-class pain . . ." He realized he sounded ridiculous and barely whispered out, "and suffering," before falling silent.

He met Graham's gaze with all the manufactured confidence he could muster. Don't let him break you.

Graham clicked his pen three times, his expression blank. "Good God, Ryan, did you read that on the Australian Theatre Guild website?"

Ryan's face burned. That was exactly where he had read it.

"I don't think—"

"And you're American, yes?"

It was a provocation, a challenge. Of course Graham knew he was American. They all did. His presence in the program was a constant source of discussion, and he fought it as best he could, but it was exhausting. After being asked again and again, he'd come up with some pat speech about the distinctive, organic quality that Australian actors had, how he wanted to tap into that, rethink what he'd learned in the States, try a new approach. And he meant it, for the most part. At least he meant it when he wasn't thinking about all the other stuff that had sent him running halfway around the world from home.

But he knew Graham wouldn't buy it.

"Yes. I'm American. Absolutely," he said, injecting a false calm into his voice, "but that doesn't define me as an actor. I believe that we should explore characters of other ethnicities and nationalities. Like I said, the character's—"

"I'm not asking for your noble theory of other cultures and places." Graham cut him off. "I'm asking because you've got a bit of work to do on the accent. You sound like you're from a banana farm in Far North Queensland in the 1980s, not an impoverished Depression-era suburb of Eastern Perth. This may be news to you, but there is not one universal Australian accent. We don't all speak like Crocodile Dundee."

A burst of laughter erupted from somewhere at the back of the theater but was quickly stifled into a cough.

Ryan took a deep breath and sat up taller. "Of course. I didn't mean to be so broad. I guess I have to . . ."

"No," Graham cut him off, the clipboard waving in the air again. "You don't have to. It's dreadful. Horrendous. Start again, from the beginning, and chuck it. You say this man's pain is universal? Then find the essence of that pain and stop worrying about the Aussie pronunciations of *brothel* and *swagman*. I can see your mental process flashing across your eyes like the stock market ticker on ABC News. Forget the technical bullshit and dig into what's real. It's there." He paused. "And while you're at it, peel off those bloody ridiculous bandages."

Ryan sank back onto the chair-bed, unwinding the sticky nonsense from his wrist, hating himself for doing it, but awash with relief. *He's letting you start over.*

Graham had only let a few others finish: Lucy of course, the only Chinese Australian girl in the class, and a clear talent; Julia, the druggie hippie girl who never studied but somehow always managed to do amazing work; and "Fat Matt" from Wollongong, who had swaggered on stage this morning having lost thirty pounds over the summer, now a dashing leading man. They'd agreed he'd have to be called "Handsome Matt" now.

All the others Graham had dismissed halfway through in a fit of disapproval, no further chances offered.

Relieved, Ryan took a deep breath, held it, exhaled to the bottom of his lungs as they'd learned in workshop. *Push it all out. Let go of Sam. Let go of last night.* He was tempted to say a little prayer but pushed that away as well. He hadn't done much praying since he'd come to Sydney. *Lose the old ways. New you.* Ironic that his monologue was about faith.

His heartbeat steadied, and he felt his weight settled into the hard plastic seats. *Focus. Forget the stupid accent. Become the character. Be him. You're a drunken waste and you've done your family wrong at every turn. And you really have, haven't you? Left your church and family without ever truly figuring out why. Turned your back on God to run halfway around the world to party on the beach and have sex with men. What were you thinking? It's better you and Sam messed it up anyway. May as well walk away. Save you both the trouble in the end when it all blows up and you can't handle it and run away, just like you did from your old life in the States.*

"Ryan?" Graham sounded impatient. "When I give you another chance, you don't hesitate. Start again this minute or book a flight home."

He stood up from the ridiculous plastic chairs and faced the auditorium, inhaling, feeling his diaphragm, willing himself to forget about the accent, letting the words flow, losing himself in it; all rehearsed intonations gone, the natural bass timbre of his voice returned. He felt himself falling into the very real pain of being rendered completely useless, his own life blending with the one on stage, forgetting the people in the theater until he came to the last line, caught up in the emotion of the moment, panting from the exertion, and realized he hadn't been stopped.

"This time's going to be different. It's my time, for Christ's sake."

The words felt completely real to him. Personal. He waited for his heart to steady again, stood up, and collected his props, afraid to speak.

Graham looked up from his clipboard. "There was some honesty there, much better. Go and sit down now." He waved his pen to the steps at stage right. Ryan started toward them. "And Ryan?" Ryan stopped and faced his teacher. "In future you might try to avoid monologues that have been done for exam requirement by every male high school drama student in the country."

Ryan's guts clenched as he walked back to his seat next to Lucy. As Graham called the next student up, she grabbed his leg and squeezed. "You were really good. Amazing," she hissed. "You know that's just his way."

"Why didn't you tell me it was a high school piece?"

"Didn't know it was. All-girls' school. Sorry." She shrugged. Her hair was perfect as always. "You were bloody brilliant."

The remaining few students fared no better, and Ryan felt slightly vindicated. Graham announced that callbacks would be Friday, and roles for the semester would be posted the following week, then dismissed them with a warning to "bloody well pick it up a thousand percent," and sent them out. They all shuffled toward the back of the auditorium, a glum lot, eyeballing each other, silently grimacing, keeping silent until they could get to the halls and bitch openly.

"Ryan?" Graham's voice rang out from the stage as if he had a microphone. "A word?"

Ryan froze at the door. His stomach did a flip. Had he screwed up that badly?

Lucy squeezed his hand without a word, then shuffled out the door with the rest of his classmates. Ryan walked back toward his instructor, conjuring up his best "pleasantly open to feedback" face. "Yes, Graham?"

"The thing I don't understand"—Graham pulled an apple from his bag and took a big bite, splashing onto Ryan's face—"is just how polarly opposite the two performances were. Like two different people were on that stage. Where were you at first? Who was inhabiting that body?"

"I'm so, so sorry. I had a bad night. Some stuff happened at the flat. I got no sleep."

"I didn't ask what happened. I couldn't care less about the sordid lives of my students. I asked who was up there. I saw two different people. It's not the first time I've seen it, and it won't serve you in the end, so I ask you again. Who are you?"

"I think I'm—"

"It's not a question to be answered on the spot with what you think I want to hear. It's a question to be considered over time with some serious reflection and honesty. Think about it. We'll talk again."

"I will. I'm sorry."

"Stop bloody apologizing. You've nothing to be sorry for. It's possible you might even be quite a good actor, but you've got to start digging deeper. Figure this all out."

"I will. I promise."

"I hate promises even more than I hate apologies. I want action. Now go."

Graham went back to his notes and waved his hand toward the door without looking up.

"Yes, sir." Ryan walked slowly to the door in the now empty auditorium.

4

Ryan

They walked along the busy footpath past the stucco archways of the old surf club, skirting round the mob of gym boys on the outdoor fitness track and the mobs of tourists posing for selfies. Clear of the crowd, they took the last set of stone steps down to the sand, pausing below the deep red tidal pools and wind-carved cliffs of Ben Buckler. It was one of those glorious Sydney autumn days that felt like high summer. The beach was packed, the surf a relaxing roll, and Ryan felt the warmth of the sun turn to a sharp burn on his scalp. He'd forgotten sunscreen.

He pointed to a spot slightly back from the crowd and looked to Katrina for approval.

"This work?" He unfurled his towel and kicked off his flipflops.

She dropped her shoulder bag onto the sand. "It's not that I mind the location," she said, hands on hips. "It's a lovely spot, but must we always do the North Bondi gay thing? Couldn't we take it a little further down the beach so I at least stand a chance?" She pointed south toward the bustling strip of sand beneath the smart pubs and cafés of Campbell Parade. "Thousands of eligible straight men mere meters away, yet every weekend I'm up here playing sassy old auntie with half of Darlinghurst."

"Come on, Kat, it's not really half of Darlinghurst."

A group of well-muscled young men passed them shouting and laughing, tossing a football back and forth, their deep voices ringing out over the surf.

"See, there are straight guys here too." Ryan tugged at the corners of his towel, spreading it evenly over the sand. The football landed at Ryan's feet, and a fit young man in salmon bathers jogged toward them waving.

Ryan picked up the ball.

"Thanks for grabbing that, mate," he called out. Physical perfection. Classic Aussie bloke out for a day at the beach with his mates.

Ryan held the football toward him, pleased that he'd proven his point.

But the young man stopped short. "Oh my God, it's Katrina King!"

Ryan waved the football at him again. Nothing. He stood frozen, staring.

"Miss King. I'm a huge fan."

"Thanks, love. That's kind of you to say."

Katrina was always so gracious when people recognized her. Ryan promised himself he'd always be as kind as she was, that is if he ever made it.

"In fact, we just binge-watched the entire first series of *Changing Tides* this past weekend." He pointed at the mob of gym bunnies he'd just jogged away from, the lot of them messing with towels and pulling off shirts, a scene straight from a softcore porn video. "Different themed cocktail for every episode. You're just amazing in it."

Katrina pushed her sunglasses back and smiled warmly at him. "Goodness! That's some commitment. You must have been in nappies when the show was on. How did you ever see it?"

"Primary school. Year five. Used to watch with Mum when Dad was out at the pub."

"Now that's a bonding experience. Soapies after school with Mum. What's your name, love?"

"Kevin," he said. "Just like your boyfriend on the second series. In fact, the year he showed up, I used to imagine myself on the show. The fashion! The hair! It was all so phenomenal!" He twirled his hands around his head, fluffing some imaginary disco chic coiffure.

"Oh, that hair! We went through cans of hairspray every episode. Probably singlehandedly brought about climate change."

"Course my dad came home early and found us watching together, giggling and repeating lines. He forbid it from then on. Told her that I'd turn into a sissy."

"Oh, I hate hearing that, Kevin. Aussie blokes and their masculinity issues."

"Well, Mum got everything in the divorce, and here I am meeting you on the biggest gay beach in Sydney. Joke's on him, I'd say!" He gave a little kick at the sand.

Ryan cleared his throat and waved the football again.

"Oh! Sorry!" He grabbed the ball and chucked it in the air, spinning it perfectly. "Thanks, Tiger," he said, his voice dropping into a growl.

Ryan looked him up and down again, those perfect muscles, that deep sinewy brown. He busied himself with his towel and thought of skin cancer.

"Did you bring sunscreen, Katrina?"

Katrina nudged her bag with her toe. "Course I did. It may be buried under sandwiches, but I'm sure you'll find it."

"Thanks." Ryan dragged the bag toward him, leaving a track in the sand.

"But I should leave you two alone," Kevin said. "Last thing you need is some silly fanboy chatting you up when you're trying to enjoy your day out." He tucked the football under his arm.

"Oh, it's fine. Lovely to know people still watch the old relic."

"You're hardly a relic. You look amazing," Kevin said. "You still set the standard, you know. Any projects coming up?"

"Not acting. No. I'm done with that. I write for—"

"*Another Lifetime*! That's right! You won the AACTA last year. We were all scream-ing for you."

"Thanks. It's nice to be recognized for my mind rather than, well . . ."

"Well, rest assured we watch it religiously too. Still, it would be so lovely to see you on screen again."

"Oh, it's unlikely," Katrina said. "I really enjoy what I do now, but you never know."

"Kevin!" A shout cut through the crash of the surf.

He turned and waved at his gang. "I've gone on long enough, haven't I. G'day, Miss King. Enjoy your day out." He spun the ball again and trotted back toward his mates, who huddled around him immediately, hopping and gesturing, their excited shrieks carrying across the surf.

Katrina waved her hat at Ryan. "Throw me my towel, will you?"

"Here you go." Ryan pulled her neatly rolled beach towel from the bag and pitched it to her.

She unfurled the towel and spread it lengthwise next to his. "Now, what were you saying before he turned up? Something about all the straight boys who fre-quent this end of the beach, was it?"

"You can't fault me for trying."

"Well, don't hold back on my account. Might as well go get his number. I think he quite fancied you."

"He barely noticed me. Too busy diva worshiping."

"I'm not blind. Or deaf for that matter. I heard him call you Tiger. He practically growled at you. Seems to me that might be worth following up on."

"Oh, I don't know, he's a bit of a scene queen, isn't he? A bit nelly?" He knew he was being a bit harsh, but how could he tell her how badly he was missing Sam? That a date with a stranger was the last thing he wanted? It had only been two weeks, but the topic had been dismissed. On her advice, he'd told him he needed a break, needed some time to figure it out, but in the back of his mind, he was long-ing to run back to Kings Cross. They just needed to find the right time to talk. He hoped it hadn't passed.

"What's wrong with him being who he is? He seemed like a lovely guy."

"You're right. I'm sorry. Guess I'm just not quite—"

"There's enough homophobic abuse hurled at you and yours from the outside world without you adding to the problem from within."

He silently watched a flock of seagulls, swooping and diving, screeching as they gobbled up the dozens of tiny crabs exposed by the retreating waves. She was right, of course.

"I don't always think it through."

"I suppose that makes sense, given your past." She took a drink from her water bottle and dropped it back into her bag. "Shaking off a nineteenth-century fundamentalist religion takes time."

"Oh, now you're being ridiculous."

A child in a bright-blue bathing suit ran toward the gulls, shrieking with delight, scattering them from their meal. She ran on, giggling and twirling, while the birds returned to their original spot, pecking and gulping.

"Fair enough, I'll spare you the lecture on religion and homophobia, but I do worry about you sometimes, my dear," Katrina said. "You might try to break the cycle is all I'm saying. Go and say g'day. What could it hurt?"

"Not today. Not now. Still a bit raw about things."

"Of course. I should be more sensitive." She rolled her skirt into a pillow and lay back on her towel. "It's a lovely day. Let's enjoy it."

Ryan scanned the crowd. Men. Men with other men. Packs of men. Perfect bodies and not-so-perfect bodies, reveling in the sun and water. She was right, of course. But wait. There they were. A straight couple, at least for all appearances. Lounging on a towel and snuggling.

"There," he said, pointing.

"There what?" She shielded her eyes and tilted forward.

"Straight couple. Dead ahead."

He tugged his T-shirt past his ears and crumpled it into a ball.

She sat up. "Well spotted." Katrina grabbed the shirt out of his hand, shook it out, folded it, and placed it in her bag. "But we're still at losing odds."

"You still want to move then?"

"No. We're settled now."

"Yay! No packing up then!"

She flung a handful of sand at his knees. "Next time though. And I mean it. We don't have to go traipsing down to Mackenzie's Point or anything. Just edge our way down from here a wee bit? Find the dividing line." She held her arm out straight, palm sideways, chopping the air. "Where it naturally segregates. You can be on the gay side and I'll be on the straight side. We could set the marker, figuratively and literally."

"Oh God. Please don't write that in a scene."

"It's going in right after the line about all the straight blokes at the gay beach."

"As long as I get to play myself."

"Done. Then we'll have two AACTA winners in the house."

"As we should."

It was a perfect afternoon. The sky a deep blue he'd never seen in the States, waves crashing along the perfect crescent of sand. If only it wasn't so crowded.

"Of course, we could try Bronte or Coogee. It's become such a mob scene. It was a totally different thing when I moved here. A little bit hippie. A little bit rundown. Relaxing."

"Sam surfs at Bronte, you know. Religiously. Been a couple of times with him, but I've always thought of it as his thing. Like it's sacred to him or something."

He pushed more sand under the towel, building up his makeshift pillow, then flopped over on his back, the sun warming his forehead.

"Sam doesn't own Bronte. But if you don't want to run into him, Coogee's a nice change. Down to earth."

"Isn't it a bit bogan?"

"Don't be so quick to pick up our local insults. You sound mean."

"Sorry. Sorry." He had no idea about Coogee really, only that people he knew didn't go there.

"It's a perfectly nice suburb with a lovely beach and some really nice cafés that cost half of what they're charging on Hall Street, but that's beside the point." She fished her water bottle out of the bag again and popped the top. "As an actor, you should embrace difference. Sneering at a working-class beach? For God's sake, Ryan."

"You're right. I'm being horrible. So many parts of Sydney I haven't seen. I guess I found my little niche right off and never ventured beyond it. Newtown to Kings Cross, Darlinghurst to Bondi. I guess I just found what worked and stopped exploring."

"That settles it then. Coogee next weekend."

"Coogee it is." He squirmed a bit to get more comfortable. "Here's hoping Mr. Right awaits you."

"Awaits both of us, perhaps. You just might meet someone new once we stray away from all this."

"We'll see," Ryan said. "I still need to talk to him."

"Yes. In good time."

"In the meantime, we'll go to Coogee and find you a boytoy."

A gust of wind swirled around them and Katrina grabbed her pale-blue beach wrap as it fluttered across her towel. "I'm not fantasizing about meeting a surfie half my age, if that's what you're thinking. I just needed to remind you that I'm not dead yet."

"Of course. Sorry."

Out in the water, a few dozen surfers took advantage of the warm weather and rising tide, their wetsuits sleek and dark against the bright blue of the Pacific.

"And for your information . . ." Katrina stared out at them, her hand shading her eyes from the sun. "I had a date last week. Dinner and drinks at a little garden café in Paddington."

"Why didn't you mention it?"

"I wasn't sure I was going to see him again. But I think I will. Just decided it, actually. He was good fun."

"Who is he?"

"Nathan. An actor who just did a bit on the show. Three-episode arc. Rachel's estranged brother resurfacing to help with the funeral. Dubious past. We're seeing how he plays and then maybe extending the arc. Might give him a quick romance with one of Rachel's mates. Course he doesn't know that yet."

"Well, that's a bit of news. What's he like?" Ryan turned back onto his belly.

"Smart. Funny. Talented. You know I'm a sucker for talent."

"Handsome?"

"As it happens, yes, not that that's the most important thing."

"Helps though."

"Or hinders. I think sometimes you're too concerned with all that."

"Maybe." Ryan felt his shoulders starting to burn. "We should get in the water."

She rummaged through her bag, papers and bottles appearing, then pulled out a manila folder and waved it at him. "Later. I've got scripts to review and I've got a detective novel in here somewhere I've started and restarted at least five times."

"Well, my back is scorching."

"So have a quick swim. I'll cheer you on from here. And when you get back, let's get some more sunblock on you."

"Sounds good."

"Wait." She grabbed the hem of his knee-length floral board shorts. ""You're not swimming in these, are you? Two years in Sydney and you're still turning up in these ridiculous things?"

"Mormon modesty, I guess."

"But it's not just Mormons, is it? Some weird prudish American thing. What's the point of wearing knee-length trousers into the water? Afraid of the sight of your own bodies?" She gestured at the fit young men in Speedos and short shorts splashing in the surf. "You better get with Aussie style, or you'll still be lying here alone, waiting for your dream man in your old saggy daks when winter sets in."

"Yeah, well, I haven't done too bad so far, have I?"

"Suit yourself. Your tan marks will be awful, though."

"Part of my American mystique." He hopped up from his towel and wiggled his hips at her, then trotted toward the water, picking up speed, psyching himself out for the inevitable cold shock at entry. The trick was to run at it like a maniac and throw yourself in so you were submerged. If you went in slow, you ended up tiptoeing and mincing in like the Japanese tourists in their rolled-up suit trousers.

He splashed through the sharp chill of the first baby rollers, kicking and lunging, raising his feet higher as the depth increased, than dove head-first into the swell, the shocking freeze over in a second. Swirling along with the curve of the current, he stayed under as long as he could, breaking the surface a few yards further out. Breathing deep, he ducked under again and kicked hard, pushing further and further away from the shore, the cold water soothing his burning forehead, his body temperature kicking up, adjusting to keep him warm. His lungs about to burst, he pushed up and bobbed with the swells, out in deep water now, counting his breaths. He was closer to the surfers now and watched them with interest. The guy just ahead of him lay flat on his board, body perfectly tanned, wet suit hugging his fit frame, his head up like a prairie dog scanning the horizon for a predator. He hopped up suddenly and angled north away from Ryan, leaning effortlessly into the swell as it curled. It was a beautiful sight, and he sighed in envy. He'd been loving his lessons with Sam, but hadn't quite gotten the hang of it yet, and, well, at this point who knew when his next lesson might be? What did "taking a break" mean? How long? New territory for him. And being with Katrina was so easy, so effortless. Like having a bohemian surrogate mother, an Aussie Auntie Mame.

He splashed around for a minute, ducking and turning, staying under as long as he could. Pushing out further, alternating strokes, ducking under again, letting the current carry him. He'd been on the swim team in high school, been really good at it. And it had gained him a little bit of status in the rigid stratification of his high school, elevating him from drama geek to athlete.

He loved being in the water. It was the thing he and Sam had bonded over that first weekend at the beach. The beauty and peace of it. The rhythm and force. The exact opposite of the electricity of the stage, the water soothed him like nothing else in his life.

He felt it now, freeing him from everything that was dragging him down here. Here in Sydney, where everything was supposed to be perfect but wasn't. Scarce money. Auditions that went nowhere. Exhausting shifts at the café that saw him getting home at four in the morning smelling of spilled beer and fried food. And men. Sam. He had imagined when he arrived that he'd be the toast of the town, the hot American on the market, the one they'd all be clamoring for. But he'd not quite tapped into how it was done, been nervous and fumbly, letting his theater nerd tendencies and his first-timer insecurities ruin many a first chat.

And the Mormon thing. As much as he played it off as a thing of the past, he found he often went back and forth between regret, guilt, and indignation over it. As a younger man, the whole no-sex-before-marriage thing had created the perfect rationale to continue ignoring his awakening sexuality, but now that he had decided to embrace it, leave his supposedly straight Mormon life behind, he was finding it more and more difficult to navigate.

Of course, he'd messed around with a few guys during those first months, sure he was embarking on a new romance each time he hooked up, only to discover that "let's do this again" meant "let's do this again, but only if we happen to run into each other out and neither one of us has picked anyone else up yet."

After a particularly hot hookup, one guy had drunkenly invited him to a footie night at his local pub before passing out, then seemed utterly surprised when Ryan turned up. He'd made an awkward show of including him, but he and his horde of mates had gotten carried away with the shouting and drinking and Ryan had slunk off humiliated.

Mates. The whole mateship thing baffled him. Men traveled in packs here. The more the merrier, the louder the better, and if you didn't meet approval with the mates, you didn't get a call back. He didn't. He hadn't. And it seemed nobody really wanted a boyfriend, so he'd started sleeping around. That at least he could figure out. Go to the bar, have a few beers—now that he'd gotten past the shock and horror of his first taste of alcohol—then hook up with the guy who made the best joke about your accent. They were all sort of interchangeable, handsome, fit, so it didn't matter who he chose. Go home for some fun, prattle on about acting as they fell asleep, then the next day find his way home in the hot Australian sun, any sort of romantic inclination he had fading into regret and a burning shame for betraying his religion as he wandered the streets of yet another unfamiliar neighborhood hoping to see a CityRail sign sooner rather than later.

Katrina had expressed concern the third or fourth time he'd stumbled in at dawn. "Revel in your freedom, darling, but at least text and say you're not coming home."

And then he'd met Sam. And Sam had asked him to spend the night and then actually called him a few days later. Ryan had been giddy but still a bit suspicious. They'd gone to dinner that night and he'd stayed over again, then gone to the beach the next morning. And he'd tried surfing for the first time. Glorious. Exhilarating.

The next weekend, they'd gone to a movie instead of the bars, and pretty soon were spending all their time together. He was relieved to be free of the bars, thrilled to be falling in love (maybe?). He really just wanted to settle down after all, hang out, have a quiet coffee or meal with someone he liked, and Sam had been the first one willing to do that, the first one who had noticed him beyond the superficial. He didn't even mind that Sam still got good and drunk now and then, well, every weekend these days, because he always got really affectionate when he did. But now this drama. This limbo. He hadn't even intended it to go on this long, but the first day or two had gone by with him still angry, then three or four, and being back at Kat's was so lovely, so relaxing.

And now it had been long enough since his last voicemail that he felt frozen, embarrassed to call back. He was still shocked by the unannounced three-way thing, the casual ease with which he was meant to play along. It had hurt him deeply. How do you explain that to someone who's taken that sort of thing in stride for years? He ducked under the water again and wished he could be lost at sea, holding his breath while he let himself drift, his lungs beginning to burn. He'd moved thousands of miles from home to this big beautiful city in the tropics to be an utter nobody.

He surfaced and pushed back toward shore as another surfer paddled past him and gave that silent nod that he'd at first thought was cruising but later realized was just a blokey way of saying g'day without speaking, a masculine signal of recognition. Yet another Aussie-ism that threw him off, made him feel alien.

He reached the shallows and kicked his way up to the sand. Katrina was lost in her book, so peaceful amid the pack of tanned bodies.

He lay back down next to her on his lumpy towel. At least she felt like family.

A rowdy bunch of teenage girls, their bare legs caked with sand, hair blowing in the wind, pushed past them toward Campbell Parade, rattling off some intense conversation in Italian. Ryan realized he was incredibly thirsty. He held out his hand. "Toss me that water, will you?"

She rummaged in the bag and tossed him a bottle. It bounced off his shoulder and landed in the sand.

"So when you seeing this Nathan again?" He cracked the seal and took a long drink.

"Don't know. Might play mysterious for a day or two. But likely this weekend."

"You'll have to keep me posted. Or maybe I could tag along and sit at the bar or something, you know, keep an eye. Intervene if it goes badly."

"I can take care of myself." She turned a page and stared at her book for a moment. "He's a bit younger, you know. Not that it should matter."

"How much younger?" His curiosity was piqued. Katrina hadn't dated since he'd moved in, said her last divorce had killed any and all desire for romance.

"A bit. A big bit. Young enough that I could be his, well, I could be his aunt I suppose, not quite a big enough gap to play schoolmistress and naughty scholar if that's what you're thinking."

"What? Course not. I was just—"

"I am a bit nervous, to be honest. He's a solid fifteen years my junior, and there's the added complication that I pull sway on a show he very much wants a bigger part on. I honestly don't know if I should trust it."

"But of course he likes you. What's not to like? If he has motive, well, you'll suss it out and send him packing, right?"

"It sounds so easy. Just walking away from someone when you don't like something about them."

"What?"

"Sorry. Not trying to make this about you and Sam."

"I left a couple of voicemails. He knows where I am." The bravado felt false, but he felt like it was what she would want to hear.

"When?"

"The day after the whole mess. I even went by a couple of days ago and grabbed a few shirts and some underwear while he was at work. I'd worn the same clothes to school for two days."

He'd intended to wait for Sam to get home from work that day, had waited nervously for hours, but when he wasn't back by eight, he'd lost his nerve and left.

He turned away from her now, evaluating the crowd, hordes of them now, only thinning out at the rocks below the Icebergs Club, an emblem of stark white modernity and Eastern Suburbs privilege clinging to the bluff, waves splashing over the sides of its famous freshwater lap pool.

She set the book face down, open to her page, spine cracked from previous reads.

"Honestly. I thought you'd be back over there by now. Silly fight. Patched it up. Moving on with things."

"But I thought you said—"

"I know what I said, and I meant it. As much as I think he's a larrikin, you still owe him a chat."

"I've wanted to this whole time. I just thought—"

"I know, dear. It's been eating you up."

"Why didn't you—"

"You needed some time to cool off. But you've had it, and you can't just walk away from your troubles."

"I don't know what to say, though. It feels like more than just a silly fight. Like this whole time he hadn't been listening. Not really getting who I am."

"All the more reason to sort it out with him. You can't just ignore people you're upset with until they go away. Face the situation. Don't be so bloody fragile, so Victorian, for God's sake."

"At least you didn't say stop being so Mormon."

"Well, you are being a bit prissy about it all."

"Prissy?" But he knew she was right. He'd played the scene over and over in his head, casting himself as the wronged heroine in some kitchen sink drama. But he'd also played a part in all of it.

"Been there myself, you know. If I'd just been a little more forgiving with Bill, we might still be together. I was so smug about everything, always insisting on my way. He understandably got tired of it. Don't let that happen to you."

Her revelation surprised him. "Sorry, I didn't realize."

"It's all long ago." She closed her book and set it on her towel. "And now I'm going for a swim."

Katrina stood and stretched, the breeze tossing her blonde hair, then jogged down toward the darkening water, her heels kicking up sand as she ran.

5

Sam

The summer night was warm, the courtyard full of artfully disheveled and tattooed King Street locals chatting and laughing, knocking back pints of Cooper's and Toohey's. Sam had gotten there early, securing a prime spot at the end of the courtyard against the aging sandstone wall, the original rock just visible beneath an unreadable collage of band fliers and flatmate notices. His university days were a decade behind him, but he still knew how to pull off the look for the neighborhood—singlet under faded op-shop western shirt, cuffed jeans, boots, his beard trimmed, his surfer's tan glowing under the string of lights that wound through the branches of the gnarled old gum tree that shaded the entire patio.

He held up his empty pint and waved at the barman stationed behind a rickety makeshift work station—a raft of two-by-fours propped up on blocks, bottles lining a metal shelving unit that looked like it had been salvaged from a derelict garage. He nodded at Sam while he rattled a silver cocktail shaker around, siphoning its pale-pink contents into four martini glasses for what appeared to be a group of CBD professionals—suits and ties—looking very pleased with themselves for keeping it real with the Newtown crowd. "With you in a tick, mate," he shouted. Sam tilted his empty pint back, draining the dregs, and gave a thumbs up.

He was a little worried things wouldn't go well tonight. He'd never expected one bad night to turn into two weeks of exile. Ryan had never run off like this before, nor had he ever taken this long to respond with even the simplest message. A day or two, sure. When he was in his head about something, he rarely checked his phone, and often days would go by before he noticed things, but with the blowup of last weekend, Sam assumed he would have been anxious to talk, or at least send some message that he was okay. If Sam didn't know him better and hadn't gotten used to Ryan's frustrating communication style, he might have already given up. But he didn't want to give up. He wanted this to work. As fucked up as things were, they weren't beyond fixing. They'd been pretty good, to be honest, which was why the dramatics of the other night had so caught him off guard, not that he was going to lead with that. His phone beeped. Ryan.

On my way.

"What does that even mean?" he muttered to himself, but texted back:
Cool. On way as in leaving Bondi? Or on way as in almost here?
Just got off train. See you in five.
He sighed, relieved, and texted back: *At table on back patio. Want me to order you a beer?*
Yeah. Why not?

So that was at least a good sign. Ryan often passed on drinks, and had opinions when others (Sam) partied harder than he liked. Saying no to a beer was un-Australian, but Sam chalked it up to Ryan's Mormon upbringing and held his tongue when the occasional scolding occurred.

The barman arrived with his fresh pint, sooner than Sam expected considering the size of the crowd. Tattooed vines and flowers climbed from within his shirt, up his neck, stopping just below his ear, his moustache waxed to two fine points, an inexplicably popular trend these days. Sam handed him a twenty. "Keep it, mate. And keep 'em coming."

"Cheers. Next one's on me, mate."

Sam took a gulp of the cold bitter draft. "How's that North Shore crowd treating you over there?" he asked, wiping foam from his lip.

The barman grimaced. "Ah, you know. Blender drinks and special requests. Everything muddled, steeped, and shaken. Killing my timing. I'm Greg, by the way."

"Sam, here." He lifted his glass in a salute. "No worries. You're keeping up with me just fine. They look like a pack of wankers, though."

"They're nice enough, I suppose, but this artisanal cocktail craze is a disgrace to true Australian pub culture. Bloody nonsense."

"What's wrong with a classic pint of VB, right?" Sam asked. He leaned back in his chair and took another sip.

"Too right. But I suppose I shouldn't be so harsh. Those arseholes pay the bills, and I'm assuming they'll clear out early. Got to get back at their computer stations to continue swindling the likes of you and me out of our pensions." He stacked Sam's last two empties. "What you up to tonight?"

Sam crushed his growing collection of damp paper beer mats into a ball and dropped them into the top glass of the stack. "Meeting my boyfriend for apologies. Behaved like a dickhead a few weeks back and he's been staying with a mate. Hoping to get things back on track."

"Went through a divorce last year. Mate, I feel you." Greg looked away, his eyes scanning across tables, taking in the state of business, then made a quick swipe across the table with his bar towel. "If he's as nice a bloke as you are, he'll see reason. Just wave when you need another pint. Boost that courage." He patted Sam's shoulder, then walked on to another table.

Sam fiddled with his lighter, clicking the flame on and off, then placed it on the table. No need to be reeking of ciggies if he and Ryan ended up back at his place.

At least that's what he hoped. Get him back home tonight, let him pack his things from Katrina's tomorrow or whenever. Put this silliness behind them. Seemed like a fairly simple task, but then again, who knew what silly ideas Katrina had been filling Ryan's head with?

Katrina irked him. And funny thing was, his mum had loved her show when he was a boy. Every Thursday night tuning in to see what was happening in the perfect little beachside village of Warangata Creek, where the gorgeous locals were always up to astonishing hijinks that would have them arrested, bankrupt, or hospitalized in the real world. He had never understood his countrymen's obsession with soap operas set in small towns. If you based your understanding of Australia on what was shown on television, you'd think that every Aussie raised sheep or worked at a beleaguered coastal clinic hours from the nearest hospital.

But bad eighties show aside, he'd been excited to meet her at first. "How the hell did you end up sharing a flat with an eighties telly star?" he'd asked when he and Ryan first met.

"She graduated from the conservatory back at the beginning. Rents out her room to a student now and then and I got lucky. And anyway, she's a writer now. Doesn't act anymore," Ryan had told him. "Said she got tired of the beauty wars. Took a pay cut, but says she's happier. She's smart. Funny. Doesn't take crap from anyone. A wonderful person."

Wonderful. Wonderful if you liked judgmental greenies who couldn't stop scolding you about cultural awareness or humane farming or bloody climate change. He'd complimented her at their first dinner, telling her how beautiful she was for her age, and she'd made a crack about winning two ACTAAs for writing only to find she was still being judged on her looks. He'd sat silently at the dinner table after that, hurt by how casually she'd brushed him off, had made him feel so small.

But here was Ryan now, and there would be no criticism of his flatmate. He stood at the doors to the patio, scanning the tables for Sam, as natural and unassuming as he always was. Sam had first noticed him across the bar at a pub in Erskineville, drag queens parading around the stage to an old disco song, and he'd been instantly attracted. Ryan had been with his drama school mates, but didn't seem to belong with them, something a little manlier about him, broody, not like his mates as they waved their hands and twirled to the music without being anywhere near a dance floor. He'd walked over and said g'day, all bluster hoping to impress, then bloody well melted when Ryan answered in an American accent. A few months into dating, he'd asked him to move in and Ryan had said yes, although Katrina had not approved.

He imagined her triumph when Ryan had shown up after that disastrous night, could hear her tut-tutting to him about him finally leaving that directionless party boy, Sam. Ryan had let it slip that she had called him that, and it had really irked him. Party boy? Sure. He was in his thirties and fit and fun. Not time to hang it up just yet.

And he'd met Ryan at a pub, hadn't he? But directionless? He had been the top sales agent of the year at T. R. Booker twice since he'd started, earning him his current spot managing sales for a block of top-of-the-line renovated flats in Bronte. Granted sales were a little slow, well, dismal to be honest. But again, not the topic for tonight.

"Hey, Sammo." Ryan had picked up on Sam's old high school nickname from his sister Belinda at his birthday party. It always sounded odd in his accent, all vowelly and drawn out, but even more out of place tonight. Unnatural. Falsely jovial.

"Glad you made it. I was starting to get worried." Sam leaned in to kiss him, but Ryan hesitated, turned his head. Too soon. Okay. Pulling back.

Sam waved at Greg. The barman nodded and grabbed a pint glass from the shelf.

"Yeah, sorry about taking so long," Ryan said. He scraped his chair forward across the rough brick and leaned against the table. "I should have called sooner but I wanted to make sure I was clearheaded. I was working all week and crazy with school stuff. Auditions for the fall semester play series were last week, and I was totally in my head."

"Yeah. I even knew that. Should have remembered. I'm sorry. Probably good that you took your time. We both needed to cool off."

"Yeah. Anyway. Sorry."

"You do all right on the auditions?

"I messed it up, but so did everybody else." He looked up at the night sky. "Beautiful tonight. Nice choice, the patio."

"I remembered you like it here." He tried to make eye contact but Ryan kept shifting his gaze. The trees, the other patrons, it all seemed to be fascinating him. "So? You get any decent parts?"

"Well, yeah, decent, but not the lead. I got the third part in a Eugene O'Neill play, one of the bumbling brothers. A few good moments, a bit of stage time, not bad, I guess. We go into rehearsals next week. I was really surprised I got it, to be honest."

"Why? You're amazing."

"I really screwed it up at auditions. Graham ripped into me."

"I'm sure you were great." Sam noticed Ryan's face flush. Was he uncomfortable? Nervous? "And I'm glad you finally got back to me. I've missed you. Missed hearing about school. Theater. My boy's going to be a star, right?"

"We'll see about that."

"You lined up any other gigs?"

"Nope. Can't take outside jobs during school."

"Right. I knew that."

"So it's back to poverty for me. Nine months of it. Then graduation, and then, well, stardom or starvation."

Greg arrived with two beers. "Here you go, mate," he said to Ryan, setting a full glass in front of him. "Go easy on him, eh?"

"Thanks," said Ryan.

Sam gulped the last of his pint down and swapped it out for the other. Greg collected the empties and walked back to the bar.

Ryan took a sip of his beer and caught Sam's eye for a second, looked away. "How are you, then?"

Sam took another drink. Should he tell the truth? Let him know how badly things were going? How would that play out in getting him back? He wanted Ryan to be comfortable, to feel welcome and safe. Why trouble him with his worries?

"Great." He felt the lie forming before he told it. "Sold two flats last week. Got top asking price, too. Head office was starting to breathe down my neck about it, but I showed them. They don't get the Bronte thing. Beach is beach to them. What works in Bondi and the North Shore should work here, right? But that's not quite it. Bronte's different. Special. You have to finesse it. Sell the family thing, the quiet. No strutting your stuff with the beautiful people. No posh wine bar or Cross Fit gym. Just great surfing and serenity. They've questioned my tactics, misunderstood me, but it's paying off now. Should be smooth sailing from here."

"I miss hanging out there, you know. Meeting you after work. I miss my surf lessons."

"Nothing stopping us if you want to go at it again. I started teaching this kid. He's twelve. Smart-arse little bugger. Perry's his name. Smart-arse but great kid, and he's a right good little surfer. His mum is single and struggling, so I offered to help them out. You could come along."

"Hmm, single mum getting free surf lessons for her son from the high school champ. Sure that's all she's after?"

"Please. She's a nice woman. Whatever. What I'm saying is, I want us to be together again."

"Sam, I do too, but listen. I . . . I don't know. I felt a bit foolish the next day, you know, stomping off in the middle of the night all offended like that. Like a real drama queen. I mean, maybe it's a bit of Mormon morality rearing its prudish head, okay? It comes up now and then, sure. But it felt like . . . more than that. I don't know. Like I don't understand how we got there."

A techno song kicked in, blasting from the speakers hanging in the tree, the bass shaking the table.

Sam leaned forward and shouted to be heard. "You're right. I really overstepped. I had no business dragging home some random bloke for a three-way in the middle of the night without any sort of warning."

"Yeah, I was pretty surprised."

"Not that it changes things, but I was pretty smashed. Probably wouldn't have done it sober."

Sam glanced down at the beer in his hand. It was only his third or fourth. Whatever.

"You definitely were." Ryan continued to shout over the thunk of the bass.

"Christ, turn this bloody shit down!" a voice yelled from the bar.

The music softened a bit and Sam leaned back, wiggling his chair back to a good position. "So I was drunk, yeah, but I honestly didn't mean to start trouble. You've got your studying and your rehearsals and your waiter shifts, and I was being a shit. I forget what being in uni is like. Honestly it was all in fun. I just wasn't thinking." He paused, letting the last statement sink in. Music, chatter, and clinking glasses blurred into a shapeless cloud of sound. Was what he'd just said true? It had to be. He knew what he wanted. Ryan. Nothing else. He felt a little dorky amid all the haircuts and hipster glasses. He just needed to focus.

Ryan had been crumpling and uncrumpling his napkin. He looked up now and dropped it on the table. "Look, I don't want to sound like I'm your scolding old grandma, but it was just, you know . . . that night wasn't even that bad, it was just the third night that week you'd come stumbling home like that. Drunk, I mean, not dragging someone along." He paused. Sam felt him building up his courage. "Is sex not good enough with me?"

"What?" He slammed his glass down, sloshing beer over the sides. "Sex with you is amazing!"

A young girl at the next table, all tattoos and dreadlocks, glanced at them and giggled.

"I just. I don't know, I got drunk and wrought up and thought it would be hot. I mean, we had talked about the possibility, right?"

"Yeah, and if you remember right, that conversation didn't end with my consent." Ryan looked up at the sky, chin tight, his sign that he was frustrated, furious. Sam had grown to recognize it. "Jeez, Sam," he said. "We're only a few months in, just barely getting to really know each other, and now porn-star-hot strangers in our bed in the middle of the night?"

"To be fair, he was hot, wasn't he?"

"Not the point." Ryan continued staring off into the distance, but he couldn't help laughing. "Okay. Yes. Sometimes I'm so uptight, I drive myself crazy. You must think I'm the biggest prude, but this is all still so new to me. Don't forget that, all right?"

"Of course not! I love when you get all shy and Mormon on me. It's cute as hell."

"That's not what you said that night."

"I said that in the heat of the moment and I'm sorry. The Mormon thing has always been charming to me. You're so old-fashioned and polite, courtly almost. I just need to remember where you're coming from."

"Just picture the spires of the Salt Lake Temple every time I clutch my pearls over your antics."

"You know I've never been there. I can't even begin to imagine."

"Who from Australia has? It's beautiful. A bit boring maybe."

Sam pulled out his ciggies again and fiddled with the packet. No Smoking signs were posted around the courtyard but they didn't seem to be stopping people.

"Go ahead. You're dying to have one, right?" Ryan said.

"You don't mind?" Sam tapped one out and held it to his mouth, his eyebrows raised, asking for permission.

"Have I ever said anything before?"

"I really do mean to give up." He lit it and inhaled deeply, blew smoke away from Ryan toward the wall, the nicotine instantly lowering his stress. Ryan pushed the ashtray toward him and made a show of fanning the smoke away. "So . . ." Sam took another deep drag. Held it. Exhaled. Glorious.

He tapped the ash tray. "Can we try again?"

Ryan looked down at the table, picked up his scrunched napkin.

Shit. Had he asked too soon?

"Course we can," Ryan said. He pitched the napkin at Sam. "You're ridiculous, you know."

Sam's heart raced with the joy of the news. Fuck yes! He felt the heat of the smoke, the beer, all pulsing through him, arousing him. "Want to come home?"

"Now?

"Well, yeah."

"Of course I do."

Sam took another drag, then blurted out, "We should just get married."

"What?" Ryan sat straight up in his chair, staring. He fiddled with his still full beer, running his finger around the rim of the glass. "You serious?"

"Course I am." He realized as he said it that he was.

"Okay then." Ryan looked a little wary. Incredulous.

"Okay? So is that a yes?" Go with it, Sam. You can't back out now.

"Yes, that's a yes." Ryan's face broke into a big smile.

"Fuck yeah!" Sam pumped his fist in the air.

The dreadlocked girl looked up from her table again and imitated his fist pump. "Fuck yeah!" she shouted.

They drank the last of their beers and walked over to the bar. Sam too giddy to say much more. He paid the bill.

"Glad to see you blokes working it out," Greg said as he counted out the change. "You'll be happy as hell, mark my words."

The pub was filling up now, transitioning from the office happy hour crowd to the hardcore partiers the neighborhood so easily welcomed.

"Course we will, mate," Sam said.

They walked through the pub out to King Street to hail a cab, Sam nuzzling Ryan's ear with his chin.

6

Ryan

Ryan had slept fitfully, if at all, second-guessing his choice, zooming from elation to dread and back again, while Sam snored away in beer-enhanced ignorance, only half-waking when the bread machine began its morning ritual downstairs. At the onset of cacophony, Ryan had finally given up on sleep, kissed Sam good-bye with an assurance not to worry, and gotten the first Bondi train from Kings Cross in a daze, then grabbed the 333 to Campbell Parade, the sun just rising over the ocean.

The beach was deserted in the pale dawn except for a few die-hard surfers pulling on wetsuits, stretching hamstrings and quads before braving the cold morning water. Sam always said Saturday and Sunday mornings were the best time to surf because the backpackers and hipster beach rats were all still sleeping it off. Ryan had protested at their first lesson, grumbling and groaning to wake himself up, amazed at how capable his boyfriend could be on such little sleep. For all his complaining, though, he loved it, the cold water bracing and exhilarating so early in the morning, once the shock of it was over.

He inhaled the sea air deeply as he climbed the footpath back toward Katrina's building, hyperconscious of making any noise, cutting through the overgrowth of great gum trees and bushy Alexandra palms that gave the narrow lane the feel of a tropical rain forest. First thing he'd have to do once they were married was convince Sam to sell up and move back out to the beach, and not just to get away from the noise. He could already imagine their ocean-view flat paid for with his first big movie, Sam's real estate career booming. But not Bondi. It was getting too crowded here, especially in summer. Maybe the North Shore?

He wriggled Katrina's spare key into the tricky old lock of the mahogany doorway, holding on to a dim hope he would get in before she was up, avoiding spontaneous need for explanation. The red-tiled floor of the vestibule was forever dusty with beach sand, and he kicked a bit up in a spray as he walked past the row of surfboards hanging on the communal rack, his own board (Sam called it a stick) looking new and unused next to the well-worn boards of the other guys in the building. *You can't afford this!* and *Impulse purchase!* had run through his head when he'd bought it, but with plans to pick up lessons again in Bronte, he was glad he had it. He stopped and ran his hand over the sky-blue varnish, pristinely waxed. Theater nerd from Utah becomes Sydney surfer? Well, sort of, anyway. He climbed the stairs to Katrina's, easing the door open as quietly as he could. The smell of espresso hit him instantly. Stealth re-entry foiled.

She stood with her back to him, still in T-shirt and sleeping shorts, leaning over the sink of the small kitchen as she waited for the little silver espresso pot to boil. The machinetta del café, she called it, a marvel to his coffee-unsullied Mormon palate. Upon first sip, Ryan had declared the Italians geniuses, falling in love with the gorgeous drink, and the brilliantly simple little machine that made it, cursing his religious upbringing for yet again keeping him away from something so lovely and simple. He couldn't quite get the hang of it, though, often forgetting that the damn thing was sitting on a hot stove and had to be watched constantly or it would boil over or worse. Many a splattered mess had been hastily cleaned up, and once early in his stay while running lines for class, he'd fallen asleep waiting for it to boil, awakening to a boom as the thing exploded, the black plastic handle rocketing into the wall. She'd wordlessly replaced it the next day, and he'd felt guilty for a month. It started to whistle now, and he sighed and pulled the door shut firmly, rattling the opaque glass panels in their frame. No further need for tiptoeing. She waved without turning, her ponytail swaying and bobbing as she danced to some silent song in her head and poured two cups of coffee. Yawning, still elated from the evening, he set his keys on the table and swallowed that little twinge of guilt that had begun its slow creep from the pit of his stomach up to his chest.

"You can call off the search party." He fell onto the couch, the sweaty delirium that always accompanied sleep deprivation taking over.

"Hush, love," she said, just above a whisper, "people are still sleeping."

"Right, yeah, sorry, but I really don't think that the neighbors—"

"Here." She nodded toward her bedroom and set the coffee cups on the dining table. "People are still sleeping here."

"What!" Ryan shouted, then remembered her orders. "*Here?*" he stage-whispered. Katrina raised her eyebrows. "Shhhh."

"Sorry, sorry," he said. "So that coffee isn't for me, then, I take it?"

"As much as I am familiar with all your idiosyncrasies, I've still never been able to time your entrances to the minute. This is for Nathan. A wake-up cup."

"So I guess your date went well?" He waved his arm in the direction of her bedroom.

"As did yours, it would seem?"

"Well, yeah, I was going to call, but . . . well."

"It's not like I was going to report your disappearance to the American Embassy. You're a grown man."

"I think you'd find that errant theater students rank low on their priority list anyway." He clutched a pillow to his chest and sank deeper into the couch. "And anyway, you always seem to catch me whether you psychically know my schedule or not. It was easier sneaking into my parents' house back in high school. But tell me about you! What happened?"

"Dinner was lovely," she said, then leaned over the sofa and mouthed, "We can talk when it's just the two of us."

"Marvelous. You sound happy."

"And you smell like you slept in the pub." She waved her hand in front of her nose as she backed away from the sofa. "Sam still smokes, I take it? Or have you picked it up now too?" Her look was serious, evaluating. Still Katrina, even in the afterglow. "What would the church say now? First coffee? Then sex with blokes? And now smoking, too? Somebody somewhere is taking this all down in a heavenly ledger."

"Don't worry, I haven't picked it up. Sam still has a few now and then, and it seemed silly to take a shower only to put on the same dirty clothes."

"Sillier things have been done in the name of hygiene."

"At least I grabbed a different T-shirt."

He'd taken one of Sam's, a relic from Digable Planet's one and only decades-past Australian tour. Sam loved American hip hop, and often chanted along to whatever artist he was into at the moment, until Ryan had to beg him to shut up.

"Are you sure it was clean?"

He sniffed at his arm pits now and caught a haze of chicken soup and cigarettes. He shrugged. "Well, at least I look good."

"You and every other twenty-something actor in hipster wear. Do they hand that uniform out now at registration?"

"Unfair! What was it in your day? Black leggings and Madonna bracelets?"

"Spot-on. I believe I was the first girl who ever replicated the entire 'Lucky Star' video at a cast party unprovoked."

"Brilliant." He flipped his arms around, framing his face.

"No, darling, that's 'Vogue.' 'Lucky Star' was all about elbows and hips."

"Right. Right."

"I did worry about you for a moment, you know." She took a sip of her coffee and frowned. "Going to have to remake these. They've gone cold."

"I could do it." Ryan jumped up from the couch. "And I should have called. I should have been more gracious about you taking me back in at such short notice in the middle of the night. I was thinking maybe we could go to dinner next week. My treat?"

"You know I don't mind at all. You don't have to worry about it. Dinner does sound lovely, though. There's a new place in Mosman I want to try. Basque. Meant to be delicious. You can meet me at the studio and we can take the ferry over after we wrap things up on Friday. It should be good fun. Are you working that night?"

"Nope. Night off."

"Good, let me brew a new cuppa for Nathan, then I'll be back out to chat in a tick." The bedroom door creaked open.

"No need to bring it in to me. I've been trying to hold back, letting you two have your catch-up, but the coffee smells too good. I'm coming out." A man in his late thirties, possibly early forties, fit, handsome, hair prematurely graying, stood in Katrina's bedroom doorway in T-shirt and underwear. "And I don't mind if it's a bit cold."

"On the table." She gestured toward the dining nook.

"Lovely," Nathan said, and pulled out a chair, his dark and furry leg hair a stark contrast to his pale, pale skin. "Ryan. Hi. I'm Nathan."

"Yep, Ryan. Nice to meet you." He kicked off his flipflops and collapsed backward onto the couch again.

Nathan took a sip of coffee, yawned, and adjusted himself in his shorts. "We weren't sure if I'd be meeting you this morning."

Ryan looked away embarrassed. "Yeah, well, here I am."

"And what's this about dinner on the North Shore?"

"Well, um, I've owed Kat dinner for ages. I suppose if you'd like to come along—"

"Oh! Don't worry, I'm not trying to gate-crash. I've got rehearsal Friday anyway. A new play at Delaney Street. Kat says you're an actor, too?" He wiggled his toes into the carpet and sipped his coffee again. There was a catlike liquidity to his movements.

"Yeah, just started my last year at the conservatory. Doing the MFA."

"He's brilliant. You should see him!" Katrina called from the kitchen.

"Wonderful. Come to the show at Delaney and I'll come see your semester play. What's on this fall?"

"O'Neill's *Desire Under the Elms*. Well, that's what I was cast in anyway. They're also doing *Uncle Vanya*, which would have been really cool, and Caryl Churchill's *Top Girls*, but well, not exactly suited to any role in that one."

"What? You didn't want to do drag for your final year?" He batted his eyes, and Ryan realized he liked him. "*Desire*'s a great play. I love O'Neill," Nathan continued. "So it's a date then."

"Sounds great."

It occurred to him that he would never be having this conversation with Sam. He pushed it out of his head. Sam was trying, and he was just so damn charming, who cared if he didn't know Mamet from Molière.

"And it's a date for Friday," Katrina shouted over the hiss of the coffee pot. "We'll rub elbows with the posh North Shore set for an evening."

"You can wear that lovely blue dress I found at the Paddington Markets last week," Ryan said.

"We'll cut a dashing figure. That is, if you can find jeans without holes in them and borrow a less dodgy T-shirt from Sam." She stood in the kitchen doorway, looking him up and down, shaking her head. "That is his shirt, yes? And to think last time you showed up at this hour it was because you were through."

"You spent the night with him?" Nathan asked.

Ryan raised his eyebrow at Kat. Had she told Nathan the whole story? Well, she must have. He would have done the same in her position. "Not now, please? I'm exhausted."

"Sorry, sorry. Nothing further about it," she said. We can chat later if you like." She walked to the window and adjusted the blinds. "It's going to be a scorcher today. Thirty-six."

"Layman's terms, please." He still had a hard time figuring Celsius. Was it multiply by five or six? Divide by nine? Subtract thirty-two? A hundred Fahrenheit? Ninety?

"Scorcher," Nathan said. "Anything over thirty just figure it's going to be hot as hell and leave it at that."

"He speaks truth," Katrina said as she walked back to the kitchen. "Do you want your coffee over ice?"

"Yes, please," he said, watching her through the old-fashioned service pass-through as she poured the coffee into a tall beveled drinking glass, ice crackling and popping in the hot liquid. He squished up one of the dark-purple throw pillows and put it behind his head.

"Things end up all right?" Nathan asked, his expression one of honest concern. "With Sam, I mean?"

"Yeah, good. We've worked things out. At least I think we have. Gonna take a bit, but . . . well. I love the guy." It felt strange declaring it to this man he barely knew, but he meant it.

Katrina walked into the lounge from the kitchen and stood above him. She lowered her voice and spoke kindly, slowly. "Don't be too eager to rewrite history. Take it slow. And take care of yourself."

"Yes, dear."

Nathan held both hands up. "Think I'll jump in the shower and leave you both to it." He stood and stretched. "Lovely meeting you, Ryan. Hope I'll be seeing you around."

"You too," Ryan said.

The bathroom door clicked, followed by the groan of the water pipes and hiss of the shower nozzle shattering the otherwise silent room.

"I just worry about you, that's all."

"I can take care of myself, you know. I'm not so delicate. I've let myself play a role. The helpless American. The newly minted gay guy. The squeamish Mormon. I certainly had a part in things. But I think . . ." Ryan hesitated and looked around the comfortable room. Katrina could be harsh at times, but she was so intuitive, so understanding. She had become his family here and he realized this felt like home, like the only place he could really be himself. With Sam it was different. Not quite home. Potential? A home he wasn't quite familiar with yet, a home that left him excited and scared.

"I know you're strong. Just—"

"We're talking about moving back in together." He took a sip of coffee. Should he tell her? She'd have to know eventually. "Sam even mentioned getting married."

She set the coffee down on the side table in front of him with a clunk. The glass was overfull and the creamy brown liquid sloshed onto the glass tabletop. "Married? Here? In Australia?" She put her hands on her hips and frowned at the mess. "Let me just get a cloth." She walked back toward the kitchen. "Well, we did just pass the new law, I suppose," she yelled over the din of banging cupboards. "Where are the bloody tea towels?" she muttered. "There you are." She turned on the taps again and yelled over the splashing. "Or I suppose you could fly back to the States, or . . . Ryan . . ." Her voice trailed off.

"Here. Right after I graduate."

The tap stopped and she walked back into the lounge room. "Good God, are you sure this is the right thing? I mean, you just had a massive fight and two-week separation over the concept of basic monogamy." She swirled the wet towel through the coffee, then wrung it into the glass.

He sat up and held his hand out for the towel. "Here, let me."

She waved him away. "I've got it. You'll leave streaks." She pushed the remaining liquid into a tiny pool, then dabbed it up with the dry end of the cloth.

"*I can't take the craziness anymore*, you said." Her voice was calm and slow, as if she was addressing a child. "*It's like living with Jekyll and Hyde*, you said. The partying. The crazy friends. The reckless weekends."

"I was just upset. It was never really that bad. I've painted a nasty picture of him to you because you're the sympathetic ear I turn to when I'm upset. I shouldn't have done that. He's just enthusiastic, and I have to remember that I'm reserved. If anything, he's teaching me to be more open, more spontaneous." He leaned forward and picked up the coffee glass. She wiped the ring.

"I'll make you a new one."

"You don't have to."

"It'll take two minutes."

"Thanks."

"You're welcome, but for God's sake, Ryan, you're learning to be more spontaneous?" She swiped the table once more with the cloth and cradled the wet mess in her palm. "You've got to be bloody joking. Is that what he convinced you of last night after he got you into bed? What's next? You going to ring up that bloke, oh, what was his name? Your potential ménage a trois?"

"Alky."

"Right. You going to call him back in for another go?" She sounded exasperated. He didn't want to have the argument now, but it seemed inevitable.

"God! No. No. No." He shut his eyes and shook his head like a child. "You're making it sound so ridiculous. I mean, Kat, I love him, and I want to make it work. And you were the one who said I should talk to him. Sort things out, you said."

She reached out and touched his arm again.

"Yes, I did say that, because walking away from a relationship without any explanation or closure is a shitty thing to do to anyone, regardless of how wildly inappropriate they are for you. Look where it got you before."

"Is that where we are now? Wildly inappropriate?" He followed her into the kitchen, the half-empty glass cold and wet in his hand. "What about your new boyfriend?" He stage-whispered, *"What is he? Half your age?"*

She walked to the sink and squeezed the tea towel over the drain, her breathing deep and steady. He could hear her counting, one number after each long exhale. Her yoga trick when she was getting angry.

"Careful, young man," she said slowly, deliberately, "don't turn this around on me. This has nothing to do with Nathan, or age."

"You're right. I'm sorry." He tipped the remains of the coffee into the sink and leaned against her shoulder. Even without a shower, she smelled like coconut shampoo and sandalwood oil. "He's lovely, isn't he. I'm glad you've met him."

"He is. And I know I shouldn't be saying any of this, should respect your choices, let you live your life, but, Sam, well . . . Have you even told him about Megan? Or did you erase it all with your magical overnight transformation from closeted married Mormon to out and proud drama school star?"

"If everything goes all right, I won't have to tell him. I've sent her divorce papers. It's not ideal, but . . ."

"Have you even talked to her? Have you talked to your parents?"

"We're in touch. Yes."

But they weren't. He'd been dodging her calls for weeks, was it months? His parents too. Lots of *busy call you soon* texts, but they had to figure something was up. She was right. He still woke up in guilt-ridden panic every other day.

Ryan knew she meant well, but he was having a hard time keeping his anger down. "And Sam's a little wild, sure, but I like that. I love it, in fact. If you'd been raised Mormon, you'd like it too. He's everything I ever wished I could be but couldn't be because of all the rules and things I believed, or was supposed to believe, or . . . I mean, jeez, it still terrifies me, of course, but I have to take this chance,

Katrina, don't you see? Especially after last time. Don't you want me to be happy?" He realized he was shouting. "Sorry. I didn't mean to yell," he whispered, looking toward the bathroom.

She faced him and put a hand on each of his shoulders. "It's not the yelling. Yell all you want. What I'm trying to tell you is that you need to seriously consider what you're doing. Of course I want you to be happy, but you've just gone through a huge life change. You don't know yourself yet." She turned to the sink and fiddled with the blind until the wooden slats fell into place. "This sun is going to kill us today, I swear."

"I think I do know myself. At least I know I can't go back to what I was."

"No one's asking you to," she said. "No one's sending you back to Utah. You don't have to be a Mormon, for God's sake, although I'm sure you looked adorable riding your bicycle around in jacket and tie, but why swing to the other extreme and lose yourself in that ridiculous Darlinghurst lifestyle? Use that sense of decency and discipline, that sense of moderation they crammed into you at that church of yours. Use it in spite of them. Use it to become a better, more generous person. You're an actor, right? Use your craft to change the world."

"That sounds like new-age hoo-hah. How am I supposed to change anything?"

"It's not hoo-hah. You have a voice. An opportunity. Do shows that matter. Write parts for yourself that carry real messages. Get serious. Use it. Don't throw it away on parties and muscles. I tried that, and I can tell you it doesn't work. I see the potential in you, Ryan, you just haven't tapped it yet. Why do you think I asked you to move in? Why do you think they accepted you at the conservatory in the first place? They saw the potential for you to be something more."

The shower stopped. Nathan was humming some vague semblance of a tune, his voice a deep baritone.

"But that's enough for now." She gave the blinds a final twist and kissed him on the forehead. "We can talk more at dinner. Now go get some sleep."

7

Sam

Sam opened the driver's side door of the convertible BMW and slid into the low leather seat.

"You sure you want to drive?" Ryan said. "This traffic looks crazy."

And there it was, the worrying.

To be honest, he'd missed it a bit. Ryan's obsessing on a bad day would drive anyone mental, but when it didn't go too far, it was sweet, easily coaxed out of, and Sam loved playing seasoned badass to Ryan's corruptible school kid.

"Course I'm sure," Sam said. "It's a gorgeous night. We can drive along Double Bay and catch more of this breeze. Best do it now before it's too cold to drive with the top down. Winter hits faster than you think."

"I love that you call it winter. Spend January in the Rockies waking up to three feet of snow and you'll scoff at your three weeks of drizzle." Ryan clicked his seatbelt and tugged on the slack. "The belt's loose, you know."

"There's plenty of warmer territory in the world, you know. Never understood why so many people choose to live in cold climates."

"Well, at least we chose it. We weren't sent as prisoners."

"Worked out better for us in the end though, didn't it? Seems the Mormons drew the short straw."

"There's an old myth about that. When the Mormon pioneers finally made it out of the Rockies, Brigham Young saw the Great Salt Lake and thought they'd reached the Pacific Ocean. Declared the trek done then and there. 'This is the place,' he allegedly said. And the joke was on them. Took them years to figure out the soil and the climate. Probably why I'm drawn to tropical climates now. My collective Mormon consciousness knows I should have really grown up in San Diego."

"But then you wouldn't have been all oppressed and had to run off to Sydney, and we would have never met."

"Oh, I would have made it here still. I feel like Sydney's somehow in my blood too. The whole leaving the homeland, figuring out a new ecosystem thing." He kept fiddling with his seatbelt. "Honestly, Sam, you've got to get this thing looked over."

Sam reached over and grabbed the belt, pulled it loose with a flick of his wrist and snapped it into place. "There. You okay now?"

"Didn't realize there was an art to it."

"Only for some people."

"Probably this cold weather. Froze the mechanism." Ryan crossed his arms and gave an exaggerated shiver.

"Oh, you. Cold is cold. Chilly rain is chilly rain, even here. By next month you'll be begging me to turn the heater on."

"Then let's enjoy it while we can." Ryan adjusted his sunglasses and leaned back. Movie star pose. "We've got plenty of time. Drive along the bay as you wish. It'll be beautiful."

Sam leaned across the gear shift and kissed Ryan's cheek.

It was a beautiful autumn Saturday. Back to normal. Days like this made him forget every stupid thing they'd ever done to each other, every stupid thing they'd said. And having an excuse to get the car out of the garage made it a thousand times better. He treasured the thing, worshipped its capacity for speed, its connotations of success, even as its age was showing more and more. Last year he'd stalled out in the middle of peak-hour traffic in Bondi Junction and caused a massive backup. Turned out to be the fuel pump. The year before that it was a cracked radiator. Belts broke. Tires leaked. Even in top running condition, it rattled and wheezed like an asthmatic widower. He dreaded the next diagnostic for fear of what they might find, but driving it felt powerful, masculine. He loved the feel of it, edging into traffic, then hitting the clutch and gunning the engine as he picked up speed, catching the other commuters' eyes as he dodged around slower drivers and screeched through the tail end of yellow lights.

The car had been a gift from his father when he graduated from high school. And as much as they were at odds, he would never sever that tie. At her graduation, Belinda had been given the smaller sportier model in red but had sold it when she'd finished uni and moved to Byron Bay, embracing her new hippie save-the-Earth lifestyle. Cars were the devil. Carbon footprint and climate change and all that nonsense. It had made their father furious, triggering endless screeds on wasted money and shocking lack of respect. Together he and Lin had reveled in his displeasure, but secretly Sam hated that she'd sold it.

They were meeting at her Airbnb on the beach at seven for dinner and drinks. She was in town for a conference of some sort. Last meeting today, so they were going to relax with her before she flew back to Byron in the morning. He'd been lazing around all day looking forward to it but was also a bit nervous about skipping the office. With sales as low as they were, he should have gone in and pulled a Saturday shift, gotten some work done. Last two offers had fallen through, a couple of the smaller units, and he needed to relist them at a reduced price ASAP. He could have grabbed his board and headed in early, gotten it all done in a few hours, then had a quick surf and ducked around the corner to Lin's holiday flat easy peasy, let Ryan take the train, but why bother? Jenny had already taken new photos for the website and written beefed-up descriptions just waiting for his approval, and it was the weekend, for fuck's sake. The units would keep. The pricing and photos could go up Monday. He didn't even care what the pics looked like. Just fucking snap and upload them! He'd shouted at her when she approached him yesterday, then pretended he was joking to diffuse. He had to play boss, play the professional, so he'd said he would review them, give notes, and now here it was Saturday and nothing done, a guarantee that he'd find a snippy email in his inbox from Kyle, the wanker at head office overseeing the project. *Fourteen-hour days? Going in on Saturday? What you whinging about, Carter? Don't make me regret making you lead sales on this.*

Lin had gone on about work-life separation when he'd suggested he might be late. "Happiness is a matter of balance, order, rhythm, and harmony," she'd said. "Not killing yourself for some job."

Too right. He was all for hippie mantras when they gave him an excuse to blow off work. Fuck Kyle and his emails.

And anyway, he wanted tonight to be special. He was still wooing Ryan back, or at least in the back of his mind he was. They'd talked it out and all had been forgiven, but he didn't want to fuck it up again, so he was planning things, making an effort. There would be dinners and drives, days at the beach, footy matches, comedy shows, like they were first dating again, focused on being a couple, doing normal couple things instead of running off to the clubs. Finding that balance, that harmony. So he'd planned this night to be special, ducked out while Ryan was at the gym, given the car a thorough buffing, then pulled it around from the garage and parked at the curb, sunglasses tilted back on his head, pride bubbling under as he waited for his boyfriend to rock up from the gym and have a wow at the old muscle car.

The engine coughed and sputtered like the starting gear on a prop plane, then settled into a deep rumble.

Ryan grimaced. "Engine sounds cranky. When did you change the oil last?"

"When'd you do the laundry last?" Sam gunned the engine again, machine-gun blasts of smoke blowing out the tailpipe. "She's just temperamental. German artistry."

An older man stopped on the footpath, his work boots dirty, Aussie bush hat worn and sweat-stained, the evidence of his honest labor set off by an immaculate shirt and tie. "You're going to need to have that engine looked at, mate," he said, then walked on to whatever bar or brothel he wouldn't be telling his wife about when he got back to whatever unremarkable country town he hailed from.

"Does your missus know where you are tonight?"

The old man gave him the finger without turning back.

Sam floored it again. "What does that old bugger know?" He revved, eased up, revved again, pushing the last bad air out, playing the pedal until the engine hummed like the string section of a chamber orchestra. He gripped Ryan's thigh, honked the horn, and eased the car out from the curb into the slow line of traffic inching down Darlinghurst Road toward William Street. Clouds of exhaust swirled around them, the crowds on the footpath moving faster than the traffic. "And we're off."

Ryan gripped the top of the windshield and shook it, testing its stability. "Well, sort of, I guess. Not going to catch much of a breeze driving at this pace."

"We could take the tunnel, but then what's the point?"

Ryan gazed up at the sky, distracted, lost in thought, clenching and unclenching his fists.

"So is that a yes for the tunnel, or—"

"Are you sure she wanted both of us to come?" Ryan faced him. "I mean, haven't you just been telling her wild tales of how ridiculous I am? How I ran off in the middle of the night and left you? Went crying back to Katrina? I'm sure she thinks I'm an idiot."

"Of course she wants us both, ya knob. She'll be pleased to see you. She was glad when I told her you'd come round again." Sam leaned in to kiss him, still feeling a little bashful at the renewed newness of it. Ryan kissed him back deeply, almost desperately, his hand pressing the back of Sam's neck, a moan welling up in his throat.

Sam broke the kiss, held his gaze. "Better let me drive or I'm gonna rip your clothes off here and now."

"Why not? That old country bloke might like the show."

"One minute a Mormon prude, the next a libertine." Sam fished his sunglasses from his shirt pocket and flipped them on. The Sydney autumn sun was brutal even at dusk. He patted Ryan's leg and edged the car forward, the dark-blue metallic paint a striking contrast to the platoon of white cabs.

"Do you think she ever wishes, they, your family, do you think they ever wish you still dated women, that you were still straight?"

"Where is this coming from?"

The car in front of them jerked to a stop as a pack of kids about Perry's age ducked across the street laughing and jabbing at each other as they dodged and ducked around the barely moving cars. "Perfect! Block that lane for me, boys! See if you can keep us here all night!" Sam yelled at them.

"I don't know. Family. It's all complicated."

He nudged the pedal again as the line eased forward. "I was never straight, for Christ's sake. It was high school. I was terrified my surfing mates would find out I was a poofter and push me out of the group."

Truth was there had been a string of girls back then. Surfie chicks. Rebels. All sexy. All cool. He'd even quite enjoyed sex with them now and then, it's just that his tastes had leaned more strongly toward men. He thought about his last couple of girlfriends sometimes, wondered if they'd blamed themselves when he'd dumped them for no reason. But why dwell? So much fucked-up shit going on in high school, having a closeted gay boyfriend was just another day's business. He was sure they were fine or he would have heard about it.

"And what about you, Mr. Mormon? I'm sure you had to play along too. How many girlfriends did you root in high school? Oh wait, no sex before marriage in your little happy clappy church, right?"

"Nope. None," Ryan said. "The cult forbade it. No time for it anyway. We were too busy playing tambourines in airports and asking for spare change." He waved his arms in the air and bobbed his head like a member of some holy roller chorus. "Better be nice or I'll start speaking in tongues."

"Promise?" A breeze blew through the trees and Sam felt the sweat cool on his neck. It was a beautiful night. Ryan leaned into his hand and growled, more relaxed now. They drove on in silence for a moment, the sky just beginning to darken as the sun set behind them.

"Lin's super cool about it. Always been that proud PFLAG sister. Sometimes I wish she'd tone it down a bit."

"It made it easier, you know," Ryan said.

"What did?" The car ahead of them hit its brakes as a gang of blokes stumbled out of Mr. Booze's bottle shop and into the street. Party was already getting started. Nothing new for the Cross. Sam jerked the wheel to the left to avoid tapping his bumper. "Shit. I need to pay more attention."

"No sex. The morality thing," Ryan said. "Maybe you're a little frustrated, but then there's none of those crazy emotions before you're ready, none of the impossible scenarios that kids can get themselves into. I guess," he said. "Of course there's the whole grievous-sin guilt trip thing, but I still think it saved us from a lot of trouble, like by the time you do it you've actually thought about it, and hopefully even love the person. That part at least makes sense to me."

"I suppose in a way that would have been a relief. If all of it was a sin, then there would be no pressure to bang chicks just to prove you weren't a poof."

"That's such a horrible word."

"Sorry. Sorry. You know what I mean. If kids at your school knew you couldn't have sex because of your religion, then that pressure to bang chicks just to prove you were straight would have been alleviated."

"I guess it was."

"You never say much about that—"

"Watch it, mate! Bloody hell!" Sam slammed his brakes, narrowly missing a delivery truck pulling out of Cole's loading zone. The young driver yelled out his open window. "Had my flashers on bright as day."

"Sorry!" Sam yelled and gave him a wave of acquiescence. Ryan's eyes were shut, his hand clutching the door handle.

"Not going to jump out on me, are you?" Sam said.

Ryan opened his eyes and relaxed again. "Nope. We're in it now for better or worse."

New South Head Road was chock-a-block with cars as it wound through the posh shops and flats of Double Bay, people leaving the city for the beach, people leaving the beach for the city, people just trying to get home from work. Sydney's eastern street grid was narrow and windy and there were traffic lights at every other cross street. Sam longed to drive up on to the sidewalk and blow past all the traffic like he was in some macho stupid American action movie, knocking over fruit stands, sending pedestrians scrambling for doorways, but he inched forward with the rest of them. At least when they drove home later, they could get a little speed along the cliffs.

Sometimes he felt trapped in Sydney. He loved the 24-7 party lifestyle and the constant parade of people out for a good time, but it could be exhausting. He had often thought of chucking it in and moving to the country. Walking away from it all. The bills. The massive headache of redoing the flat. His job. Fuck his job. Fuck the hipsters for invading Bondi while ignoring Bronte. Fuck Kyle for setting the prices too high.

Maybe he should just quit. They could join Belinda up in Byron Bay now that her divorce was final. Place was booming so work would be available. Small enough to have that slow country town pace, away from the party scene but still close enough to civilization, with the Gold Coast and Brisbane just up the road, that Ryan could easily get some acting gigs. Seemed every damn cop show was shot up there these days, right? And the surf was amazing.

He was holding that one back though. They'd barely gotten back together, needed to find their footing again. After tonight went well, a trip motoring out to the Blue Mountains would be a good next step, he thought—renting a cabin somewhere, opening the car up on some empty country roads, showing Ryan how beautiful rural Australia could be. Leaving the city for good was a conversation for another day.

They descended the hill into Double Bay, the pubs and curry stands of the Cross now replaced by bespoke wedding-dress shops and artisanal patisseries. "It's still not too late," Ryan said, pointing toward Edgecliff Station.

"Aw, come on. Where's your sense of adventure? We'll be out of this mess as soon as we get to Ocean Avenue and it'll be smooth sailing."

Ryan was right, of course. At this rate they'd barely make it on time. Not that Lin was a stickler for punctuality.

They eased past the endless row of restaurants along New South Head Road and turned east. Rose Bay came into view, a deep blue cove dotted with sailboats and fishing craft. Gorgeous.

"See? If we'd taken the train, we'd have missed all of this." He grabbed Ryan's hand and squeezed it, then let go and shifted up as he picked up speed.

The traffic had thinned out a bit and he accelerated as they turned up O'Sullivan and passed the stucco mansions dotting the hillside above the Woolhara Golf Club. "Belinda's a really good cook, by the way. And tons of fun. And she's honestly more forgiving about any of this shit than either of us are. It'll be a good night."

"If you say so."

They crested the hill and Sam gunned it toward the generic cluster of skyscrapers at Bondi Junction, gaining speed, edging around the other cars, the scent of sea air growing stronger and stronger as they approached the beach. At Bronte Road he pulled onto a back street he often used during rush hour. The traffic thinned to nothing; he accelerated, winding past the hodgepodge of brickworkers' cottages and fifties flat blocks, the deep scent of eucalyptus mixing with the sea air. He slowed to a crawl as they approached the beach and found a parking space just a few meters past Belinda's flat.

They got out of the car and he pulled up her text with the flat info while Ryan grabbed the wine from the back seat. *Ring number 3A. Kendrew.* A fifties brick block. Not ramshackle, but definitely in need of a tune-up. Tenant names written on sticky tape adorned a row of buzzers crookedly bolted to the left of the doorway. Sam found the name and punched the button.

"Is that you, Sammo?" Belinda's voice crackled through the old intercom system. "Come on up. Third-floor right."

"Yep. See you in a tick."

Sam pushed the door open. Cracks spiderwebbed down the plaster walls, and the carpet was stained and worn. The whole place needed a deep clean and five gallons of paint. Of course this was Belinda's choice. Her fuck-you to anything corporate or posh.

"I thought Bronte was supposed to be nice," Ryan said.

"You having a go at my job?" Sam jogged up the stairs two at a time. "This is yonks away from my building, and you'd be surprised. Even grotty places like this are a fortune out here. It's all about the views. Walking distance to the beach. Rehab heaven."

"Said the estate agent."

"So I did."

He mentally logged repair lists as he climbed, wondered about the foundation, the plumbing. The lot of them would probably just be razed when a buyer came in, but he didn't want to give Ryan the satisfaction of calling it correctly.

They reached the top of the stairs, the dim wattage of cheap lightbulbs casting shadows across the plaster. The door flew open and Belinda—Lin—stepped into the hallway, hair still wet, her ankles crumbed with sand. A gauzy hippie skirt wrapped around her bathing suit.

"Sammo!"

Sam hugged her tightly, breathing in the sandalwood oil that clung to everything she wore.

"So so so good to see you."

He stepped back and took both her hands. "Come straight from the surf, did you? Flat owner's not going to be happy about all that sand."

"For the cleaning fee they charge, they can certainly sweep up a little sand."

"There's my sister. Hippie only till there's work to be done."

She brushed a bit from her shin. "I was planning on cleaning. Just making a point."

He leaned through the doorway. "Food smells great."

"Course it does. Get that table set while I change?" She waved at Ryan. "Come on then, love. No use standing in the hallway."

Sam pushed past her into the flat.

Ryan waved the bottle of wine at her. "We brought this."

"Lovely." She grabbed his wrist and pulled him along, herding him inside.

"Cutlery and plates are in the—"

"In the cupboard?" Sam yelled from the tiny kitchen. "Brilliant. Would have never guessed."

"Yes, yes. Brilliant, Sam." She ducked down the hallway and a door clicked shut.

Sam set his keys down on the Ikea basic countertops and pulled open the top drawer. Cutlery on first try. Well done.

"See? She's perfectly happy to see you."

"I suppose."

"Relax, and see if there are any plates in that cupboard."

Ryan pulled open the laminate cupboard door leaned forward. "Two plates. Two bowls. Two glasses. And about twenty coffee cups."

"Same situation with the cutlery. Two seems to be the magic number. That's what you get with these places. Grab whatever works. Salad fork'll do for me."

"At least there are four chairs."

"Are you mocking my holiday flat?" Belinda entered the room in a pair of jeans and peasant blouse, towel-drying her hair.

"Not exactly posh, is it?" Sam wagged a plastic goblet at her. "I think we have these same plastic cups for events at the office. They come in packs of one hundred."

"Right on the beach though. Had a lovely swim, and will sleep well tonight knowing that I have not contributed a single cent to any fucked-up neocolonialist American hotel chain." She stepped to the stove and stirred whatever was simmering in the oversized aluminum soup pot. "No offense, Ryan."

"You're fine. Not particularly proud of my country at the moment. Always wanted to live overseas anyway. When theater school presented itself, I jumped."

"So when do we get to watch you accept that Oscar?"

"I don't know about that. I'm just a student. You never know who's actually going to make it." He held the bottle of wine toward her. "Grabbed something Australian. Hope you like it."

"Lovely. Just pop it there and we'll open it with dinner."

He set it down, his shoulders tensed, and turned back to Lin, hands clasped in front of his chest. *Relax. Calm down*, Sam silently urged him.

Lin lifted the wooden spoon from the pot, cupping her palm beneath it. "Taste, brother."

Sam took the spoon in his mouth and savored the sweet spicy curry. "Really nice. Vegan?"

"Why? You worried about your protein intake?"

"Not in the slightest."

Ryan slid one of the rickety chairs back from the little bistro table and sat down. Good. He was letting his guard down.

"And don't be so modest, Ryan. Not everyone gets into the conservatory." She dropped the spoon back in and turned the flame down. "I think we're ready."

Sam grabbed the chair next to Ryan, their knees touching. "He's already killing it. He was 'nervous businessman' on an episode of *Harbour Cops* a few weeks back, and he was smashing. The Silver Logie is all but his."

"Not that anyone watches *Harbour Cops*. They're on, like, season seven thousand." Ryan grabbed a paper napkin from the stack and sat next to Sam. "At school they only let us accept commercial work our final year, and then only during breaks, so you take what you can get. I wouldn't mind getting into more theater here when I graduate. Forget the Oscars, I'd settle for a Helpmann. Keep it local."

Belinda brought the pot from the stove and set it next to the rice on a trivet embossed with a photo of the Opera House with Welcome to Sydney! scrawled across it in glitter.

"To your point, I don't think I've ever seen *Harbour Cops*. Mum watches it, I think. She would have seen you. I'll ring her and tell her I know you." She took Sam's plate and filled it with rice and curry.

"Yeah, she'll get a kick out of that. Bragging at the tennis club that her son's boyfriend is a telly star."

Sam had been nervous when Ryan told him he was an actor, braced himself for the onslaught of egotism, worried he'd have to lie about how good he was, but a few weeks in he'd gone to a play and been bowled over. The shy, self-deprecating young man who could barely look you in the eye at the bar became magnificent on stage, confident and full of swagger. He just didn't seem to quite have a handle on talking about it. Sam was happy to do the boasting for him.

"Honestly," Ryan said. "It's just a few lines. Not exactly Shakespeare." He scooped a bit spoonful of curry and blew on it. "How's work for you?"

"Fair enough." Belinda filled her own plate and sat down. It smelled amazing. "I'll never be a millionaire, but I like what I'm doing. There's a serious stigma around mental health care, even in a place like Byron. People are happy to rally for a cause, but then don't take care of themselves. If people get comfortable enough with it, you know, see it as preventative and not just a last resort when they can't cope, then we could address some real problems before it's too late. Save people a lot of heartache and trouble. Change things."

"I'm sure you're great at it."

"She's fantastic, of course," Sam said, "and this is bloody delicious."

Belinda took the bottle of wine and filled their assortment of cups and plastic goblets. "I'm offering couples counseling now, did I tell you? Got my first clients last month. Gay couple as well. You two might consider it, you know. Get some stuff out on the table and process what you just went through."

"We're fine. We've done a lot of processing, if that's what you call it," Sam said.

"Couldn't hurt. Give you a fresh start."

"We've already made a fresh start," Sam said. "Going well."

"So glad to hear it. I was gutted when I thought you two were done."

"Then you'll be happy to hear our little bit of news. We're getting married this spring. It's my graduation present to him."

"You're kidding me!" She slammed her hand down on the table. "That's amazing!"

"We've had our rough patches." Sam leaned in and kissed Ryan's ear. "But I'm sure he's the one. Couldn't be happier."

Ryan squeezed his hand under the table.

"Well, congratulations! I had no idea you were going in that direction. A toast is in order, yes?" Belinda waved her plastic goblet.

Sam thrust his forward, and Ryan met them with his *I Hate Mondays* coffee cup.

"Cheers to us," Sam said and took a big gulp of wine.

"Well done." Belinda took another swallow and grabbed the bottle, splashing the remains equally among them. "Ryan, be a dear and grab that cab sav on the bench behind you?"

Ryan swiveled, knocking Sam's knees, and grabbed the bottle. "Corkscrew?"

"Should be a screwtop," Belinda said.

Ryan cracked the cap and set the bottle on the table.

"Do you have a solicitor?" Belinda said through a mouthful of rice.

"Haven't gotten that far just yet."

"Might want to get on that. Things are booming now that marriage is legal here, courts getting backed up, especially when it concerns residency status. I have a friend who specializes in marriage visas. Danielle Chin. She's fabulous. She'll love you."

"Is she a serious lawyer? I mean, did you meet her at a silent retreat or vegan baking class?"

"Ah, Sammo, the jokes never get old, do they? I knew her at Sydney Uni. You've probably even met her. She's brilliant. Of course we could just call Dad. Have him ring up his old business solicitor? I'm sure Leo Higgins would love to take a break from setting up corporate monopolies and evicting honest farmers to help out two young blokes in love."

"Text me her number. Anything to keep Dad out of it."

Belinda fished her phone from under her napkin. "Good as done." She poked at the screen, then waved it at Sam. "You know you'll have to see him at Christmas, right?"

"I think I'm busy."

"It's April, Sam. Do you generally book appointments eight months out? You've got no excuse. Just think, your first Chrissie as newlyweds out at the old homestead."

"You know he'll turn it into a big production. Throw a party and pretend we're best mates. Turn it around to make him look good."

"Would that be so bad? Past issues aside, you know he means well. He'd love to talk to you. If you rang him and told him you and Ryan were getting married, he'd not only pay for the whole thing, he'd take out a full-page ad in the Sydney *Morning Herald* and buy you a float in the Mardi Gras parade."

"That's what I'm afraid of."

"Why can't you let go? He means well."

"You have a foggy memory of our childhood."

"I remember it as well as you do. Things were weird. So what?"

"Things were fucked up."

"Fine, fucked up. But look what he and Mum were dealing with. I know he'd love to talk to you."

"I don't know how you even—"

"I choose to let people evolve. You should try it some time."

"And the therapist has arrived."

"At your service."

Sam picked up his glass and drained it. "Pass us the bottle, Ryan."

He filled his glass and waved the bottle toward Belinda.

"Still full," she said.

Ryan held his hand over his cup. "You know me. Haven't quite got the hang of it yet, to be honest. One glass'll do. Or one coffee cup, that is."

"That's right," Sam said. "The old Word of Wonder forbids it. Right, Spunky?" He set the bottle on the table and pushed his chair back.

"Word of Wisdom, you dork," Ryan said. "But, well, I'm not . . . I mean, not that I care, I suppose. I'm not really much of a churchgoer these days. I guess I just never developed a taste for it."

"Well, I'm not Mormon. Word of Wisdom be damned." He took a long, deep drink. It went down easy, beautifully. "Time to loosen up. Get the party started." He took another swig and waved his glass at Belinda.

"Slow down, Sam. The wine isn't going anywhere." She frowned and poured him half a glass. "And we've still got Pavlova. I picked it up from—"

"Don't tell me it's bloody vegan too."

"Chickpea brine functions the same as egg whites so it's—"

"It's fucked is what it is. I'm not having chickpeas for dessert."

"All the better for me and Ryan, then." She stood. "Like a slice? It's just in the other room. Not enough bench space to keep it in here."

"Yes, please," he said.

She pushed past Sam toward the lounge room and gripped his shoulder. "Play nice, brother." She returned with a pink box wrapped in white satin ribbon. "So, Ryan, will your parents be coming down for the wedding?"

"Um, I don't, well—"

Sam shook his head. "No, no, no. No Jensens at our wedding. Far too churchy for that, aren't they, Spunky? Wouldn't want to disappoint ole Joe Smith and have a gay son, right?"

"It's Joseph Smith."

"Joseph. Right."

"And they're just doing what they think is right. What they believe God wants. They don't mean any harm."

"But somehow they cause it."

"But they're good people. They're my people. They just don't understand."

"Well fuck 'em, I say."

"Sam!"

"Sorry, sorry. Not your parents. You know what I mean."

"Still." He grabbed his glass and drained it. "Hope you have a third bottle, Lin. This one isn't going to last very long now that Spunky's having his share." He glugged a few splashes into Ryan's cup, then took another big swig.

"Sam, I said I didn't—"

"Won't kill you. Come on then. It's a party."

Belinda set three slices of pavlova down on the table, the snow-white meringue set off by toasted golden ridges. "Put your glass down and just try it."

"Rather just have the drink, thanks."

"Ryan, I hope you're driving home."

"Aw, now the nanny shows up."

"I'm serious, Sam, do you really want to get done for drink driving?"

"You're just jealous I have the old Beamer still."

"Not in the least. Sale price paid for a year of postgrad."

"But you miss it just a bit, don't you?"

"Not really. I mean, yeah it got me some attention that summer, but—"

"So come for a ride with us."

"I'm flying out in the morning, you know that."

"I mean now."

"Absolutely not. You're a drink away from blotto."

"Listen to you. Knocking them back yourself, aren't you? Always liked a drink, right, Lin?"

"Sure, but not like this."

"Well, excuse me for wanting to enjoy my weekend."

"That's what I was hoping for anyway, not this."

"Well, we won't bother you any more then."

"Don't be silly. Crash here. You're welcome to."

"That settee wouldn't sleep a child, let alone two grown men."

"Take the bed, I'll take the settee, really."

"We should just be going."

"No, please stay. I haven't seen you in months. Let's not do this."

"Promised my boy a ride up the headlands."

"So take him tomorrow when it's light out. See more that way."

"It'll be fine."

Belinda held up her hands in surrender. "Fine. Just be careful, please."

"Right then, we should be going."

"Thanks for coming again. You guys really need to think about Christmas back in W.A."

Ryan reached in and hugged her tightly. Sam stood back, still angry about the scolding.

"Come on, Sam, big hugs." She held her arms out. "No hard feelings for an over-protective sister?

"Yeah, yeah." He leaned in and hugged her tightly. Why not. Better to get along. "Love you, Lin."

They walked back to the car. A chilly seaside fog drifted in over the Tamarama rocks, obscuring them in the moonlight.

"Bloody Belinda," Sam muttered.

Ryan stepped around a menacing-looking flock of ibises pecking for trash on the sidewalk. "What are you talking about?"

"Being so pissy about the ride. And all that nonsense about making happy families with Dad. Fuck that."

"She didn't mean any harm, Sam."

They arrived at the car.

"So how about it?"

"How about what?"

"A drive over the headlands?"

"It's so foggy we won't be able to see anything."

"Fine then. We'll just head home." Sam yanked the door open angrily and slouched into the seat. Everyone seemed to be gunning for him tonight. What the fuck was wrong with people?

"Come on, Sam, don't be such a baby."

"I'm not a baby, it's just . . ."

"It's just you're a baby. It can wait. In fact, why don't you let me drive. I've been dying to try, you know."

"Really? You sure?"

"Well, you did have a bit of wine. Just being safe."

"You had a bit yourself, Mr. Mormon."

"True. Should we just leave it? Come back for it tomorrow?"

"Look, I didn't have that much, honestly. Maybe one glass more than you. Fog is probably just patchy here and there. You know how it is out here. Bronte shrouded in fog while Bondi's perfectly clear. Can we at least give it a shot? If we get to the point and it's still foggy, I'll just turn up Bondi Road and get us back to the city."

The conversation was beginning to annoy him. He just wanted to go on a damn drive.

"Promise?"

"Yeah, yeah. Come on."

Sam jolted forward into the empty road, playing the clutch in and out with the gas, revving up to a high whine, the floor rumbling under his feet before he shifted up and shot forward into the night. The fog still clung to the road but traffic was thin as he rounded the park and shot past the pubs and petrol stations on the way to Bondi, slowing and gunning at the lights, then shooting forward again onto Old South Head Road toward The Gap and Laing's Point. As they climbed and twisted to the top of the North Bondi Hills, the fog lifted, and the dark waters of the Pacific reflected the moon back at them from a hundred feet below Dunbar Head.

"Gorgeous," Ryan said.

"Too right it is."

Sam knew the next stretch like the back of his hand, and he instinctively pressed the pedal down further, the engine responding beautifully, not a hiccup. The low body of the car swung and tilted with the contours of the road as if they were one, and he careened toward the dimly lit mansions of Watson's Bay. He gunned it once more as they approached the traffic circle that marked the end of Old South Head, his foot reluctantly poised over the brake.

"Dammit, Sam, slow down!"

He hit the brake and swerved right, slowing into the constant flow of traffic circling the row of restaurants along the waterfront.

"We were fine, Auntie, I mean Ryan."

"What? You almost ran straight into that house!"

"What? Not even close. Where did my fearless boyfriend go? I thought you'd get a kick out of it. Fucking Christ, Ryan."

"*Fearless* doesn't cover what you just did." Ryan pressed himself against the passenger door.

Sam hit the horn, three long blasts startling the crowd on the patio at Wilson's. "Let yourself go, mate. You've been spending too much time with Katrina."

"Hey now. She's my best friend."

Sam waved to the patio diners. "Don't I know it. And she doesn't approve of me one bit."

"That's not true."

"You know it is, but I don't care. All I care is I have you."

Ryan unclenched, moved back to the center of his seat. "So are you sure about it?"

"Course I'm sure."

"I mean, I know we've talked about it before but I didn't think . . . well. It kind of caught me off guard hearing you say it in front of other people. Made it feel official."

"Don't you want to?"

"Of course I do. I love you. You know that."

"I was hoping so. Figured if I announced it in front of my sister, you couldn't back out."

"Why would I back out? You're all I ever wanted," Ryan said.

Sam looked over at him and Ryan met his gaze. Locked eyes with him. Sam realized that he really meant it. He leaned over the seat and kissed him, then blasted the horn again.

"I'm getting married!" he yelled at the crowd.

No one looked up. They either didn't hear him or didn't care.

8

Ryan

Lucy stared into Ryan's eyes, her face blank, emotionless, inscrutable. Her mouth widened slowly into an O and he mirrored her, raising his eyebrows in unison with hers as she contorted her face into a clown's mask.

"Aaaaaaeeeeeeeeeiiiiiiiiioooooooouuuuuuuuu," she drawled, her tongue extended. Ryan wallowed with her, conscious of the timbre of his voice, matching every rise and fall in tone, every nuance of diction.

"GGGGGGGGGGGGGrrrrrrrrrrrrrrrrrrrrrrrr," she continued, her eyes narrowing, and he followed, mimicking the form and sensation, blocking out the sound of the others around him engaged in the same senseless mooing.

"Take your voices as low as possible," Graham called out as he walked among the pairs, his heels thudding on the hollow boards. "Scrape the bottom of your vocal range."

Ryan sunk lower, his throat vibrating and rasping.

"Deep in the chest. I want to hear the growling of bears, the gnashings of wolves."

"Aiiiiiiiiiiiiiiiiiiiiiiiiiiiii," a high voice screeched above the low gurgles. "Yiiiiiiiiiiiiiiiiiiiiiiiiiiiaaaaoooooo."

Lucy broke her growl and turned to stare.

"Christ, not yet, Paul," Graham shouted. "We're still on low register." He stomped past them to the back of the stage where Paul stood, clutching Charlotte's arms, a loose scrim wafting behind them.

She pushed him away. "Wasn't my idea."

Someone laughed, and the growls dissipated into chatter. Ryan focused forward, eyes locked on Lucy, hearing her breath, matching it. Focus.

"Sorry, sir." Paul's voice. "But I was feeling the wolf. Feeling the American West. I was at the top of a cliff, surveying the ravine, hunting for prey. The howl was pure instinct. The sound existed outside of me."

"While I appreciate your commitment to the Stanislavski method, you might consider listening to a wolf or two before you screech like that in future. You sounded like a chihuahua."

Lucy's eyes widened at Ryan, but she remained silent.

"Sorry sir."

"Keep it up and you'll be out of the show and on your way to a kennel. Everyone back to it. Start low, low as you can, hit bottom, then we'll start working back up to the top. And do your best to eradicate Mr. Capelli's yelping from your brains."

Ryan felt for him. They'd all been there. Graham could be incredibly harsh when he was displeased. But this is what it is, he told himself. This is what being an artist is about. Learning to take criticism is just as important as learning your craft. The meanness of it still sat wrong with him.

"Begin!" Graham yelled.

Ryan and Lucy leaned in again, their faces almost touching. Scattered props and costumes disappeared into the periphery. Lucy raised her eyebrows at him, a challenge. His growl matched hers exactly, their tones vibrating together, voices blending with the others around them to one massive rumble. She leaned further in, her eyes narrowing, voice feral, guttural. Ryan couldn't imagine how the sound was coming out of her. She was so small, so bubbly. But she was good, amazing, her focus burning so intensely he could feel the heat from her forehead. He leaned in closer, his forehead an inch from hers, hot breath mingling with her growls, and he sunk lower, pausing for breath only to avoid passing out. He could feel his hands digging into the planks of the stage, weighing down as he called forth every ounce of anger and aggression to match hers. Together they sounded like wild dogs, then buffalo, then a sea of diesel engines.

"And up, up, not too fast, rise . . ."

His rumble became a growl again and he kept her gaze steady. He could no longer hear her. They had all blended into one. He rose to a hum, then a whine, holding, waiting for the signal.

"And scream!" Graham stomped his foot on the stage, the boom shaking through the floor and up through his spine.

And he let loose with it. The pain and frustration of all the past. Utah. The church. Pretending to be straight. Screamed. Wailed. Like a lost soul, sure of death, frozen on a mountain, lost at sea. The final scream of lost hope. A good-bye to it all.

"And stop." Graham stomped his foot again, and the wails cut short.

"Intense, Ryan," Lucy whispered.

"You," he said. "Insane."

He stood up and gave her his hand. She grabbed quickly, again showing strength beyond her size, and pulled herself up.

"Who needs therapy after that?" she whispered to him.

"Miss Zhao. That was well done."

"Thanks, Graham."

"But don't get too carried away with it."

She gripped Ryan's hand harder. The sting with the compliment.

"Well done," Graham addressed them all. "But remember, this isn't some primal therapy exercise. Contrary to the opinions of certain of our graduates who can't resist making asses of themselves in the press, acting is not some mystical woo-woo or embodying of the spirits, although some may say it is. It's a practical craft like any other, and one that requires knowledge, skill, and discipline, not out-of-body experiences. You're no different than any plumber or hairdresser who takes their work seriously. Get over yourselves."

He clapped his hands sharply and Ryan's shoulders tensed. He supposed Graham had a point. Still, it had felt amazing.

"Places for act 1, scene 1. Ryan, Paul, and Abel. And I expect you all to be off book."

"Nail it," Lucy whispered.

"I intend to, even if I'm only playing the other bumbling idiot," he muttered back.

"But you're bloody hilarious, and you've got more lines than I do. You're all over act 1."

She was right. He hadn't gotten the part he wanted, but the prologue act with him and Abel as the bumbling brothers allowed them not only to narrate the backstory but to set up a deceptively comic tone that made the violent vicious ending all the more shocking. O'Neill definitely knew what he was doing.

"Ryan! Center stage now!"

Ryan hustled center with his castmates and grabbed his chair at the makeshift farm table.

Graham went from actor to actor, fussing with shoulders, pushing on foreheads, leaning, poking. He messed up Abel's hair, then came to Ryan.

"Shoulders down, Jensen, remember you're a slouch. A lazy lout. Show it. Sink into the chair."

Ryan imagined every schoolboy on the back bench of the bus and flopped his legs and arms out, claiming all the physical space within his reach. He slung one leg up over the table and pushed his chair back.

Graham leaned in.

"You've been listening. It shows."

"Thanks, I really appreciated the feedback. I know I wasn't doing my—"

"Stop. Take the compliment. Don't be so obsequious."

"Sorry." He instinctively straightened his posture.

"There it is again!" Graham's voice was curt, sharp. He grabbed Ryan's shoulder and shoved him back down. "Just do the work. It's in you."

He stepped to the front of the stage. "Begin."

Ryan scraped his chair further back from the table, sank deeper, and became the lazy young farmhand, ready to abandon his family at the first mention of gold.

9

Sam

A large woman laden with shopping bags pushed past them on the escalator. "Stand to the left, love," she called out as she wriggled around them.

Sam grabbed Ryan's shoulder and pulled him to the side as more commuters rushed past them. They stood together now, at the end of a perfect row of uniformed schoolgirls exiting the station, all plaid dresses and sunhats, phones out, texting madly. He felt Ryan's body against his own, rigid and tense, willing himself further out of harm's way.

"Sorry," Ryan said, under his breath.

"It's all right, mate," Sam said. "They'll all get where they're going."

A disorienting Rubik's cube of tracks, escalators, and mobbed multilevel platforms, Town Hall Station still threw Sam off even ten years in. The underground labyrinth often sent him in the wrong direction, backtracking up stairways and down passageways to finally catch the right train and get where he was going. That first month of uni, he had often found himself waiting on the wrong platform watching his own train pass by on the opposite tracks. Nerve-wracking. He still hated it, avoided it at all costs. But today, he wasn't going to give in to it. If they were a minute or two late, so be it. It was their day, and he didn't want any stress while they got things sorted out. Ryan was obviously feeling the overwhelm, clinging to his arm like a child holding on to his mother in the supermarket.

They reached the gates and Sam tapped his Opal card, triggering that delightful squeal that told everyone in the vicinity your card was low on funds. May as well just have the station voice shriek out "deadbeat can't pay his fare." He eyed the readout: remainder $1.40.

"You need some cash?" Ryan asked. His card dinged normally, the pleasant chime of a full fare-payer, as he followed Sam through.

"All good. Just forgot to top up. Get it on the way back."

Except he didn't have any cash. Bankcard was overdrawn. And a buck forty wouldn't get him on the bus tomorrow to work. Have to scrounge couch cushions for change tonight. No way he was going to ask Ryan for his pocket change. As much as he complained about money, he always seemed to have it. His restaurant shifts did him well. Probably didn't hurt that neither Sam nor Katrina had ever charged him much rent. Maybe he should . . . but that was a thought for another day when they combined accounts and hit the big time. For now, just get to the solicitor's and see where they stood.

They climbed the last flight of steps to the street, and Sam eyed Ryan up and down again. He knew he was coming straight from school and going back to rehearsal, but for God's sake, not even a polo shirt? Sam had come straight from work, ditching out early to make their appointment on time, and was dressed in a crisp dress shirt, dark-blue trousers and tie, a jacket slung over his arm, every bit the Pitt Street businessman, making Ryan look extra slouchy in his jeans and T-shirt. Ryan had caught his look when they'd met at Kings Cross, but Sam had recovered his composure quickly. Any friend of his sister's wasn't going to care about their dress sense. She'd probably like him for it. The casual American thing.

That was another thing that worried him, if he was being honest. Belinda was probably a ripper of a therapist, but she was a bit of a new-age flake, lost in a world of weed and waves up in Byron, where deadlines and consequences didn't seem to exist, and it stood to reason her mate might be the same. Still, he'd been at it for weeks, calling firm after firm, anyone who advertised as gay-friendly, and the best he'd done was two months out, and the fees were astronomical. Lin's mate had agreed to installments and had a booking open that week. Danielle Chin, however hippy-dippy she might be, was a blessing. Remember that.

They took the next set of escalators to street level, Sam leading the way, ducking in and out of the endless stream of cabs and buses, cutting around the mob of smartly dressed city workers mobbing the Queen Victoria building, its namesake monarch cast in bronze, her famous frown guarding the entrance to the repurposed posh shopping center. He checked the address again and turned into York Street, stopping at a stark concrete tower set back from the street behind a three-tiered brutalist fountain. Sam cut quickly past the splashing stack of gray blocks, Ryan behind him, and pushed through the glass doors, the lobby of the building shockingly quiet after the street noise.

"This is it then." He punched the up arrow.

"Are you sure? Do you think we're rushing?" Ryan hung back from the elevators, dwarfed by two giant potted palms.

"What? You having second thoughts? Are you kidding?"

"No. No. Sorry. It's just . . ." He held both hands up. Palms out. Defensive. "I can't believe we're really doing it, that's all."

"Believe it, Spunky. We're really doing it."

Just nerves. They'd be fine. A big step, after all.

They stepped into the first open car and the doors slid closed. Sam leaned in and nuzzled Ryan's neck, ruffled his hair. "You've made me the happiest guy in Sydney."

Ryan's eyes were squeezed tightly shut. "Me too," he said.

They reached the seventh floor. A young man greeted them at the reception desk. Well groomed. He looked familiar. Probably Oxford Street. "May I help you?"

"Here to see Danielle Chin. Sam Carter and Ryan Jensen." Sam continued in his role of director, sensing Ryan's silent gratitude.

"She's expecting you. Just down the hall. Third office."

"Ta."

They walked past a row of photographs of happy couples kissing in front of various Sydney landmarks—the bridge, the opera house, the Anzac Memorial—then proudly signing documents in front of an Australian flag. Miss Chin's door was half-open. Sam tapped lightly.

"Come in."

A slim Asian woman of about thirty-five sat behind her desk wearing a dark blazer and silk blouse. Her shining black hair was pulled back in a ponytail. Professional. Serious. Not at all the hippie type Sam had imagined. A relief. Lin must have met Danielle Chin in another life.

"Just coming from the beach, are we?" She looked Ryan up and down. "Embracing the Aussie lifestyle?" So that was working. Well done, Ryan.

"Oh, yeah. Um." Ryan fumbled to find his words. "I'm sorry— it's just that I'm on my way to rehearsal later, the conservatory, we do—"

"I told him to dress smart," Sam said, relaxing now. "But, well—"

She waved her hand, cutting him off. "Not a problem. Just having a go at you. Suit and tie not required. At least not until you face the judge."

"We'll be facing a judge?" Sam felt his stomach kick.

"Relax! Joking!" She gestured toward the chairs in front of her desk. "Don't worry. No courtroom in your future."

His shoulders relaxed. His breathing steadied. Fair enough. She had a sense of humor. Now it made perfect sense she was Lin's mate.

She shuffled through some paperwork and picked up a folder. "Have a seat, gentlemen. I've got your application files here."

Sam folded his jacket over his arm and sat down slowly, while Ryan slid into the chair beside him and leaned forward, the surefooted confident actor having replaced the nervous Mormon schoolboy. That dual nature was part of why he loved him. Made him real.

"How're we going then?" Sam asked. He fiddled in his suit pocket for the pad he'd brought. Better to write things down. A trickle of sweat ran down his forehead, instantly icy in the air-conditioning. "All ducks in order?"

"Well, the initial bridging visa should be no problem. We grant those without too much trouble, so you won't have to leave the country when you finish school, Mr. Jensen." She waved an orange formal-looking paper at Ryan. "The final relationship claim takes longer, and it's a bit trickier, but shouldn't be a problem provided a few things are sorted before you get married."

Sam clicked his pen, ready to write. "Just let us know. Anything that needs to be clarified should be an easy task. We've been together now for a good bit and we really want this."

"The shared address is key, your income statement, Mr. Carter, is sufficient, and Mr. Jensen's part-time employment and two-year stint at an Australian university serves you well, so on that score you're picture perfect," she said.

Sam sighed with relief and Ryan visibly perked, sat up in his chair. Sam reached over and grabbed his hand.

"You wouldn't believe some of the issues that come up here." Miss Chin sat on the edge of her desk, legs crossed. "Profit-driven marriages between strangers. Lengthy criminal records in foreign countries. Even had one where the couple were underage and using forged passports. That one was quite exciting, actually. Had to bring in the state police. You two are a dream compared to all that, so long as you've brought along your divorce decree? Put that all officially in the past?" She ended her sentence in that conversational uptick many Australians used that made direct statements sound like questions.

"Right! Divorce! You got us there." Sam leaned forward in his chair. She had to be kidding around.

But she wasn't smiling. "You do have it with you, yes?"

So she was serious?

"What divorce decree?" he asked. "I'm gay, Miss Chin. Came out at eighteen. Don't think you're going to find any ex-wives running around Sydney." He laughed at his own joke. "And this one here's barely out of missionary school. You've got to be mistaken."

"I'm referring to Mr. Jensen's divorce decree, from his marriage to Megan Mortensen in January 2016?" Again the questioning uptick. She fished through the file, held out a slightly blurred document—a fax?—State of Utah Certificate of Marriage emblazoned across the top in rococo lettering. It looked like some shoddy document you'd get online, like an online ordination or something. "You do have it?" Her tone remained matter-of-fact and she continued shuffling through papers. "We'll need it for proof of your single status, or your interdependent relationship claim will technically amount to bigamy in the eyes of the Australian government." She gave a slight chuckle. "But then again, you are from Utah, Mr. Jensen, so I suppose the misunderstanding is forgivable." She set the file down. "*Big Love* was amazing." She chatted on as if at a backyard barbecue. "I never knew the first wife had to give permission. At least a touch of feminism, I suppose. Who would have thought that in this day and age . . ."

Sam's brain caught up with his mouth. He turned to Ryan.

"You were married?" he said, cutting Miss Chin off, his voice rising in confusion. Ryan stared straight ahead in silence. "Apparently still fucking married?" He gripped the arms of his chair and his knuckles turned white. He stared at Ryan, his eyes wide. "What's going on?"

Ryan looked straight ahead. After a moment, he spoke, so quietly that Sam had to lean toward him to hear. "It was supposed to be taken care of already. It was only for a year." His voice fell to almost a whisper. "I sent her the papers after my first year. When I was sure. She was supposed to take care of it. I would have told you but I figured it was over with so why dredge it up. Best left in the past."

Sam's mind jumped to a million places. Who was sitting next to him? This sweet aw-shucksy Mormon kid was married? But of course he was. Weren't they all? Like at eighteen? And just the one wife? Jesus. But his mind moved quickly from incredulity to a sense of betrayal. He'd been straight up with Ryan, hadn't he? Aside from the tight money, which was going to sort itself out, he'd been up front about all his baggage. This whopper of a lie of omission felt like a sucker punch, and he was reeling from it.

"Seems a pretty significant fact to leave out," he said, "so, I'll be your second . . . well, spouse, I guess?" His felt his voice rising in sarcastic anger now. He didn't care. "But you've filed for divorce so I suppose that makes it all right then." He leaned as far over in his chair as he could without standing up. Ryan's face was inches from him. His eyes were closed. "Couldn't have any bearing on our relationship, now could it." He was shouting now. "No, not at all. Not like anything in your past does."

Miss Chin put the state document back on the pile, shock registered in her eyes. She looked at Sam and spoke calmly. "Try to stay calm, Mr. Carter. I realize you may be in a bit of shock. Goodness." She stood up and started pacing behind her desk. "This certainly makes things a bit more difficult."

Ryan stared at the floor, still silent.

Sam felt it welling up in him, tried to swallow it, but the dam burst. "Just look at me!" he screamed. "Am I just some ticket to citizenship so you can party on the beach and prance around on stage, then divorce me after the requisite two years and move on with your fancy actor friends? Dinners with the Blanchetts? Holidays with the Jackmans? It was Katrina's idea, wasn't it? Do you even love me at all?"

When Ryan spoke, his voice wobbled with raw emotion. "Of course I love you. You know I love you! I know I should have told you. It's just, it's in the past. It was the church. There's so much pressure. I thought it would fix me. They told me it would fix me. I prayed and begged and did everything they told me and, well, it obviously didn't work. Why do you think I moved halfway' round the world to go to school? I could have just as easily gone to school in the States, but I wanted to have a new life. Leave it all behind. Remake myself. You're everything I've ever wanted. Finally. I get to be who I really am now. With you. I didn't want to start with baggage."

Ryan's last comment fell flat, as unconvincing to Sam now as a promise of a phone call from a drunken hookup. His jacket had fallen to the floor, and he picked it up, folded it over the arm of his chair.

Miss Chin walked out from behind her desk. "Let's all try to remain calm. We don't want to alarm anyone else in the building. Keep it between us. I'm sure we can figure out what's going on."

Sam wondered if she'd go running to Belinda to tell her about the spectacle. But this wasn't her fault.

"And you just thought it wouldn't come up? Magical disappearing marriage license?" He realized he was shouting and adjusted. Quiet. Slow. Deliberate. "We could have figured it out together, avoided this mess."

"I assumed she'd done it."

"That was smart." Sam felt himself heating up again.

"I'm sure your intentions were good, but these things follow you. Surely you're aware of that," Danielle said. She held the document up again. "My husband and I are considering moving to Canada, you know. I certainly hope we would still be considered married in Vancouver. He has family there, an auntie and cousins. The last generation of Chinese immigrants went to Vancouver and Seattle, you know. Things didn't always go smoothly, but they worked it out." She stopped pacing and looked at Sam, shrugging her shoulders. "The younger ones are coming here now, or going to New Zealand."

He appreciated her efforts to calm things down, but it was too late. "You hear that? Maybe you can try Auckland next, Ryan. Find a new mark . . ."

"This is obviously a more complicated matter than I realized," Danielle said.

No one spoke. Sam's breath was ragged, the sounds of a storm.

"I'll just give you two a moment to chat." She brushed past them but paused in the doorway. "I'm sure we can sort this out. Remember, civility is key here, gentlemen." She stepped into the hallway and pulled the door closed behind her.

Ryan looked at the floor. He reached out and put his hand on Sam's knee, but Sam pushed it away.

"It's not even the fact that you've got a wife back home."

"Had. Past. I signed the papers and sent them to her ages ago. She said she filed them."

"Filed or not, you flat-out lied to me about it all. Young Mormon boy shedding his past and coming into his own. Finding his true self on the stage. Lovely tale of self-actualization or whatnot. But you're really just some damn religious hypocrite cheating on your clueless wife while you're away at school?"

"I'm sorry."

"Unless she knows about me? Does she? You two having a laugh? Have three-ways with other confused missionaries, do you?"

"No. That's ridiculous. I haven't—"

"So neither one of us knows about the other? Bloody brilliant!"

"I know I should have—"

"The way you talk I just assumed you'd burnt down the church at fifteen and never looked back, mister hip actor and world traveler, right? Shake off the shackles of religion and march down to Sydney gay and proud and ready for the big city, right?"

"There was so much pressure from our families, the church. We met when I got home from my mission, when I still thought I could do it. She was in theater with me. We had a lot of fun together, and I figured if I had to do it, may as well be her. It just seemed like the right thing to do. We even did okay for a while."

"Assuming you've banged her then. Got any kids stashed away up there?

"Come on, Sam. You know I don't."

"Problem is, I don't know. I feel like I don't even know who the fuck you are!"

"You know exactly who I am. I just, well, I just didn't know how to tell you."

"This is insane." Sam stood, pulling at his tie. "Good thing you still left some shit at Katrina's. You can head straight there from here." He walked toward the door, then stopped, turned back to face Ryan. "Are you rooting Katrina too? Seems you're full of surprises today."

He walked out of the office, slamming the door behind him, the glass rattling in its mahogany frame. Anger seethed through him, but deeper than any anger, his heart was broken beyond anything he'd felt in his life. He stomach churned, and he held back tears, unwilling to let any of these people see him cry. The elevator opened and he stepped in, breathing steadily, counting: One, two, three, don't lose it. Four, five, six, stay steady.

The doors shut and he descended to the street.

10

Ryan

Ryan stood up, still in shock. He felt tears welling up but forced them back down. Should he follow? And say what? Explain things how? Why should Sam take him back? It looked exactly like what he said, that Ryan had lied about everything and was simply using him for citizenship. But he wasn't. He had been afraid. Worried it wouldn't work, but most of all just so anxious to make a clean break that he'd kept it all to himself. And now look. He was screwed.

"Goodness. He seems very angry. Are you all right, Mr. Jensen?" Miss Chin stepped back into the room and approached him slowly, tentatively. "I'm very sorry about all of this."

"It's not your fault."

"I just hate to see this kind of trouble get in the way of things. You're such a lovely couple."

"You're very kind." He looked at the floor, his eyes watering.

She set their file down on the desk. "Perhaps you just need a little time? Sometimes these things are more easily explained when everyone is calm."

"Sam doesn't do calm very well."

"Yes. He does seem to have a temper, although you—"

"It's my fault. He had no idea what hit him."

"You say you've filed the divorce papers?"

"Yes, well. I didn't technically file them. I signed them and sent them to her. You can download them from a dozen different sites. I didn't even call her. Haven't spoken to her since." He walked to the window overlooking the street, scanning the crowd for Sam. "I came here to reinvent myself. Clean slate. Leave the past in the past. Look what that got me."

She came to the window and stood next to him, a hand on his shoulder. "After years in this line of work, I find that the truth is always the best answer. Now that it's out in the open, you may be able to rebuild things. Would you like to sit for a moment? Your appointment was booked for an hour. I can leave you to collect yourself before you go."

"No. I think I'll go. I imagine he's out of the building at this point?"

"I imagine so. It's been a few minutes."

"Thank you, Miss Chin."

"Call me Danielle."

She leaned in and hugged him, and, surprised, he hugged her back, fiercely, desperately, holding on for everything he was worth.

"There, there," she said.

He felt tears running down his face and onto her blouse and pulled back, embarrassed. "I'm sorry. Gosh. Didn't mean to crush you."

"It's fine." She took the box of tissues from her desk and offered them. "Just stick to the truth."

He grabbed a tissue and blotted his eyes, then crunched it into a ball in his palm.

"It will all work out," she said.

"Thanks. I think I'll go now."

"Of course."

He walked slowly to the elevators, unable to process the buzz and hustle of busy people around him.

"Parking validation?" the receptionist asked as he passed his desk.

"Train," he said without stopping.

He rode the lift down with a group of chatty office workers making plans for the pub, then walked out of the building to face the business crowd of George Street again. At the entrance to Town Hall station, he hesitated, then walked on. Rehearsal wasn't for a few hours, and he wasn't quite ready for rolling around on the floor willing his body to transform into the characters Graham insisted they become. Didn't know if he could do it at all today. He walked on through the cavernous rows of high-rises across the CBD—the breezy Aussie term for "Central Business District"—glad he was dressed so casually now, no jacket and tie to make things worse now that everything had fallen through.

A few turns through side streets and he found himself in Hyde Park, his favorite place in the city. He'd wandered over from his hostel in Kings Cross that first day, jet-lagged and overwhelmed, astonished by its meticulous beauty, the perfectly symmetrical flower beds, the immaculate lawns. Hundred-year-old wrought-iron benches lined the manicured stone walkway that ran the length of the park. He walked slowly now, sheltered by a massive canopy of weeping figs, in shade and silence. A cathedral of trees. A whisper of serenity in the wild city.

Dozens of Mormon missionaries milled around at the south end of the park, setting up shop near the solemn grandeur of the ANZAC memorial. A common enough site here. The local ward—Mormon-speak for congregation—was in a building just across the street. He'd gone to church once that first week, had sat in the back, close enough to the doors to leave without being noticed, and had never been back.

They walked around in pairs, trying to engage picnickers and tourists with conversational openers he was well familiar with. He'd spent two years as a missionary in Ecuador, intent on curing himself through sharing the gospel and giving service to others, but nothing had changed. Still, he refused to believe that God had forsaken him. There had to be a way. He had proposed to Megan his first day back in the States, and they'd married six months later. He had thrown himself into the marriage wholeheartedly, but deep down he knew he was embarking on an elaborate lie.

He'd been with his wife right up to the day he got on the plane, his plan for escape and reinvention a secret he hadn't dared tell a soul. He'd only sent her the papers a few months after he arrived in Sydney. After he felt confident enough he could make it here. Afraid to face her, he'd simply downloaded the forms for a no-contest divorce, filled out everything but her signature, and mailed them. He'd dodged her calls and emails since then. They'd been hourly, then daily, then weekly. He'd deleted the voicemails unheard, moved the emails to trash without opening them. It was just too much to process. He was too terrified to hear her disapproval, her disappointment, or worse, her heartbreak.

And then they'd tapered off completely. That had been about six months ago.

His parents had never mentioned it, so he at least knew she hadn't told them.

He'd seen the elders there in the park on his first day, nostalgic but exhilarated by the idea that they had no idea who he was, no idea where he was from, or that he had until just days before been one of them. His reinvention then had felt seductive and exhilarating, like anything was possible. He had simply gotten on a plane and left it behind. Shedding his identity as he lost sight of the North American continent. Yet he had failed. Sam hated him now. He was hated back home. He had nowhere left. Nobody except Katrina, and she'd warned him about this for months.

He sank down onto a bench and watched the young men take to their work without thought or worry.

He hadn't thought about church in months.

He hadn't prayed in months.

He closed his eyes.

"Dear Heavenly Father," he whispered, the words feeling like treachery on his tongue.

"Dear Heavenly Father, I don't know what to do." The solid metal slats of the bench dug into his back. He leaned into them.

"I have made a total mess of everything and I need your help."

He looked up to see if anyone was staring at him . . . not that someone muttering on a park bench in Hyde Park would be that remarkable. No one was watching. No one cared. Why should they?

"I've lied to everyone," he continued. "I've misrepresented myself to the world. I've deserted the people who loved me most. I've turned my back on my family. I've turned my back on my faith. I thought I could make something better here, something wonderful, but instead I've ruined everything. I'm a failure as an actor. I'm a failure as a boyfriend. I'm a failure as a husband. I'm a failure as a son.

"What do I do?

"What do I say?

"Where do I start?

"I just wish I'd never gotten on that plane.

"Please guide me to the right decision.

"Please help me to do what is right.

"Please help me to know what to do to fix things.

"I know I've been a disappointment.

"I am who I am and I can't change it.

"I've tried. I've tried and tried and tried.

"I thought this would work.

"I thought if I just moved to another country where nobody knew me.

"But it didn't work.

"I'm so lost.

"I need help.

"Anything.

"Guide me, please.

"Show me what to do."

He took a deep breath, unsure if he should go on. What more was there to say?

"I say these things in the name of Jesus Christ, amen."

He kept his eyes closed for a moment and let the reality of it all sink in, filling his lungs as deeply as he could and holding the breath in—a meditation exercise from school—expelling it, pushing, pushing, until he couldn't get another wisp of breath out. His heart slowed and he took another breath. Deep. As deep as he could go, and as he held it, a thought came to him, forming itself on his tongue. "She's right. Tell the truth. To everyone. It's the only way you're going to fix this. You have to come clean."

He opened his eyes. The sun was setting over the western edge of the park, orange and purple rippling across the reflecting pool.

Two missionaries stood in front of him. "How are you today, sir? Everything all right?"

"I'm fine, thanks."

"You just looked, well . . ."

"Yeah. Well, it hasn't been the greatest day." He'd been crying into his hands and he rubbed them across his jeans now, leaving dark streaks across the blue denim.

"We'd be happy to help if we can," one of them said. He was a tall lean kid with the blond hair and perfect white teeth of a Utah native. Elder Bingham, his name-tag read.

"I appreciate it, but it's something I have to do myself. You elders don't need to worry about me. I'm sure there's someone here who would be interested in the discussions, someone golden." The old lingo felt strange to him now, a foreign language.

"Are you a member of the church?" The other young man was shorter, thin. He clutched a Book of Mormon to his chest. Elder Roberts.

"I was. I used to be, but I haven't been active for a bit."

"Our ward is right here," Elder Bingham said, gesturing past the war memorial. "You'd be welcome to come with us on Sunday."

"Oh, I know," Ryan said. A group of tall gangly ibises strutted around the bench, picking at anything that looked like food. "I've known. The church and I don't really get along anymore."

"It's never too late to come back, you know. What's your name?" His face was warm, open.

"Ryan. It's Ryan Jensen. I'm from Salt Lake. Here in grad school. Theater." He looked up at the memorial again, its understated grandeur breathtaking.

"Well, I'd offer you a Book of Mormon but—"

"Yeah, I already have one. Somewhere, anyhow."

"You know where to find us," he said.

"That I do," Ryan said, "but I've got to be going." He stood and held out his hand to the tall one who had first spoken. "I wish you two the best in your work, though."

He walked back to Town Hall Station in a daze, swiped his card and numbly found the platform for Bondi. Another fight. Another flight. This was seeming too familiar, sickeningly so.

He found a bench at the far end of the platform, away from the midafternoon crowd, and pulled out his phone. Now or never. Three p.m. in Sydney, so, nine in Utah? He pulled up Megan's contact page on Facebook. Would she even talk to him? He waved his finger over the call symbol, inched it closer, closer, a millimeter from connecting. The wind kicked up from the tunnel and the train screeched up to the platform. A group of school kids tumbled and chased each other off the escalator and surrounded his bench, their ties pulled loose, jackets slung over arms and shoulders.

"This far down the end we'll at least all get seats," yelled one of the boys. "Come on."

Ryan put his phone back in his pocket, his heart heavy with guilt, but relieved at being interrupted.

11

Sam

After their meeting at the solicitor, Sam had walked south, fuming, furious, then ducked into a dark bar on the edge of the CBD, one he assumed Ryan would never find. He'd been there for hours, knocking back bourbon after bourbon, forgetting that he and Jenny had promised Kyle that they'd be in on Saturday to flog these damn units.

Her text the next morning had been a rude awakening. *Where are you? It's 10:30????* *Kyle will be here at 11:00!!* He'd slugged down some coffee, grabbed a ninety-second shower, thrown on the first shirt he grabbed from the wardrobe, and was running down the stairs when he had to run back up and vomit. Kneeling at the toilet, sweat pouring off his brow, he got another text, this time from Perry. *We still on for surfing when you finish work?*

Fuck. He was already so hung over he could barely think straight, his head hot and pounding, his guts roiling as if he might have to puke again. He typed in *sorry mate—too crook to surf today*, then immediately deleted it. He hated disappointing the kid. Perry still hadn't made many friends, and Amanda certainly wasn't going to teach him anything.

He ran back upstairs, his head pounding, his stomach in revolt, grabbed his surfboard, and ordered an uber, crossing his fingers his credit card would cover it. Sick as he was, the water might do him good, and focusing on something else might get his mind off Ryan and the whole fiasco. Double fucking life. Right? Mormon wife? Jesus. Why not just tell me? Was I your bloody first?

He'd slogged through the day with Jenny. A few potential buyers had strolled in but balked at the prices, and left when Sam said they were nonnegotiable. He'd shut up shop at two and grabbed his board. Just get in the water and forget.

He watched as Perry staggered up onto the beach, surfboard dragging behind him, tossing in the shallow breakers, his dark-blue wetsuit speckled with patches of wet sand. He picked the glossy new board up, tucked it under his arm, and walked to where Sam stood squinting into the afternoon sun, his head pounding, the scattered palm trees of Bronte Park behind him. "That wasn't bad, Perry. Just a little fine-tuning and you're going to be solid."

"Bullshit. I stuffed it up again, Sam." The boy's hair hung in his eyes, a starburst of scabs formed across his chin where he'd scraped through some rough gravel at last week's lesson.

"You didn't stuff it up, mate." Sam's own surfboard lay beside him on the ground, the once bright red and gold paint faded and scuffed. "You've got great form. You're just going a second too late. If you pop up late, you miss the best part of the wave, and end up getting buried in the curl." He mimicked the action as he described it, squatting and hopping like he was doing calisthenics. The kid really did have chops. The moment it clicked, there would be no stopping him.

"I know. I know. Two seconds. I just never quite catch it. I suck," Perry said.

Sam pushed his sunglasses up onto his forehead and rubbed a bit of sunburnt skin off his peeling nose. "You don't suck. I wasn't great when I started either," he said. "The thing you have to remember," he said, trying now not to sound like a schoolteacher, "is that it takes a few seconds to get everything situated, you know—your body, the board—so if you wait until the wave's on you, it curls before you catch it and you get dragged under. Trick is going two seconds before you think you have to."

"How do you know two seconds?" Perry said. He tugged at the zipper on his wetsuit.

"Trial and error. It works. Believe me." Sam took the boy's darkly tanned shoulder and shook it playfully. "You can do it."

"Should I do a few more practice runs here first?" He dragged his board around next to them and laid it flat, then crouched down to go through the pop-up drills again.

"Nah. Your form's fine. Honest. Really good even. It's just timing. Go try again." He nudged Perry's board with his foot and pointed out to the water. "You'll get it by the end of the afternoon, I promise."

Perry turned away from Sam and picked the board up, balancing it on his head as he broke into a jog. As Sam watched Perry hit water's edge, a woman approached. She was young and heavyset, topless, her breasts round and plump, her shoulders burnt a bright red except for two pale stripes where her bathing suit had been. She held out a tube of sunscreen to him and said, "Would you mind?" in a British accent. Her towel lay crumpled in the sand a few feet away, a book open next to it, face down. She was alone.

Sam looked at her, keeping his gaze eye level, trying not to stare at her brown nipples, and pointed out to Perry. "I'm just teaching him how to . . ."

"Please?" she asked, and giggled. "I'm already burnt to a crisp."

"Why not." He held his hand out, and she gave him the tube, then turned to face the water.

As Sam slathered lotion on the woman's burnt shoulders, Perry ran a few more paces, high-stepping over the breakers at the water line until he was out several meters, then dropped the board and jumped on head first, pushed out into the water, and paddled away from the shore with a confidence and grace to his movements Sam had never had at that age.

He massaged the crisp flesh, wiping bits of white lotion from her neck, remembering for a fleeting moment the days when he used to still hook up with girls. With Ryan gone, what was stopping him from doing it again?

Shut up, Sam. That was back when you didn't know who you were.

Still, he thought about Amanda for a moment. She'd been keen the moment they'd met on the beach but covered it up when he mentioned he was gay.

Christ, you're half-drunk and crazy pissed off at your boyfriend.

He shook it off and looked up toward the row of shops and restaurants along Bronte Road, sidewalk tables already filling up for the afternoon, the metal railing that kept traffic from careening off into the rocks rusted and peeling from a rainy winter. The midwinter day was clear and brisk but still warm enough to surf and get a bit of sun. Lots of locals getting into wetsuits or lying out in the sun, but too cold for the suburban picnic mob.

"Ta," the woman said, and took her tube of lotion from Sam. She walked back to her towel.

He turned to watch Perry, small for his age but fit and fast, nearly eclipsed by his too-big board and the other surfers out in the water, his back to Sam as he watched the line. A swell formed, bowing the surface, and Sam felt that rush that a perfect wave always gave him.

"Come on, Perry," he muttered. He watched Perry turn and paddle north along the line. "Up on your knees. Now. Come on!" he said, louder now, although the boy couldn't hear him. Perry was already crouching on his knees, gripping the board. "Up!" Sam yelled.

Perry popped up a half second late. He stood, wobbling for a moment, steadied himself, then leaned into the curl, his board cutting perfectly through the water past a group of surfie chicks who had missed the moment. He had it.

"You fucking beauty!" Sam yelled. He picked up his own surfboard from the cool, damp sand, hooked it under his arm, and walked down to the shallows to where Perry was hopping up and down and yelling. "I did it! I bloody well did it!"

The British woman cheered from her towel.

"Awesome, mate," Sam said.

"Two seconds. You were right. It was perfect."

"Absolutely perfect. Proud of you." He leaned down and splashed Perry with a handful of water. "And it only took you two hours,"

"Aw, shit," Perry said. "Didn't take me two hours. Don't be an arsehole, Sam."

"Watch your mouth, Perry. Do you want to run a few more?" Sam asked and looked at his watch. He was thinking Ryan would be home soon, then realized that he wouldn't be, that he'd kicked him out and told him to never come back. But he couldn't focus on that now. It would just make him sick all over again. Besides, the kid had really done it.

"Or better yet we could go grab a burger or something? I bet you're starving after this. You've earned a meal, I reckon." He needed a meal himself. Still shaky from the night's indulgences and the morning upset, he hadn't been hungry enough at lunch time to eat but now he was ravenous.

Perry coughed. "Is it six yet? Mum says I have to be home by then."

Sam looked at his watch again. "Not quite five. We've got plenty of time if we head out now. Do you want burgers or curry? I'm buying. We can lock the boards up in my office."

They walked through the park past the changing rooms, the outdoor showers, and the bars and beams of the various fitness trail stations, and started up the steep concrete steps that led to the street. Two high-school-aged girls walked beside them, eyeing Perry slyly.

"I should really just go, Sam," Perry said. "Mum will be wondering. She's a nutter. Panics about everything if I'm late."

"Come on, mate, she knows you're safe with me. Let's get a burger to celebrate that perfect wave."

"Sam. It sounds cool, but . . ." Perry looked at the ground. "Look, Mum says I'm not supposed to be alone with you. Surfing's fine, but nowhere else." He looked up at Sam, his eyes squinting shut. "'Cause you're gay and all that."

"Are you joking?" Sam asked.

"I told you she's a dipshit."

Sam stopped walking. "Fuck," he muttered. "She really thinks I'd do that." They paused at the traffic lights under a cluster of golden wattle trees that rustled in the faint breeze, obscuring the view of the street. He turned to face the boy. "Are you afraid of me, Perry?"

"Course not. She's an idiot."

Sam stepped off the curb into the road and tightened his grip on the varnished surface of the board.

"You have to be careful!" Perry said in a high voice, imitating his mother. "Men like that, well, they may be nice, but sometimes they want to do things." He spat on the sidewalk. "You should hear her. Talks to me like I'm a toddler. Like you're some kind of perv or something."

"Christ, Perry. You really know how to put things, don't you?"

"I've already fucked a girl at school, you know," he said, and narrowed his eyes. "Mum thinks I'm still eleven or something. And anyway, Spaz's uncle Rhys is gay. He flies for QANTAS. Spaz says gay blokes come to their flat a lot for parties, and my mum is always up there for drinks, carrying on, calling Rhys her boyfriend. Says she gets super drunk and silly."

94

"Well, that's a crock of shit. Tell your mum she . . ." He stopped himself. No good would come from calling Amanda a crazy bitch in front of her son. A furniture delivery truck going too fast came toward them and Sam jumped back up onto the curb. "Bloody idiot," he yelled. He looked at Perry. "Tell her I think I can resist the urge to kidnap you and drag you to my cave, if that's what she's afraid of."

"Yeah, right. Big scary Sam. There's a cave under the cliff walk, you know. That's where we went. Me and Sophie. Lots of kids go there to smoke or chill-out or whatever. It used to be cool, but some homeless bloke lives in it now. It smells like my dog. I think he shits back there and leaves it." Perry made a face and plugged his nose.

"Yeah, I know those caves. I haven't been out there for a while, though," Sam said. "I guess it's a good enough place to hang out if you haven't got anywhere else. Stay away if some homeless bloke is camping there, though, all right? You never know when someone like that is going to go off."

"Yeah, whatever. I know. I can take care of myself. He had a bunch of shells in a circle, like he was making something with them. I took one and gave it to Mum. She says I can't go there anymore either. She says the homeless are mostly addicts and perverts."

"Lovely. So at least it's not just gay people."

"Nah. Mum hates pretty much everybody who isn't just like her or who doesn't agree with her," Perry said. "I should go." He gestured toward the Greek café.

"Yeah, I reckon you should."

"Next Saturday again?"

Sam scanned the row of cafés, looking for Amanda, wondering if she was watching somewhere. He realized Perry was waiting for an answer. "What? Sorry. Yeah, of course."

"Cool." Perry started across the street, past the row of cars idling at the lights, his board wobbling as he walked. "Bye, Sam," he yelled without turning back.

"Bye, Perry. You're doing awesome!" he yelled at the boy, then muttered, "and tell your mum to pull her bloody head out of her arse."

Breathing deeply, Sam watched Perry walk until he was out of sight in the crowd. What the fuck was Amanda pulling? It didn't make any sense. She'd invited him to dinner that first day on the beach. They'd had a glass and a laugh and talked about their hometowns, their jobs, surfing. After a few drinks, she'd even admitted she'd fancied Sam when she first saw him and that she'd been a little embarrassed when she realized she was barking up the wrong tree. Then with Ryan back, they'd gone over again and things had gone well. So he thought. There was that moment that she'd scolded him about the PDA but surely that wasn't that big of a deal. He had been surfing with Perry for a couple of months now, and it dawned on him. Two-faced bitch was apparently just wrangling surf lessons for her son. "Goddammit!"

he muttered. He threw the board over his head and trotted across the street and down the block to his office. Out front, the new signs he'd ordered had tipped against the building in the breeze, a sandwich board that read "Luxury Units!!! Sea Views!!! Display models open now!!!" He walked through the 1950s retro-chic lobby and past the front desk. Jenny had stayed late following up on emails and booking the food and furniture for the next viewing. He'd assumed it wouldn't take her long, but she was still here gabbing on the phone. He waved at her curtly, not slowing as he went back toward his office. She put the phone down. "Hey!" she called after him. "What's the rush? How was the surfing?"

He stopped and turned back. "Sorry. Brilliant," he said, affecting cheeriness. "Perry's getting really good."

She waved a pale-blue slip of paper at him. A check? "His mum stopped by, left this for you." She'd painted her nails black to match her overdyed hair. Goth this year. Last year it had been hippie, but hippie blokes were always high, she'd said, and she didn't like weed, so she'd given all her organic-cotton peasant blouses to charity shops and now squeezed herself into corsets and vinyl and went to raves and dance parties, had even dragged Sam and Ryan to one last Mardi Gras. "I'm stopping at the bank on my way home. Shall I take it with me when I go?"

"Christ. I told her no charge." He grabbed it from Jenny and looked at it.

Pay to Sam Carter. 200 dollars. Amanda Rosalind Lewis.

Surf Lessons was written in the memo line in curvy script. "Bunch of bullshit," he said.

"So just send it back to her," Jenny said, her voice defensive. "Christ, Sam, I'm sure she meant no harm." She lowered her voice. "Even if she is a bit of a bitch. Hoity toity that one."

"Yeah, sorry, Jen. Didn't mean to bite your head off. Just worried about sales, I guess. We've got to figure out a way to move some of these units faster."

"I told you what you need to do. Do like that bloke did in Brisbane and make a video of yourself touring the units in your bathers," she said, giggling. "We'll sell the whole building in a day. You and Ryan coming to the pub tonight?"

"Yeah. I don't think so." Sam set the check back down on her desk on top of a stack of leaflets that had to be sent back to the printer. They'd gotten the phone number wrong.

Should he tell her about the mess at the solicitor's office? No. Too soon.

"Oh, come on, why not? It's Saturday night, for Christ's sake," she said.

Sam stared at the check.

"Sam?" Jenny waved her hand in front of his face.

"Sorry, what?"

"The pub."

He shook his head.

"Well, if you change your mind, come down," she said. "Carlos is coming out tonight. I want to go home and pick out something to wear, you know, sexy but not too slutty, so I'll be off now, if it's okay with you."

"Of course," he said.

She started the business of closing up: stacking papers, shutting off computers. "I've told him all about you. He'll want to meet you, I'm certain. And Ryan too, of course."

What had happened at the solicitor's was just too much to unload right now, and he didn't want her asking a million questions, so he started flipping through a stack of files, feigning busyness, sand crumbling from his hands onto the desk. "Yeah sure," he said.

"Are you really okay?" she asked.

"Fine. Yeah. I'll be fine," he said.

"Carlos really wants to meet my friends, Sam," she said, getting up from her desk and grabbing her handbag. "You're going to like him. Please come."

"All right, all right."

"Ta," she said, and walked out to the street.

See you at the pub," he said.

He watched her go, his head still screaming from the night before. He fished in her drawer for where he knew she kept a packet of Panadol, popped a couple in his mouth and crunched them dry, then looked down at the check from Amanda again. No way he was turning up at the pub. Good enough to teach her son how to surf but too queer to be a friend to him? He was seething. He needed a swim. Maybe that would clear his head. He stomped back to his office and wriggled out of his wetsuit, pulled on his boardies, and headed back to the beach.

Icy and rough, the water still clung to the cold of fading winter, but Sam splashed into it without flinching, diving under as soon as he was waist deep. He cut through the curling waves that were faster and stronger now in the evening tide, and came up for air past the break line. The sun was setting, reflecting off the orange sandstone of the cliffs, blinding him for a moment. He kicked into the standard crawl that all Australian kids learn by the time they're five, and swam north toward the promontory that separated Bronte from Tamarama.

He reached the tidal pools at the base of the cliffs breathless but exhilarated, and pulled himself up onto the sea-polished stone ledge. Sea anemone and kelp wavered with the slight current as a wave washed over his legs. Balancing with one hand on the rock face, he crept along the ledge, and climbed up to the cave. A storm had driven him there years ago when he'd been out surfing alone in the rain. It had made him feel like a young boy discovering a secret. Buried treasure. It faced out to sea, no real access except by water, and by one narrow, steep trail that led up to the cliff walk. Homeless camped out along the cliffs occasionally during the summer, but the tropical rainstorms of Sydney winter were far too much for anyone to manage with much comfort, so it was empty the rest of the year.

He stooped a bit, turned sideways to move through the crevice that led inside, and saw the shells first. A sundial pattern like Perry had described. Sand dollars and starfish, even a purple one. Those were hard to find. Past the crevice, the cave widened out and he could stand up again. A crusted tin of baked beans lay cold in a burnt-out makeshift fire circle next to a pile of filthy rags that must have been clothing. The light stopped there, giving no indication of how far back the cave went. The smell was awful. Shit, piss, rotten food, and sweat. Who could live like this? He gagged and turned to go back to the water and rinse off the filth he felt crawling over his skin.

"Get the fuck out of here," a voice yelled out of the darkness. "I'm sleeping."

Sam stopped walking and turned. It felt like a challenge. "Not your cave, mate," Sam said. "I'll go where I like."

"Just leave. I live here now." A scraping noise came from the back of the cave and a man about Sam's age came forward. He was shirtless, wearing dark-green track pants that looked surprisingly new and clean. His narrow chest was covered with tribal tattoos, his black hair pulled back. Sam looked for track marks on his arms but didn't see any. Didn't mean he wasn't an addict. The smell of human waste followed him in a choking cloud. His eyes were bright blue.

"You can't live here," he said. "You're scaring people. Scaring children. Not right that you're around them, is it? Some nasty old smackie, aren't you?"

"I'm not bothering anyone," the man said. He stood at the edge of the shadows, sizing Sam up.

"You're bothering me now," Sam said.

"Fuck off, pretty boy," the man said, and reached down to pick up a rock. "Fucking poofter."

"Watch how you talk to me, you filthy waste." The comment stung. Sam prided himself on being so butch and boofy that no one ever guessed he was gay, but this bloke had sniffed it out immediately.

"I'll say what I like," the man said, imitating Sam, and waved the rock at him. "Poofter. That's what you are, aren't you?" He stomped forward once as if he was going to charge. "I'll mess up that pretty mug of yours," he said.

Sam took another step forward, heat rising in him.

The man spit at him, a brown stringy lump of mucus that landed at his feet. "Maybe you're the one who shouldn't be around kids."

And that cracked him. Before he realized he was going to do it, Sam slammed his fist into the man's face. "Fuck you, you piece of shit."

"Jesus!" the man yelled, dropping the rock. He stumbled backward a step further, cringing, and put his fists up in a weak imitation of a boxer. "Arsehole!"

"Piece of shit," Sam said again. The anger seethed, carried him out of himself, and he grabbed the man's shoulders and shoved him against the cave wall. His eyes were adjusting to the dark and he could see a bedroll, a flashlight, a pile of books. "Get the fuck out of here," he said, leaning in toward the man's terrified face. "This is a beach community. Kids and families. Get the fuck out. Go back to Redfern or Bankstown or wherever the hell you get your drugs. I'll throw you out into the sea and you'll bloody well drown, you smackie piece of shit."

The man pushed against Sam with barely the strength of a child. "I'm no smackie, you fucking arsehole," he said. "I'm fucking clean."

"Bullshit." Sam let go and hit him again. His fist connected with the man's face, knuckles twisting skin across bone, and the man's nose popped. Blood poured down his lip and the man dropped to the floor and covered his head with his hands. "Stop! Stop! You've broken my nose!" He curled into a primal ball and groaned, arms above his head, his crying a low moaning monotone like the caw of a crow.

Sam stepped back. He should just go, go now before this got out of hand. Then the anger and humiliation of the day washed over him again. Ryan had strung him along about everything, treated their relationship like some prized possession when he was married all along. Then this bloke had the nerve to call him a bloody poofter. Well, fuck you. Fuck you all.

He ran forward as if he was on the footy pitch at school and kicked. The man's stomach gave way like a half-deflated balloon, his groan barely audible as the wind was knocked out of him. Sam stepped back and kicked again, feeling something snap, and again, and again. He stopped to take a breath, wiping the sweat and rage from his brow.

The man rolled over toward the wall of the cave, blocking his belly and ribs with folded arms. "Stop!" he begged, his voice heaving with sighs of pain.

Sam stopped and looked down at him. The man shook like an animal, his hands and face covered with blood.

"Jesus. Fuck. Sorry. Oh my God." He moved backward out of the cave, stepping on the sunburst of shells, smashing and scattering them. "I'm sorry. Really."

The man lay curled as he was, moaning. "Just leave me alone," he cried.

Sam turned and stumbled out of the cave and climbed back around to the tidal pools, his heart pumping so hard he had to stop and steady himself against the wall of the cliff. He sat down on the edge of the pool, cool water lapping at his feet, and looked at his hands. What had he done? A bit of blood on his right, but nothing more. No scrapes. Nothing. He kept breathing, and eased himself down into the sea, gasping as the cold of the Pacific froze his lungs. He kicked and thrashed as the sun continued to drop, getting used to the chill again, then pushed out from the rocks back toward Bronte. Just swim. Swim. You'll be fine.

It was really nothing worse than would have happened in a bar brawl. He looked back toward the cliffs, scanning to see any movement along the ledge. The guy would be fine. Right? He had to be. It was just his nose and his gut, right? Surely the guy had been in a fight before and survived.

He swam the length of the small bay toward the city, lights coming on in shop windows and flats as darkness fell. He stopped to rest when he got to shallow water and his feet hit ground. He stood shoulders deep, bobbing up and down with the swells, until a wave washed over his head and filled his mouth with frigid salt water. He spit the brine back into the sea and pushed off toward shore.

Back at his office, he toweled off and got dressed in the clothes he'd put on that morning: a pale-blue tailored dress shirt and flat-front black trousers. He checked his mobile. Three missed calls from Ryan. Fuck him. Two text messages from him also: *Sammo, it's me. I'm so so so sorry about yesterday. Please let me explain,* followed by *I know you must hate me. Please talk to me.*

A message from Jenny followed. *Hey, we're here. We've ordered starters. Turn off your computer and get your arse down here!!!!* He put the phone down on the desk and thought of the man crouched there on the floor of the cave, screaming, his face covered with blood. For all he knew, the guy was bleeding out. Fuck. He picked the phone up again and dialed triple zero.

"Emergency services. Do you require police, fire, or ambulance?"

"Um, I don't know. Ambulance, I guess. I think someone's hurt."

"I'll connect you, sir." The phone clicked twice. He thought of hanging up.

"New South Wales Ambulance. What's your emergency?"

"I was just swimming out at the Tamarama headlands and I heard someone yelling for help. It was dark and I couldn't see anything but it sounded like it was coming from the cliffs."

"Thank you, sir, you didn't see anything?"

"No. Just heard."

"How long ago was this?"

"About twenty or thirty minutes. I had to swim in to get to a phone."

"Not a problem, sir. We appreciate the call. Can you be more specific regarding your location?"

"Right at the point between Tamarama and Bronte. The cliffs."

"I'm sending someone out there now, sir. May I have your name?"

He thought about hanging up again but they'd just trace his mobile number if there was a problem.

"Sam Carter."

"Thank you, Mr. Carter. Thanks for calling this in. Can we reach you at this number if we need to ask you any further questions?" There it was. He was fucked. The guy would tell them what had happened and he'd be thrown in jail. He deserved it, he supposed.

"Yeah, sure."

"Thank you, sir."

He hit the disconnect key, put the phone down on his desk, and tried to imagine what jail would be like. How much time did you get for assault? A month? A year?

Jenny had put the check on top of his appointment diary, and he picked it up again. He pulled an envelope from a side drawer and copied the address from the check, then took a piece of clean white paper from his printer. "Dear Amanda," he wrote. "When I offered to teach Perry to surf, I did it as a friend, not to make a profit. I can't take your money. Perry's doing quite well, by the way. Take him out to dinner instead. Sam." He folded the note around the check, put it in the envelope, and dropped it on his desk.

For twenty minutes, he sat looking at his phone. Ryan called and he hit reject after a few rings. He expected a text to follow, but nothing.

The phone rang again. A six-digit number this time. Public services.

"Mr. Carter?"

"Yes."

"This is Irene Griffiths with New South Wales Ambulance." She had a slight accent. New Zealand?

"Yes?" He shuffled through the pile of leaflets.

"We responded to a call you made to triple zero about a call for help on the Tamarama headlands?"

"Yes. I called."

"Mr. Carter, I want you to know that we searched the headland and found nothing. There was some evidence of a homeless camp, but no one we could find in the vicinity. Are you sure of what you heard?"

"Yes. I'm sorry. I did hear someone yell." Why hadn't he just told them about the cave? Admitted it?

"Is it possible someone was having a joke at your expense?" She sounded annoyed.

"I don't think so, no." He fished in his drawer for his flask and took a gulp, the vodka bringing a touch of relief to his burning guts.

"Have you been drinking, Mr. Carter?"

"No. No I haven't." He slowed his speech down, concentrating on each word, then took one more sip and twirled the cap back on. Might have to make a statement. Can't be drunk just yet.

"Well, it appears there was no emergency. We may need to contact you again, but for now feel free to go about your business, sir."

He tilted backward in his ergonomic office chair that had cost far too much money and braced his feet against the desk. "All right. I will."

"Good night, sir."

"Good night."

He put the phone down, relieved. So the bloke had managed to run off. The office was dark now and Sam hit the switch on his desk lamp, creating a small circle of light on the mess of papers, paint samples, and photographs of the units. He couldn't be hurt too badly then. Well, unless he'd fallen into the sea and drowned. Not likely though. He'd looked reasonably fit. It would be fine. He pushed back his sleeve and looked at his hands again. A bit of blood clung to his thumbnail and he scraped it off with his letter opener. No need to tell anyone else about it now. He knew, and that was enough.

12

Ryan

A chilly wind blew up the escalator from the tunnel, and Ryan shivered in his thin dress shirt.

"You should have worn a coat, Ryan," Katrina said as she pushed her Opal card back into her wallet and dropped it into her purse. Her own coat was a beautiful black wool, worn over a low-cut shimmering blue cocktail dress, her perfect platinum hair pulled back in a classic updo. "Palm trees or not, we still have winter here, and you know it. What were you thinking?"

"It was beach weather last week."

They'd been having an unseasonably warm winter, lovely days in the seventies all through August, but tonight the thermometer had plummeted, and he wasn't dressed for it. He'd wanted to look sharp for the play tonight—cuffed sleeves on his tailored shirt, tight jeans, new shoes—but he was freezing.

"And anyway," he said, "I left my overcoat at Sam's. Haven't had the nerve to drop by and get it, to be honest. And I didn't want to wear my ratty old parka with these clothes. I'll be fine. It's not that cold."

A wave of damp air blew across the platform and he clenched his teeth.

"Your parka would have looked fine. That's what coat check is for anyway. Get rid of the damning evidence of poverty, them move into the crowd looking fabulous."

Katrina had gotten them comp tickets that night to the new show at the Canal Street Theater, a world premiere about devastation and drama in a future climate-change post-tsunami Sydney—the tsunami that everyone knew was coming any day now, at least everyone in the more earnest and intellectual circles Katrina traveled in. The planet was doomed. Love and loss among the flooded ruins of the city. It sounded a bit silly but it was getting great reviews, and apparently the set—a forced-perspective replica of a ravaged post-storm Bondi—was astonishing. New levels of professionalism in Sydney theater, people were saying.

"It's not the story, but how you tell it," she'd said when he'd sneered.

And it was a family affair anyway. Nathan had the second lead, the young husband left a widower when his wife dies trying to kill a shark for food at the end of act 1. And the director was a friend of Katrina's: an old school chum who had built a solid reputation in local theater, someone that Ryan should meet, she said, get his face in front of him for future auditions, get his foot in the door at some of the local repertory companies.

"Networking," she said. "You need to network."

He hated the word. Hated the falseness of it. Pretending to be friends with people, to love their work, all because you wanted them to hire you. He'd almost said no, still indulging himself in a bit of wallowing over the break-up, but Nathan was turning out to be a standup guy, and he wanted to show solidarity, so he'd rallied at the last minute.

Katrina stepped to the edge of the platform and looked down the tunnel, squinting for the sign of an oncoming train. "And as long as we're being honest . . ." She stepped back, looking him up and down, clicking her tongue in disapproval. "Graduation's only a couple of months away. What are you going to wear out to auditions next year? Not every day is a sunny day in paradise. You need a good umbrella, good shoes, and a tailored coat. A couple of new shirts wouldn't hurt either."

"Yes, I know, Mother. I looked at a few things at Meyer last week. A week's wages for a pair of shoes." He fiddled with his phone. Lucy was supposed to message him about running lines later. Nothing. He shoved it back in his pocket. "I can go to Kmart tomorrow, I guess, but honestly, why bother? Pretty hard to be going on auditions here when I'm going back to the States anyway."

"Don't be so dramatic. You're going to stay and you know it. It's just a matter of logistics. And your mother will send you the money for a coat as soon as you ring her, so I suggest you stop playing the sad act. Now let's get coffee." She walked toward the brightly painted kiosk, Ryan trailing behind her, hoping it was warmer near the milk steamer.

Katrina opened her wallet and fished out a twenty.

The barista wiped his hands on his apron. "Get you something, love?"

"Flat white, please. Need a warm-up."

"Cold one out there? I've been down here all day."

"Bless you for that. All day with no sunlight? I couldn't do it."

"I mostly work in the evenings, so I see plenty of sun. And they pay well. Anything for your friend?"

"Do you want something, darling?" Katrina called over her shoulder.

"Flat white. Thanks."

The barista whacked the metal brew basket against the bar, knocking the old grounds into the bin, then wiped it, filled it with ground espresso. "Where are you lot off to tonight?"

"Theater. New play."

"Nice." He cranked the silver brew basket tight and punched a button. The machine hissed and wiggled. "Haven't been to much theater myself, rather watch the footy."

"Every man has his passion. This one's an actor. We'll be seeing him on stage soon."

"Oh yeah?" He tipped the silver coffee jug into two paper cups, then dolloped the steamed milk over them. "When you're going to be on something, pop down and let me know."

"We will, thanks." She waited for the barista to skim the foam off their coffees and cap them with brown plastic tops. She handed Ryan his coffee, and he clutched it in both hands, warming them.

"I wish you wouldn't announce it," he said as Katrina dropped a dollar coin into the tip cup. "You know I'm headed right back to the States after graduation."

"Oh, you gay boys. What's a little bigamy these days anyway?" Her voice echoed off the tiles as if she were on mic and Ryan cringed. No one appeared to be listening. Still, he stepped closer, silently hoping she'd tone it down, but she was on a roll, reveling in an audience. "Wasn't he the one who was suggesting three-ways and other adventures? Open relationships? Thrupples? It's all become de rigueur with you lot, yes? As long as it's all boys, that is? But if someone's been married to a woman it's all shock and tears? He was just surprised, that's all. You'll sort it out."

He leaned in and spoke softly. "Can we spare all these good people the tawdry details of my love life? And there's nothing to sort out. You should have seen his face. Pure hatred."

"He doesn't hate you. He loves you. And that's why he's so upset. Give him a bit more time."

"It's been weeks, and even if he does come around, I'm still married back in the States." He paused, letting the statement sink in. "I'm married, Kat."

"You know you really got me with that one," she said, wagging a finger at him. "I thought you were joking at first."

"Hence your cackling when I said it."

"Well, I'd had a few wines with dinner, and you have to admit it is far-fetched. Who knew my dashing gay actor roommate was really a closeted Mormon elder on the run from his sister wife!"

"There was no sister wife! Just the *one* wife."

"I know, darling. I'm just having a go at you."

"I know, but I wish you wouldn't. The church stopped the practice of polygamy—"

"Yes, yes. Stopped a century ago. People are uninformed. You're Mormons, not monsters. I know, dear. You've explained it to me again and again."

"Sorry, I just get so tired of it."

"You need to toughen up. People focus on the silliest, most obvious bits of things they don't understand and then run with them. You know that. You wouldn't believe the nonsense that people still say when they find out I'm Jewish. On set even!

Half the bloody industry is Jewish and someone still needs to go on about guilt-inducing mothers bearing chicken soup. I usually just shrug it off, but occasionally I've ripped into people. You just get tired of it. We're supposed to be above such things in the theater. Students of the human experience and all that." She took a sip of her coffee and locked eyes with him. "But I didn't mean to be crass, my dear. I'll stop this instant if it really bothers you."

"It's fine. You're the only one who really understands."

"And it's honestly just a matter of a phone call, surely? Of course she'll sign once you've spoken."

The shriek of the train whistle sounded in the tunnel and Katrina pointed to the far end of the platform. "Come along, dear, you know I hate the crowds in the middle cars."

"Yes, your ladyship. Shall I carry your coat?"

She smacked his arm with her handbag, then led the way, pushing through the usual Friday evening hordes bound for the restaurants and pubs of the inner city.

"You know," she said as the carriage doors slid open in front of them, "you ought to write that play. Create a vehicle for yourself. Tormented, closeted Mormon boy runs from his unforgiving religious community to discover his true gay self in Sydney."

"Oh, give me a break. That's ridiculous."

"I'm serious. Have it end with true love found at the parade. So much gay theater ends in tragedy. It would be sweet. We could call it Mardi Gras Mormon!"

The doors slid shut and the prim recording rattled off the list of next stops. Kogarah, Jannalli, Kirawee, Cronulla. Exotic names. Parts of the city he'd never seen. Not missing much, Sam had told him. Cronulla and its greater environs were the Jersey Shore of Sydney. Katrina had concurred. The one and only time they'd ever seen eye to eye.

"That's the worst title I've ever heard."

"Oh, I don't know. The masses love a bit of word play." She made a sweeping gesture toward the other passengers. "What I don't understand is the whole deception thing. Why not just talk about it? It makes you more interesting in a way. Explains a lot about how you go through the world. Your quirks and contradictions."

"Well, I didn't realize I was so boring before. Thanks."

"That's not what I mean and you know it. Stop being defensive. I just wonder why you would hide it when it could actually be quite a conversation piece. Why not just be honest?"

"The conversation piece part of it was the whole reason I kept my mouth shut. I've been burned too many times. People never understand, or they fetishize it, you know. I made the mistake of telling the first guy I hooked up with I was Mormon, and all he could do from then on was beg me to wear my missionary suit, or worse yet have me strip to my temple garments. And it wasn't just him. I got so tired of the objectification. Couldn't tell if guys liked me for me or if they were just notching something new and exotic on the bedpost next to *cowboy* and *cop*."

"I had forgotten you were a missionary. Seems so incongruous to who you are now."

"Where do you think I got that cheap suit jacket you hate so much?"

"You are a mass of contradictions, Ryan Jensen." She looked out at the lights of Double Bay as they emerged from the tunnel. "I forget that it's not just women who have to put up with such nonsense. Thinking you've met someone nice only to have it all end up with the stupid dolt expecting you to wear ridiculous lingerie and talk like a sex doll, begging him for the privilege of sucking his smelly cock like you can't imagine anything more exciting in the world."

The woman seated across from them glared at Katrina and pulled her young daughter close to her.

"Kat!" Ryan hissed.

"What?"

The woman frowned.

"No time like the present for addressing female oppression!" Katrina called out, loud enough for the whole car to hear. The woman stood up, took her daughter's hand, and walked down the steps toward the next carriage. The car lurched and she grabbed the railing, shaking her head.

Ryan pulled at his shirt sleeve. The left arm had rolled loose and was flopping around his wrist. "I wasn't trying to say that, you know, that women don't put up with shit. I'm just saying, I don't know. I guess it's all screwed. People all treat each other like crap to be used or screwed or whatever and then they all just move on to the next adventure. Screwed. Fucked. There. I said it. Fucked."

Katrina grabbed his sleeve. "Here, let me do this. You're hopeless." She rolled the sleeve tightly just below his elbow. "You know that was one of my first clues that you weren't as far removed from the church as you said you were."

"What was?"

"Your squeamishness around swearing. I remember the week you moved in, I said 'bloody fucking hell' or something when I spilled my coffee, and you got all pinched, all frowns and disapproval like a librarian giving the glare to a pack of noisy schoolkids."

"I did not!"

"You did. Just for a second, but you did. And when you swear, you sound, oh, I don't know, tentative, like a seven-year-old who's just discovered the words and is wondering what he can get away with."

"I don't know. It was all pounded into us from such an early age. No swearing. No caffeine. No liquor. No drugs. No dating before sixteen. No sex before marriage."

"Well, you're certainly making up for lost time, what with your coffee addiction and spurned male lover."

"Already writing the promo for the play, I see." He folded his arms across his chest in a pout, wobbling slightly as the train rattled round the bend before Kings Cross.

"You're doing *librarian face* again."

He realized he was and unfolded his arms.

"It's funny. I figured that as long as I was committing the grievous sin of homosexuality, why worry about lesser sins? I may as well try a drink, have a cup of coffee! Silly, isn't it. But I just can't bring myself to swear every other word like so many of the guys here."

"And you're more the gentleman for it."

"Thanks." He took a sip from his brown Styrofoam cup, almost spilling it as the train jolted to a stop and more passengers poured on. Their car was filling up, definitely a younger and edgier crowd than back in Bondi. A pierced and tattooed, street-rat-esque young couple huddled on the bench across from them, both painfully thin, dirty. Junkies, Ryan thought, staring, then corrected himself to the Australian vernacular. *Smackies.*

"But it wasn't just the lack of vulgarity in your vocabulary," Katrina said. "The newness that everything held for you. That too. And I don't mean just Sydney. It was more than just being new in a foreign country. It was like you'd been let out of jail and were running at the world full tilt, making up for lost time."

The young junkie girl stared at him defiantly, pulling at a strand of greasy hair. He looked away, embarrassed.

"I guess I did go a little crazy at first."

"No worse than any Aussie kid in first semester at uni. I was just a little surprised, that's all, given you were pushing thirty and starting a post-grad course."

"Twenty-seven isn't pushing thirty."

"My dear, it will be soon enough."

"The thing is, it still means a lot to me. The church, that is. I realized that, you know, when everything came out at the lawyer's office."

"And you shouldn't have to apologize for needing some time to figure it out. A bit of faith is lovely."

She reached across the seat and held his hand. They rode on in silence.

Central was packed, and Katrina took Ryan's arm as they pushed through the crowd to the escalators. "I'm lousy at these things in heels. Be a gentleman and make sure I don't tip over."

He stepped slowly, remembering to stand to the left, and steadied her as they rode to street level. "Of course."

"And remember, networking."

"Yes, Mother."

They exited the station through the side passage on Chalmers Street. The dark-blue glossy bricks of the Bondi platform must have looked brilliantly stylish when the line was added in the seventies, but now they looked dated, a bit fast-food, in stark contrast to the sandstone arches of the main station. Cones and barrels blocked the footpath for construction on the new light rail line, so they skirted around the blockades and walked up the steep slope of Devonshire Street into Surry Hills, the array of convenience stores and internet cafés serving the station area dissipating as they climbed, giving way to a row of deceptively modest and down-market cafés and bars, all burnished and tattered to look as though they'd been there for decades. . . a trendy deception hiding award-winning chefs and astonishingly high prices.

The theater stood at the end of the street beneath the towering hulks of Sydney's notorious Northcotte public housing project. "Art meets poverty," Katrina said. "Isn't it always thus?"

"Can't we do something?" Ryan said, and held her arm as they walked up the steps and through the well-heeled, bohemian crowd to collect their tickets.

"The theater offers free tickets to local residents and admission to youth acting courses, but still—"

"Katrina!" A female voice called out from the crowd. "Katrina, how are you?" An older woman, short and stout, probably sixties, pushed forward toward them. Hair pulled back, minimal makeup, smart black pantsuit. Much younger woman at her side. Ryan wondered if they were partners.

"Raquel. You look wonderful," Katrina said, grabbing the other woman in a firm embrace.

"Flattery. You of course look gorgeous. Meet my niece, Bronwen," the woman said.

"Bronwen. That's a lovely name, so storied and English."

"Yet I always longed to be Brittany or Heather when I was growing up. Something American. Ah well." She flitted her fingers above her head, dismissing the thought.

"She's just been accepted to the conservatory," Raquel said.

"Graduate program?"

"Oh, God no. I've only finished high school this year. Undergrad for me, thanks."

Katrina grabbed Ryan's shoulder and squeezed. "Ryan here's just finishing the master's program. You two should talk."

Bronwen looked at Ryan, sizing him up.

"Oh? Congratulations, dear." Raquel swooped in and hugged him close, her breasts pushing against his rib cage. "And how do you know Katrina? Family, I presume?

We've got to keep it in the family, you know. Maintain the reputation. Apparently they're even letting Americans in these days. I was just talking to Graham the other day and he told me—"

"He must have told you what a wonderful talent Ryan is? He is the only American studying there at the moment."

"Oh! I'm so naughty!" She took Ryan's hand and patted it like his grandmother used to. "You must forgive me for having a little national spirit. You Americans have so much opportunity, while our little corner of the world barely has enough parts to go around, it seems. Of course you're talented. Graham only picks the best. In fact he was saying he saw real talent in you. I was making the silly argument that room should be saved for our own, but, then again, we do steal a lot of parts from the Hollywood elite, don't we?"

"Many an American actress would be happy to see Nicole Kidman sent packing, that's for sure." He squeezed Raquel's hand.

"True, true. And how are your studies going?"

"Fair enough, I suppose."

Katrina nudged him gently. "Don't be so self-deprecating, dear," she said, her classically trained voice rising above the murmur of the crowd. "He's doing brilliantly."

"I imagine he is."

He was still uncomfortable with this level of attention. It was something Katrina had constantly coached him on. Always take a compliment in stride. He always told himself he'd do fine, but here in the moment, he felt ridiculous. He urged his heartbeat back down and looked around at the well-dressed theater crowd. This was what he wanted, yes? Of course it was. Absolutely. He squeezed Raquel's hand and leaned toward her. "I'm always telling Katrina you Australians don't give yourselves enough credit." Her collection of rings and bracelets felt cool against his skin. "The quality of the work here is unquestionable. Australian film and theater are a great proving ground. It's why I chose the conservatory in the first place. I wanted to really have to earn it. I see it as an honor to be here and would consider it a true achievement to make a mark here."

"Well then, I take back what I said. I wish you the best of luck." Raquel turned to Katrina. "And I understand we'll be seeing you back on the screen again soon, my dear. You know the public has long hoped for Katrina King's return. Bernard over at SBS was almost screeching about it, he was so excited. I know you were keeping the reboot hush-hush, but he spilled."

"Oh, we'll see how it goes. We're keeping it to a limited series for now. Just ten episodes. We'll shoot over the summer and show it in the fall. I almost didn't do it, you know. Those days in front of the camera feel like another lifetime ago. *You're a writer now, Katrina* . . . But then I thought, why not write it myself? Show them they don't need an ingenue once and for all."

"Exactly. Brilliant. Don't hesitate to call the office when you're ready to cast."

"You're top of my list, dear."

"And you, mine."

The five-minute bell rang and Raquel waved toward the door. They walked across the deep-purple carpet together, the two older women huddled together continuing their chat, Ryan trailing slightly behind with Bronwen.

"You're going to love the conservatory," he said.

"Too bad you'll be gone."

"Oh, you'll make plenty of friends."

"Most drama school kids are wankers, though, aren't they?"

"Well, now that you mention it . . ."

"But I've known Uncle Graham since I was a kid. It'll be fine."

He couldn't imagine anyone calling Graham "uncle," and for a moment he considered bursting her bubble. But why? It was a beautiful night and they were doing what they all loved. Theater. He breathed in deeply and took it all in.

"You'll be brilliant," he said.

They came to the doorway and Raquel held up her ticket. "We're in the next section."

"Ta, then. We'll see you inside," Katrina said.

"I meant what I said, Katrina. Talk to Bernard and send me the casting list. It's going to be a smash." She brushed a bit of lint from her niece's blouse. "Come, Bronwen."

"Lovely to meet you both." Bronwen elegantly twirled away from them and followed her aunt, her skirt flaring.

"You didn't tell me you were rebooting the show. Amazing!" They stood behind an older couple showing their tickets to the usher.

"You've had a lot going on."

"Still."

"I would have told you, but we're playing it really close to the vest. Confidentiality on pain of death. You understand."

"I can't wait to see it."

Katrina presented their tickets. The usher was a painfully thin young man, all elbows and knees in his oversized jacket and tie.

"Thanks for coming tonight, Miss King, it's an honor."

"That's lovely of you to say, dear. Are you an actor?"

"Trying to be," he said, his voice cracking.

"Best of luck to you."

He tore their tickets. "Row C is the third row. You're in the first two seats on the aisle."

"Yes, thank you."

They walked down the sloping floor toward the stage.

"So now you've met Raquel Winston."

"What a delightful old broad."

"Broad is right," Katrina said. "She casts half the network shows on the air. This is what it is to play the game. I was going to suggest you drop her a line offering to show that niece around. Get in her brain as a good bloke. Auditions coming soon."

"But surely she's got that lined up."

"Doesn't matter. Do it. It's about getting noticed, not actually doing the favor."

"So cynical."

"Not really. It's how things are done. You signed up for it. Do what's needed."

"Well . . ."

"There's no well. Do you want this? Or do you want to go running home back to Utah?"

"I want it. You know I want it."

"Of course you do. I knew it from the moment I met you. We're alike in more ways than you realize. Now let's sit down before they dim the house lights. I want to make sure I don't snag my dress."

He held her bag as she adjusted her skirt and eased into her seat.

The sconces dimmed and conversation ended.

13

Sam

"Come on, Sammo," Luke yelled up from the pavement. "If you don't come down now, I'm getting in a taxi and going without you!"

Luke looked ridiculously prim and reserved amid the Friday night blast of car horns, club music, and drunken partiers. He paced nervously on the footpath, a schoolboy out on holiday, not quite comfortable with the older kids.

Sam leaned further out the window. "Go right ahead, mate," he shouted down to him over the din. "If you want to waste fifty bucks and miss out on a ride in a vintage luxury automobile, be my guest."

Luke gave him the middle finger. "I'd be better off. That car is a death trap."

"Fuck off," he yelled. "Down in two ticks."

The street noise had swelled to its usual screech. It had seemed so cool when he bought the place. Federation-era flat with crazy rehab potential. Victoria Street and Darlinghurst Road both lined with cafés and pubs. Five minutes' walk to the train, fifteen to the gay clubs on Oxford Street. That first year had been a shitload of fun—parties, guys, all-night access to anything he wanted. What's not to love? But now, as he looked over the streetscape of the Cross, he shuddered. Another year had taught him there were many things not to love—nonstop noise from the pubs, drunks and druggies passed out in the laneway, an almost weekly need to paint over new graffiti on the front door and facade, and everything twice the price it was back home. He'd thought about selling and moving out to the beach, but with the reno job only halfway done—fits and starts and a weekend here and there—he couldn't resell yet for anything close to what the place would be worth once he was finished. Best to stick to it. At least with Ryan gone, he'd get more work done and get it on the market sooner. Good bloody riddance. Well, okay, he missed him. Of course he did. But he was learning to shut up about it. More pressing things to deal with.

"Don't you dare bring him up tonight," Luke had shouted into the phone. "Party's on tonight. No moping over married American wankers."

His mind kept flipping back and forth, running through it all again, from storming out of the solicitor's office to bashing the shit out of that smackie at the Bronte cliffs. He knew he'd gone too far. Blamed it on the situation. The booze. He'd gotten good and drunk at the office afterward. Was the guy okay? He'd rung the police, but had they come? Panic set, something he was lately more familiar with than he would have admitted to anyone. Everything seemed to be caving in. He was two months behind on the mortgage, had rung and given the bank a bullshit story about needing a week. Truth was he didn't know how long he needed. He hadn't sold a single unit that month. Increasingly nasty emails from Kyle were suggesting he light a fire under his arse or consider another line of work. But what could he do? He had no qualifications. Couldn't even make coffee or tend bar. He'd bullshitted and charmed his way into the job, logical choice while he was on break from architecture school, learn about the market, learn about design hands-on, but now they were demanding results he just couldn't give. But weeks had become months had become years, and he sucked at it. Hated it. Sure, it was fun now and then, and he loved Jenny to pieces, but he hated the grind, dragging his arse in there every day at dawn, bullshitting with bougie Eastern Suburbs newlyweds whose parents were paying their deposit, pretending the prices were in line with the market just to get a damn commission check. And those were coming in less and less frequently.

The whole thing was draining—financially, mentally—so tonight was essential. Mental health night. Who cared if he only had a couple hundred bucks left in his account? Tonight would be a blast. Relax, have a laugh, maybe get some much-needed action, and first thing Monday he'd ring back everyone who'd toured the building in the past month and offer them all a 10 percent discount, Kyle's insistence on set pricing be damned. He just needed to reimagine the marketing strategy, make it sexy somehow. Stop worrying about the banal realities of sales and spend some time strategizing. The money would come.

He opened the fridge and grabbed a VB, but put it down again. You're going to take it easy, remember? No pre-gaming. Might even go the night without a drink, hey? Couldn't hurt.

But he couldn't do anything about it now anyway, could he? So why not enjoy the evening? It was the first truly warm night of spring, he was single again, and it was time to blow off some steam. "Fuck it!" he shouted at the walls. He checked his reflection in the bathroom mirror, messed with his hair a bit, and growled at himself, *You'll sell a million on Monday and that damn smackie will be fine.* Probably turning up at hospital was the best thing for him. Got him in front of the right people and got him into rehab or something. Likely did him a fucking favor. He flexed to check that his T-shirt was the right fit—perfect—walked to the fridge and picked up the can of beer again, ice cold against his palm. What's a couple of beers? He tapped the top, caught his finger under the tab. It'll feel good. You need it. Except it was never just a couple, was it? Nah. Never a couple. Always an ocean. And the hangovers. Brutal lately. Even more so than normal. If he was going to get into the office early tomorrow without feeling like death, there was no way he could start drinking now.

He squeezed the can as hard as he could, willing it to crush under his grip. Superman stunt. It remained stubbornly intact, rigid as steel. "Fuck you," he muttered, "you're not taking me tonight." He slammed the can down on the cutting board, then flew down the stairs two at a time, pushing through the street door with his bull-in-a-china-shop strength, the glass rattling behind him as the door slammed shut.

He grabbed Luke in a bearhug and squeezed him as hard as he could. "Ready for a big night, pal?"

"Christ, Sammo." Luke wriggled out of his grasp and pushed back a step. "I thought you said you were changing." He waved a hand at Sam's chest. "That's the same T-shirt you had on when you went upstairs."

"And what's your look tonight? Daggy old uni lecturer? Playground pedophile?" Sam grabbed Luke's bowtie and tugged on it. "Old Professor Pedo. Jesus bloody Christ."

Luke slapped Sam's hands away and straightened his tie. "There is no evidence that Jesus was a pedo. He just consorted with prostitutes."

Sam gave the tie one more flick. "Noted. You still look like a pedo."

"I'm brilliantly stylish and you know it. You'll be begging to borrow this next week."

"Fat chance," he said. "American hipster shit. Togs for wankers."

"Perfect for you, then. Didn't you just knock one out? You were upstairs long enough." He jerked his elbow back and forth and waggled his tongue.

Sam grabbed his crotch and squeezed. "Yeah," he said, gyrating his hips. "Rubbed out a quickie while gazing in the mirror."

"You're a pig." Luke grinned like he always did at Sam's silliness. "Seriously, though. I want to get there before the show starts."

"Let's get the car and get a move on, then, if you're so determined."

"Fine. Lead the way."

Sam walked up the laneway toward his garage. "Drag shows never start on time, you know," he called over his shoulder, "especially at the Royal. So you can chill out." He picked up the pace, trotting the last steps, his keys already out. The padlock popped open and he rolled up the door of the dark and narrow garage. "Wait 'til I back out," he called. "Don't want you scratching the doors on the side wall."

"You're worried about scratching that old heap?" Luke yelled in at him.

"It's not a heap, it's a classic," Sam called out from the depths of the garage. "It's a privilege to even gaze upon it."

"Silver Service taxis are classic enough for me, thanks. You waste heaps of money storing that thing and paying for repairs. Why bother with the hassle?"

"Because driving it feels amazing. And I don't see you turning down the lift."

Luke was right, though. A hundred bucks a week was a shit-ton for a garage, but he hadn't been able to find anything else. Yet another expense he was behind on. He shook it off. Sam turned the ignition and gunned the motor. A combination of heavy exhaust and cold engine shivers made the car rattle and growl, smoke shooting from the tailpipe.

Luke gave an exaggerated cough and stepped back from the curb. "Maybe I'd better take a cab after all. Seriously mate, get that engine checked!"

Sam revved it until the growling softened to a purr. "She'll be fine, and you know it. The best cars are always a bit temperamental. Just takes a minute. Come on." He stopped in the drive, back end still half in the garage, and Luke dropped into the passenger seat. "I'm waiting."

Their teasing went back to first year at university, when they'd both pledged St. Andrews College and been assigned as roommates. Sam's dad was a legacy, so his place was assured, and he arrived with all the confidence he was accustomed to, but Luke was on scholarship from a country town near Goulbourn, a working-class kid who was a whiz at maths and was getting his degree despite his parents' wish that he manage the family shop. He was an accountant now with one of the biggest firms in Sydney.

They'd gone for beers that first night, Luke shy at first, hardly able to talk, but Sam had liked him, sensed a kindred spirit, and drawn him out. A few weeks into the semester, they were palling around everywhere together, joking and smart-arsing with everyone they met. Midsemester, Sam had suggested they go out on Oxford Street, just to have a look, right? Of course he'd already researched which of the pubs catered to the gay crowds, and Luke had put up no objection. By the end of that first year, they'd both come out to their closer circles, and moved into a share house in Bondi so they could surf and party, live the beach lifestyle away from all the pierced-nose-protest-sign wankers on campus.

They'd been best mates ever since, putting up with each other's nonsense and screw-ups and short forays into the dating world, but neither one of them had had anything like a long-term, so they'd pretty much been each other's constant companion through it all. Until Ryan, that is. Luke had made it clear from the first that he didn't like him, and they'd had a bit of a falling out over it.

Tonight was a reconciliation of sorts.

Sam backed a little further out into the laneway, steering with one hand and fishing for his cigarettes with the other. He clicked his lighter and sparked the tip of his cigarette. "You want one?" He held the pack out to Luke.

"You're not going to smoke in the car, are you?" Luke shouted over the music pumping from the pub across the street. "It's too cold to put the top down."

"Oh, listen to old auntie," Sam said. "She's nervous about secondhand smoke or whatever." He blew a thick gray cloud toward his friend. "You used to love a ciggie now and then. What happened?" He hopped out of the car and pulled down the garage door, then dropped back into the driver's seat, the engine purring beautifully now.

"Lot about me you don't know lately." Luke reached for the radio dial, fiddling with it until he found some thumpy club song. "Once Captain America moved in, you vanished off the face."

"Yeah, sorry about that." Sam lurched the car backward into the laneway, then pulled forward into the heavy Kings Cross traffic. "And you know I thought he was the one."

"Well, maybe he is, just not for you."

"Sorry to be a romantic cliché." Sam honked his horn at the taxi idling in front of him. "I honestly thought this was it."

"It's all right. You just don't seem like the heartbreaker I used to know, I guess."

"Maybe I've changed."

"Fair enough. I just missed you, that's all."

A break in the oncoming traffic and Sam whipped around the cab, cutting back into his lane just in time to miss a bright-red tour bus, country folk and foreigners gawping from the open-top tier.

"Jesus Christ!" Luke grabbed Sam's leg and dug his fingers in.

"Sorry." He waved at the bus driver and eased forward. "Look. I'm sorry I let the friendship drift, but I'm making up for it now, so let's just have some fun, okay?" Traffic started moving and they picked up speed past the lights. He cranked the volume, and the two of them yelled along to ridiculous lyrics about dancing naked in the street, Sam zigzagging through the late-night city traffic, weaving in and out of his lane, narrowly missing two girls on a scooter cutting across from behind, wobbling so close to the driver's door he could have touched them.

"Chinga tu pinche madre!" the driver shouted as she revved past. Her friend hunched behind her grabbing the sissy bar with one hand while she flipped him the middle finger with the other as they sped off, cutting down the middle line between the rows of cars.

Sam hit his horn. "Go back to bloody Brazil!"

"I think they were speaking Spanish," Luke said.

Sam accelerated again and moved back into his lane.

"Listen to mister smarty pants. Well then, go back to bloody Spain!" he said, laughing a bit now that the tension was gone. The girls were long out of earshot anyway.

"Nice to know you haven't lost that welcoming Aussie spirit."

"Always, mate. A credit to my country."

Luke cracked his window, letting in the crisp winter air, waving his hand at Sam's cigarette smoke.

They sped on through the city and arrived at the Royal in no time, a massive line already forming outside, music thumping from open windows clashing with the blasting radio in the car. Sam eased into a spot in the pay lot behind the Ezymart and cut the engine. "It's on then," he said. "Let's go."

They walked toward the club, shuffling around a pack of girls decked out in pink feather boas and crowns. Hens' night. They hooted and catcalled at Sam and Luke. "What's on tonight, boys?" A blonde in a white skirt and jean jacket eyed them up and down. "Come to the Cross with us, you two, this place is too dull." Her tiara had tilted slightly, pushing her hair into her eyes. She twisted and spun it, but it still fell lopsided. She tugged at it again, then gave up. "We're out for a good time! Rhonda's getting married. I promise you'll get lucky."

Sam nudged the crown back into place. She was beautiful. "Good on Rhonda, but we're looking for a different kind of luck."

"I suppose we all are," she said. "Seriously though, you boys look like a lot of fun, and these slags are boring the shit out of me," she said.

"You'll be right," Sam said.

"As will you, I'm sure." She slapped his arse and turned to her friends. "Forget it, girls. He's looking for dick!" she yelled. Her friends had swarmed a pair of taxis. She smiled at Sam, then pushed past him and squeezed into a cab.

They queued up with the rest of the crowd beneath the crumbling brick facade. A neon sign offered rooms to let, from back in the day when drinking establishments were required to offer accommodation or be denied a liquor license. The line moved quickly enough, though, and they found themselves inside in minutes, maneuvering through the crowd toward the bar. Traditional down to its green-tiled walls, rows of pokie machines, and portrait of Queen Elizabeth above the bar, the pub was decades older than any of its patrons, a classic Aussie hotel, now a renegade drag destination and pickup hot spot for the more rough-and-tumble Inner-West gay scene, an anti–Oxford Street institution. It reeked of beer-soaked carpet and hundred-year-old plumbing, far too grimy to be considered even remotely retro-chic. The real deal. Sam loved it.

They had missed the first show, and Sam was silently pleased, itching for Luke to bring it up so he could tease him for being a pissy queen. Best mate as he was, he could be a bit caught up in being at the right place at the right time, fancy-schmancy this and that, and who would be there to see and be seen in a way that Sam just couldn't be bothered with. A second show started in half an hour, so they nudged and prodded forward into the main bar past the pool tables, the grungy cool crowd the exact opposite to the dance clubs in Darlo. Bearded uni boys drank pints of dark beer, tattooed lezzos ruled the pool tables, fashion-forward freaky queens spun and dipped around the tiny dance floor in the corner.

Sam edged up to the bar and caught the bartender's eye, a younger guy, fit. Sam hadn't seen him before.

"What'll it be?"

"Lemon lime bitters for me and a VB for my friend."

"Ta." He turned to the taps and pulled a beer, another, then dunked a couple of glasses in the soapy water and set them on the drying rack.

"Ten dollars, mate." He set two beers in front of Sam.

"Lemon lime bitters, right?" Sam yelled over the music.

"What?"

"Just the one beer." Sam held a couple of fives out.

"Five then." He grabbed one of the bills and pushed Sam's hand back. "Already poured though. Yours if you want it." He turned to the till and slapped the five into the drawer, then dunked two more glasses into the sink.

"Lemon lime . . ." Sam stopped. The guy couldn't hear him. Couldn't care less anyway.

It's right in front of you. What's the harm?

"Fuck it." He picked up one of the glasses and took a deep drink. Perfect. He'd just have the one then.

An out-of-place older couple in matching windbreakers played at the pokies, eyeing the showroom door. Sam imagined them in from Bankstown for the thrill of it because they'd seen the *Priscilla* musical. And good on 'em. A huddle of young guys stood next to them, all decked out in their best retro punk T-shirts and matching haircuts, clearly on a cross-town field trip from Darlinghurst. The tallest one jerked his thumb toward the couple and mouthed something to his mates. The all burst out laughing, and Sam scowled. He hated the whole too-hip inner-city Sydney scorn for working-class people. *Bogans*, they called them. *Westies*. Ryan had even picked it up. It drove him mental, the nastiness of sneering at honest hard-working people. As stiffly upper crust as his parents could be at times, they had still insisted that he treat everyone with respect, regardless of income or manners, and he'd held onto that value, even as he'd chucked many others and run off to Sydney to party with the big boys. Sam lifted his drink to the couple now and gave a quick nod. The man lifted his as well, returning the Aussie salute.

The gaggle of snitty boys had already lost interest, preening and chatting among themselves. "I love drag, but I hate poofters, ya know?"

"You are a poofter, mate." Luke leaned back against the bar, surveying the room. "Play butch all you want, but it's Saturday night and we're at a gay pub for a drag show. Doesn't get poofier than that."

"Maybe so." Sam set his drink down and watched the boys continue to twirl and chatter. "But we don't have to bloody well act like screeching teenaged girls, now do we?"

Luke took a sip of his beer and wiped the foam from his mustache with a paper napkin. "You're safe then. No one's going to suspect the surly bloke growling in the corner."

"Best way to get lucky, anyway, isn't it? Be the blokiest one in the room."

"Ah, you're an endless source of insight and good advice, Sam," Luke shouted over the music, "although you might want to work on that. You're not nearly as butch as you once were, you know. Marital bliss softened you. You're out of practice."

"You saying I've gotten nellie?"

"Would it be such a bad thing if you had?" Luke grabbed Sam's shoulder and shook it. "Drop the facade. Be yourself. Let's just have a good time."

"Deal."

A young girl edged through the crowd, waving a twenty at the bartender. Bomber jacket and bleached short hair. Maybe twenty. She was tiny, barely able to move through. Sam noted her frustration and turned sideways, pulling Luke with him. He gestured for her to move up. "Come on, then. He won't see you from out there."

"Thanks, mate." She squeezed in and waved her money again.

Luke wriggled out of Sam's hold and pointed across the room. "See those sportos against the far wall? Now there's the blokiest guys in the room over there. They're definitely having a perv at us." He gestured toward a group of young men, late twenties, looking more like builders having a post-shift pint than poofters out for drinks and a drag show. One of them in a Bond's singlet, well-muscled arms, raised his pint glass to them, then drained it. Sam thought he looked familiar.

"I'll take the tall one and you can have the burly one," Luke said. "Looks like a builder who wandered in from Parramatta. He keeps checking to see if his wallet's still there. Hot as shit, though."

Sam looked around at the dingy old bar that felt like a second home. "Don't be so hard on him. We were scared shitless the first time we came here."

"Bullshit!" Luke waved his beer at Sam, sloshing the foam across his sleeve. "That first night out I lost you half an hour in, looked for you everywhere, only to find you'd ditched me and gone home with some bear couple for a three-way."

"Yeah, well, those first few minutes were still terrifying," Sam said.

"You're amazing."

"I still love a good three-way, you know. You should try one sometime. Well, you should try getting laid some time at all. Might tone down those nerves."

"Ah, fuck you. I get laid plenty, not that you'd know it lately. All coupled up and all that. No room for your mates."

"Yeah, you already said that, sorry. I did miss out on some fun. I know it."

"How was it dating a Mormon anyway? Can't imagine the rooting was all that inventive? All monogamy and missionary position, was it?"

"Don't be nasty, mate. You know he was a missionary, right? Like for real?"

120

"Yeah, yeah, bad suit, name tag, bicycle and all. Would you like to hear a message about Jesus Christ? You've told me a thousand times. The part you didn't mention was the wife."

"Enough." Sam slammed his beer down on the bar and turned away.

Luke grabbed his shoulder and squeezed, pulling him back toward him. "I'm sorry buddy," he shouted over the music. "I'm not trying to make you mad, Sammo. I'm just telling you the truth. Look at this bar, full of fit local boys. You can have your pick. No closet-case Mormons. No secret lives left back overseas. Just true-blue Australians. You said it yourself tonight. Keep it Aussie, mate."

"You're right." Sam swigged his beer. "And we should start with those blokes over there." He waved at the burly bearded guy by the pool tables. The guy motioned him over.

Sam looked back at Luke. "Well?"

Luke shoved Sam forward. "What are you waiting for? After all that talk, get on with it or I'd think you were nervous."

"Ah, fuck. Not nervous at all, just getting warmed up."

"Good, because for a second there I thought you still might be crying over lost Mormons."

"Nope." Sam held up his glass to Luke, who clinked his own against it. "What's done is done. Cheers."

"Cheers, mate. Go get some."

Sam walked across the bar, puffing out his chest as his confidence returned. It was going to be like riding a bike. Easy peasy.

The guy smiled as Sam approached. "How you going?" he said, his Western Suburbs accent pronounced and thick. "Sam, isn't it?"

But of course. It was Alky. The Greek guy from their failed three-way.

"Ah, mate. Wow. Didn't recognize you at first. Been a bit, hasn't it?"

"Yeah, last summer, was it?" He was wearing a singlet that accentuated his dark shoulders and arms, a massive new tattoo of a dragon curling out from under the fabric. "You guys get things sorted out?"

"Yeah. Fine. Moved on." Sam traced his finger up the dragon's tail. "That's new."

"Yeah, been working on it a bit. Had my last session just two weeks back. She's just healed."

"Sexy."

"Thanks, mate. What are you up to tonight?"

"Oh, you know. The usual. Out for a good time. A celebration, I reckon."

"Oh yeah? What you celebrating?"

"Being single again. That, and, yeah, well, fuck Americans," Sam said. He sloshed his beer to his mouth and took a long drink.

"Too right. Fuck 'em," Alky said, draining his glass.

"I'll be honest. Been hoping to run into you again." Sam caught the glint in his eye and knew it was on. Foam stuck to his beard. "I need another one, though." He lifted his empty glass. "You?"

Alky sidled in closer, his leg pressed against Sam's. "Sounds good."

"I'll just head back to the bar for us."

"Na. You sit tight. I waved you over here when you had a perfectly good spot already. I'll go get 'em." He moved around the pool table in the direction of the bar, turning sideways to slide past a trio of young girls who had created an impromptu dance floor next to the jukebox. "Don't go picking someone else up while I'm gone," he yelled back at Sam.

Sam had forgotten how easy it was. How perfect when it clicked. They'd barely exchanged a few sentences and he knew it was happening.

He thought back to the night he had first met Ryan. It had taken him hours of wheedling and sweet talk to get him to agree to come home, pry him away from his daggy drama school friends. But it had been worth it, right?

Stop it.

Luke gave him a thumbs up from back at the bar. All good.

Alky returned with a couple of beers and handed one to Sam. "VB okay? I forgot to ask."

"Yeah, perfect. Can't stand those fancy crafty beers anyway."

"Fuck, me neither. Don't need to chew my beer or worry about what it pairs with, just want to have a drink, right?"

"Too right."

"Was wondering how long it would take you to recognize me. Hadn't seen you out in a while."

"Yeah, sorry. Luke and I've been having a catch up. We used to rage here all the time when we were at uni." He waved at Luke, who was now talking to a handsome guy at the bar, fit and older, mid-fifties probably. Luke's taste skewed that way often. They were deep in conversation and Luke didn't catch his signal. "Glad I ran into you, too. Regretted the way that all went."

"Long forgotten. Just glad to see you again. You're dead sexy." He leaned in and kissed Sam, his lips dry and cracked, like he spent his days outdoors. Was he a tradie? Sam couldn't remember.

Sam broke the kiss and took a drink. "You too. Have to say, I—"

But Alky kissed him again, cutting him off, beer and smoke mingled with the sweat of his lips. "Glad we got the opportunity to give it a go again."

"Opportunist, are you?" Sam said.

"Too right, and looks like you're my opportunity tonight." His hands moved over Sam's chest, down to his waist, his grip powerful, insistent.

"Yep. All yours . . . in fact, why stand around chatting about it when—"

"Hey, your mate over there is waving at you."

Sam looked up at Luke, who was flagging him and mouthing *Showtime*.

"Right. I promised him we'd see the show. You guys coming in?"

"Na, we're just here to play some pool, have some beers. You should skip the show. Hang with me."

"Promised. I owe him. I'll come and find you when it's finished."

"Right. Mates come first. But don't be too long."

"No worries, I won't be." Sam kissed Alky again, his mouth open this time, their tongues interlocking, tasting of beer and smoke.

Alky grabbed the top of Sam's jeans and pushed his fingers just past the waistband.

"Wait. Wait. I gotta go," Sam said.

"Hurry back, sexy."

Sam was blushing, felt himself getting hard. Couldn't have picked a better rebound, if that was what this was. "I will." He pushed through the crowd to where Luke had joined the queue to get into the showroom.

Luke grabbed them a table at the back—perfect spot for watching the crowd—while Sam ordered a couple more beers. At this point it was on. Why not? Screams and cheers rang out as the lights went down and a six-foot-tall queen in Raggedy Ann / Hillbilly drag—overalls, red pigtails, and a couple of teeth blacked out—stomped on stage and started to lip-synch to a dirty song about farm animals.

Sam sang along with gusto, consciously enunciating to not sound drunk, "go tell a chicken, suck my dick, and give him chicken pox."

"How the fuck do you know the words to this daggy old song?"

"*Saturday Night Live*, 1970s. Gilda Radner. My dad had the album. Look her up, she's brilliant."

"It's filthy. Delicious."

"Shut up and watch the show."

The curtain lifted after her number to reveal half a dozen queens dancing around dressed as sheep and dairy maids, while a few hunky guys, oiled up and shirtless, played Jackeroos, pretending to shear cuddly stuffed sheep, rubbing them all over each other's bodies.

"I'll take a couple of those, thanks," Luke said.

"I've already had a couple of those." Sam pointed at a bloke at the back who he'd spent a random Mardi Gras with.

"Course you have. Big swinging dick. There's my old Sam. Welcome back."

"Yes, sir. I think I still have his number. I could text him a pic of you if you want. He'll be all over you."

"I think I'll be fine on my own. Already caught a guy's eye a couple tables over."

"Good on ya."

"I'm gonna send him a drink in a minute, but in the meantime, shut up. Felicia Von Felchinbum is up next."

"Silence and respect for your diva. As you wish."

"Ta."

The show continued on its merry filthy way, and Sam hooted and cheered and sang along with the crowd. It felt nice not having Ryan along, to be honest. As game as he was, he always had to comment on the character work, the sets, the arc of the narrative. Sam had lost it on him one night early on in their relationship. Told him to shut the fuck up with his drama school crap, that it was just bloody drag, and they were there for a laugh. Ryan had pouted the rest of the evening. Yeah, it felt good to just be able to relax and be himself.

"Missed you, Lukey," he said, and shook his friend's shoulder.

"What?" Luke shouted over the music.

"Nothing. Just . . . nothing. I'll grab us more beers."

The show wrapped up with a big production number set to some country song he didn't know, the queens now dressed as slutty cowgirls in sparkles and bustiers simulating various sexual acts with the Jackeroos, ending with them all barely dressed, whipping their lacy lingerie around like lassos. The crowd screamed and cheered.

As they slogged toward the doors to let the next mob in for the midnight show, Luke tapped Sam's shoulder and nodded toward the guy he'd made eyes at earlier.

"Go on, then," Sam said. "Got someone waiting in the bar as well."

His spirits were soaring. A few beers in, now. Seven? Eight? Fuck, who was counting? What mattered was the alcohol was doing its job, freeing him up, wiping his emotions, giving him a sense of euphoria he hadn't felt in ages. Thoughts of Ryan pushed to the back, replaced by the urge to let go and have a good time. An urge he was just now realizing he'd stifled far too often these last few months. And why should he? He was a single guy now. Young and good-looking. Wasn't going to last forever. Best to take advantage.

The main barroom was even more tightly packed now. Midnight crunch time. Regular crowd now boosted by people drifting in from earlier commitments, dinners and cocktails, birthday parties, drinks with coworkers, to really get down and dirty. He headed toward the pool tables, scanning for Alky, the crowd parting for his big frame.

And he stopped short. There was Alky, the guy he was banking on, the guy who had just had his hands down his pants, there he was in a full-on pash and grope with a thirty-something guy who was basically a taller version of Sam. At least he had a type.

Sam's gut clenched and he stopped walking. The shame of rejection welled up inside but quickly turned to anger. Figured he'd walk over and tell him straight out what a dickhead he was. Couldn't even wait an hour for a sure thing? That fucking horny?

But why fucking bother? Weren't they all like that?

"Fuck all of you," he muttered, and pushed his way back toward the door. Stupid idea anyway. Night out with friends, forget about his troubles. Fat fucking chance. He wasn't sticking around for this. Luke could find a ride with whoever he picked up.

Sam knocked forward through the crowd and out the door to the street. The line was now triple what it had been when they'd gotten there, and he had to walk in the street to get around everyone. A car blasted its horn at him as he walked toward the garage.

"Out of the road, you bloody idiot!" the driver shouted through his open window.

Sam flipped him the finger and kept walking. The garage was another street back and he muttered to himself as he walked along, thinking of all the shit Luke had said, all the garbage that had spewed from his mouth as soon as he was sure it was over—what a killjoy Ryan was. What a prude. How stuffy and boring and pseudo-intellectual he was. How he'd sapped all the fun out of Sam, and Sam had played along and agreed with him. Adding his own bits about things he'd held back from Luke previously, about Ryan's silly modesty, even when they were alone, his initial naivete about sex and his refusal to curse. What he wouldn't give right now to hear Ryan say, "Gosh darnit, Sam!"

He got into the car and sat for a moment. Breathing deeply. Calm the fuck down. Last thing he needed to do was bust out into a crying jag in a parking terrace. He turned the keys and jumped in shock as the still-cranked music blasted from the speakers. "Holy fuck!" The knobs felt slippery and wobbly as he fumbled to notch the noise back down, and he howled involuntarily until he'd gotten it shut off.

It was still early. He could go somewhere else. What? No. Who are you fucking kidding? Go home. Get some sleep. Have another drink and cry your eyes out to Adele or something back in the flat where no one can see you. Fine. Yes. Beer in the fridge. Finish it off. He eyed the traffic and pulled out of the garage onto Erskine-ville Road, away from the hubbub of Newtown. Turned up Mitchell Street, dark and quiet at this time of night, and cut through the residential streets of Alexandria to the M-1 at Moore Park. Easy enough. Straight shot through the tunnel back to the Cross. He turned the music back up and started singing along, his spirits lifting a little now that he was out of the pub, the brightly lit tunnel giving him focus. What about calling him? Too late. Tomorrow? Exit approaching, he turned the volume up and sang with even more gusto.

And . . . fuck.

Of course there was a drink driving checkpoint at William Street. There was every weekend, for Christ's sake. What was he thinking? Was it too late to swerve out and get back on the distributor? Absolutely too late. Already ten cars in. No way of turning around. Fuck.

He rolled up to the lights, all thoughts of calling Ryan gone.

"License and rego, mate?" The officer was tall, young, his uniform loose on his scrawny arms.

Stay calm. Just talk to the guy. He's just a bloke like you. Maybe he won't pull out the breathalyzer.

"Mind blowing into this?"

But of course.

"Look, mate," Sam said. "I'll be honest. I've had a couple of beers. I'm sure I won't go over, but just wanted to be up front about it. Happy to take a warning or what have you."

"Good to know, Mr. Carter," the officer read from the license as he clicked on his torch. "But let's just have a go anyway. If you've only had a couple, then there's likely nothing to worry about."

Sam took the apparatus, his hand shaking, and blew into the mouthpiece.

"Keep blowing 'til you absolutely can't blow any more, please."

Sam wheezed a bit, and stopped to wipe his mouth, held out the kazoo-like thing to the officer.

"Not a full read, sorry. Go again, please." The officer flashed his light around the car, lingering on the glove box, the floor. "Deep breath. Full lungs please, and expel it all into the mouthpiece."

Sam inhaled as deeply as he could. May as well play along as nicely as possible, might make a difference. Then pushed his lungs, forced every last bit of air out until he felt like he was drowning. He let go and gasped, handed the device to the cop.

"Mr. Carter, I'm going to ask you to step out of the car."

He was fucked.

His mind raced. He couldn't spend the night in lockup. It was a bit late, but he could call Belinda and have her post bail if need be. They had a pact from high school. Call me first. Don't call Mum, and especially don't call Dad. They'd never had use for it up until now, but he realized she was his only lifeline.

Sam had made a point of staying away from home for years now. Yeah, there were the odd phone calls, but he hadn't seen his parents or been back to Margaret River since New Year's three years ago when Mum and Dad had insisted the whole family get together. He'd been planning on surfing in Bali with Luke, but Belinda had called and begged him to come, so he'd changed his ticket at the last minute and showed up a day late. Dad had made his announcement after dinner with a glass of champagne, composed and camera ready, as if he had just won another architect's prize. "Your mother and I are divorcing," he'd said, his voice quivering as he leaned on the carved ironbark mantle in the dining room he'd designed himself. "I'm gay. I've known for years but didn't have the courage to stand up and be myself. I've decided I can't live a lie any longer." Sam was stunned. "I'm moving to London to join a firm there and start my new life." He paused for just a second then, expectant, as if they should all break into applause at his admission, then went on about realizing this might come as a shock, that he still loved their mother. At this point Sam tuned him out, anger and frustration filling his head. He turned to his mother for a cue, but Helen remained unreadable, simply shaking her head a bit and muttering, "Just get on with it."

His father had spent the rest of the holiday wandering around the house mistyeyed, as various family members came and went, having deep-and-meaningfuls with anyone he could corner, but Sam managed to dodge him whenever he saw him coming. When his dad packed and left for London, they all lined up dutifully and said good-bye. "You and I have got to talk, my boy," he said as he grabbed Sam by the shoulders. "The others don't quite understand."

After dinner, Sam and Belinda had gone to the patio to have a drink, finally able to speak freely. "At least he's not becoming a bloody hairdresser or a flight attendant," Sam said. Lin was on her third glass of wine and had started smoking again. She curled her feet up beneath her on the paint-peeling Adirondack chair. "Dad could never do hair," she said. "Look at that tie he was wearing today. He has no sense of style."

Sam lay back, listening to the surf. "I can't believe the bastard had the nerve to think we'd all flock to him with sympathy and support. I mean, come on! You run around this house like a crazy man for thirty years, barking orders and shrieking over petty disappointments, and now we're all supposed to just understand? Fuck that. I hope he is a dismal bloody failure as a gay man, that no one will touch him with a ten-foot pole, but then that's pretty much guaranteed at his age, isn't it?"

"Holy shit, Sam," Belinda said. "Give the guy a break."

"Sorry," Sam said, "I don't mean to sound like an arsehole, but I can't help being a bit thrown."

"Of course you're shocked. So am I," she said. "But just think how Mum feels, and the crazy shitstorm that must be going on in his own head. We can't be cruel. Can't you try to be sympathetic? Remember when you went through it? Just think if we'd all turned our backs on you when you came out."

"Thing is, he did," Sam said.

"Can you give him a chance?"

"He was a bastard. Told me I wasn't a man."

He'd agreed to try that night, but after his dad left for Melbourne, more and more time passed between calls and emails. Sam hadn't spoken to his father in

14

Sam

Dwarfed by the nondescript glass and steel towers of Bondi Junction, the little brown church on Adelaide Street seemed lost, a remnant of another era, its hundred-year-old sandstone facade pockmarked and faded from decades of exposure to tropical storms and blinding Australian sunshine. Sam had caught the train from the Cross and jogged the ten blocks from the station, worried about being late, cars whizzing above his head along the Syd Einfeld bypass. Overheated and out of breath, he stopped across the street and leaned against an overgrown fig tree, assessing, his once-pristine polo shirt splotchy with sweat.

Unpleasant errand aside, he loved this neighborhood. His first apartment out of uni had been just a few streets over in one of the worst, most decrepit units in a row of seriously dodgy old terrace houses full of surfies, students, and Poms on gap year from Oxford or wherever. A compromise for the lot of them, not beachside, but a reasonable walk down Bondi Road whenever they wanted a surf, and near enough to the train to get to work quickly at their underpaying desk jobs in the CBD if hangovers had them running late.

The main draw of course had been the price. The grotty old thing was far cheaper than any of the increasingly posh reno jobs along Bondi's main surfing drag, and none of them could see giving up partying and getting serious enough about life to manage real rent. Of course that entire row had been knocked down now to make way for a new gym, a new mall, a twenty-story apartment tower with rooftop pool. He'd lost touch with all of them except Luke. Had they sold out? Gotten their shit together and moved up in the world? Or kept it real and followed the ever-dwindling supply of cheap surfing flats out to Maroubra? Cronulla? It didn't matter. Life moves forward.

There were AA meetings closer to home, of course, meetings all over the city according to the website, but he didn't want to run into anyone he knew and have to explain why he was ducking into a church on a Friday evening when he should be out enjoying himself. What would he do? Tell some lie about Bible study? No one would believe him. Anyone with eyes and half a brain would suss out it was for one of these god-awful meetings.

At least there were gay-specific meetings. As long as he had to sit and listen to people moan and groan about their sad lives, there may as well be the possibility of getting laid. This one was a bit out of the way—Bondi Junction, not a conspicuously gay spot, while the rest were smack in the middle of Darlo or Surry Hills—high risk of being seen. So, spot chosen, he'd picked out a tight-fitting polo shirt that showed off his biceps, and jumped on the train at Kings Cross.

He watched as a few people wandered into the church, fuming at himself for being so stupid that he had to be here. "Get to as many meetings as you can," his solicitor had told him. "Take a pocket diary with you and get them to sign on the days you attend. It will look better in court. Addressing the issue before you're ordered to. Show them you're remorseful." He'd picked up a diary at the newsagent next to the station, and he pulled it out of his pocket now, crumpled the cellophane wrapper into his pocket, then bent the spine to loosen the pages.

He hadn't even been that drunk. Or at least not by his standards. He'd blown a .14, almost three times the legal limit, the cop had told him. Sure, he'd intended to stay sober that night, but he'd been far worse on other nights. All of this hoopla seemed a bit ridiculous. With these new stricter laws, one beer put you over the limit. He hadn't hit anyone, had he? Made it straight home if he'd just taken a different route.

Jail was far too crowded with weekend warriors to make room for a regular bloke with no police record (the cop's words), so he'd been let go after initial booking and walked home from the police center, stumbling along the bottle- and paper-strewn streets of Surry Hills just as the sun was coming up. He'd chucked his clothes and collapsed on his bed feeling filthy and sick, then slept through the entire day, only stirring and stumbling to the window as the sun went down across Elizabeth Bay. He'd wept quietly, but only for a moment, pushing it back. He would fix things.

The following Wednesday, he had received a letter apprising him of his court date and an advisory that his license was disqualified for the next three months, pending intervention by his legal counsel or the results of his hearing in six weeks' time. He also received the towing and storage bill for his car and a request for prompt retrieval. The cost stood at seven hundred dollars, with increasing fees the longer he left the car. He didn't have the money, so he'd rung Belinda and feigned a breezy ease with her, talking about the weather and the world before finally telling her what had happened and asking for her credit card number. He played it as a boys' night out, funny story, can you believe it? Can't believe I'm having to use the "call me first" rule. He assured her a commission check was on the way so it would only be a matter of days before he paid her back, just a bit of a tight spot at the moment. She'd tutted a bit—her Byron Bay indignant social justice warrior persona kicking into high gear—had gone on about psychological trauma, the unfairness of it all, and said of course she'd loan him the money, asked if he needed anything, if she should come down, stay with him while he healed. He'd assured her he wasn't traumatized, just hung over. As she signed off, she said, "Be careful, Sam, but don't let this shame you. The legal system only exists to oppress the weak and to make money. Fuck the police."

"Yeah. Fuck the police," he'd agreed, his indignation rising at her encouragement. "Can't a bloke have a few drinks on a Saturday night? I didn't hit anyone. Didn't damage any property. Right? Fuck 'em."

But they were cracking down with the new law, making examples of people, his solicitor had said, so he'd better look suitably penitent, which meant these meetings. Basically, he was fucked.

Everything he knew about AA came from American movies, where many a star had taken on the addict role and won awards. An otherwise boring businessman crashed his car and left someone crippled for life yet somehow managed to elicit forgiveness in the final scene, a dirty cop saw the light and got off the cocaine after almost losing his job, or a brash young woman ruined her sister's wedding and embarrassed the family, remorsefully giving up alcohol after a heartfelt intervention. Inevitably there was a scene of the newly reformed character, the drunk in question, still devastatingly handsome or gorgeous, sobbing in a church basement in a circle of folding chairs full of pathetic bogans in Kmart track suits. It all seemed so bloody American. Labels. Judgments. Panicky solutions. Australians didn't worry about a bit of drinking. It was a way of life in Sydney. Any Aussie who was showing up at these things voluntarily had to be a complete twat, he figured, but even the slightest chance of getting a lighter sentence for show of proper remorse seemed worth it, so he'd fake it, play nice, say what they wanted to hear, get his diary signed and go to court a changed man, at least in the judge's eye.

But there was still that little bit of doubt gnawing at him. He'd meant to stay sober. Promised himself. Yet all resolve had flown out the window on a barman's simple mistake. And once it was on, there was no turning back. There was no such thing as a couple of beers anymore. And people had noticed—Belinda, Jenny. He really needed to get it together. Just need to be a little more ready next time. Maybe stay away from the bars for a few weeks and break the cycle. Hit the gym. Get in some more surfing time. Who needs a bunch of wankers in a church basement?

He hung back a bit longer, feigning interest in a band flyer stapled to a telephone pole, lighting a cigarette, messing with his phone. A steady trickle of people spilled into the building now. A young guy—slim build, close-cropped hair—stopped and looked at him, pointed at the church door, then walked through. Kind of hot in a nerdy sort of way. Looked a little like Ryan, to be honest. He'd be the one if there was any chance of hooking up.

He walked across the street and ducked inside, eyes to the ground, following the sound of footsteps down a dark stairway to a small tiled room where he was immediately struck by the smell of stale coffee and lavender floor polish. The room was mostly full, mostly men, mostly middle-aged. A circle of folding chairs, just as he'd imagined. No Kmart track suits, but lots of shorts and flip-flops and T-shirts, like anyone out at a barbecue or doing the weekend shopping at Coles. One fastidious older gent in a smart jacket and pocket square cooled himself with a black lace fan, and a couple of skinny twinks dressed for the club whispered to each other and giggled, but other than that there were no outward signs that this was a gay meeting. There were a few chairs set back against the wall, out of the circle, and he slunk across the room and sank into one beneath some children's drawings of Jesus. A couple of seats over, two women chatted, looking like any of a thousand office workers in the CBD.

The guy who'd noticed him on the street sat on the far side of the circle facing him. He looked nice enough, like he had his shit together, even hip, wearing a T-shirt for some new Aussie techno band that Sam had just heard on Triple J. He nodded at Sam again and smiled. Shit, had he been that obvious? He pulled his phone out, acted as though he hadn't noticed, busying himself with texting and looking at profiles on Scruff. Two more women entered the room. Big dykes. Classic butchies down to the flannels and Tevas. Real old throwbacks. He typed a message to Luke, *Mate, you wouldn't believe the collection of crazies here,* hit send, then regretted it. Who's to say these weren't nice people? His nerves were getting him. Breathe. Calm down. Luke texted back. *Groan. Meet me in Darlo after? Dinner and drinks?*

Chatter diminished as a heavy-set guy with close-cropped hair stood up from his chair and cleared his throat. Sam looked up and caught his eye, quickly looked away.

"Hi. I'm Patrick and I'm an alcoholic."

"Hi, Patrick!" they all sang out in cheerful unison.

Sam groaned inside. This was going to be awful.

The guy remained standing and read some statement from a paper—welcome, desire to stop drinking, no outside issues. Others stood and introduced themselves to more cheerful shouts. One of the old lesbians near him stood and read more sappy-sounding stuff—powerless, God, steps, amends. It all drifted over Sam, not really connecting. He zoned out and texted back to Luke. *Yes! This thing is excruciating.* Perfect. He could meet Luke out. Catch up. Even stay sober. Show he could do it. That he didn't need these meetings.

The room had fallen silent. Sam looked up and found all eyes were on him. Patrick was still standing, He seemed to be in charge. "I'll ask again, then. Any newcomers? Don't be shy."

Sam slipped his phone into his pocket. "Oh, um, sorry. Hi, I'm Sam," he said, remembering his solicitor's admonishment to play nice.

"Hi, Sam," they all shouted. Applause burst out around the room. Faces that were all grins and google-eyes stared at him, making him so uncomfortable he found himself looking at the floor.

The meeting leader spoke again: "Welcome, Sam. You're in the right place. Keep coming back."

They all echoed, "Keep coming back," then the meeting leader rambled on about donations needed for a raffle, a sober campout in the Blue Mountains, a new Saturday night bonfire meeting on the beach, then said the meeting was open for sharing. Silence for a few moments, then a voice called out from the front row, thin and higher pitched, but masculine, crackling with nervous energy.

"My name's Robert, and I'm an alcoholic."

"Hi, Robert," they all shouted.

"I'm pretty fucking grateful to be here. I've been sober for eleven months today," he said, and they all applauded. "I've been at my job since July, and I've just managed to get a bond down on a flat in Randwick. I'll be moving in on Monday. No more couch surfing or sleeping rough on the beach," he said. The voice had a familiarity to it, a certain whine that made Sam think of Perry when he missed a wave and cried about it. "But seriously, I'm grateful to be here. Grateful to all of you for putting me up on your sofas for the night, taking me to dinner, and listening to me rant and ramble while I got this figured out. I feel different now. Truly amazing. I know now it's all due to turning it over to my higher power."

"Thanks, Robert," they all murmured, then fell into that awkward silence again.

Good lord, thought Sam. Has it come to this?

A deep voice interrupted the stillness. "Hey, I'm Damon and I'm an alcoholic." It was the cute guy in the band T-shirt, and Sam leaned in to listen, shaking off his annoyance. This could be interesting. The guy mentioned hard work and amends, then launched into a story of trying to make things right with his ex-girlfriend and getting his family back, seeing his daughter again. Sorry for the wrongs he'd done them. Asking forgiveness.

So the only cute guy at the gay meeting was straight. Straight and whinging. Bullshit. Sam tuned out again. No eyes were on him in the back row. He texted through the rest of the meeting, only stopping to drop his diary into the collection basket as his solicitor had told him, then fishing it out with a signature on today's date when it came back around. After what felt like hours, they all stood and joined hands for a prayer. He moved his mouth as they all chanted something about serenity and courage, the guy on either side of him squeezing his hand and rocking rhythmically. As soon as they broke grip, he shot toward the door. Enough of that. A few shouts of "keep coming back" followed him as he left.

So, that was that. He supposed he could get through a few more if it meant a lighter fine. Maybe even learn something about moderation, get a little perspective, things were a bit messy after all. Shit. They were a hell of lot more than messy. But he was sure he didn't need this.

The sun was just setting, and he stopped in the cool shadows of the church court-yard to light a cigarette, then began his walk back toward the station. Frangipanis lined the block, and he took their scent in, breathing deeply, enjoying it for a moment, then took another drag, drowning it out with the smoke. He flipped through the pages of the diary. Counting the weeks from now until his court appointment. Six bloody weeks. Fuck.

He texted Luke back. *Walking to train. Dinner? Where?*

Oxford Patio, then we can go to ARQ?

Oxford, yeah, but no ARQ. Probably should have an early night.

Aw, don't be a bitch. Don't let that meeting scare you. Come out!

But it did scare him. It scared him a lot.

I don't know. Sounds like a bit too much for tonight. Ring you tomorrow.

So now what? Fifteen minutes' walk to the beach. Sitting alone on the balcony at Russo's taking in the sea air while having a burger would be the perfect thing to shake this all off. Might even get a swim in. Hadn't brought his bathers, of course, but no one would notice his undies in the twilight, or if they did, they wouldn't care. He left the courtyard and walked toward Bondi Road and the beach.

"Sam! Hold up, mate." That whiny high-pitched voice again. Robert, was it?

Sam stopped on the footpath and turned back to face the guy, took a drag on his cigarette. "G'day, mate," he said, not sure what this guy wanted, but just curious enough to listen.

Robert was small and dark, thin. Sam wondered if he was getting enough to eat. His tight T-shirt only made his weight more pronounced, his delicate arms criss-crossed with thick veins, his hair pulled back in a ponytail like some aging lothario stuck in the nineties. "I'm Robert," he said, and held out his hand.

Sam shook and nodded. "Sam. Pleased to meet you."

"So how'd your first meeting go?" he asked, taking a step back and waving Sam's last puff of smoke away from his face.

"I guess it was all right, thanks. Lots to think about."

"Surprised to see you here, I must say." As he spoke, he exposed the cracked and gray teeth of a longtime addict.

Did Sam know this guy? He didn't think so, but he'd had many a night out with many a bloke. They must have partied together at some point.

"Ah, well. Didn't have much choice, I guess." He waved the diary, then shoved it in his pocket with his phone and smokes.

"You don't remember me, do you?" Robert stepped closer, looked into Sam's eyes with an intensity that made him uncomfortable. "We had quite a night once, you and I. Blocked it out, did you?"

Sam racked his brain trying to place this strange intense guy, looked him up and down again. Still no recognition. "Did we, um . . . ?" Sam left the obvious question hanging in the air. This guy wasn't his type, but you never know, might have been a night he had really tied one on.

Robert laughed, his cackle almost lost in the sound of the traffic. "No, mate, we didn't fuck, if that's what you're asking. But you should remember me." He was smiling, but a note of sarcasm, almost malice, had crept into his voice that made Sam's stomach clench. Robert took a step closer to Sam and growled. "You gave me quite a bashing a few months back. Kicked the shit out of me quite nicely, you may recall." His eyes narrowed and he took another step forward.

That voice. That was it. *Leave me the fuck alone!* He still heard it in his dreams, pictured the man hunched on the ground screaming for mercy. The face, The hair. Of course it was him. Robert stepped closer. Sam felt panic rise in his throat.

"Don't try to tell me you don't remember," Robert continued. "You know damn well it was you," he leaned in and hissed. "The bloody caves out at Bronte. I was crashing between homes, and you decided to beat the fuck out of me for no reason whatsoever. I'm trying to stay safe and dry, trying to stay sober, bothering no one, and some stupid surfie boofhead stumbles into my camp, and just kicks the bloody shit out of me for no goddamn reason at all!" His voice had risen to a shout, his breathing rapid. He stepped closer and stared Sam down.

Sam took a deep breath and looked around to see if anyone had heard the yelling. "I'm . . . I'm sorry, mate. I don't know what happened to me. Fuck. I'm so so sorry."

A few people from the meeting shuffled past, moving toward the train station, fiddling with phones or chatting among themselves. The man who had led the meeting—Patrick, was it?—paused for a moment, looking at them, evaluating the situation. "You blokes right?"

"Yeah, mate, thanks. Just turns out we know each other." He gave Robert a look that hopefully transmitted the need to stay calm.

"Happens a lot. First meeting I went to my old dealer was the chairperson. You'll get used to it." He stopped next to Sam, looking at them both, oblivious to the tension.

"Right. Small world," Sam said. He imagined the guy had told that story a hundred times.

"Anyway, I'll leave you guys to catch up. See you next week, Sam?"

"Sure, yeah."

He wandered away from them, meandering, stopped at an overgrown jasmine hedge and plucked a sprig, smelling it deeply, waved at them once, then headed off toward the station, tucking the flower into his pocket. The rest of the meeting-goers were gone, the street empty, the setting sun reflecting orange and red off the windows of the Junction skyline.

"I called it in, you know," Sam said. "Called you an ambo." He reached out to touch Robert's shoulder but the other man stepped back a pace. He pointed a finger.

"Yeah, well, I never saw one. Never even heard a siren. I climbed out myself. Walked over to emergency at Prince of Wales. Barely made it. You cracked two of my ribs, you fucker. You really fucking hurt me."

Sam felt all the horror and nausea of the moment well up in him again. His voice shook as he spoke. "I'm sorry. I'm really sorry," he said. "God, you don't know how many times I've played that scene again in my head. I was drunk. Shitfaced, as a matter of fact. Not that that's an excuse. God, I just, I mean, I'm just so fucking glad you're okay."

He reached out again. Robert didn't flinch this time, but leaned into his grip. Sam felt warm flesh through his T-shirt, the angles of his bony but muscular build. He had almost killed this man.

"Well, yeah. I'm okay now. I mean, you didn't sever an artery or bash in my skull. Not strong enough for that now, are you." Sam could feel the man shifting from victim to tough guy, withdrawing his vulnerability. "If you hadn't caught me off guard, you might have been a little worse off for it yourself."

"Yeah, you definitely feel strong." Sam gave his shoulder a squeeze.

"Want to go for another round and see what happens?"

"God no." Sam laughed, but the man's face was serious.

"Thought about what I would do if I saw you again many a night," he said, looking him up and down. There was a nervous edge to his voice, the slightest quaver. "Just didn't imagine it would happen here."

"I've wondered too," Sam said. He really had. He'd even gone back out to the caves a few days later to check but found no one. "Called every hospital. Had nightmares about it." Feeling the tension lessen, he let go of Robert's shoulder, still wary, but calmer. "Can I make it up to you? Buy you a drink? No. Wait. That's not the right thing to do, is it . . ." An overwhelming sense of remorse and regret for that night still ran circles in his head, but he kept breathing and felt his heart settle back to its regular speed. "Anything, mate. Name it. I've felt so fucking horrible about that ever since. Didn't know who you were or how to find you."

"But you did know." Robert had both his arms in a vice grip before Sam knew what was happening. "You knew exactly where to find me. You could have swum yourself right back to the cave where you'd done the damage and fucking helped me, but you left, abandoned me to whatever was going to happen. I could have bloody died."

His hands were incredibly strong, digging into Sam's biceps. He tried to wiggle his way out but Robert only gripped harder. He stumbled back and felt the iron fence rails scrape across his shoulders. Sam looked up for a church straggler. Would someone intervene? The courtyard was empty.

"Mate, I'm sorry. Really." He leaned into the fence, feeling the points of the spikes. There was no way out of this and the guy wasn't taking his apology. "Whatever I can do to make it up to you. I swear."

Sam's restricted pulse thumped painfully as Robert squeezed even tighter. The man brought his face so close to Sam's he could see the pores in his nose.

"You know I wanted to call you out when I saw you in there," Robert said. A threat was still present in his voice. "Maybe give you back a little of what you gave me. But I didn't want to cause a scene."

Sam's heart was beating so quickly he thought he might hyperventilate. Was he going to have to fight this man again? He couldn't imagine it. The pain was already so great, the guilt already so intense.

"You have every right to want to kill me," he said, keeping his voice as clear and level as possible. "I was a total monster that night and you did nothing to deserve what I did. No one could possibly deserve what I did. If you want to bash my head in, do it. Go ahead. I've got it coming to me. I'm all yours." He realized he was crying, his last words coming out in a choked vibrato. He squinted to keep the tears from pouring down his face, and let his body fall slack, waiting for Robert's fist.

"Not going to do that, mate." He released his grip and Sam felt the blood flow through his arms again. "Beating you up isn't going to make anything better. I guess I just . . ." He stepped back. "I guess I just wanted you to understand how badly you hurt me."

Sam sighed with relief. "I understand. I'm just . . . I'm just glad you're okay."

"You're not okay, though, are you," Robert said.

Sam said nothing.

"It means something that you came here, you know. Maybe you're just here to get the signature. Maybe that's what got you in the door, but you're here. You came for help."

"I suppose I did," he said. But had he? The whole thing had felt like such an obnoxious inconvenience at first. Still, there was a sense of relief he felt now having done it, but that was probably more just relief that he wasn't going to get the shit kicked out him. "At least I want to make it up to you."

Robert spat on the footpath. "No drinks, mate," he said, "but you can buy me dinner to make up for it. If you're really trying to get sober, we could have a talk, if you promise not to punch me, that is."

He thought of his original plan for dinner alone at the beach, throwing himself into the water, shaking the whole thing off, but his gut made him stop. Fuck it. Do the right thing for once. "Promise."

They chatted as they walked toward the center of Bondi Junction, turning away from the crass sameness of the giant shopping mall toward the old-school surfer vibe of Bondi Road, Robert seeming more and more at ease. He told Sam he'd been a builder for several years but had gotten into heroin with his girlfriend at the time and lost his job. He'd been crashing with mates in Redfern when they'd booted him for skipping rent and behaving like an erratic fuckwit. He'd couch surfed for a couple of weeks but it was harder and harder to fix when you didn't have any privacy, so he'd ended up living rough on the beach. The caves were his final resort. He said he'd gotten clean there on his own, sweating it out, howling and crying, before he'd managed to get to a meeting and ask for help.

They stopped at an Indian takeaway, sandwiched between a flower shop and a barber, barely wide enough for a row of tables across from the counter. Without thinking, Sam told him to order whatever he liked, then panicked, doing a quick calculation in his head to make sure it would clear his account. Thankfully, Robert only ordered a vegetarian curry with naan and a coffee. Sam ordered chicken korma and a water. Twenty-five bucks total. He sighed with relief when his card cleared.

"Where are you living?" Robert asked Sam, tucking a napkin into his shirt like a bib. Country manners in the big city. Where was he from?

"Flat in Kings Cross, Federation-era storefront just down from the station on Bayswater. Rehab I've been working on myself. Quite proud of it." He looked around. Thought he recognized someone at another table, then told himself he was being paranoid. Put it out of his mind.

"Lots of meetings over that way," Robert said. "Darlinghurst and the Cross are full of them. There's a nooner I like tomorrow around the corner from your house. The big church off Victoria Road, just past the hospital."

Sam stuck his hands in his pocket, rocked on his heels. "Suppose it couldn't hurt."

The food was simple and delicious, and Sam felt the edge of the evening wear off as they swapped war stories.

Robert spoke of his first days in Sydney as a young man from Queensland. "Once, I woke up in a house I didn't recognize and stumbled around to find the bathroom, only to walk in on a middle-aged woman on the loo who I'd never seen in my life. I stumbled backward, waiting for her to scream, but she simply said, 'Hello, you must be with Maria,' and offered me a joint . . ."

Sam caught back a laugh and hit the table, rattling the cutlery. "Been there, mate. Woken up in so many places I didn't recognize with so many hot guys I never got the name of. Even when I was dating someone. Couldn't seem to keep my dick in my pants. Then when he moved in, my boyfriend, well. I tried to spice things up a bit. Dragged home a guy for a threesome once, turned out he wasn't so interested and ended up single for a couple weeks. Then it turns out he's still married and I was the one being lied to. Shit's crazy. So yeah, I know what you mean."

Robert pushed back in his chair. "Yeah, I've more than once been run out of a flat still pulling me pants on. It's good to have a laugh, but it's serious business, an alcoholic getting sober. We don't realize it but it's not just the drinking or using, but all of it. Running ragged. Burning the candle at both ends. Demanding more of our fair share of everything without doing the work for it."

Sam felt uncomfortable at the mention of the word. Alcoholic. It sounded so cheerless, so puritanical, so permanent. "I'm trying to wrap my head around it," he said. "Just focusing on my court case at the moment. My solicitor told me to hit these meetings as much as I could before my appearance."

"Right. Compelled to attend. The meeting as necessary evil. Well, maybe after you're done with court, you'll want to come back on your own."

It felt too strange. Too much to think about in any kind of permanent sense. He'd been able to knock off for short periods here and there in the past. Dial things down, save a little cash, get more productive at work, hit the gym extra hard, what have you. He'd even gone a month once, well, twenty-eight days. Four full weeks. He'd made it—granted, with a little anxiety—and he'd rewarded himself with a weekend in Melbourne just for proving he could do it. Luke had gotten them a deal on the hotel through work and they'd gone on a bar-hopping, pill-popping bender. And he wasn't the only person who'd thought about it. Ryan had mentioned it here and there. And Jenny too. Just the other day, he'd been standing at her desk asking her about an appointment when she'd waved her hand in front of her nose. "You smell like a brewery!" she'd scolded. "Have a coffee and a mint before the next client arrives."

He took a sip of water. "I'm wondering if maybe there's something there for me. I mean, I'm bloody tired of the hangovers, if nothing else." He felt that old emotional seize-up happen again, that anxiety that gripped him for no reason when he talked about things openly. "Just kicked my boyfriend out. Sales at work suck. Emails from the boss getting nastier. No commission in a couple of months, and without Ryan's bit in rent, I'm falling behind on my mortgage."

"I hear you. When my girlfriend split, I couldn't make ends meet anymore. It was only a month later I was on the street. Found the meetings about a month in. Saved my life."

"So why the gay meeting? In fact, why so many straight people there at all?"

"Ah, poor Sam, did you hit the gay meeting so you could get laid?" Robert shook his head but was still smiling.

"No. I mean, well, maybe." He couldn't believe how quickly Robert had sussed him out. "But then there were so many straight people there. This shit is confusing enough already without me thinking some hot guy at an allegedly gay meeting is up for it and then finding out he's straight."

"*Gay meeting* doesn't mean others can't attend, just that it's a safe space for gay issues or whatever. Basically means that a few poofters started it up when they felt like the other meetings were too blokey, back when gay people couldn't speak freely. It's different now, at least I hope it is. This one's been around for yonks, and now it seems to be about a sixty-forty split, you know, still mostly gay but definitely not all. I just go because it's close to my house and the people are nice."

"Fair enough. Still, all you straight blokes threw my mojo off."

"Well, you threw me off first time around. Didn't peg you for a poofter. Thought you were some stupid surfie musclehead who thought with his fists instead of his brain." He fiddled with the last of his food, dredging a crust of naan across a smear of sauce. "Damn, mate, you really knocked the wind out of me."

Sam felt his gut clench again. "Like I said, mate, I'm truly and deeply sorry for all that. Really. Had a really fucking shitty day and you were the last person I expected out in my little sanctuary."

"Forgiven. Well, after a few more dinners maybe."

They walked back toward Bondi Junction and said good-bye on Grosvenor where Robert's bus stopped. Robert leaned in for a hug and Sam hesitated, then went with it, feeling so strange in the arms of the man whom he'd only months earlier beaten to a pulp. He found himself clenching harder and harder, holding him with all his might, and he began to weep, great wrenching sobs for all that he'd done and all that had gone wrong. Robert held him just as tightly.

"It's going to be all right," he said.

"Is it?" Sam asked.

"I promise," Robert said.

Sam broke the grip and looked him in the eye. His face was deadly serious.

"Here, give us your phone so I can put my number in." Sam held it out to him. Robert tapped the screen and started clicking away. "You're just lucky I didn't go with my original plan and step into the lobby to ring the police when I first saw you." He handed the phone back to Sam and shoved his shoulder. "There you go. Call me when you want to go to another meeting. I'm serious. And don't go drowning yourself in sorrow in the meantime. It isn't good for us. Gotta start fixing things."

Sam didn't even know what that meant. Where to begin. He just said, "Okay," as he stared dumbly at Robert for another second, then turned and walked toward the station, riding the escalator down to the platform in a daze.

15

Ryan

He spotted it from a block away. A late eighties model, a bit smaller than its American counterparts, but identical in all other ways—plain orange brick chapel, simple white steeple, two small wings of high-windowed classrooms. No stained glass, no crosses, no statues, the only identifying element a dark gray sign in plain lettering—The Church of Jesus Christ of Latter Day Saints, Marrickville First and Second Wards—the middle-class austerity of it emblematic of that no-nonsense Mormon philosophy of life. No money spent on extravagance that could otherwise be used to spread the gospel.

As he approached the building, he was hit with both anxiety and a sense of comfort. As much as he had chafed under its restrictions, especially during the last couple of years, the church still represented home and family to him, and he felt a gut punch of remorse, longing for the way things once were. He hadn't been back to Utah since he started at the conservatory. Almost three years now. More time than he had spent on his mission. Megan had agreed it would be okay, the extravagance of a flight home not worth it for such a short time away, and he could work during breaks, take extra shifts at the café, and still get out on auditions. His parents had offered a flight home at Christmastime, but he'd convinced them to save their money. His family wasn't poor, by any means, but international flights weren't in their normal budget, and the appeal to Mormon frugality bought him more time, freedom, a postponement of a conversation he didn't want to have.

And what was home? Sydney had started to feel like home now, especially once he'd found Sam. Home. A new life. A new Ryan. At least that's what he'd thought until that day in the solicitor's office. He had almost dialed Megan a dozen times, but he just couldn't bring himself to do it, couldn't get his mind off what he'd done to her, what he'd done to Sam. He'd tried meditation, incense (Katrina's), surrounding himself with friends, swimming until he was so exhausted he could barely float, and reading every new play he could get his hands on, but it wouldn't go away, this sense that he'd totally and utterly screwed up, that he'd hurt the people he loved.

Church was the only thing left he hadn't tried.

He had a few minutes, so he held back at the corner, getting some relief from the sun in the shade of an ancient Moreton Bay fig tree, its leathery limbs weaving a spider's web of green and gray. It was all so familiar. Families in their suburban Sunday best. Men in dark suits. Conservative, but good quality. Women in modest but well-made dresses. Mormon fashion was uncomplicated, unassuming, nothing at all like the Amish or the Mennonites, although people often confused them with those more fundamentalist sects. He'd once had an argument with a guy at school who kept insisting that if Ryan was from Utah, he was therefore Amish and to just stop denying it. When he'd told the guy he was about seven states too far east and to check his history book, the guy insisted Ryan was lying to escape his past. To be fair, he'd been right, just a little mixed up on exactly how.

And it wasn't only Australians. Misinformation came at him from all sides in the States too, at least any time he left Utah. How many wives do you have? (The church had stopped the practice of polygamy in the 1890s.) How many mothers did you grow up with? (Just the one, thanks.) Where were the golden tablets buried? (Plates, golden plates, not tablets.) Have you ever read the Bible? Have you ever considered becoming Christian? Is it true Joseph Smith was a Satanist? And on and on and on.

A guy he was chatting with at an Oxford Street pub one night had lit up when Ryan mentioned he was Mormon.

"You know the Australian gay community owes the Mormon Church a great debt of gratitude," he'd said.

"How so?" Ryan indulged him. He was kind of hot. "You might be confusing us with the Unitarians. My church is pretty clear on their stance with—"

"Not that. Not that doctrine bullshit. Churches all say the same thing. I'm talking about those fit spunky boys in suits and ties wandering around Hyde Park. Damn. Like a porn movie just waiting to happen. Were you a missionary? I bet you looked hot in that suit."

"Yeah, well. I meant it at the time. Sincerely. It's only now that I—"

"And that crazy strange underwear! You wearing them? Do you ever log on to Mormonguyz.com? Super sexy. You should check it out."

It made Ryan angry, almost sick, the disrespect of the sacred, the disregard for other people's beliefs, but he had more recently found himself blaming the church for his troubles, for preaching sin and punishment from the pulpit, for spinning that spiritual catch-22 that same-sex attraction in and of itself was not a sin but a struggle to be overcome. Acting on it, of course, was a grievous wrong in Heavenly Father's eyes. These ideas had eaten away at him for years, eroding his self-esteem, and pushing him into deeper devotion to his faith, into his marriage with Megan to prove he was normal. Yet, through all the praying, the scripture study, the agonizing denial, nothing had changed.

He had downloaded a hookup app about a month after their wedding, chatting with a few guys but never meeting up, then just before he left the States for school, he had broken down and had a short and awkward hookup with another returned missionary whose wife was out of town. Guilt had paralyzed him immediately afterward, and he'd almost confessed, but one day passed, then two, the guilt faded, and he realized that this was who he was, and had been all along. Nothing was changing it, and Australia presented itself as the perfect opportunity. Get as far from Utah as he could get, where nobody knew him, nobody knew his past, and completely reinvent himself.

He still held on to the basic goodness of it, that love of tradition and home, the idea that a loving God was watching over us, and today he needed it, felt it missing. He had gone through so much with Sam, but it was his past that was doing him in. He'd lied to Megan so completely, so unforgivably. His insistence on getting married, even when he knew he wasn't sexually attracted to women. The thing he had clung to as proof he was spiritually sound had been his undoing, and he had hurt everyone involved in the process, even if they didn't know it yet, and it seemed he had also ruined his own chances at happiness.

It struck him that he would be entering a chapel for the first time since the week he'd arrived in Australia. He felt himself tearing up, but shut it down immediately. Don't want to draw attention to yourself. What do you even want here? To make peace? To prove them wrong? To find a way to forgive yourself?

At least he had dressed the part. He still owned all the elements of the costume— dark jacket, white shirt, tie, leather-bound scriptures. The curious gazes were benign. He clearly fit in, but from where?

A man in his mid-thirties, paunchy, slightly balding, looked at Ryan as he walked through the double glass doors into the foyer. "G'day, mate," he said, "you new to the ward?" the familiar question sounding so out of place in the man's Australian accent.

"I'm visiting from the States," Ryan said, holding back for now, not sure he should let them know he lived in Sydney.

"From Utah?" He held the hands of two small children, a boy and a girl.

"Yeah, I'm from Salt Lake."

"Right," he said. "We were there last year. Right up against the mountains. Beautiful. My wife's American. Her family lives in Draper."

"Home sweet home," the woman said, her American accent startling.

"Beautiful. Amazing houses out that way. I'm from Cottonwood Heights."

"Just up the road." She held a baby, barely visible through folds of pink blanket.

"Yeah. Her family has an awesome spread there on the bench. They've done better than mine ever did, but I keep pushing ahead. We were there for two weeks last year. Went through a session at the Salt Lake Temple. So inspiring! And the skiing. Alta and Snowbird both. Amazing powder. Puts New Zealand to shame."

"He didn't believe me," she said. "Had to fly seven thousand miles to prove it."

"I always believed you. But we still have to have a little home pride, don't we? Stick up for the Kiwis?"

"I grew up skiing at Brighton. Just up the road from my parents' house, er home."

Home. The preferred LDS term. He was hyperconscious of the switch. It implied a place for family, a sanctuary, not just a physical structure. He supposed it was nice, in a way.

"I'm Malcolm, by the way. But call me Mal." The name sounded so un-Mormon, again so foreign. "And this is Rebecca, my wife."

"Nice to hear another American accent," she said. "I'm worried my kids are all going to grow up sounding like Crocodile Dundee."

"Mum!" the young girl said. "You're the one who talks funny." She was four, maybe five, and carried a quilted bag over her shoulder that certainly contained picture books and snacks—the standard LDS keep-the-kids-quiet kit.

"We both talk funny," Ryan said.

"It's all right if you do, I guess." She tugged at her tights. "Can we sit down?"

"Just a moment, Maddie." Rebecca patted the child's head. "It's so nice to meet someone from home. Are you here long? We should have you over to dinner."

"Ripper idea," said Mal. "Name a night this week and it's yours. We can fire up the barbecue, have you meet some of the other members."

"That would be awesome. Have to figure out my schedule for the week but I'd love to." Even as he said it, he knew he'd give them an excuse when the time came. But it felt so good in the moment. So familiar. Like this place. Even the foyer that was identical to the ones back home. Same reproduction of Warner Sallman's austere *Head of Christ.* Glass case with ward announcements and pictures of all the young people who were serving missions. Simple modern sofa and two small armchairs for parents who needed to take their kids out of the meeting.

"Of course. You must be here for work. We can exchange details after the meeting. Will we be seeing you in elder's quorum? What's your name?"

"Ryan. Ryan Jensen."

"Right. So many Jensens in Salt Lake."

"Church did some good missionary work in Sweden back in the day."

"Ha. Too right," Mal said, then dropped his voice to a low almost-whisper as they entered the chapel. Ryan had to lean in to hear him over the prelude music coming from the pipe organ at the front of the room. "Come and sit with us, if you don't mind the terrors here." The toddlers were getting a little restless, tugging at their father's hands.

"Sounds good."

The family chose a side pew near the back, and lined up in traditional Mormon Sacrament Meeting family configuration. Mother first, kids next, then dad, the parents serving as disciplinary bookends with dad on the aisle seat should someone need to be taken outside. As they shuffled to a stop, Mal looked up at Ryan, scooted in a bit further, and patted the seat next to him. Ryan grabbed the dark wood of the pew ahead of them and sank down onto the hard but comfortable bench, the simple organ music sweeping him back to another time.

The meeting proceeded exactly as it would have at home, just with different accents. He knew that the Sunday school class here would be on the same lesson as his class in America. All so uniform. Regimented. Unoriginal, perhaps, but it was comforting, knowing that every Mormon church around the world would be doing the same thing over the next twenty-four hours.

The opening hymn was one he loved, and he sang along enthusiastically. Pushing through the verses effortlessly by memory, and breaking into harmony at the closing line "Hence forth and forever, amen and amen."

"Nice voice," Malcom whispered. "We should keep you down here to help our choir. They're a little ragged."

"Dad!" his daughter hissed. "Be reverent!"

"You've got me there. Sorry, Maddie." He patted his daughter's head and put a finger to his lips.

After the welcoming and announcements, they opened the hymnbooks again and sang "There Is a Green Hill Far Away" in preparation for the sacrament. Ryan held back this time, aware of the reverence needed for the slower piece, and also remembering his promise to himself that he wouldn't draw more attention than necessary.

The sacrament tray came to their row, the young deacon in white shirt and tie holding it out to him to take the bread, and for one moment he thought of abstaining, passing the tray straight to Mal, but it was better to fit in, to pass scrutiny, than to continue to be the outsider who not only was a stranger but had refused the sacrament. He felt a twinge of guilt as he swallowed the bread, but in his head offered a prayer of repentance and a promise to make things right again. He felt a sense of relief and passed the tray on to Malcom. The water followed the bread and he again pondered his situation. It was crazy. He'd told so many lies. But it could all be fixed. He could be forgiven. He just needed to take action.

When the last deacon had returned to the sacrament table, the bishop stood again and announced that today was fast and testimony meeting, and that microphones would be brought to members who stood to bear their testimonies. He'd forgotten it was the first Sunday of the month. Fast and testimony could be a bit of a wild card depending on who got to the microphones first. He'd sat through many an embarrassing confessional back at home, and many an inspiring message. But this wasn't home. These people were lovely Australians. Their perspective might be different. What had he come for if not to hear the message again?

The bishop pointed to the two far corners of the room where young men stood ready with the mics, thanked everyone for being there, and sat down. As often happened, the first member of the congregation to stand was a child, a young girl, maybe five or six. She held the microphone close to her mouth, her heavy breathing causing a bit of feedback. She spoke while her mother whispered in her ear, "I know the church is true. I know Joseph Smith was a prophet. I love my mommy and daddy and my brothers and sisters. Amen."

It had often bothered Ryan when young children did this at home. How could they have a testimony of something they didn't understand? But today it felt natural, sweet really. He felt his worry fading.

After a few more children spoke, a middle-aged woman stood up a few rows in front of them. Her voice faltered a little as she spoke. "Good morning, brothers and sisters. I stand before you this today to bear you my testimony of the power of the gospel in my life. I have faced some serious challenges, but the Savior has been there for me and eased my burden. As many of you know, my husband left me and left the church just a few weeks ago." Ryan felt the room grow even quieter.

Malcolm whispered, "Terrible thing."

The woman continued. "I have no idea why he did it. He won't speak to me or our children, not even his own parents. He's gone. Off to Melbourne to do whatever it is he's doing with whomever it is." Her words came slowly, and her voice shook with emotion. "I must say I've struggled to understand why this is happening to me. How could I survive something like this? I thought we had a happy marriage. What have I done wrong?" Tears were in her voice now and she stopped speaking, sobbing audibly. "I thought my life was over," she continued. "The bishop has been so kind, and so many of you have reached out to me, so many of you have been so kind, and I have spent many hours in prayer, and I have found peace and solace, knowing that my husband has his own free agency and is walking his own path, whatever that may be, and that what I must do is continue to pray and to praise the Lord and to live in the knowledge that I will be happy again one day, that answers will be revealed, that a solution will come into focus. I know this to be true, but only if I stay true to the gospel and to the teachings of the Savior." She paused and breathed deeply, the microphone picking it up as if she were playing a dramatic role in a film. "I am in so much pain right now." And she broke down weeping again. "But I know that my testimony of the gospel will carry me through. In the name of Jesus Christ, amen," she said, racked with sobs.

The woman sitting next to her stood up and put an arm around her shoulder, taking the microphone from her and holding it out to the young man waiting for it at the end of the aisle. Ryan felt his stomach heave. He thought he might throw up.

He stood up to go to the bathroom, and the young deacon came walking toward him, holding out the microphone to him. He held up his hand and shook his head, then walked toward the back of the church. A few people made eye contact as he passed them. Questioning. Who was he? Where was he going?

Don't rush. Don't show any emotion. Just keep walking. You're just going to the bathroom. He made it to the double wooden doors and pushed quietly through to the foyer, easing the doors shut behind him, then walked quickly out of the church and down the steps toward the street, not breaking stride as he turned back toward Marrickville station. The dark wool fabric of his jacket had become a heat-conducting blanket, searing his shoulders in the ridiculously hot summer sun. His tie felt like a noose, and he pulled it loose as he walked, balling it up and putting it in his pocket, He walked past a kebab shop, hairdresser, newsagent, chemist, all the standards found near any Australian railway station, and ducked into the EzyMart, grabbing a cold bottle of water from the cooler.

The Middle-Eastern shopkeeper said, "Three dollars, mate."

Ryan fished a five out of his wallet and lay it down, pocketed his change, and chugged from the bottle as he walked back out to the street. He had no intention of returning now. He knew that. He didn't deserve what had been done to him, but neither did anyone deserve what he'd done to them. By grasping at straws, by cling-ing to appearances, he'd ruined everything for everyone. He had to call Megan. He had to call her now.

He swiped his Opal card at the turnstile and pushed through, walked to the end of the platform. Near empty on a Sunday afternoon. He'd imagined the conversa-tion happening in person after graduation, over dinner, carefully prepared, a chance to show how truly sorry he was. He'd spent many an evening rehearsing his speech, emoting to the windows and walls, writing draft after draft of it, crafting it to per-fection, imagining himself a character in a heart-wrenching modern drama. Mamet. Stoppard. Shepard. But this wasn't a play. This was people's lives, and any furthering of the lie would only make it worse.

It was early evening in America yesterday, well, Saturday, yesterday according to the calendar. It always struck him as weird that the person he was talking to on the phone could be living in a different day. She might be out to a movie or dinner with her family or some of her friends, but she more often stayed in.

He pulled her up in his contacts, and his finger hovered over the call symbol, his pulse racing, his stomach high in his throat, his own grim face reflected back at him in the glass. He was tempted to just throw the phone back in his pocket, but he had to do it. He just hoped it wouldn't go as horribly as he knew he deserved. He found a bench under the eaves of the old station house and sat down in the shade. Just do it. Finger poised over the green dial symbol, he closed his eyes and urged himself forward.

At least Katrina wasn't coaching him from the wings. For someone who was so concerned with the human condition, it was sometimes astonishing how obtuse she was about her own place in things. She'd asked to come along today, to buffer him through it, but he'd said no. She'd been hurt at first, but gotten over it, and now she was away for the weekend with Nathan, off to the Blue Mountains, going all hippie-dippie in Katoomba, nesting in some rustic holiday house, bushwalking, meditating, and raving over the cuisine at some farm-to-table vegan restaurant. He knew he'd lose patience with her if he'd gone along. He'd tried to hate Nathan, been jealous of the work he was getting, of the time he was taking with Katrina, suspicious that he was using her for her industry connections. But he'd had to admit, after a few more lovely dinners and a great day at the beach where they'd surfed themselves crazy, that the guy was all right. She'd texted pictures already. Beautiful countryside. Beautiful food. The two of them all smiles and hugs.

But he needed to focus now.

The whole sham marriage thing aside, his relationship with Megan had been good. They were friends first, both theater-mad, and she had a silly sarcastic side that brought him out of his brooding overseriousness just when it was needed most. They'd been good for each other in many ways. The sex hadn't even been bad—at least, not at first. He had tried his best and managed to enjoy himself now and then, and she assured him it was good. Not that either of them knew anything about it prior to their wedding night. They'd both been good Mormon kids and waited until they'd been married. Temple marriage. Sealed for time and all eternity. If either of them had been sexually impure, they wouldn't have been able to be married in that most sacred of places, and to have a secular service in a regular chapel instead of the temple was as good as taking out a billboard announcing you'd done it before the wedding night. So they'd been good. And they'd loved each other. Really. He had to remember that. But then he'd dropped the divorce bomb on her and, like the coward he was realizing he was, he'd run.

Shielding his phone from the sunlight with his hand, he opened her last text. Six weeks ago. Six weeks and he hadn't responded.

So, I guess you're not talking to me. I'm so confused right now, but I'm not going to chase you down anymore. Call me when you're ready.

His finger hovered over the call button. They had always Facetimed at the beginning, but he wasn't sure he could face looking at her. He tapped the screen, his heart racing. The phone rang half a dozen times, and he was about to hang up when she answered.

"Wow," she said. "I'd just about given up."

"Meg. Hi. I'm sorry I took so long to get back to you."

"Three months isn't a long time, Ryan."

"No?" Her answer surprised him. She was such a forgiving person, maybe . . .

"No. It's abandonment. Plain and simple."

"I'm so so sorry."

"You're going to be saying that a lot over the next few minutes, I think."

"As many times as you need."

"And not even a video call? What, too guilty to look me in the eye?"

"I just thought, well, after so much time . . ."

"Switch to video and talk to me like my husband or I'm hanging up."

He hit the camera symbol and her face came into view.

"That's better," she said.

Her hair was shorter, dyed a darker brown than normal, striking against her pale complexion. Was she doing a play? He could see the familiar wall of her parents' kitchen behind her, oak cabinetry that hadn't been updated in decades. Pictures of Joseph Smith and of the current prophet hung next to each other on a cork board by the refrigerator. Familiarity washed over him. She really was beautiful, her face comforting, even in the middle of the mess.

"You're right. This does feel better," he said.

"Mm, hmmm." She stared at the screen, waiting. This was on him, after all.

"I've been meaning to call. But—"

"Don't say that. You haven't been meaning to call. You're been dodging me for months."

"Honestly, Meg, I just—"

"Rule one," she said. "If we're going to talk this out, you can't lie to me. No more stories. No excuses. You ran away to Australia, mailed me divorce papers with no warning, and then went silent. At no point in that story does 'I've been meaning to call' sound believable."

"Agreed."

A train on its way out to some suburb he would never visit slowed into the station, the screech of metal on metal hissing and whining as the brakes engaged.

"What is that?" she asked. "Where are you, I can barely hear you!"

"I'm at a train station. I was at church. I'm on my way back to the flat and I'm sitting on the platform."

"So you still go to church?"

"Well, it's been a while."

She turned her face away from the phone. "I thought so."

He could hear shuffling and clanking, someone in the kitchen, see the window behind her, the trampoline in her backyard that had been there since he'd known her. She leaned back into the picture and waved a manila envelope at him. Australian postmark. Nausea gripped him.

"What's going on? These papers? Are you serious?" She shoved the envelope in front of the phone so it blocked out the picture.

"I'm so sorry about just sending them. I should have—"

"Are you serious or not?"

He shut his eyes for a moment. There they were. This was real. "Yes, Megan. I'm serious."

"Would you mind telling me why? What did I do?"

Another train screamed into the station. "Hang on! Another one, but I'm getting on this time," he shouted. "It'll be quieter once I'm on board. I'm taking you off speaker . . . so I'll have the phone to my ear instead of looking at you, just FYI."

"Okay, fine. I will too then, I guess."

He hit the camera button again, canceling the video connection as the doors slid open, then climbed the narrow half staircase to the upper section. It was almost empty. One couple sat at the front speaking Chinese. A young man with long dark hair listened to music through headphones, mumbling tunelessly along to some song Ryan couldn't make out. This would be fine, especially now that he was relieved of the intensity of eye contact.

"There. It should be quieter now."

"I asked you a question."

"I know. I'm just, well, it's just hard figuring out how to say things."

"You've had months to figure out how to say this."

"And then it all goes sideways."

"What did I do? I really need to know."

"You didn't do anything! No! I'm so sorry I let you think that! Honestly, it's really just about citizenship and getting more work and—"

"Stop. You're lying. That's not the real reason. Don't forget how you and I pored over all the permanent resident details. As long as you're still under thirty, it's not that difficult and you know it. Do you want me to hang up?"

"No! No. I'm sorry. You're right."

"Turn on your camera. Look at me and tell me the truth. I don't care if the train is full."

"All right." He hit the button and faced her again. Where he had anticipated anger, he only saw pain. "This is going to be hard."

"Harder than getting divorce papers in the mail with no warning and no explanation?"

"Of course not. Megan, you didn't do anything wrong at all."

"Now you're buttering me up. 'It's not you, it's me.' Is that it?"

"Well, to be honest, yes."

"What are you talking about?"

"Well . . ." He paused, lowered his voice. "Gosh, this is so hard."

He could hear her mother talking on the phone somewhere in the background. This was really far too awkward to be doing in public, but he had to forge ahead.

She looked into the phone intently. "Okay, now you're scaring me. What's going on? I could forgive you for needing to sort some things out, you know. I get that you needed some time and space, that things got confusing. That's why I haven't signed those darn papers yet, but honestly, what are you doing? What are we doing?"

"Megan. You know I love you."

"Oh, Ryan. That's what people say before they leave you."

"Well, to be fair, we're already on a break."

"News to me. All this time, I thought I was supporting my wonderful husband who had gotten into a wonderful drama school in another country, and who knew? Maybe I'd even eventually join him there, and then this? We were on a break?"

"Of course all of that's true and I love you for it. I just meant we're on different sides of the world. A geographical break, I guess."

"That's ridiculous."

He paused and looked out the window at the endless stream of mid-rise apartment blocks that lined the railway tracks to the horizon, trying to figure out what to say next. "Okay, maybe so, but, well, things have changed for me here."

"What do you mean?"

He looked around him to see if anyone was listening to him. Of course no one was. Why would they care?

"We really need to talk about divorce."

"I hate that word."

"My life is here. Your life is there. Surely you've met someone you want to go out with, haven't you?" Dammit. He was pussyfooting, deflecting from his own involvement. He had made himself a promise he wouldn't, yet here he was, encouraging her to be the one to end it.

"That's what people always say when they've met someone themselves."

She wasn't buying his ruse. She was too smart, and this was not going at all as planned. It all sounded terrible, so predictable and canned. Like a breakup speech from a movie for Lifetime Television. Drop it, Ryan. Just get honest. You owe her this much!

"Megan, I'm gay."

She said nothing, waiting.

"I've known for a while. I didn't know how to tell you."

"I'm listening now."

"I've lied to you and lied to myself and it's been awful and I need to make a clean break and be myself. I love you. I love you so damn much it hurts, but I have to do this. I even had a boyfriend but he dumped me because he found out I was married and that I lied about it. Dammit. There. I said it."

Megan was silent for a moment. He could hear her breathing.

"Well, I guess in the back of my mind I knew this was coming."

"I'm so so so sorry. I wish things were different."

"What do you want me to say? That it's all fine? That I understand? That I support your struggle?"

"I don't know. That sounds a little—"

"A little insincere? A little self-deprecating? Yeah. I would agree. So I'm not going to say those things."

"I've been a total asshole. I wouldn't expect you to."

"I really love your new swearing habit, by the way."

"Sorry. I don't even really swear, I'm sorry."

"Please stop saying that."

"Okay. What do you want me to say?"

"Tell me how it happened. The truth. How long have you known?"

"I don't know. A long time."

"Well, which is it? A long time or you don't know?"

The train stopped at Sydenham, big bustling station, and transfer point for the eastern suburbs, but he decided to stay on, not disrupt the conversation with all the noise and hubbub. He could switch later at Central. A few more people got on, backpackers, a few young kids, and an older man drenched in sweat, dragging several pieces of luggage behind him.

"I've known for years, okay? I guess I've always felt this way but the church told me I was wrong and sinful and I couldn't figure out why it was happening to me so I kept praying and kept trying and . . . well. And I really loved you. Love you. Here and now. I mean, I love you. I just can't be married to you. It's not fair to you or me."

"Honestly I think you're more worried about you than me. So what have you been doing down there? I suppose you swear up a storm down there and drink and party now. Running around with guys? Hooking up? You said you had a boyfriend. So, you're cheating on me?"

"Yes. I am. You can hate me all you want."

She heaved in a deep breath and broke out sobbing. "The thing is, I don't. I get it. The church needs to evolve. I try so hard to follow the prophet but the whole gay thing has never made sense to me. I really do understand that you were suffering."

"Thank you. You don't know how hard it's been to deal with this."

"But this is my life too. You say it's been hard. Hard for you running off to drama school in a fabulous big city on the beach? Hard for you exploring your sexuality with no consequences while I'm up all night wondering what I did to make my husband hate me?

"So many of my friends kept asking me why I wasn't down there with my husband, and I gave them our story, our agreed-upon narrative. I couldn't get a work visa since you weren't a resident. I was focusing on my own career goals. We would reunite soon and share our great successes. It was all lies, wasn't it?"

"Not all of it. I really did want the best for you."

"You wanted the best for yourself. I was never a consideration."

"That's not true." But it was. Stop pretending. Come clean.

"I was really hurt when you said you needed to go alone, but I believed your logic. You needed focus. We couldn't afford it. Deep down I wanted you to ask me to go with you, but you clearly had an agenda and I fell for it. What an idiot."

"Don't be so hard on yourself. You're absolutely right. I ran off with no concern for how you would feel or what might happen to you. I hate myself for it. All I want to do is make it right."

"I don't know if it'll ever be right. I need some time."

"Of course. I'll give you as much time as you need. We can have my uncle George file the papers. He'll do it free, and, well, they're all going to find out eventually."

"I don't want your uncle doing it. It feels too personal. This will be handled by a neutral party. You owe me that. And you'll pay whatever they charge. Beyond that, well, we own nothing and I'm not going to contest. Then, what, mail these forms back to Australia? File them here?"

"I don't know. We'll have to see what the—"

"No. Wait." She shut her eyes and rocked back and forth. "Why am I bending over backward to accommodate all this? You're still living with that Katrina woman? I've got that address. I'll sign and send. Everything else is up to you. You figure it out."

"I'm so—"

"I know. You're sorry. Maybe one day I'll accept your apology. I need to go, Ryan."

His phone went dead as the train pulled in to St. Peters, the doors hissing open onto an empty platform.

16

Sam

Sam sat in his ergonomic desk chair stripped to his underwear, his surfing towel draped around his shoulders to catch the hair as Jenny trimmed, the clippers buzzing and tingling as she worked behind his ears. He felt a sudden sharp bite and yelped.

"Dammit, Jen! You sure you know what you're doing?"

"Sorry, just a little giggly at seeing my boss in his undies. Slip of the hand." She adjusted the guard and restarted, a bit slower. "Composure regained."

Sam felt the prickle of falling hair along his shoulders and back. He'd have to shower in one of the empty units. Wouldn't be the first time. He tugged at the towel for better coverage. "Sorry for barking," he said, "but I only decided to grow it out this year. Finally ditched the boofhead footy player look and now you're buzzing it all away."

She tugged at his curling bangs. "I'm doing you a favor. You haven't been at it long enough to hit the tousled surfy look, and this long bit in back isn't enough to be retro. The judge will just think you're a metho. Seriously daggy, Sam."

"Gosh, thanks." He relaxed his shoulders and accepted his fate. "Then please undag me. Just be a little more careful, please?"

She pinched his ear. Hard. "I was only one unit shy of my cosmetology license when you hired me, you know, and that was a coloring class, nothing to do with scissors. I passed all that with top marks."

"Didn't mean to insult your skills." He pried her fingers from his ear.

"It's all good." Hair sprinkled down his towel as she blew the last clippings from his shoulders.

"I thought it was odd, you know, jumping ship from cosmetology school like that, but you were super enthusiastic and you nailed it with the office software so I snapped you up. Never figured I'd be calling in your hair-cutting skills."

The scissors snipped next to his ear again, and he jerked involuntarily.

She grabbed the top of his head and clenched. "If you don't stop wiggling, I'm going to hit an artery and you won't make it to court at all. Hold still."

"Sorry. Sorry." He clenched his shoulders and sat up straight. "Do you ever regret it?"

"Not finishing the cosmetology thing? Not in the least. Short-sighted goal, I'm glad I put behind me. This is a far better job. Next step real estate license and then watch out, world!"

"Careful what you wish for."

"You don't like what we do?"

"I don't know. I was all set on being an architect. Or at least my dad expected me to be. Knock out my coursework with distinction and join his firm as the golden boy, but the uni course was a nightmare. Dropped out second year. He was furious." Not looking back, though. He looked around his office. The leather armchairs, the mid-century modern teak desk. Palm trees and sea view just outside the floor-to-ceiling windows. Success, or at least the aura of it. No one walking in off the street would guess he was drowning. "Selling the stuff is the next closest thing, I suppose. It gets me by. Not my dream come true, though, no."

"Tilt your head back." The buzz of the clippers stopped. She grabbed the scissors off his desk and took a handful of his bangs. "Have you thought about interior design?"

"What about it?" He squinted against the falling hair.

"You. Doing design. If you're not happy here, that is."

"Nah. Too gay for me, thanks."

"Right. Big butch Sam. Too cool for throw pillows and wallpaper." She let go of his bangs and set the clippers to his neckline. "Thing is, you're really good at it."

"I told you. Not my thing." He turned to face her. "We done?"

"Hold still!" She grabbed his chin and held it for a moment, like she was scolding a naughty child. "Your flat's gorgeous, though. I've never seen a better reno job. And the touch-ups you've done on the flats here, even after the stagers have tarted them up with pillows, chrome, and blonde wood."

"That's different."

"How so?"

"Well, work is work, and home is home. If the stagers are going to muck things up here, then who else is going to fix it? I just open up one of those decorator magazines and re-create something that looks okay. But the flat's mine. My baby. And it's all architectural elements, right? Wood. Glass. Metal. Framework. Wallboard. Ryan chooses the girly stuff. You know, the curtains and throw rugs. Well, chose, anyway."

"Right, sorry. Didn't mean to bring it up."

"You didn't. It's fine. I'm fine with it."

Another chunk of hair fell to the floor.

"You thought about dating again?" She ran her hands through his hair, pulling and twirling as she snipped.

"God no."

"You might—"

"Jen. No."

"Sorry. Just a bit more to do here. It's looking good." His towel started slipping again, so he tucked it into his waistband so it would stay.

"Are you happy here?"

"What do you mean? Happy in Sydney?" She handed him a handled barber's mirror. "Have a look."

"No. I mean here. Working for me."

"Course I am. Don't be ridiculous. Best boss I've ever had. Who else signs off on two-hour lunch breaks?"

"Well, you're the best—"

"Don't say I'm the best assistant you've ever had. We both know I'm your first and only."

He held the mirror closer. "Still. You really are." The haircut was good. Neat and professional. "I mean, who else would give her boss a haircut so he can appear in court on drink driving charges?"

"Life happens. I like you better for it. Makes you human. More like a friend than a boss. Now hold still while I touch up your shoulders. Bit hairy there, aren't you?"

He relaxed into the warm buzz of the clippers again as she shaved the stray hairs from his shoulders. He loved working with her. But wasn't that the problem? It was easy to be popular when you started the day at ten and spent half the day bantering like school kids. He couldn't say when the last time he'd checked her timecard was. Nine to five for head office. Who cared if they closed up early now and then for drinks on Friday afternoons? Who wouldn't enjoy that? But was he actually a good boss?

"All done for real this time." She produced a lint roller from her purse and twirled it across his neck and shoulders.

Sam jumped out of his seat and flipped the towel over his shoulders, rubbing at the itch of dry hair clippings.

"You're a bundle of nerves, Sam. Calm down. You'll be fine. It's a first offense."

"Second offense." He walked to the wall and adjusted a painting.

"What do you mean?"

"Got pulled over for drink driving when I first came to uni."

"You didn't mention that. How long has this been a . . . ?" She paused. "Sorry, no, not judging. What happened?"

"No jail. Dad rang up his attorney—that was when we were still speaking—got the charges reduced to reckless driving. No drink drive charge. Paid a fine and took the bus for a semester. Record still there though." He remembered the humiliation of that weekend. His dad yelling at him that if he hadn't been as successful as he had, there wouldn't be attorneys to call. That larrikins like Sam simply ended up in jail.

She rolled the chair back behind his desk. "Still, your solicitor says it should be fine, right?"

"Yeah, first time drink drivers generally don't do time, but the prosecutor may argue the reckless as precedent, and then I'll likely get a few days or a week." He realized he was pacing and stopped, facing her. "Good thing I still have vacation time."

"That was so long ago. Be optimistic."

"Trying, but I'm bracing for it anyway. Regardless there'll be a fine, and I'm going to have to come up with the money for it. Shitter is, we've only sold two units since before Queen's birthday weekend."

It was the first time he'd said it out loud. Queen's birthday was in June. He'd been drunk that entire week, first for the New South Wales observance, then again for the Western Australia oddball observance a week later. "This queen, how many birthdays does she have?" Ryan had asked that first year. Not that Sam needed an excuse. Queen's birthday, Christmas, or just Tuesday. Any day was good for drinks, and nothing had happened in the office that week except sleeping off hangovers in his office with the lights out. But it was August now. They had to step it up.

Jenny zipped up her barbering kit. "No need to jump to conclusions. Hold off the panic if you can. Monday will tell."

The whole thing made his stomach clench. He'd been telling himself it would turn around, had emptied his savings while waiting for that next commission. He knew Jenny was struggling too. A portion of her pay was meant to come from sales as well. But it was all going to turn around. They'd get these sold. She'd get her license. They'd be an unstoppable team.

Out in the main office, the front door rattled.

"Bugger," Sam muttered. "Can't they read?"

"Likely a few jetsetters gagging for a luxury beachside condo. Financial problem solved." She walked to the door. "Now get your clothes on while I stall whoever it is. You can shower later."

Sam grabbed his shirt and trousers from behind his desk, neatly hung at a safe distance from flying bits of hair. She was right. A deal now would be a lifesaver, but it was four o'clock on a Friday. Who honestly wanted to start a real estate deal with the weekend looming? What he really needed was a swim.

He slipped on the gray tailored trousers and tucked his shirt in, smoothed it around his waistline, eliminating any pucker or wrinkle, then pulled his belt tight and glanced at the mirror behind his door. He stepped into his shoes and opened the door, ready to talk up the view of the last rooftop unit. Jenny had done a bloody good job on the hair. Sharp. Professional. At least he'd look the part for whoever it was.

But he stopped short. Kyle stood next to Jenny, holding the Back in an Hour placard.

Sam's gut clenched.

"Back in an hour, is it?" Kyle asked. "What were you two doing back there?" He chuckled, but it didn't sound like he was in good humor.

Jenny stood silently. This was on Sam. He needed to say something. Lie? Tell the truth? She shrugged at him. Had she said something already?

"Sorry, Kyle. I thought it was late enough."

"Knocking off time seems to be set at five over at the main office, Sam. Didn't realize it was up for negotiation." He tapped his watch and looked around the office. "Not that there seems to be much going on here to keep you open. In fact, was hoping to have a word to you about that. Your office free?"

"Of course. Sorry."

Jenny stood silently at her desk, her eyes pleading, barbering kit still in hand.

"Wouldn't have normally shut the doors, but been meaning to get a haircut for weeks. Wanted to look sharper for the clientele. Jen objected but I—"

"Right. Right. Only thinking of the clients, were you? Well done."

"Kyle, really. I'm sorry."

"But why stop at a haircut? How's about a shopping trip while you're at it? Lunch at the club?" He walked to Jenny's desk and clicked her mouse. "How's the appointment book?"

Sam turned to Jenny and mouthed sorry.

"Empty, I see." Kyle took a step forward. "Your office, Sam. Now."

Each step felt like he was slogging through mud as he led Kyle to the back. He felt sweat dripping down his back as he opened the door.

"I hope you weren't leaving this mess for the cleaners." Kyle gestured at the scattered hair, the towel on the floor.

"Sorry. No, of course not. Jenny gave me a haircut. I needed it." He was trying to sound casual, jovial, looking for some kind of connection with Kyle, but his boss's face remained blank.

"Not only shutting up shop early but coercing your assistant into providing you with free grooming services, then?"

"Of course not. I'm paying her fifty bucks." He wasn't, of course. She'd refused, as he'd secretly hoped she would.

"Well, then, of course that's fine."

"Sorry. Friday afternoon and all. It won't happen again."

"Damn right, it won't. Things are out of control here and it's going to stop."

"I'll just grab the broom."

"Leave it. Stop futzing around and listen to me."

"Have it done in two ticks." Sam's voice cracked with nerves.

"Don't bother." Kyle stood over his desk, picked up a file, then threw it back down. "I'll have the cleaners come in on Monday before I start."

Sam leaned the broom against the wall. "Start what?"

"Start selling these bloody units since you seem to be incapable of it."

"What? Kyle? I'm not incapable. I'm busting my ass, in fact. The market is ridiculous. This isn't the neighborhood for this type of—"

"Enough. It's most certainly the type of neighborhood."

"But the prices are too high. People's offers are too low."

"What offers? You didn't tell me about counter offers!"

"You said the developers were dead set on price. I didn't think . . ."

"No, you didn't think, did you? But you certainly got in some surfing time." He nodded toward Sam's board, leaning against the file cabinet, then opened Sam's desk drawer and pulled out his flask. "And some drinking."

"Kyle. Honestly. I haven't had a drink in weeks. Not since—"

"Since you were arrested? I would hope not."

"How did you . . . ?"

"I'm not stupid, Sam. When the court called to verify your employment, I assumed it wasn't for laughs. It's astonishing how easy it is to get information from a clerk when you tell a few jokes. Makes sense now, why you smelled of booze at the last few staff meetings. I figured you were just having family shit going on or something, but here we are."

"But why now? Just let me get through this. I'm going to turn it around."

"You're kidding, right? Your budget request just arrived. Raises for both you and Jenny? New furniture for the model units? Doubled catering budget for viewings? For what? You haven't sold a unit in weeks! Months! What are you playing at? Lord of the Manor?"

"Just please don't sack Jenny. It isn't her fault."

"No, it isn't. In fact, if it wasn't for Jenny, this would have blown up ages ago. She seems to be the only one capable of closing a sale or registering any documents."

"But I—"

"You put your name on a sale that took place when you were out of the office, Sam."

"I'm the registered agent."

"Yes, but you weren't here. Registered or not. Jenny sold the unit while you were off doing God knows, and you took the sale. Sums up your entire experience here nicely. Sister down from Byron, was it? More likely you sitting in a jail cell. Not the first time, I imagine."

So Jenny had said something after all. Fuck. He'd done all that groundwork with that couple, just asked her to fill in at the last when Lin had come down for her birthday. And he'd been so kind to her. Given her a chance when she had no experience.

"Yeah. No. Not the first. You're right. But I guess you probably already know that. We've all done it, right? Honestly. If you just give me a chance—"

"You don't get it, do you? It's not the arrest. That's just the icing on the damn cake. You're incompetent, Sam. Delusional. I don't know what you think you're doing over here but you won't be doing it any longer. Clean out your desk. Today. I'll give you some privacy, assuming you won't trash the place. Leave the keys with Jenny when you go."

Kyle walked out of the office and Sam picked up a stack of brochures from the desk. He was tempted to hurl them across the room but he set them back down. Control. Calm. Breathe. A drink would suit him. He picked up the flask and shook it. Still full. He'd been such a self-righteous little shit lately he'd left perfectly good scotch in his desk. He snapped the cap and took in the aroma. Wood. Spice. Beautiful. He brought it to his lips. Fuck them all.

"Sam?" Jenny called. "I've got the hoover from the maintenance closet. I'll just come in and clean up the hair if you don't mind."

"Fine." He set the flask down on the table. Later.

The doorknob rattled and she pushed through, carrying the vacuum cannister, the hose thrown over her shoulder. He wanted to strangle her. Call her out for being a rat, but, honestly what good would it do now.

She set the hoover down and pulled the cord along to the outlet. He turned away from her.

"Sam, I'm really sorry."

He picked up his Salesman of the Month plaque from his desk. Four years old now. Cheap plastic, the painted-on gold scratched and peeling.

"You don't have to say anything."

"If it makes any difference, Kyle called me. Demanded I account for your schedule, the time of sale. Told me my job depended on it. He threw me off. Got me so confused I can't remember what I said. I never would have done anything to hurt you."

Of course she hadn't meant to cause trouble. He'd always loved her. Felt a camaraderie that had never happened with a workmate before. Didn't fix the immediate problem though, did it? He set the plaque down and faced her.

"Of course not. I know you wouldn't rat me out."

"I'm so so so sorry." She dropped the hoover to the floor with a clatter and walked over to him.

"What am I going to do?" Sam realized he was tearing up and squinted his eyes to stop.

"You'll get things sorted out. You're brilliant. Figure out what you want to do and do it."

"It's all such a fucking mess. Everything I ever thought I wanted. Boyfriend. Job. Gone." He kicked his surfboard and it clattered to the floor.

She rushed to pick the board up. "No need to damage this while you're upset. It's going to be okay."

"Don't bother. Probably have to sell it."

"Things may be tight for a bit but you'll find something else. Maybe something better."

"I'm already months behind on the mortgage, Jen. They're going to repossess the flat."

"Shit. So crash with me. We could be flatmates."

"In that tiny studio? We'd never make it. You'd kick me out the first week."

"I happen to like my tiny studio, but fair enough. Surely there's something . . ."

"There's nothing."

He started to cry, big heaving sobs.

"I'm fucked."

She pulled him into a hug, smothering his face against his shoulder. "There, there." She squeezed him tighter. "You're a wonderful talented man, and you'll find whatever it is you're meant to do. Give it time. Give it time."

He hugged her back tightly and sobbed silently into her shoulder, her skin warm through the silk of her blouse. She patted his head and he broke the embrace, wiped his eyes on his sleeve. "I suppose I should collect my things."

"Do you want me to—"

"No. Need to do it myself. Just give me a minute."

"All right then. You can still leave the hoovering to me. Call if you need something." She stepped back, straightening her skirt. "It's going to be all right."

The click of heels on hard tile echoed as she walked back to her desk.

He pulled open his drawers. Almost empty. He had never really moved in, never committed to the place. He took out what personal effects were there. His keys. Sunscreen. A novel Belinda had loaned him. His surfing boardies and his wetsuit rolled up like a yoga mat. He threw everything in his gym bag with his laptop, crammed his towel in on top, then pulled out whatever work-related paperwork he could see and piled it on the desk.

He picked up the flask again, could already taste the first swallow. He popped the cap. He thought of calling Luke, or just heading out alone. (Luke had been a bit standoffish since the whole drink driving thing.) It was Friday, after all. The smell hit him as he waved it in front of his face. Familiar. Beautiful. Sick.

You know how this goes.

For God's sake, Sam. This isn't the time to have a fucking hypothetical conversation with yourself.

But you do. You know how it goes.

Right. Maybe you can get blotto and go kick some other junkie's arse, right?

His heart pounded faster and harder. He waved the flask in front of his nose again.

Fuck.

Robert had told him to ring, but Sam was sure he hadn't meant it. They all have to say that, right? Part of the performance? I'll be there for you, just give a ring. Yeah, right.

Thing was, he'd been meaning to call. Processing things. With a few more clear-headed days behind him, he thought that he might be able to just do it on his own. Not sure this whole zombie cult thing was for him. But fuck, right now he didn't know what else to do. He could feel it consuming him.

He pulled up Robert's name in his contacts and hit dial.

Robert answered on the second ring. "Sam. Mate. How you going? Was hoping I'd hear from you."

"Yeah, sorry about that. A lot going on here." He looked down at the mess. He'd spread the hair even further pacing up and back. It was going to be hard enough for Jenny to clean without grinding it into the floorboards. He'd run the hoover for her before he left. Least he could do. "Shitty fucking day, to be honest."

"Life of a drunk is pretty dramatic, yeah. Been there. What's up?"

"Fuck, mate. I just got fired from my job, and I'm standing here with a flask of whiskey in my hand. You said that if ever I felt like I was going to take a drink to call you before I did. So, I'm calling. I'm bloody well fucking calling."

"Good you did. Where are you? Still at your office?"

"Yep, Bronte."

"I'm just over in Randwick. Hop and a skip. Fancy a meeting? There's a five o'clocker at the Anglican church on Swindon. Get in a goddamn Uber or whatever it is you fancy boys ride around in and meet me there. You've got about forty minutes."

"But an Uber this time of day will be too—"

"Then don't come. Fine. Cry about Uber fare and go get drunk."

"Wait, what?"

"Do you want to get sober or not? You want some help?"

"I don't know. Fuck!" he screamed into the phone. Then stopped and caught his breath. The answer came from deep down and felt like broken glass in his mouth. "Yes. Yes, I do."

"Good. Then walk. Jog. Get on the damn bus. I don't care. Get your arse over here and meet me. And stop shouting."

"I've got my surfboard."

"Perfect. Maybe someone at the meeting will give you a few bucks for it and you can start paying your bills."

"How do you know I'm behind—"

"Every bloody drunk's behind on his bills, Sam. It's a joke. Lighten up. Just get your arse over here."

Sam paused. Was this it? He could just go, right? Just walk out, drop the keys, be done. Start over?

"You coming or you having a wank?"

He popped the lid back on the flask and thunked it into the trash can.

"On my way."

"Good. See you shortly."

17

Ryan

"Move, Ryan," Lucy hissed. "We're done. No more curtain calls. Go."

He stared blankly at the heavy, deep-blue curtain in front of him. The auditorium had fallen silent. It was over. They'd done it.

Handsome Matt leaned past Lucy and yelled, "Bloody hell, Ryan. How long do you need to bask in the moment? Move!"

"Shit, sorry." He squeezed Lucy's hand, then shuffled off with the other actors to shouts and cheers backstage.

"Well done, everyone!"

"We did it!"

"Amazing, Ryan!"

"Lucy, you were brilliant!"

"Matt!"

He ducked to the side and leaned against the cinderblock wall, grabbing onto a fly rope and tugging at it absentmindedly as he scanned the room. They'd done well. Really well. Maybe now these bastards would give him a little respect and stop treating him like the American idiot.

Matt approached him. "You fucked up your cue in scene ten." Streaks of sweat ran through his stage makeup. They'd played lovers on stage. No such relationship off. Apparently his nationality was still unforgiveable.

"What? Sorry. I don't think I—" But he knew he had. It had been his one glitch, but they'd recovered. "You're right. I did. Sorry."

"I had to improv my way back in. It was fine, but I just—"

"Ryan!" Katrina's voice shocked him out of the moment. She stood at the stage door with Peta, dressed in her usual head-to-toe black, leaning on the banister in a pose that could only be called theatrical.

Matt stared at Ryan, apparently waiting for an answer. Why did he have to be such a dick and have a tiff about it right now? They'd all been excellent. Ryan wasn't going to give him the fight he so obviously wanted. "But you saved it. You're brilliant. Spot-on instincts."

Matt smiled at the unexpected compliment, then blurted out, "You were awesome too, otherwise."

"We all were," Ryan said. He shifted around Matt and waved at Katrina.

"Bloody good show, Mr. Jensen," she shouted over the crowd.

A crowd of first years ran back and forth with props and costumes getting things reset for tomorrow's performance. A young guy Ryan had never seen before pushed past him, lugging the heavy wooden bedframe that dominated the stage for much of the show. "Behind you," he muttered.

Ryan saw a break in the crowd and pushed toward the door, dodging costume racks and prop boxes, his heart pounding in his chest. "Was it all right?"

"Brilliant, my dear." Katrina pulled him into a hug. "When you put your mind to it, you can really pull it off."

"Fair job, Ryan," Peta said, her gruff affect no different than ever, then leaned in and gave Katrina a peck on the cheek. "Good to see you, doll."

Ryan stared in shock as Peta wandered off with her clipboard. "I expect a strike and reset for tomorrow in thirty minutes, no more," she shouted. Back to business as usual.

"But you know it was good, surely," Katrina said. "The applause went on for ages."

He pulled his tie off and shoved it in his pocket, unbuttoned his shirt another notch. "Everyone's mother and uncle were in the audience. They would have applauded at anything."

"Don't be ridiculous. There were critics out there. Agents. You were phenomenal."

It had been on his mind all day, of course. The opening night of his last play at the conservatory. His graduation role. The culmination of three years of frustration, elation, hard work, and painful self-analysis, all in hopes of being able to do this thing for a living. Calls from agents and casting directors were not unheard of following a good graduation performance. But he had to push it out of his mind. Without residency, it meant nothing. Focus on the moment.

He hugged Katrina and kissed her on the cheek. "How did you get back here, anyway? Peta's a drill sergeant at that door. She blocked David Winters last month when he was here to see his niece in the one-act series, told him hell no, pushed him back out to the street, and slammed the door. I assumed she'd make you wait in the lobby with the other plebs yet here she is giving you a peck on the cheek?"

"A little kindness to the staff goes a long way. A lesson Winters never learned, and one you should remember."

"Yes, Mother."

The lights came up to full stadium blast, destroying the illusion of the set, the flats and props flimsy and cheap in the glare.

"And anyway, Peta's girlfriend is a costume designer on the show. Known them for years. Even had them over to dinner once or twice."

"Not since I've been around."

"Well, Judith's a bit tricky, always looking to blame the patriarchy for the state of her career. And you know I'm a sympathetic ear. Male bastards who run this industry step on women all the time. Thing is, she's done quite well, and what jobs she's missed out on have been due more to her prickly nature than her gender. Bit of a malcontent, if I'm telling the truth. Peta could do better."

"You saying you're switching teams?"

A rope swung in Katrina's face as the flats started coming down. She batted it aside. "Please. I think if I was going to be a lesbian, you'd know it by now. Just saying a little courtesy goes a long way. Don't ever be that kind of person who lords it around when you make it. It's simply bad form."

"His niece isn't all that good anyway, you know. Winters." Ryan said, lowering his voice in case someone who liked her was around. Not likely, but still. "She's a name-dropping party girl. We always joke about her connections getting her in rather than talent. Probably good he wasn't allowed backstage to blow her ego up even more."

"Stop!" Katrina held up a finger. "Look at all this." She swept her hand toward the mass of people: actors congratulating each other while futzing with costumes, techies striking set, professors scribbling notes. "You're all brilliant, but there aren't enough parts to go around so you tear at each other. Don't fall into the trap. It's just petty jealousy, and it ruins friendships. Remember, you're a family. You've been through something together and that bond is unshakeable. Be kind. I'm still mates with everyone from my graduating class. You never know who you're going to end up working with, or hoping to work with. Opportunity knocks when you least expect it. Treat everyone with respect and it isn't a problem."

"Lovely bit of preaching there, Katrina. And what were you saying about David Winters?"

"That he's a brilliant actor you'd be fortunate to work with. He just doesn't always wear his success well. Learn from it."

"You coming to the cast party, Ryan?" Julia waved at him from the back of the room. She stood on the replica of Bethesda Fountain, the brilliant white wings of her own angel costume already shed in favor of her standard hippie-chic uniform of peasant blouse and jean shorts.

"Yep. Dinner first, but see you there."

She blew him a kiss, then grabbed on to Matt's shoulder and jumped down.

"She was excellent," Katrina said. "Made a small part astonishing."

"She really was. That booming voice. The way she syncopated her speeches. No one knew she had it."

"I think they did, actually. She made it here, after all. And you, my friend." She looked him up and down. "You were inspired. Did you bribe them to do *Angels in America*? It's written for you with a bow on it."

"A little too spot-on, if you ask me." He slipped his jacket off and chucked it on top of a crate full of hats. He wanted to get to dinner and avoid another rehash of the Mormon conversation, but when Katrina was on to something, you let her speak.

"It was perfect."

"Role of my lifetime. You're right." (She was, he knew.) "Who knew I'd get to play a closeted Mormon scoundrel who abandons his family and faith for money and sex and basically sells his soul to the devil? Couldn't be more spot-on."

She ruffled his hair. "I meant symbolically, of course."

"It was a stroke of luck, to be honest, playing Joe Pitt. I did just about everything he did, was able to really build from experience. Just hope I stopped things before, well . . ." Thoughts of his family surfaced, his trepidation over doing what needed to be done.

"You're going to be fine. I believe you've emerged from all of it with your soul intact . . . maybe even found it for the first time. You'll really be able to heal things over Christmas, now that things are out in the open."

"One can only hope."

"Are you going to see him before you go?"

He waved at Lucy and held up a finger, mouthed *One minute*.

"He called. Said he wants to talk to me. I don't know."

"Are you at peace with it?"

"I don't think I'll ever be at peace with it."

"See him. You need closure."

He grabbed the railing and clenched, pressed his forehead to the wall. "God, I hate that word. *Closure*. It just makes it worse, I think. Pretending we're going to be friends, that my heart wasn't broken, that my entire future hasn't changed. Why can't we just agree to not see each other and let it be?"

"Time heals."

"It's only been a few months."

"Still. I think you'll feel better if you see him. At least you'll know where you stand."

"Can we just . . ." He let go of the railing and faced the crowd.

"Of course! It's your night. I'm being ridiculous. Forgive me. Choose the restaurant and we'll be on our way."

"Is that Katrina King?" somebody yelled.

"Here I am facing an existential crisis, and they're still more interested in you."

"I've earned a few gasps and shouts. Worked hard for them." She faced the other cast members and crew and applauded energetically. "You were all amazing. Well done!"

Her approval got them rolling again and the room echoed with cheers and whistles. Ryan felt the beginning of tears but pushed them down. This was it. He was going. All dreams and plans aside, he was done. Leaving. And regardless of Katrina's schemes, he would likely never see this place again.

"You were the most brilliant of all, my dear." She leaned in and kissed his forehead.

"I can't believe this is it."

"Not 'it.' Just home for the holidays, yes? Make things right with Megan? Talk to your family? We'll figure something out and you'll be back here before you know it."

"Assuming something works out."

"Have you told them anything yet?"

"Not yet. Better in person. Anyway, I'm sure Megan has. Why wouldn't she?"

"They need to hear it from you, though. You do owe them something of an explanation, even if they were part of the problem."

"They're nice people, you know. Not nearly as rabidly right-wing as Mormons are made out to be."

"Of course they are. How many people are really the embodiment of all the worst traits of a church or political movement?"

Peta stomped by, waving her clipboard. "If you're not on-stage crew, I need you to clear the area. We've got some lifting and moving to do and we all want to go home." She stopped by the door with them for a moment. "Doesn't apply to you, love. I'm sure Graham would love to see you." She walked over to a huddle of actors by the curtain. "All of you. Out!"

Lucy broke from the huddle and rushed toward them. Dropping her usual cool reserve, she grabbed Ryan in a fierce hug and kissed his forehead. She was playing Harper in the production, and the performance had transformed her. "Don't worry," she said as she squeezed tighter and tighter. "It's just me, your pill-popping wife."

Ryan lifted her off the ground and swung her back and forth. "You were so wonderful. I felt like such a bastard treating you that way, even on stage."

"Well, you should have." He set her down and released her. They both smoothed their hair, their clothes, regained composure together, scene partners always.

"You were brilliant, dear," said Katrina.

"Thank you, Miss King. I've always loved your work." Cool and collected again, she gave a little bow.

"Well, thank you, dear, but surely you can't remember the old thing when she was working."

"I grew up watching your show. Knew I wanted to be an actress in primary school. Spent many a night with my mum, taking in the way you did it, noting everything. Judy Smith was excellent too. You were brilliant together. Collin uses one of your scenes in first-year workshop, you know."

"Which one?"

"The one in court where you speak out against your attacker and break down in the witness box. Judy's the solicitor browbeating you? He says it's the definitive example of how a courtroom scene should be done. It's bloody brilliant."

"Well, I guess we did all right on that one."

"I guess you could say you did all right." Graham stood next to Katrina in sweat-soaked T-shirt and jeans, his face flushed. "You won the bloody AFI and the Silver Logie that year." He kissed her cheek. "Forgive the sweat. It's hell-fire hot up in the box, but I can't watch properly from anywhere else. How are you, love?"

"Thrilled to be here. Excellent work."

"Well, I wouldn't go that far." He turned to Ryan. "I almost leapt to the stage and strangled you when you upstaged Handsome Matt. Stayed behind him so long we couldn't see his face when he gave his line about the doctor, and you missed your next cue."

Graham. The man Ryan both loved and feared. He'd done everything he could to do his best tonight, but that moment had caught him completely off guard. He'd hoped no one had noticed, that Matt would get over it and keep it to himself, but of course his director would know. And bring it up. "My shoes were slipping, and I was holding on to the bedframe to not fall over. I got out as quickly as I could."

"I told you to get better shoes. And you, Lucy. The vocal intonation shifted too much in the final act. Remember, Harper has found *her* voice, not someone else's entirely."

"Good God, Graham." Katrina tugged at his sleeve. "The heat really is getting to you. Let them enjoy their achievement for a minute!"

"Fair enough. Well done, all. Really. And Ryan, I only criticize because you were this close to being bloody brilliant." He held his hand up with thumb and forefinger miming a pinch. "You're at the point where the little things really matter now. Good work."

Ryan was startled by the compliment. He couldn't think of anything to say.

"And well done, Lucy," Graham continued. "I had great faith in you, and you didn't disappoint. Your drug-addled state was so convincing I was thinking of asking who your dealer is."

"Well, if you want a little weed, Caleb from second year—"

"So I've heard," Graham said, "but I prefer mine from more reliable sources." He pulled a handkerchief from his pocket and wiped his forehead. "I've gone through a dozen of these tonight, and there are miles to go before I sleep." He leaned in and kissed Katrina on the cheek. "Lovely to see you as always, my dear."

"You pulled it off as always," she said. "Ring me when you get a moment. You owe me dinner."

"As soon as this bloody semester is over." He walked toward the stage, pointing and gesturing wildly for people to do his bidding. "I want everything stacked and cataloged tonight without a single item broken or scratched," he yelled.

"What he said," Peta shouted.

Katrina laughed. "There he goes."

"How is he so casual with you? So relaxed?"

"Seriously, Miss King. That was not the Graham we know."

Katrina leaned back against the railing. "Darlings. I graduated twenty-five years ago. He was in the class behind me. He wouldn't dare give me attitude. In fact, he's quite good fun, if you give him the room to be."

"I can't imagine."

"He does impressions of all his famous former students. You should see his take on Daniel Gentry."

"Oh, he does it in class with first years. Gets them laughing, then tells them they'll never be as good," Lucy said. "I made the mistake of laughing loudest that day. He singled me out for a week."

"Ah, Graham. One day he'll learn the difference between intimidation and motivation, although his style suited me."

"Sometimes he scares the crap out of me."

"As he means to." She waved toward him hunched over a broken spotlight that they'd had to kill after act 1, two light techies listening intently as he pointed at the lens and shouted at them, his withering insults lost in the clang and bang. "But we should get out of everyone's way and get out to the auditorium." She pressed herself further back against the railing as the spotlight was carried past. "Pavel's here tonight. He said he'd wait. Let's not keep him."

"And I need to get out of this costume." Lucy tugged at the collar of her dowdy dressing gown. "You too, Ryan. They'll want these logged back in."

"Pavel?"

"My director friend? The night we went to see the tsunami play?"

"Oh God, yes. That!"

"It's possible the critics were blinded by their fascination with climate change, but he's done good work in the past, and I know he likes to recruit new faces. You could do worse than joining Canal Street."

"That would be amazing, of course."

"For both of you. Anything is possible."

"You're too kind, Miss King." Lucy unclasped her hair and shook it out. "I'm heading to the sheds, then. It was lovely meeting you. See you at the party, Ryan."

"You too, dear, a pleasure."

"Stellar work, my friend." Lucy kissed Ryan's cheek, then walked toward the dressing rooms.

Ryan grabbed his jacket from the pile of hats and threw it over his shoulder. "Not joining Canal Street with a visa that expires in five weeks."

"Relax, darling. We'll figure something out."

"I think the Australian government needs something more definitive than 'we'll figure something out.'"

"Oh, sod them. I'll marry you if it comes to that. God knows we have a better case than you and Sam ever did. You've lived with me for the better part of three years."

"You'd do that?" He grabbed her hand, then let go, realizing how childish he must seem.

"Course I would. Not like I'm looking to get married to anyone else. Nathan's lovely, but one mistake was enough for me. I intend to enjoy living in sin for as long as he'll have me."

"Please say you're joking, or I'll be up all night planning my future successes."

"I'm not joking."

"But every inch of me wants to stay. There's got to be a way. I've worked too damn hard for this." He waved his arm at the busy theater as three crew members dragged the giant flat of the New York skyline from the stage. "I'm going to make it, Katrina."

"Of course you are." She waved her arm toward the stage he'd just left. "And you've already made some amazing inroads here. What about the playwright's program here? Work out all that Mormon stuff on the page. Paired with your acting, there'd be no stopping you."

"Believe me, I've thought about it. I'd have to get a killer scholarship, though. No more international tuition checks in my future. I'm barely making it as is." He nodded toward the dressing room door. "I really should get out of these clothes and let the costume manager get home."

"Of course. But money isn't the problem. There's funding for gifted students." She took his arm and they walked together across the concrete floor marked with decades of spilled paint, arrows, and directives in permanent marker. "And you can live with me for as long as you like. You're the first student lodger I've ever had who I didn't want to kill. I kick most people out after a semester or two. But you made it the entire run, well, minus that misguided moment in the Cross. I don't know how you did it."

He reached the door marked Male. "Mormon manners. We may have some backward ideas about the world, but we're very well brought up." He placed a hand behind his back and bowed to her in his best imitation of royal protocol. "But seriously, I've still got to go and make things right with my family."

"Of course. Of course. But I'm dead serious. Family is one thing, but you've evolved, left it behind. Making peace with the past doesn't mean you have to rejoin it. Your real family is here now. Fly home, make amends, then get back here."

"And in exchange you want?"

"Just your soul, darling." She took his arm. "Now get dressed so we can go meet Pavel."

"Won't be a minute." He swung the door open and pushed past Matt and Jacob to his locker, his heart pounding with nervous energy.

18

Sam

Sam was late, so they settled for the last rickety table out at the curb. The morning breeze wasn't doing much for the unseasonably hot day, and he could feel the rubber strap of his flip-flops cooking the top of his foot, his legs and arms roasting in his wetsuit. He wished he had just brought his gear along to change into after their meeting, but it was never this hot at 9 a.m. He'd have to suffer through. As much as he was aching to get wet and cool down, business had to be handled.

"I almost didn't recognize you," Sam said. Jenny's transformation was complete. Goth was gone, replaced by professional. Hair pulled back. Dark blazer. Sharp, especially in comparison to the bunch of breezy casual Bronte mums having their post-kid-drop-off coffees at the table next to them.

"It's still me. Don't be silly. Drink your coffee." She gestured at the stack of documents sitting on the table between them, colored tabs indicating where signatures were needed. "But let's finish these up so we can talk about nicer things."

Sam shielded his eyes and grabbed the top sheet off the stack. "Just never thought I'd be handing it over to you, you know."

"You hate me for taking your job, don't you?" She had wound her pen around a loose strand of hair, twirling and twisting it, then dropped it and straightened her blouse. "I'm going to have to learn to stop fidgeting if I'm going to run things now, aren't I."

"Your fidgeting is lovely, Jen. It's you. And you're welcome to the job. I sucked at it anyway. You'll do great. And congrats on the license."

"You didn't suck when you applied yourself, Sam. And I've never had a nicer boss." She sipped her coffee and clattered it down in the saucer nervously. "I did worry about you, though."

"I must have been a monster."

"You always treated me like gold. Although I watched you behave like a rat bastard with a client now and then. I guess I knew how to talk to you when you were in a bad mood."

"You did. You're the only person I liked at the whole damn agency. How are you going to feel having Kyle breathing down your neck now?" He leaned back in his chair and looked up the road at the block of flats, remembering how excited he'd been that first day. Head sales agent at a posh remodel. Minutes from the beach. Surfing at lunch. But it had all fallen to shit. He took another sip of coffee. At least it was over. He lowered the volume and tried to speak a little more calmly. "How's it been?"

"He's honestly not that bad. He's a little uptight, sure. Wants efficiency with no questions. But it's only been six weeks. I'll work my voodoo on him. Chill him out. Still got a few tricks, I suppose. In the meantime, there's a lot of yes-Kyle-right-away-Kyle, but he doesn't ask for anything unreasonable."

"Yeah, he's always rubbed me wrong. I'd even convinced myself it was homophobia, at one point, you know, why he hated me so much, but I guess I just have to face up to it that I did a shit job."

"Chalk it up to experience and do better next time."

"I know, sorry. Case closed."

The table of mums next to them got up, hugged and air-kissed, fiddled with ponytails and sun hats. One had a newborn and made a big show of strapping her into one of those huge runner prams, the big contraptions with bicycle wheels, pushing past them and rattling their table, her perfect body accentuated by her tight yoga gear. Eastern suburbs snobs. Sam started to sneer, then caught himself. They had every right to be here. He was the one who had blown it. He eyed the now-empty table in the shade. "Jen, do you—"

"Move? Yes. Grab it before someone else does."

He jumped up and slid into the built-in banquette below the window, dipped one of their napkins in a water cup, and spot-wiped the table as Jenny gathered papers.

She sat down across from him. "Much better. I could feel my scalp burning out there."

"And this thing is just a heat conductor masquerading as a surfing kit." He stacked the leftover cups together and waved at the waitress.

Jenny spread the papers out again and passed the pen to him, holding eye contact, her eyes as kind as the first day he'd met her, when she'd strolled in for her admin interview in torn leggings and a lace corset.

"Just sign them and we're done. The client assumes your mortgage and you're off scot-free. Even making a bit of a profit."

"As are you. Glad to give you the commission, love."

"Sorry it took as long as it did. You'll get your check this week. You been getting by?"

"Yeah, sold the Beemer to a car collector. Living on that 'til this came through."

"Oh, but you love that car!" She grabbed his hand. "It's irreplaceable." She really had no idea how bad it had gotten.

"Just a piece of machinery. There will be another when I get on my feet."

"Well, we did get you top dollar. All that work you and Ryan did turned out well. Really raised the value. We had offers the day it went on the market. Well, you know that, of course."

"Yeah, well, I did the lion's share of it. Granted, he carried a few buckets and hammered a few nails, but mostly he just stepped on things when I needed them. That and picked out the damn pillows. I just think it's crazy that first day on the market my unit's sold, yet these things sat here for months."

"It was the pricing, not you. I convinced Kyle to contact the developers. They're in Dubai, going off random numbers they pulled from the web. Their refusal to budge was based on some memo no one remembered writing. We're dropping them this week. Finally should get snapped up like they should have all along."

"Just my luck."

"Oh, don't worry about it. You said yourself you were miserable there. Let it go. I'm honestly super jealous you're going back to uni. You're going to dazzle your lecturers."

"Let's hope."

"And think of all the hot young blokes running around campus. I'm sure you'll dazzle a few of them, too."

"Now there's my Jen."

Sam looked back down at the papers and paused. School. Uni. Holy shit. After fifteen years. His breathing got agitated and he felt sweat running down his forehead. But this was it. Normal life. He had to give it a try. Just do the next right thing. That's all you have to do, Robert said. They'd been working together for a month now. At first he'd thought that sponsorship meant some kind of therapy or rule-riddled regimen, but it turned out it was just two guys talking about sobriety, comparing notes. Of course there was a bit of reading, but he found he was enjoying it, that he was relieved he could finally be honest about what was going on. He'd worked through the first three steps and was picking up his two-month chip later that evening. Jenny was the first person he'd told.

"Fuck it," he said, "here goes," and scribbled his name across the bottom line.

"You'll do great, you know."

"We'll see."

"You know you will. Now go have your surf. You sure you don't want your copies now?"

"Nah. At this point I'd end up just chucking them into the water, expecting some kind of catharsis like in a bloody movie. Just mail them to my mum's house like we said. I'll be back in W.A. at the end of next week."

"Consider it done."

He stood up and hugged her, holding her close. He realized she was crying. "I'm sorry this all happened," he said.

"Don't be."

She leaned into the hug, grabbing him tighter, and he felt her heart beating, her chest rising with each breath. She was amazing. "You're amazing," she said. "Remember that. And, well, whenever you get to the apology part, you know, what are they?"

"Amends," he said slowly, almost in a whisper, still holding her tightly.

"Amends. Yeah, that. Well, when you get to that part, we're good. No need."

"You're the amazing one."

"Love you, Sam."

"You too."

"And I've got to get back to work." One final fierce squeeze, so tight he could feel her ribs against his, then she let go, kissed his cheek, and walked back up the road without another word, the paperwork that severed his final ties with Sydney tucked under her arm.

19

Ryan

Ryan jog-walked down the moss-covered stone footpath, cutting through the euca-lyptus and bright-purple jacaranda, zigzagging down the steep slope toward the beach. At Hall Street, the heat radiated from the pavement in visible waves, and he ducked to the other side to avoid the direct sunlight. He was drenched in sweat.

They were meeting at Café Marseille in Bondi. Neutral ground, Sam had said. Months had gone by, and Ryan had given up hoping he would hear from him again, but here they were. He knew he shouldn't expect anything, but his heart had done a little flip when he'd agreed to meet, then immediately fallen into doubt, suspi-cion. Why now?

He thought of canceling but knew he needed to keep his word, even with the storm warning. The weather service had cut into the morning television broadcast as he and Katrina were laughing at an old episode of *Neighbours*—Kylie Minogue in her tomboy days, big hair and all. An earthquake off the coast of Fiji had created what the newsreaders were calling a wave-train, swells five times the normal height and growing, picking up speed, heading toward the Australian coast. It might run out of steam offshore, or it could gain traction and hit the Sydney beaches, a full-fledged tsunami. Risk was fifty-fifty. By noon it had picked up speed and the watch had been elevated to an advisory. Beach closures followed shortly thereafter, from Kiama to Nelson Bay, three hundred kilometers of coastline, all to be evacuated. No warnings beyond the beaches themselves at this point, though, so Ryan assumed that the weather service was simply having a heyday, overreacting on a slow news day. *Not afraid of a little tidal wave, now, are we?* Sam had texted. *Tsunami be damned,* Ryan had typed back. Beyond that, Sam wouldn't say what he wanted to talk about.

The street was mobbed. Even busier than usual. Young and fit beachgoers crowded the sidewalk, tourists and locals, dressed in as little as possible for the sum-mer heat, babbling in at least half a dozen languages, abandoning the shore as life-guards barked evacuation orders. Beachgoers wandered up Hall Street, figuring out what else to do with their afternoons, shopping, ducking in and out of cafés and bookstores as if they had all the time in the world, regardless of the state-wide warnings. Ryan angled out into the street and jogged around a steady stream of cars still inching toward the beach in the weekend traffic. The lack of urgency was palpable.

"He'll lay on the charm and you'll just fall for it again," Katrina had said at dinner the previous night. "I don't understand how you're so blind to his bullshit."

"I'm taking him at his word. He's dodged my calls ever since the whole mess with the solicitor, but this feels real. If he wants to get back on a friendly footing, I'm all for it, even if it's just to explain things a little better."

"He has an agenda, I guarantee."

"I hope he does, honestly."

Katrina looked surprised.

"We weren't just some casual thing that didn't work out, Kat. We were serious. We were living together, for God's sake. Regardless of his flaws, I still love him. Aren't people allowed to change?"

"Course they are," she said. "I'm being unfair. I suppose I just want you all to myself."

"Even with Nathan moving in?"

"I don't know. It's cozy with the three of us. I sort of think of us as a family."

"Same. You're the family who finally accepted me when my real one couldn't, but I've got to move on. You don't want me growing old and bitter here, do you? The aging single guy who lives in the spare room with his straight-couple besties, right?"

"It's Sydney. Everyone has flatmates. And twenty-seven is hardly aging. You can live here as long as you like."

"But who knows when or if I'll be back? We haven't heard back on my playwright's application yet, and I'm not even sure if it's, well . . . Honestly, what's the harm in saying good-bye?"

"I suppose there is none." She picked up her knife and focused on her lamb chop. Conversation over.

And now he walked toward what felt like fate. He had dressed strategically—the right tank top, some old cargo shorts with a split over his thigh, flip-flops. Show off his tan, keep it casual and cool, play it off like he was catching up with an old mate without a care, while underneath there was still that last bit of hope that they would sort it out.

Sam stood on the sidewalk in front of the café having a smoke. He wore jeans and an untucked dress shirt, sleeves rolled. Handsome as always. He waved and pointed at the café.

"Hey, Sammo!" The old nickname sounded forced. Pull it back.

"Thanks for meeting me, Spunky." Sam grabbed him in a bear hug. "You want to grab a table?" He sounded genuinely pleased to see him. Relaxed.

A dark wood banquette ran the length of the restaurant along the sidewalk, but there wasn't a seat in sight. It was packed full of chattering people catching the sunshine, looking over their shoulders toward the beach, waiting to see if a tidal wave was really going to hit. Sam pointed at the doorway, and Ryan followed him inside, blinking and squinting as his eyes adjusted to the cool dark café. The room was empty except for staff. All action on the street. The young girl behind the counter waved at them.

"How you going, Ryan?" she called out as she arranged sandwiches on a serving tray. "You braving the warnings with the rest of us?"

Ryan knew her from coming in with Katrina on weekends. Emma, was it? She was Irish.

"Yeah. We'll be fine, I think." He walked to the window table furthest from the doorway. "You still serving?"

"We're still serving for a bit, I suppose. They're recommending that businesses start to close up in case we go to a full warning, but so far it's only an advisory once you're off the beach."

Joel, the owner, sat at a corner cracking eggs into a blue ceramic bowl. "Bloody joke if you ask me, mate," he said. "There has never been a tsunami in Sydney. Never. I reckon there never will be. Newsreaders just like saying the stupid word. *Tsoo Naaaaa Meeeeee.* Tidal wave isn't good enough anymore. Fucking airy-fairy bullshit."

Katrina always swore that Joel's nonstop commentary was what made the place.

Sam slid into a booth. "Spot-on, mate. Bloody end of the world climate change panic is giving me the shits. Was thinking of walking down to the shore after lunch. See if I can coax the fucker out."

Emma arrived with menus. "Now's not the time to take a stand against science, is it? I think we should all be getting home, if you ask me." She set cutlery and napkins in front of them, adjusting them to perfect symmetry. "Who's your reckless friend here, then, Ryan?"

"Sam Carter. Nice to meet you."

"G'day, Sam," she said. "You're not going to get our Ryan into any trouble today now, are you? I'm sure there are other ways you can impress him rather than risking his life."

"Ah, no worries. We're just catching up," Sam said. "If I do any cliff diving, it'll be on my own."

"Careful with this one, Ryan." She eyed them in that way that people did when they knew you were gay. Two blokes on a first date. At least she had chosen the sassy response and hadn't gotten all stiff.

"I'll be on my guard," he muttered.

"I'll be back in a moment to get your order." She walked back to the service window, added two more sandwiches to the tray, then hoisted it over her shoulder and walked toward the door. "That is," she called over her shoulder to Joel, "unless we're swept away by a tsunami—excuse me, tidal wave—before I get the chance." She stepped out onto the sidewalk, letting the door slam behind her.

"We'll be fine." Joel swooshed the bowl around and poured the yellow clumpy mess into a pan. "Course if we go full warning, we'll shut down. Don't see it happening though. I'll manage your order while she's busy outside. You boys hungry?"

The rich smell of grilling sausages hit Ryan. He usually ordered the full English breakfast, but he had butterflies in his stomach, too nervous for food. "Just toast and coffee, Joel. Iced?"

"And how about you, young fella?"

"Yeah, plate of eggs would be lovely," Sam said. "Turkish and haloumi? And a coffee, thanks. Flat white."

Ryan set his menu down and looked across Hall Street, nerves kicking in, avoiding eye contact with Sam while he collected himself. He pulled out his phone and snapped a few pictures of the crowded sidewalk.

"Are you going to look at me?" Sam asked.

"Sorry, yeah. That was rude." He put his phone away. "Never seen a beach evacuation. Wanted a record of it."

Emma returned from the sidewalk, her tray tucked under her arm.

"Joel get your order?"

"Yep. Good to go," Ryan said.

She walked behind the bar and started wiping down the espresso machine.

"Didn't mean to scold you, seeing how it's the end of the world and all that," Sam said. He reached up and lowered the blind against the harsh sunlight, then settled back into his chair.

"It is pretty ominous if you think about it."

"Right. If we went to the right church, I'm sure we'd be hearing about the second coming." He angled his chair so he could lean against the wall, pleased with his own joke.

"Latter-Day Tsunamis," Ryan said. "It would definitely be a thing if Utah had a coast."

"Christ finally returns, but it's to Bondi Beach, not Salt Lake City. A cry of foul play erupts over Utah." He waved his cutlery in the air, eyes wide in mock panic. "Maybe we should have met in the city after all. Don't know if I'm ready to list all my sins just yet."

"I figured you would already have pushed past the barricades and gone for a swim just to prove you could get away with it. You serious about the cliff diving?"

Sam leaned back in his chair. "I thought about it of course, but, well, I've been reevaluating things, I guess. Danger junkie wasn't really working for me. I think you know that."

He reached across the table and grabbed Ryan's hand. The only sound in the restaurant was the hiss of the milk steamer as Emma made their coffees. "Kind of why I wanted to see you today, to be honest. Couple of things I want to tell you," he said. "First of all, of course, is to say I'm sorry I haven't returned your calls. I've been really going through some shit and I needed a breather to evaluate."

"It's okay. Really. I suppose we both did."

"Thing is," Sam said, "I've quit drinking. Been sober nine weeks." He leaned forward and locked eyes with Ryan as he said it, gripping his hand, then let go abruptly, as if he realized he'd gone too far. He looked down at the table. "I realized drinking was killing me and I admitted I was powerless over it." He fidgeted with his fork, pressing the tines along the edge of his paper napkin. His voice had taken on a strange, stiff tone. Theatrical. "And in admitting that, I realized I'd hurt a lot of people. I know I've caused you great pain, and that I behaved horribly. I want to apologize for all of that and ask if there's anything I can do to make it right." He looked up, his eyes wide, like a child asking for an extra helping of ice cream.

Emma arrived with their coffees. "Enjoy these." She looked at Ryan with a raised eyebrow and walked back to her post.

Ryan took a drink from the tall cool glass, already coated with beads of condensation from the heat. "You're sober? Wow. Congratulations. I mean, I guess I didn't realize it was that bad." But of course he had realized it. Sam's drinking had been bordering on nightmare territory when he lived there. Why was he lying? Playing the manners game? Be honest. "Well, though, I guess it makes sense. You were really struggling there. So did you go to rehab or something?"

"No, I quit on my own, but I've joined AA."

"Is it working?"

Sam sipped his own coffee and wiped his lip. "It's a lot to take in," he said. His gaze was fixed on something out the window. "But yeah, I think it might stick. At least, I hope it will."

"A lot to take in?" Ryan asked. The street traffic had come to a dead stop. They must be blocking off Campbell Parade. He wondered if they should cut it short.

"Lots of stuff to read. Lots of information to process. The first step tells me I have to admit that I'm powerless over alcohol and that my life has become unmanageable. Basically, that my problems were all of my own making, that I caused damage to the people I love. In a nutshell, I can't drink again, and I have to make amends to those I hurt and start over. Live a spiritual life."

"Wow, that's all in the first step?"

"Well, no, just the powerless and unmanageable part. Amends is step nine. I'm not quite there yet. My sponsor even told me not to worry about it yet, that we'd get there, but I knew I needed to talk to you. Especially since you're going back to America now."

The words stung. This wasn't what he had hoped for. "How did you know I'm going back?"

"Well, since you've graduated now and we're not getting married, I just assumed . . ." He averted his eyes as he let the sentence drop.

Ryan fished through the sugar bowl for a sachet of fake sugar and poured it over his coffee, turning the foam a pale yellow where it touched.

"Well, you shouldn't assume."

"What? You staying?" He leaned forward, his voice rising slightly.

"Well, no, well, I don't know. I'd like to, yeah, but seems my options are pretty limited. Katrina offered, but, well, that isn't really realistic."

"Katrina offered? Offered what?" Sam's voice rose even further.

Ryan looked around the room to see if they'd drawn anyone's attention, but the café was still empty.

"You know. Marriage. I mean, I think she was only half-serious, but still . . ."

Sam pushed back in his seat. "So you went from marrying your boyfriend to marrying your old theater auntie? Nah. Immigration wouldn't see through that at all."

"She's not my old theater auntie. Come on, Sam." He stirred his coffee and set the spoon on the paper table cover, a light-brown stain spreading around it. The ridiculousness of it hit him. "But yeah, I mean, of course they'd see through it. Nothing suspicious about that, right?"

"Too right they would. Be cool if you could stay, though."

Emma arrived with their plates, sizing up the situation. "Just let me know if you need anything," she said.

"Ta, thanks," Sam said.

Emma walked back to the counter and started a conversation with Joel, apparently satisfied there wouldn't be any trouble.

Sam poked at his scrambled eggs, cut a browned slice of haloumi in two, and took a bite. "Smart boy, saying no," he said. "I knew I hadn't been dating a dummy. Yeah, that would get you kicked out faster than lightning and then you'd never be able to come back. Marriage fraud or whatever."

"Yeah, the last thing I need is a felony record in Australia." He took another sip of his coffee and looked down at his toast, deep brown and dripping in butter. He wished he had an appetite. "Might get me some street cred, though. You know, no publicity is bad publicity and all that?"

"Silly."

"Completely." Ryan felt the tension lessening, like it was just them messing around and being ridiculous like always,

"But honestly, I feel like this is all my fault. This situation," Sam said. "If I had given you the space to be honest with me, maybe we'd be married and this wouldn't even be an issue. And God, wow. Did I overreact or what?" He tried to play it off with a laugh but Ryan could tell he was nervous. It was in his voice, his eyes. "And I really want to fix things. I truly want to make amends to you. Like I said. I know that what I did harmed you. Putting all those expectations on you, then kicking you out. Ending things so abruptly. Can you forgive me?"

"Of course I can," Ryan said. It was an easy answer to give, he found. Easy as ordering another coffee, but now where? Why not ask? What did he have to lose?

"You know, we could try again," he said, tossing it off casually as he looked out the window.

"What?" Sam slapped his hands down loudly on the table, then looked around sheepishly, embarrassed by the noise. "You mean us together again?" he said, leaning forward, dropping his voice.

"I mean, we both admit we did foolish things. I love you, Sam. This could be our last chance. I'm going back to America next week to sort out the divorce. I'll be home for Christmas. And then what? Starting my rounds of auditions in LA as if Sydney never happened? Or maybe just maybe jumping back into school here with the debt that comes with it? I love it here. I love being with you here. What's to say it wouldn't work this time, now that we've faced a few things?"

Sam shut his eyes. "You know I'd love to. I'd love to just pay for the coffee and walk out that door and drag you home and never look back, but, Ryan, . . . I . . . God, I just don't know how it would be any better. I just don't know. I mean . . ." He stopped talking and looked down at his plate, pushed at the eggs with his fork. "And that's not why I came here today. This isn't why I'm here. I'm honestly here to put things right, but we've got to move on, put a proper end to things with no hard feelings. I mean, of course I've entertained fantasies of us again, but we didn't work. No matter how hard we tried. We need a sense of completion. I don't know. Isn't that what people say? Completion? Whatever that is?"

Ryan felt himself pulling away, leaning back further in the banquette. This wasn't his old Sam, this droning, self-help mantra spewing man-child. "So, you asked me here just to say that?"

Sam's face remained emotionless. "Yeah. I was a monster. I need to make it up to you. Please tell me what I can do to fix things."

"I would love to talk this out, but . . ." Ryan hesitated, not sure if he should say what he was thinking, afraid to lose the chance, but they had to get honest or nothing was ever going to change, so he shut his eyes for a moment, then spoke. "It's just that your speech sounds so rehearsed," he said. "You sound like a kid who's memorized his lines. You're making amends to me because that's what . . . remind me what step this is?"

"Nine." Sam held up five fingers and four, like a child telling his age.

"Not that I don't appreciate it, honestly, but can we just talk? Does this have to be something on your checklist?"

"To be honest, I didn't know how else to start the conversation." His knife and fork scraped at his eggs, but he didn't take a bite.

"I'm sorry. I guess that's on me, too. I made it pretty difficult."

A motorcycle blasted its engine and Sam looked out the window, startled.

Joel walked to the window. "Looks like someone's going out with a bang," he said. "You boys all right?" He stood in the doorway facing them, hands on hips, his apron flecked red, brown, and green, evidence of a day's cooking.

"Lovely, thanks," Ryan said.

Sam waved a bit of toast at Joel. "Food's perfect, mate." He leaned closer to Ryan. "I didn't mean it to sound stiff. I wanted to talk to you, honestly. But it's something I need to do for my recovery, so . . ."

"It's okay. I get it. I just don't want this to be a checkmark and then off you run to apologize to the kid you bullied in primary school."

"Ha! Yeah, that'd be Jimmy Chambers. How'd you know?"

"I remember you telling me about him! Chasing him around the playground and having to apologize in front of the whole class?"

"That's him. Still makes me cringe when I think of it. We called him poofter when we didn't know what it meant, or, well . . ."

"Of course."

"Yeah, in fact he's meant to turn up here in thirty minutes for my next appointment. Gotta get this done."

"What?"

"Aw, come on, Rye, you know I'm fucking with you." Sam reached across the table and touched his arm.

"Shit. Okay. You know how gullible I am."

"Sorry. All joking aside, I did want to talk."

"I'm glad. And I'm glad you've quit drinking, if that's what you needed to do."

"Well, yeah, couldn't deny it was causing a shitstorm in my life. Jail, my job, you gone. Fuck. I mean when it comes down to it, I had to face I was prioritizing the grog over anything else."

"How's work?"

"Ah, shit, you haven't been around. Got fired a few weeks back. No sales. Excessive absenteeism, closing the office early. Basically got accused of using the office as my personal changing room for my surfing hobby and a place to stash my flask."

"Sorry. Wow. That really sucks."

"And they gave my job to Jenny. I bloody coached her through her certification." His face scrunched up in reproach, then softened. "Course I love her, you know that, but still."

"Shit, really?"

"But I can't complain. I brought it on myself. Had chance after chance, really."

"As did I with my own shit."

"Look, I get it, you were confused and scared and didn't know how to tell me. I could have seen that if I hadn't been so wrapped up in my own bullshit."

"I still should have told you, and I'm really sorry."

"I get it."

"So, what now? Is he going to give you a reference?"

"Ha! Not bloody likely."

"Have any leads?"

"Yeah, well, that's also one of the big reasons why I'm here."

"Career change?"

"You could say that."

"You really should get your contractor's license, you know. You've done such great work on the flat. You've got such a great eye and everything you touch seems to just install itself. God, I was hopeless about that shit. You must have wanted to kill me."

"Nah. I get it. Some people have the touch with carpentry and tools. Others don't."

"I'm useless."

"You're amazing at what you do."

"Ah, well. I'm learning. Trying."

"You were amazing in your graduation play."

"What? You saw it?"

"Of course I did." He stared at the TV above the bar. "Looks like they've lowered the warning."

"Told ya," Joel shouted to the otherwise empty room. "Bunch of wankers panicking over nothing."

Emma walked back in from the sidewalk, a tray of dirty dishes balanced on her shoulder.

"You need anything?" she asked.

"We're good, thanks."

Ryan bit into his toast. He'd found his appetite again. Knowing that Sam had been to the show had given him a surge of hope.

"What did you think of it?"

"You were amazing. The play was brilliant. As much as you talked up and down about how you'd kill for a part in it, and then you got a lead role? Couldn't let you go through all that hard work and not see the results. Even if I couldn't bring myself to call you yet, I was still barracking for you."

"Where were you sitting?" He crunched into the bread again, raining crumbs into his coffee.

"Oh, a couple of rows behind Katrina. She didn't notice me."

"Ha. Sounds like her." Ryan knew Katrina's focus was always intense when she went to the theater. She'd shushed him more than once when they'd been out to see plays together.

"Anyway, I was really proud of you. Great way to cap off your program."

"Thanks."

"So now you're going?"

"Well, I sort of have to, at least for now. My visa runs out in a few weeks. Thinking about the playwright's program but it's more money than I have right now. Might just do some work at home for a year and save up. Come back then."

"Shame you can't stay. You'll make it, though. You're destined to, I think."

"Got some other stuff to sort out first."

"As do I."

"Right. Sorry. I didn't mean to make it all about me again."

"No. It's fine. This is about both of us, not just me."

The bell rang over the door and a family of four struggled in with backpacks and towels. Two tired-looking parents with a teenage boy and primary-school-age girl. All deeply tanned. The girl's nose was peeling.

"Table for four, please?" the father said to Emma in an Italian accent.

"Take your pick." She gestured across the empty room.

"Grazie," the mother said, and guided her children to the table at the next window.

Sam waved at the kids, then turned to Ryan.

"I'm leaving as well."

"Leaving Sydney?"

"Yep. Makes the most sense when you think about it."

"Does it? I guess I thought you were pretty settled here. What about the flat? All that work you've done?"

"Already sold it. Got a generous offer from some suburban couple hankering for the inner-city life. Signed the papers last week. They take possession three days before Chrissy."

"So, back to W.A.?"

"Yeah. Family putting me up for a bit. Aunt Kate. Mum doesn't have the room but Aunt Kate's in that big old house all alone." He pushed his plate to the side and clattered his knife and fork on top of his crumpled napkin.

"What'll you do for work?"

"Back to work for her. Lumber business is thriving out there."

"You'd make a damn handsome lumberjack." Ryan took the last sip of his coffee and sucked up a piece of ice, crunching it loudly.

"Ah, well. Don't get too excited. I'll mostly be doing office stuff. Managing accounts. The real goal is to head back to uni and finish my architecture degree."

"But that's amazing!"

"It feels right."

"But then . . ."

"You could come with me, you know."

"Right." Ryan paused and looked down. He'd often wondered what it would be like out there. Had entertained a few fantasies of married life in the wealthy suburbs on the western coast. But those ideas were long gone. "Are you sure?" he asked.

"I don't know. But I want to be."

"I would love to think we could try, but . . ."

"I love you so much, I just, I don't know how it all got so fucked up."

"Mormonism," Ryan said.

"Can't blame them for everything . . ."

"I know. I'm joking. They're doing their best. I just, I don't know . . . I wish I'd been raised by agnostic parents in New York or something."

"I love exactly who you are."

"Even with my stupid modesty and secret marriages? I still laugh at the ridiculous naivete of it all. Thinking it wouldn't come up in a background check here. Of course it would, and even if it hadn't, was I going to honestly be married to two people and not tell either one of you?"

"Yeah, things would have gotten tricky eventually, although who knows? We might have learned to share like those sister wives on telly?"

"Right, she would have loved that."

"Although it would have been a race to the finish, really. Who knows what shit would have hit the fan first? Your wife showing up on the doorstep? Or the bank changing the locks on the flat and chucking us into the street."

"What?" Ryan's voice rose and the Italian family stared.

"You know that flat was going to be repossessed if I didn't make the payment this month?"

"Seriously? Why didn't you say—"

"How could I and still be your hero?"

"You'll always be my hero."

"Hero who drank himself out of a job and a house."

Emma stopped at their table again. "Finished with these?" She stacked the plates and grabbed the cups.

Sam threw his napkin on the stack. "Ta."

"Another coffee?"

"I've had plenty," he said.

"Ryan?"

"All good, thanks." He jiggled his glass, rattling the ice. "May just keep this to crunch on, though."

"Suit yourself. Just pay at the bar when you're ready." She walked the plates back to the bar. "Food'll be out in a tick," she called at the Italian family.

"You're a good man, Sam," Ryan said.

"And so are you." Sam grabbed his hand again and squeezed, hard, as if he wasn't going to let go.

"So what do we do? Is that it?"

"Unless you want to, um. Never mind." Sam looked down at the table and let go. He sighed, stood up, and pulled his wallet from his pocket.

"Unless what?" Ryan pushed his chair back and stood, clenching his calves as he found his balance.

"Program says don't embark on any new ventures during your first year of sobriety. Sponsor says moving home and getting back into school isn't a new venture, it's properly finishing an old one, but, well, I was going to say . . ."

"What?"

"What if you called me in a year? What if we could get all this shit behind us and try again once we were both stable? It just sounds so lame, I guess. Like you'd wait for me. Like there isn't bigger and better just around the corner for you."

"Who's to say there is? And even if there is some hot guy out there waiting to sweep me up, who's to say I would be interested? You're in my blood, Sam."

They walked to the bar together.

Joel set his phone down and fished through a stack of handwritten tickets.

"You blokes had enough?"

"Perfect." Sam fished a fifty from his wallet. Joel handed him back a couple of fives and a few dollar coins. Sam clinked them into the tip jar. "Thanks."

"Any time. Come back when we're not facing the last days."

"Will do."

They walked out the door. Emma stood at the banquette chatting to a group of young women, all fabulous hair and sunglasses, and didn't see them leave.

Ryan stopped on the sidewalk. Unsure of what to say next. He wanted to hug Sam but didn't know if he should or what would happen if he did. He leaned forward, half-raised his hands, waiting for a signal.

"For Christ's sake, just hug me." Sam grabbed him in his arms and held him tight, rocking back and forth in front of the café as half the city pushed around them.

"I will," Ryan said. I'll call you in a year, Sam, and I hope you'll be happy to hear from me." He leaned in and held him tighter, face buried in Sam's shoulder. "I love you, Sam."

"I love you too," Sam whispered in his ear. "And I will be happy to hear from you. Always. Guarantee it. You're going to be famous as fuck, ya know."

"Maybe we both will," Ryan said.

Sam kissed his cheek, then broke the embrace and walked up Hall Street toward the Junction. At the lights at O'Brien, he turned and waved, then disappeared into the mass of people evacuating the beach.

Ryan turned toward the water and walked, pushing back against the crowd, his hand shading his forehead until he reached the railing at the edge of the street. The scene down at the waterfront resembled some nuclear apocalypse movie from the seventies, the main stretch of Bondi Beach bizarrely empty in blazing summer sunlight, while hundreds of people walked up the hill or milled around along the railing on Campbell Parade, staring, waiting. Waiting to see what a ten-meter-high wall of water looked like rushing up to the shore. Lifeguards and police officers waved people away from the area. "Move on. We're still on watch," someone shouted, "No one allowed on the beach yet," so he walked toward the north end of the beach, the place he'd come that first day, where the Dover Heights headland jutted out into the water. He climbed up the steep rock face and walked out across the sandstone ledge.

Two boys around twelve years old were hanging out along the edge of the rocks. The blond one, cigarette clenched in teeth, struggled with a packet of matches, losing each new flame to the wind.

Ryan walked toward them and sat on a wooden bench worn smooth by years of wind and rain. "What are you two doing up here? Having a smoke before the world ends?"

"Ah, we're high enough up here no tsunami'll hit us. What you doing out here?"

"Might just go for a swim."

"They've evacuated. You'll get swept away," the blond kid said, sucking in on his cigarette frantically as the match caught.

"I won't. Watch me," Ryan said.

"Cool," the other said.

"Mind holding my mobile in the meantime?"

"Got any games on it?" the other one asked. He was shorter, darker, hair cropped close.

"Yeah. Tons." Ryan unlocked the screen and handed it to the boy. "Meet me at the bottom of the cliff with it and I'll buy you another pack of smokes."

The blond kid's hair blew and tossed in the wind. "Make it two."

"Fine, two. Get hiking."

"Awesome," the shorter one said. He fist-bumped his friend and they started the climb down. "Careful, mister."

Ryan climbed down the rock face and hung by one arm over the ledge, weighing his chances. A whistle blew. Someone yelled, "Mate, there's a tsunami warning.

What the fuck are you doing?" He dropped onto the lower ledge and steadied himself against the cliff face. Joel was right. Fuck the tsunami. If it was going to happen, he'd already be dead.

He inched along the rough ledge, past pools full of purple starfish and anemones, ignoring the call of the lifeguard. He reached the last outcropping of rock before the rough sea below him, the Tasman gray-blue as far as he could see. Behind him, the hills of Bondi were green and lush.

"Fuck it," he said, the profanity he'd once cringed at feeling natural, suitable.

He pulled his shirt off, kicked off his flip-flops, paused for a moment to gauge the distance, then threw himself over, only ocean now, brilliant blue. He hit the icy deep water and shot down deep. The fabric of his cargo shorts swirled and tugged in the rough current, pulling him deeper below surface and spinning him around. Don't panic. He remembered Sam's advice from surfing lessons. If you're twisted up, stop kicking, look up, you'll rise.

He let go now and felt himself begin to float upward, adding a kick or two as he regained his sense of direction. Through the clear water, he looked up and saw sunlight sparkling in the waves. Kicking and thrashing, he felt himself rising, when a surge spun him around and pulled him down again. He gulped a bit of salty water, the sea rougher than he'd ever experienced. Panic almost winning, his lungs began to burn, but he let go again, began rising upward again, caught the light, then kicked and paddled like mad until he broke the surface, gasping and sputtering just as another wave crashed over his head and knocked him against the cliff. He reached for the ledge but was pulled back in again, the waves sinking and rising at alarming heights, just allowing him to gasp for breath as another crashed over him. He kicked and kicked and managed to get a few feet closer to shore, rounding the ledge, then was pulled under again, sand swirling in his eyes, his sense of direction spinning. He kicked up again, moved in a bit closer, ducking under before the next wave could spin him around. Finding his pace now, he pushed and kicked, straining forward, methodical, determined. Shore loomed closer.

Three lifeguards stood on the beach ahead of him. Waving. One rushed in, his bright-yellow rescue float dragging behind him on a rope. Ryan kept kicking, relaxing into his exhaustion as the guard grabbed him, pulling them both in on the float.

"What the bloody hell were you thinking?" the guard asked after he'd looked Ryan over for cuts and bruises. He lay on the sand of the empty beach. The two other guards and a police officer stood talking a few feet away. "Didn't you hear me yelling at you to stay out of the water? You got a death wish or something? There's a bloody tsunami warning."

The surf looked perfectly normal from where he lay.

"Yeah, but it didn't come, did it?" He was still gasping for breath as he said it.

"Water not exactly calm as glass though, is it? There's still fallout. Undertow."
The lifeguard sat down on the sand next to him, took Ryan's wrist, and counted slowly. "Your pulse feels fine. What were you trying to prove?"

"Nothing. I don't know." His breathing had returned to normal now. "Just that I could do it, I guess."

The sun was just beginning to set and the breeze felt cool on his wet skin.

"Just promise you won't do anything that stupid again. And when that officer talks to you, show a proper sense of remorse." He nodded toward the other men. "Get too mouthy and they'll haul you in. Act like you didn't know."

Ryan sat up. A crowd had gathered along the steps, watching the scene. "I'll tell him I was heartbroken over my divorce or something and didn't see the warning."

"No!" the lifeguard hissed. "You don't want that either. All it takes is one mention of suicide attempt and next thing you know you're spending a lovely weekend under observation in hospital. Do you want that?"

"No. Of course not. I'm sorry. I really am."

"You mean it?"

"Yes."

"All right, then. If you say you won't do it again, I'll let it go. You look fine to me." He grabbed Ryan's arm and pulled him up, then waved at the police officer. "He's all right. On your way."

The crowd applauded as Ryan approached the steps and walked back up to Campbell Parade, avoiding eye contact.

"Nice dive!" someone yelled.

He crossed the street toward the bus shelter. The boys from the cliff walked toward him through the crowd, the blond one holding out his phone.

"That was wicked," he said.

"Thanks, guys."

"What you doing now?"

"I guess I have a plane to catch."

"You going back to America, mister?" The boys stared at him as if he were a prophet.

"Yep," he said. "America."

He dusted the sand from his feet and started the long walk back up the hill to Katrina's flat.

20

Sam

First train of the day and the station was empty except for a few poor souls headed to some ungodly early morning shift somewhere. Luke was home in Goulbourn for the holidays, and Jenny's parents were in from Singapore, so he'd dropped the keys in the lockbox as instructed and dragged his suitcases to the train. It was a given he had no cash for a cab.

The platform sparkled from a fresh mopping and his suitcase flopped and wobbled as the wheels skidded through soapy film. The train pulled into the station, his last train ride in Sydney, at least for now, and he stepped into the freezing car, air-conditioning already blasting in anticipation of crowds and summer heat. He sat on a bench beneath a large photo of a hairless pig, blind eyes staring from a cage barely large enough for it to move its head in. "Join the Royal Australian SPCA and help stop factory farming," the sign read. Sort of thing made him sick, until he wanted bacon for breakfast. The summer she'd crashed with him and Luke before she moved to Byron, Belinda had tried to convert him to vegetarianism, told him he was killing himself and the environment by eating meat. He'd played along for a few days, swallowed as much of her eggplant-lentil-tofu concoctions as he could stand, assuring her it was delicious, then told her she was nuts and ducked into the pub across from their flat for a burger before meeting his mates for drinks.

The train picked up a few more passengers as they hit the busier stops, and he pushed his suitcases under the bench as best he could. A young woman in jeans and tank top, school bag on her back, clung to the rush-hour strap as the train entered the tunnel at Redfern.

"Home for Christmas?" she asked.

"For good," he said, giving his bag a final kick.

He slept through most of the flight, then hugged Belinda in a daze when he found her in the terminal. Her flight had arrived half an hour before his, crack of dawn, not his idea of comfort, but she'd paid for both of them and he was truly grateful. They headed south from Perth toward Margaret River, Sam driving the rental car, Lin humming along to the radio, her seat pushed back, tracing patterns on the dash with her big toe, the familiar brown hills of Western Australia dotted with sage-brush and scrub jarra.

"I can't understand why Dad feels he still has to fly home for Christmas," Sam said as they passed Bunbury and he pulled onto the Bussell Highway for Augusta.

"Neither can Mum," said Lin. "She's skipping dinner with us to do something with Tom's kids. Says she'll have a makeup dinner with us once Dad leaves."

"Still making every holiday uncomfortable years later," Sam said. "Wonderful."

It was so easy to fall back into the old narrative about their father that he and Belinda had been perfecting for decades. What was digging at him was not so much that his father would be there but that there would be an expectation of reconciliation—whatever step he was on was irrelevant—and he knew it was the right thing to do. The idea terrified him. Talking to Ryan had been easy. This was an entirely different story.

They drove on in silence until they reached Keenan Forest and Sam pulled off the highway toward home. Aunt Kate still lived in the old family house on the river and they had agreed that Sam would stay there for now. It was impressive. Built by his great-grandfather when he came west from Sydney after World War I to cash in on the timber boom. A two-story Australian red brick, its peaked roof enhanced by the intricate ironwork of the Federation era, double doors with huge bay windows on either side, six dormer windows across the top, and a veranda that wrapped around the entire house. His own family had lived in the house until he was six, when his father had given it to Aunt Kate and built the seventies-modern beach house out at Surfer's Point. Huge modular squares of white stucco clustered on the hillside sur-rounded by gum trees and eucalyptus, invisible from the road. Sam had loved their house with its walls of glass that faced the sea; he could surf almost every day, but he somehow felt, still, that they'd been cheated out of living in "the manor." His dad lectured him on the concepts of modern design and minimalism, joking that Aunt Kate would like it better anyway since she was stuck in the past, still managing the lumber business. The new house had won that year's Robin Boyd award, but they'd sold it after the divorce, the year Sam dropped out of architecture school, the year his dad moved to London. His mum now lived with her new husband in a gated community eighty kilometers to the north at Bunbury. Closer to the city and civilization, she said.

Sam pulled the car into the familiar circular drive, the tires popping and crackling over the gravel as he came to a stop. The smell of eucalyptus was stronger than he remembered, and he breathed deeply, stretching, shaking off the hours of cramped travel.

His dad walked down from the porch, arms spread, the welcoming patriarch. "Samuel! Belinda! Come. Give us a hug, then," he called. His hair had thinned con-siderably but he still looked fit and young, as handsome as ever. It was unfair.

Sam groaned at the performance. They had never hugged growing up, and Sam tensed up as he was groped, squeezed, and kissed wetly just below his ear. Belinda of course leaned into her hug on tiptoes, rocking back and forth, humming some odd tune. Very Byron. Very one with the universe.

Sam turned and grabbed a suitcase from the car.

"Hello everyone," a man called from the porch. He was dark and small, his voice sharp, urgent, almost shrill. He shielded his eyes from the sun as he walked down the steps. The new boyfriend. Aunt Kate had mentioned him over the phone. Apparently Dad had met him during a stopover in Malta on an all-gay cruise of the Mediterranean the year before. Aunt Kate called him "The Maltese."

"Sam, Belinda, this is my partner, Marcus," their dad said, emphasizing "partner" in that modern gay way that Sam hated so much. *Partner.* It sounded so clinical, so sexless, like they were opening an accountancy firm together rather than fucking.

Marcus hugged Belinda and kissed her on the cheek. "Just as beautiful as your father described you," he said. He stepped back and looked at Sam. "And Samuel. Just as handsome as your father. You've done well, Anthony."

"Oh, uh, thanks." Sam was caught off guard by the compliment, but more so by this man using his father's name with such obvious affection. "Nice to meet you."

Marcus leaned in for a hug, his grip surprisingly firm. "Thank God you're here," he whispered in Sam's ear. "We need some gay sensibility. Your aunt is driving me crazy." He let go and spoke normally again. "And where's that cute boyfriend we've heard about? Lin says he's delightful."

"Um, Ryan couldn't make it." Sam glared at Belinda over Marcus's shoulder.

She shrugged and made the same too-cute apology face she'd made since they were kids, then grabbed her father's arm and walked him toward the house.

Aunt Kate waved from the porch. "Did you survive the flight? I just hate being cooped up like that for so long. I swear, each year they've crammed more seats in. Soon enough we'll be standing."

"Lin popped for business class," Sam said.

"Very civilized of you, Belinda," Aunt Kate said, and motioned them into the house.

That night they gathered in the formal dining room, around the table their grandfather had carved from local Australian blackwood. Aunt Kate had made a seafood stew with fresh crab and spotted prawns she had gotten from the fisherman's stalls on the pier.

"Tell us how things are going in London then, Dad," Belinda said.

Sam grimaced. His father didn't need any encouragement to talk.

"Ah, thanks for asking, Lin. It's going wonderfully."

Sam turned to Aunt Kate to ask her about her last trip to Melbourne as his father launched into a story about getting a bomb threat from a group of separatists while building a new post office on the Isle of Wight.

"Tell them about that awful place we stayed at last year in Nice," Marcus said. His voice was loud and unfamiliar in the old house. Shrill. Sam and Kate stopped talking and looked up.

"The plumbing was so old we ended up having to carry water in from the well. We tried to explain to the caretaker but he wouldn't do anything about it. Very uncivilized," Marcus said. "Just like the French."

"Really? I've always found the French quite lovely," Aunt Kate said. "Maybe your French isn't up to the task of explaining a plumbing problem."

"Well, maybe in the finer hotels your family is used to," he said, "but this was an old farmhouse in some little village outside the city. We were getting to know the people. Can't really do that at the Four Seasons, now, can you? Your brother's idea." He patted Anthony on the shoulder.

"Always a man of the people, my brother," said Kate.

Sam heard the edge in his aunt's voice—always one for the subtle dig.

Marcus scooped more stew. "This is delicious, Kate, so lovely and old-fashioned. You'll have to teach me before we head to Hong Kong."

The conversation drifted into small talk, and Belinda and Sam cleared up the plates. Aunt Kate took the massive coconut cake she'd ordered weeks ago from the bakery in Donnybrook and carried it into the dining room. Belinda set the dessert plates down, and Kate raised her glass. "To my dear family on Christmas. May your lives be long and fruitful."

"Hear hear," they all shouted.

"Believe me, Kate, ours is fruitful," Marcus said, leaning in to nuzzle Anthony's neck.

"It appears it is." Aunt Kate sipped her wine. "You'll have to tell us more, Marcus. What do you two get up to? I haven't been out on the London scene since Tony and I went to university. What's this year's dance? This season's trendy cocktail?"

"Dowager's Punch is all the rage, Kate dear. You'd really enjoy it," Marcus said, forking a bit of cake into his mouth.

Kate wagged a finger at Marcus, the signal that she was about to let loose.

Belinda dug her fingernails into Sam's thigh. "Do something before she lays him out," she whispered.

Sam shook his head, his eyes wide. "You."

Belinda kicked Sam under the table, then stood. She tugged at Sam's shirt and he stood as well, the light from the old chandelier making patterns across his forehead. "To Aunt Kate, for hosting us and for preparing such a lovely meal, and to Dad and Marcus for making the trip. To everyone, happy Christmas."

"Happy Christmas." Sam raised his water glass.

Belinda began singing "Hark the Herald Angels Sing," her voice lovely and clear, waving at them all to join in, "jollying them along," her mother would have said. Her father stood and joined in, his deep voice in sharp contrast to her soprano, and the party relaxed again into the beauty of the song and the pleasure of the holiday.

Belinda finished her cake, then gestured toward the doorway. "Come have a smoke with me, Sam."

He stood, grateful for the diversion, and followed her out through the French doors to the back patio. She pulled out her ciggies.

"Not just yet," he said. "I want to breathe the eucalyptus."

"What, did you quit smoking now as well?" she said, and clicked her lighter on and off.

"Maybe. I don't know. Get rid of all the vices in one go, right? Aren't you supposed to be all healthy anyway? Do real hippies smoke?" He slid down into one of the old wrought-iron lawn chairs and looked up at the night sky.

"God, Sam. Forgive me if I like a smoke now and then. You're such a dipshit sometimes." She waved the packet in his face, the government warning glaring at him over the vivid picture of a gangrenous foot.

"You know I'm just having a go at you."

It had been a lovely dinner, really. He and Belinda had fallen so easily into their old ways of teasing and poking, it felt just like high school. Still, he was a bit on edge.

"And no one even says *hippie* anymore. You think you're so cool, but you sound totally clueless. What's happened to my cutting-edge big brother?"

"Well, what do you call yourself then, if you're not a hippie?"

"I don't know. Clued in? Aware of global issues?" She tapped the packet and pulled one out. "Dying for a smoke?"

"Go ahead," he said. "Indulge if you must, dear sister."

The doors opened again and their father stepped out carrying an overfull glass of red wine. Music drifted out with him, Aunt Kate playing the piano, something complicated and percussive. Prokofiev? Not in the least bit Christmassy.

"Mind if I join you?" he asked.

"Come on, it's a gorgeous night," Belinda said. "Look at those stars."

He rattled another chair across the patio and sat across from them. "Lovely meal, yes? So good to see both of you."

"It was perfect, Dad."

Sam took a sip of his water. "Yep. Lovely."

"No wine tonight, Sam?" His father sloshed his glass at him. "You still on that health kick? You certainly look fit, son." His dad grabbed his bicep and gave it a squeeze.

Sam pushed his hand off. "Lay off, mate." His father's grip was still unbelievably strong. "Yeah, um, no wine for me tonight."

The array of alcohol that night had been astonishing—three wines with dinner, champagne with cake, brandy afterward for those who wanted it. It hadn't bothered him to that point, but his dad's glass was on the verge of tipping onto his trousers. Should he tell them? Might be good to just get it out. "To be honest, Dad—"

"So, I was thinking Marcus and I would swing over to Sydney for New Year's, then up through Byron before we leave the next week," his father pressed on, forgetting his question. "See you both in your natural habitats, so to speak. What do you two think?"

"Wonderful, Dad," said Belinda. "You'll love our cottage, it's in the forest outside town and you can't hear a thing at night. But Sam—"

"What about it, Sam? We'd love to meet Ryan and see the city with you. I've never been out in Sydney as a gay man, never really seen Darlinghurst, would love to go to the pubs there and meet your friends. And New Year's Eve must be a big show. We could crash at yours? What do you say?" His dad set his glass on the wrought-iron table next to him, the same one that had been there since they were kids.

Sam wasn't planning on this new ambush. Telling his dad about his sobriety felt necessary, but Ryan? The flat? A breeze kicked up, rustling the leaves of the ancient gum tree that hovered over the drive. Sam shut his eyes and breathed deeply of the scent.

"Why so silent, Sammo?" His dad took another swig of wine.

Oh, just get on with it. No need for fibs and evasion anymore, right? Just tell him. Rigorous honesty, right? "You're welcome to come to Sydney, Dad, but I won't be there. I'll be—"

"What do you mean, you won't be there?" his father said. "You dodging me again? Frankly, I'm getting a little tired of the bullshit, Sam. Shouldn't have to get a damn hotel when my son lives in the middle of it all. You'd think you were embarrassed of me."

"He's not lying, Dad," Belinda said.

"What? What do you mean? Why didn't you tell me?"

Sam realized his father was asking Belinda, not him. Anger rose up.

"Wasn't my story to tell, Dad," she said. "Anyway, Sam lost his job."

"Thanks, Lin. Why not just drop the whole story on him?" Cigarette smoke curled around his face and he waved it away.

"Well, it's not like he wasn't going to find out."

He stood up. She was right, of course, but the invasion of privacy had him seething. "Why not tell him the whole thing then. Give him the whole last year. I'd probably leave something out." He walked across the patio but stopped at the stone steps that led to the shore. Calm down. You want this to work. Belinda's often overstepped out of concern. No need to lose it.

"Sorry. Yeah. Still a bit raw, I guess." He walked back toward them and stood behind his sister's chair.

"It'll be all right, son. Sit down, let's talk. Get a glass and have some of this Shiraz. You really need to relax. All is not lost. I'll just put a call in to Gerald at—"

"If it's all the same, Dad, I don't need any more favors, and please stop pushing the wine at me. I don't drink. I quit. Gave it up." The confession was supposed to feel freeing, but he felt the heat rising again.

"What? You've quit drinking? Well, how am I to intuit that over one meal? You should have said something," his father said. "Should have said something about all of it. We could have talked it out. Come to a solution. Why did you let it go so far? If you would have just answered my bloody calls!"

"Last time I told you anything about my life, you called me a lazy idiot. Tell me who would want to hear more of that?"

It still felt so awkward. He hadn't had a drink in months but the emotions kept coming. He tried to focus on what he'd learned. Remember it isn't all fixed in a minute. Putting down the bottle is just the beginning, It's all a work in progress. Stay calm and be kind.

But Robert had never met his father.

"I only meant it in the moment. I was shocked you'd dropped out of uni, that's all," his father said. "Then that firm in Bronte just seemed a bit too good to be true, and I worried about that mortgage. Hung you out to dry, did they? Your boss is a fool."

The lights from the dining room cast a shadow across his father's face, and for a moment he looked exactly as he had when they were young.

"You've had a few rough years, I guess I just wanted to push you back on track. Circumstances. We'll fix it. And I don't know why you thought you had to quit drinking, anyway. We all enjoy a pint, son. There's nothing so shameful about enjoying a few pints. Did Ryan tell you to quit? He's American, yes? They're so dramatic about those things. Ridiculous!" He patted the chair next to him. "For God's sake, sit down, son. Relax. Have a drink and forget about this nonsense. We'll come out for New Year's and have a ripper of a time."

Sam sat down again, remembering to breathe, giving it over to the universe or whatever nutty idea of God he'd come up with. Sam paused, trying to think of the right thing to say. Pull back from the anger built up from all those years. "It wasn't Ryan who told me to do it. I quit on my own. Ryan and I aren't even together anymore. He moved back in with bloody Katrina because I'm a drunk and I fucked up our relationship." It was the first time he'd put it so succinctly, taken the full blame himself. It felt freeing, emboldening. "Anyway, everything has fallen to shit, and I won't be there again for God knows how long, let alone for a New Year's gay pub crawl with my dad and his sassy new boyfriend."

His father stiffened. "Mind your manners, son, I'm trying to patch things up here."

And he meant to, to be polite, to try to see the other side, but it just grabbed hold of him and ran. The anger, the pain from his past. "So am I, Dad, but Jesus. I don't know why you think that now that you're out and proud, all is forgiven and you can just show up and inflict your embarrassing gay midlife crisis on us and we can pretend we're just mates running around the city hitting the pubs and looking for cock together." The heat rose to his face, just like in high school when they'd have it out over a bad grade or a late night out. The sense memory was perfect down to the glass of wine. Dad tipsy. Dad going on and on. Dad telling him what to do yet again. How to live his life. All thoughts of taking the high road were now gone. "You can do whatever you want, old man. Dance all night at the clubs and get as drunk or drug-fucked as you like, and you and Marcus can go troll the saunas and the nude beaches to your heart's content, but I won't be there. I'm perfectly capable of getting my shit together, and I don't need your bloody input."

"I don't want to listen to this," Belinda said. She stood up and pitched her cigarette to the ground, grinding it out with her foot. "If you were capable, we wouldn't be having this conversation, Sam. Get a grip." She walked inside and pulled the door shut, dampening the sound of the piano.

"Samuel Carter, you are being absolutely vile," his father said, his voice deepening into that angry growl that Sam knew so well. "Mind your tongue, son, or we're going to have a serious problem."

"You're the one who's being vile," Sam said to his father. "You and that pissy queen of a boyfriend prancing around here like—"

"That's enough!" His father stood, slamming his glass down on the table. "I have done nothing but bend over backwards for you. Put up with your nonsense through high school—smoking weed, staying out all night, failing classes. Made phone calls and letters to make sure you got into architecture school. Cashed in a favor with the best firm in Sydney when you dropped out. Cars. Holidays. Checks when you came up short. All I wanted was to see you finally behaving like an adult, finally succeeding. And now I want to get to know you a little better now that I've come out, but I guess that isn't possible. I've saved your arse a million bloody times, yet you treat me like a bloody fucking pariah. Well, good luck with that, son. Hope UWA doesn't expect much from you. Be surprised if you make it past your first semester." He picked up his glass and took a big mouthful.

"You're such a bloody arsehole."

"Yes," his father said, "I may be, but I'm still your father, and you owe me some respect." He stepped forward, towering over Sam, leaning in, as if Sam were fourteen again and about to get the belt. He felt the adrenaline rise, his defense instinct kicking in, but his dad stepped back. "You will not ruin this holiday. I expect better behavior from this point forward." He walked toward the house, stopping at the patio doors. "Now go apologize to your sister."

As his father shut the door, Sam's heart sank. What he had meant to be a moment of reconciliation had turned into a scene as ugly as any from his childhood. He felt sick. Flesh-crawlingly hungover, but without the benefit of a drink. Fuck. A little late for a prayer, but he chanted one anyway. It still felt so foreign. What was God anyway? At least he could wrap his head around the serenity prayer, around the idea of letting go and recognizing what you can't control. He repeated it like a mantra, the words falling into rhythm with his feet as he climbed the stairs to Belinda's room.

She sat at the foot of the bed wearing shorts and a T-shirt. Aunt Kate had stacked dozens of file boxes along one wall and there had been barely enough room to squeeze through the door.

"Hey, sorry."

"Can't you just try?" she asked. "He's trying, Sam."

"He's not trying. He's full steam ahead telling everyone what to do and how to do it, just like always. Surprised he didn't try to paddle me for old time's sake."

"You pushed him to the limit. And you're fine," she said. "It's not like you guys have never fought before."

"Right, because he was horrible to us."

"Sam, he wasn't that horrible," she said, stroking his arm, "Sure, he can be a bit of a dickhead now and then, but that's parents, right? You know I honestly could never really figure out why you two fought so much. You'd lose your shit at the slightest provocation, and run off screaming into the night with no one knowing when you'd turn up. He spent a lot less time yelling at you than he did searching the neighborhood for you and calling round to friends. Yeah, he was pretty damn stern sometimes, but we all turned out okay, didn't we?"

"Well, he was horrible to mum, and there's no excuse for that." Sam realized he sounded like a teenager, and wished he hadn't said it.

"You're grasping. You don't know what their marriage was like," she said. "I know you're upset, but you've got to try, especially now that you have this commonality . . . It should be a bond, not a point of contention."

"I really meant to try. I did, but he just gets under my skin and all of a sudden I'm screaming."

"Fair assessment."

"Let me ask you something. When they got divorced, did you and Mum go out pub crawling looking for blokes together?" He stood up and tossed the pillow back on the bed.

"Of course we didn't, she was grieving."

"She should have been bloody celebrating, Dad's such a wanker." He paced back and forth at the foot of the bed, clenching and unclenching his fists.

"I don't want to fight," she said. "I'm not the enemy here. Sit down. Relax."

"Remember when Robbie Williams's dad would hang out with us at parties? Awful, right? And Robbie hated him. Dad's doing the same thing."

Belinda patted the worn old quilt on the bed next to her and Sam sat down. "We were in high school and Mr. Williams was a perv. And dad lives in a different hemisphere. It's not like he's following you around Sydney. He just thought it would be nice to get to know his son again. Calm down." She reached to the bedside table and pulled a rolled-up baggie out of her woven jute handbag. Sam could smell the weed immediately, pungent and fresh. "Want some?"

He shook his head. "I quit. No more for me."

"I thought it was just the drinking. Oh, and the smoking."

"All mind-altering substances. It's complicated."

"Gateway drug. Got it."

"Something like that. No, it's . . ." He waved the baggie away. "It's too hard to explain."

"You've got to stop feeling so sorry for yourself over all this. If you don't find a way to get past this, your head is going to explode. Talk to Dad."

Sam realized she was right. Regardless of what had happened, they needed to start somewhere. He wanted to call Robert, but it was three in the morning in Sydney. Tomorrow would have to do.

He woke up to his dad shaking his shoulder. It was barely light outside.

"What's wrong?" he asked. "Did something happen?"

"I thought we'd go surfing, just the two of us. Maybe have a talk." His dad looked tired, a bit disheveled, but he was dressed for the beach already, board shorts and a dark-green T-shirt, a towel slung over his shoulder.

Sam shut his eyes and tried to pull the covers up. "I'm barely awake, Dad, and I'm not really . . ." He was about to say he wasn't in the mood, but he caught himself. They needed to talk, and he knew it. He just didn't know if he was ready.

"I shouldn't have gotten so angry last night, and I'm sorry." His dad tugged at the blanket. "We used to go surfing after we'd had a fight when you were a boy," his father said. "Remember? It always seemed to do the trick."

His dad was right. The ocean healed. The current. The cold. The unpredictability. Turning your fate over to that crazy energy whose plans you could never predict. It was just what he needed. "All right, can you give me half an hour? I'll need a coffee and a moment to surface."

"Fair enough. The old boards are still here gathering dust. Kate's stepkids never really took to surfing."

Sam scrunched deeper under the blanket. "God, they were wankers, weren't they?"

"Absolute gremlins, as was Steve."

"Too right."

"Your aunt is better off now. She seems quite happy. So get up and let's find those boards."

"Just give me some time, right?"

"Would it help if I brought you some coffee?"

"Thanks, but I'll come find you when I've had a minute."

"Fair enough." His dad grabbed Sam's foot through the sheet and squeezed. "Proud of you, son," he said, "this drinking thing, by the way. Nothing like a fresh start." He picked up an old picture book from the shelf and set it down. "I'll check on your sister. Coffee brewing."

Sam put his face in the pillow and inhaled deeply, breathing in the scent of home, of cedarwood and cooking and of packed linen closets that might need a little airing out. He waited until his dad's footsteps hit the bottom of the stairs, then sat up again.

He pulled on his boardies, walked down the narrow staircase to the kitchen, and grabbed a cup of coffee. It was still early enough that mist clung to the trees, obscuring the water's edge. He finished his cup and headed out the kitchen door, through the trees and down to the beach, the sand like ice on his bare feet.

His father stood waiting at the shore, hand shading his eyes as he scanned the horizon.

"Good. You made it."

"My wetsuit's in one of the boxes I shipped. They haven't arrived yet. Didn't think I'd need it first day."

"Indian Ocean's much warmer than the Pacific. Did you forget that? Or have you gotten soft on me over there in Sydney?" His dad jogged in place on the cold sand, limbering up. "Just get your blood pumping. You'll be fine."

Sam kicked up one foot, then the next, found a rhythm. The coffee started to work and he shrugged off the chill. "Dad, I'm really, well, I shouldn't have spoken like that to you—"

"Hello, my handsome boys!" It was Marcus, waving from the trees as he walked out onto the sand. He was wearing a purple and green kaftan.

"Bloody Christ, Marcus," Anthony shouted over the surf. "That getup! Will there be a fashion show later? I hope you found me one as well."

"Oh God, this isn't mine. I didn't have any sunscreen, so I borrowed it from your sister, well, stole it from one of the guest rooms. Hippie chic, yes?" He grabbed the skirt with both hands and twirled. "But don't mind me. I know you two need your bonding moment, Anthony. I promise to sit here silently. It's a beautiful morning."

"Just don't go rummaging through any more cupboards without supervision. Who knows what you'll end up wearing to dinner."

"Your sister has impeccable taste. Don't tempt me."

Sam's dad picked up his board and ran down to the water and plunged in. "You coming, Sam?"

"Yeah, wait up."

Sam grabbed the other board and ran down to the beach, the cold of the water catching his breath. Indian Ocean warmer, my arse. He went under again to get acclimated, swimming further out, dragging his board along, surfacing out past the baby breakers. His dad knelt on his board, paddling out toward the line. Sam hung onto his board, kicking to move further out, and ducked his head under again, the freezing water still shocking his skin. When he emerged this time, his dad was already up, carving through a barrel with the precision of a surgeon, his legs bent squarely, his posture as perfect as on the day of their first lesson.

Sam pushed out further and saw his opportunity, catching a midsized wave just as it curled, the tide rumbling beneath him as he leaned forward and cut across the crest. It broke before he was ready, though, and he went under in a swirl of sand and seaweed. He came up coughing but exhilarated. His dad pushed out again, but Sam realized he still wasn't awake enough for the task, hopped up to the beach, and sat down next to Marcus.

"You two looked great out there."

"He did, maybe. That was a pretty shit run I just pulled." He shuddered and pulled his knees up to his chest.

"He's good, isn't he?" Marcus waved out toward Sam's father, hopping up on his board again. "He's been talking about this since we planned the trip. Surfing again with Sam."

Sam turned and looked at Marcus. "Really?"

Marcus nodded. "He adores you, you know. Belinda too, of course, but he went on and on about you and your accomplishments, and surfing with you when we got here."

"Yeah, he taught me how. He's brilliant at it." Sam patted his board. "You ever?"

"Me? Oh please. I can barely swim. I'm happy to be a housewife who chooses the flowers and throws the dinner parties. Frankly, I thought I'd be able to do a bit of that while we were here, but your aunt has been a bit distant."

"Yeah, Aunt Kate's a bit stiff sometimes." Sam leaned back on his elbows and shook his wet hair. "She's witty as all hell when you get to know her, though."

"I've felt some of that wit. A bit sharp, isn't it? I've tried my best but I'm getting tired of the glares. She thinks I'm going to steal the silver and come to dinner in a harness and chaps."

"Now that would be a sight." He looked at Marcus in his swirling kaftan and realized he'd underestimated him. He dug his heels deeper into the sand. "I suppose I'm afraid that's how they see me," he said, "some silly gay boy who moved to Sydney to dance in parades and dress up in women's clothes. Everything I do, they judge. My job, my flat, dropping out of uni, the drinking, and now I've lost it all. 'Oh, isn't

Sam a disappointment. Dad's a brilliant architect, but Sam dropped out of school and can't even hold a job selling real estate. And poor boy goes to those alcoholic meetings. And gay! Such a shame.'"

"Well, he thinks you're doing fine. Says you'll be who you'll be. You'll figure it out. We talked last night. He trusts you. Don't worry about what the others are saying."

"Mum's worse, to be honest, but Aunt Kate's been great. Promised me room and board while I get on my feet, and part-time work with the lumber company while I get sorted back into uni."

"Kind of her." Marcus dug his toe into the sand. "You know she calls me the Maltese?"

"Um, yeah, I did."

"I heard her on the phone the other night." He fluttered his hands toward Sam's father. "Tony said I can't say anything since we're in her home and all. She thinks I've corrupted him, you know. Group sex. Rent boys. Like Joe Orton and what's-his-name cavorting in Morocco with hashish and male prostitutes. But really it was the other way around. You know, before I met your father, I'd never—"

"Don't!" Sam shouted, then laughed as he realized how loud he'd been. "Sorry, I'm just not quite ready to think of that sort of thing involving my dad, you know."

"Don't want to hear about the sex life of someone who read you bedtime stories?"

"Oh, believe me, there were no bedtime stories. But he did teach me how to surf."

The sun had finally risen above the trees and warmed the sand at Sam's feet. He stretched his legs and stood up. "I think you should just go ahead and steal something, put Aunt Kate over the edge." He brushed a patch of drying sand off his ankle. "You know, something she'll really miss. Start with that glass fish on the piano. She's really particular about it. It's Venetian. I'll help."

Marcus fluttered his kaftan and smoothed it around his ankles. "Perfect."

Sam looked out to the water where his father bobbed and floated, eying the horizon. "I guess I'm going back in then."

"Yes. Go. He's so happy to see you again. Just give him a chance."

"I will. Promise."

Sam jogged toward the water, board balanced on his head, sunlight reflecting off the waves.

Acknowledgments

I started the Master's Program in Creative Writing at the University of Sydney with no clue what to expect. I had cobbled together a few stories for my application portfolio and was somehow accepted but was far more interested in partying on the beach than really working on my writing. That quickly changed as my inspiring and challenging instructors shook me out of my tropical daze and gave me a new respect for the craft. Thanks to David Brooks for giving me that first inkling of a real work ethic, and to Sue Woolfe for teaching me to let go and let the story tell itself. I am especially grateful to Alex Kendrew, my first and dearest friend in Sydney, for saving me from my grotty flat in Redfern and offering me his beautiful and peaceful spare room steps from the beach in Bondi, a life-changing experience that set me on a better path and became an inspiration for parts of the novel.

After Sydney, I went on to the Center for Writers at the University of Southern Mississippi. There I found an invaluable cohort with the likes of Fae Dremock and Damian Dressick, and I thank them for always supporting me with good humor and honest advice. I also had amazing instructors there: Jim Robison, Frederick Barthelme, and Andrew Milward all contributed greatly to my progress, and I thank them all from the bottom of my heart. But it is Steven Barthelme to whom I owe the greatest debt of gratitude. He is a true Texas gentleman, a brilliant storyteller, and an insightful and dedicated teacher. Without his unwavering support and guidance, I would not be the writer I am today.

Friends and family have given great support as well. Thanks to my mom, who smiled and stayed positive through the string of random colleges and ever-changing majors before I finally settled on English. Thanks also to fellow writer/academic Bonnie Clark for her sage and calming guidance, to Quincy Norris for grounding me in the real world, and to Michael Mitchell for always believing in me, no matter what hairbrained scheme I embarked on.

And finally, many thanks to Dennis Lloyd at the University of Wisconsin Press for seeing something in my manuscript and helping me get it across the finish line.

All of you played a part in this and I hope you enjoy the results.